DREAMLAND
DUTY ROSTER

LT. COLONEL TECUMSEH "DOG" BASTIAN

Once one of the country's elite fighter jocks, now Dog is whipping Dreamland into shape the only way he knows how—with blood, sweat, and tears—and proving that his bite is just as bad as his bark . . .

CAPTAIN BREANNA "RAP" STOCKARD

Like father, like daughter. Breanna is brash, quick-witted, and one of the best test pilots at Dreamland. But she wasn't prepared for the biggest test of her life: a crash that grounded her husband in more ways than one . . .

MAJOR JEFFREY "ZEN" STOCKARD

A top fighter pilot until a runway crash at Dreamland left him a paraplegic. Now, Zen is at the helm of the ambitious Flighthawk program, piloting the hyper-sonic remote-controlled aircraft from the seat of his wheelchair—and watching what's left of his marriage crash and burn . . .

MAJOR MACK "THE KNIFE" SMITH

A top gun with an attitude to match. Knife has a MiG kill in the Gulf War—and won't let anyone forget it. Though resentful that his campaign to head Dreamland stalled, Knife's the guy you want on your wing when the bogies start biting . . .

CAPTAIN DANNY FREAH

Freah made a name for himself by heading a daring rescue of a U-2 pilot in Iraq. Now, at the ripe old age of twenty-three, Freah's constantly under fire, as commander of the top-secret "Whiplash" rescue and support team—and Dog's right-hand man . . .

continued . . .

NIGHT OF THE HAWK
The exciting final flight of the "Old Dog"—a shattering mission into Lithuania, where the Soviets' past could launch a terrifying future . . .

"[A] gripping conclusion . . . A masterful mix of high technology and *human* courage."
—W. E. B. Griffin

SKY MASTERS
The incredible story of America's newest B-2 bomber, engaged in a blistering battle of oil, honor, and global power . . .

"*Sky Masters* is a knockout!"
—Clive Cussler

HAMMERHEADS
The U.S. government creates an all-new drug-defense agency, armed with the ultimate high-tech weaponry. The war against drugs will never be the same . . .

"Whiz-bang technology and muscular, damn-the-torpedoes strategy."
—*Kirkus Reviews*

DAY OF THE CHEETAH
The shattering story of a Soviet hijacking of America's most advanced fighter plane— and the greatest high-tech chase of all-time . . .

"Quite a ride . . . Terrific. Authentic and gripping."
—*The New York Times*

SILVER TOWER
A Soviet invasion of the Middle East sparks a grueling counterattack from America's newest laser defense system . . .

"Riveting, action-packed . . . a fast-paced thriller that is impossible to put down."
—UPI

FLIGHT OF THE OLD DOG
Dale Brown's riveting debut novel. A battle-scarred bomber is renovated with modern hardware to fight the Soviets' devastating new technology . . .

"A superbly crafted adventure . . . Exciting."
—W. E. B. Griffin

DALE BROWN'S

DREAMLAND

armageddon

Written by
Dale Brown and Jim DeFelice

JOVE BOOKS, NEW YORK

DALE BROWN'S DREAMLAND: ARMAGEDDON

A Jove Book / published by arrangement with the authors

PRINTING HISTORY
Jove edition / August 2004

Copyright © 2004 by Dale Brown
Cover art and design by Steven Ferlauto

ISBN: 0-515-13791-X

A JOVE BOOK®
Jove Books are published by The Berkley Publishing Group, a division of Penguin Group (USA) Inc., 375 Hudson Street, New York, New York 10014. JOVE and the "J" design are trademarks belonging to Penguin Group (USA) Inc.

PRINTED IN THE UNITED STATES OF AMERICA

10 9 8 7 6 5 4 3

DREAMLAND
DUTY ROSTER

LIEUTENANT COLONEL TECUMSEH "DOG" BASTIAN

Dreamland's commander has been mellowed by the demands of his new command—but he's still got the meanest bark in the West, and his bite is even worse.

MAJOR JEFFREY "ZEN" STOCKARD

A top fighter pilot until a near-fatal crash at Dreamland left him a paraplegic, Zen runs the Flighthawk program and has now accumulated more air-to-air kills than any other active pilot in the air force. But he's got a grudge bigger than the wheelchair life has confined him to.

CAPTAIN BREANNA "RAP" STOCKARD

Zen's wife has seen him through his injury and rehabilitation. But can she balance her love for her husband with the demands of her career . . . and ambitions?

MAJOR MACK "THE KNIFE" SMITH

Mack Smith is the best pilot in the world—and he'll tell you so himself. He left Dreamland to reshape the Brunei air force in his own egotistical image.

CAPTAIN DANNY FREAH

Danny commands "Whiplash"—the ground attack team that works with the cutting-edge Dreamland aircraft and high-tech gear. Freah's wife and friends want him to run for Congress. The war hero would be a shoo-in—but does he want to give up the excitement of Dreamland?

JENNIFER GLEASON

Computer specialist Jennifer Gleason is one of the creative geniuses at Dreamland, responsible for the multi-mode combat computer that helps control the Flighthawks. She's also

Dog's lover—but her emotional and intellectual sides don't always get along.

JED BARCLAY

The young deputy to the national security advisor is Dreamland's link to the president. Barely old enough to shave, the former science whiz kid now struggles to master the intricacies of world politics. Zen Stockard is his cousin—and Zen still can't figure out how the skinny kid who used to follow him around on a tricycle grew up and got a real job.

LIEUTENANT KIRK "STARSHIP" ANDREWS

Starship flew through flight school and was on the fast track to a career flying the air force's frontline interceptors, like the F-15 and F-22. But family commitments made him change his plans. Now he has a post at Dreamland flying the U/MF-3 Flighthawk robot planes, where he's finding that no amount of training can prepare him for real combat.

AND IN THE SOUTH PACIFIC . . .

PRINCE PEHIN BIN AWG

The nephew of the sultan of Brunei and the unofficial protector of the air force, bin Awg has an enviable collection of Cold War aircraft—and a well-earned reputation as a partier. Can he mature in time to save his uncle's realm . . . and his own neck?

CAT MCKENNA

A one time Royal Canadian pilot, McKenna has found work plying the skies for a shadowy Russian arms dealer. But when her paycheck bounces, she looks for a new job—and ends up locking horns with Mack Smith.

CAPTAIN DAZHOU TI

Years ago, Dazhou's Chinese grandfather was disinherited by the sultan of Brunei. Now he wants revenge—and has a secret Malaysian warship to insure that he gets it.

SAHURAH NIU

A devout believer, Sahurah is convinced that he has a place in Paradise—and is willing to kill thousands to reach it.

I
Paradise

Malay, Negara Brunei Darussalam (State of Brunei, Abode of Peace)
6 October 1997, (local) 1302

BREANNA STOCKARD TOSSED HER BACKPACK TO THE GROUND, put her hands on her hips, and took a deep breath. The Pacific Ocean spread out before her, a blanket of azure silk. A few white clouds wandered casually in the distance, drifting across the sky like a pair of vacationers easing across a solitary beach. Civilization might lay in the distance—there were oil derricks somewhere offshore, and merchant ships did a brisk trade at the nearby harbor—but from where she stood Breanna had no hint that she and her husband Jeff "Zen" Stockard weren't the only people in the world.

This is what God looks at everyday, she thought to herself. Paradise.

Breanna took another deep breath. A month ago, she had found herself stranded in the Pacific during a fierce storm, tossed back and forth in a tiny life raft. It seemed impossible that this was the same ocean now.

Maybe it wasn't. Maybe that hadn't even happened. Ten days here in the wonderful paradise of Brunei—helping train pilots to fly the EB-52 Megafortress "leased" to the kingdom as part of an eventual three-plane arms deal—had purged her of all unhappy memories.

One more week and it might even be impossible to have an unpleasant thought ever again.

Zen had surprised her yesterday by turning up for a weekend

visit. They had twenty-four more hours together before he had
to return to Dreamland, their base back in the States.

Breanna smoothed out the blanket she'd borrowed from the
hotel and spread it down on the white sand next to the path. She
dropped her bag and Zen's small backpack and turned to go back
up the path.

"I'll bring down lunch, then I'm going to take a swim before I
eat," she told her husband, who was negotiating the bumps down
from the parking area in his wheelchair.

"Yup," said Zen.

"You don't sound very enthusiastic," she said.

"Yup."

"Jet lag getting to you?"

"I'm fine."

She leaned over and gave him a kiss on the cheek, then trotted up the hill for the rest of their things.

BEFORE THE ACCIDENT THAT HAD COST HIM THE USE OF HIS
legs, Zen had considered going to the beach a useless waste of
time and a dreadful bore. In his list of things to do, it ranked
right above lying spread-eagle on Interstate 15 at rush hour.

Now it ranked somewhat lower.

He had tried talking Breanna out of the idea back at the hotel, when Prince bin Awg had called to say he and his family
couldn't join them on the planned picnic. His Royal Highness
Pehin bin Awg was nephew of the sultan, a royal prince and
government minister; he owned the beach and had insisted they
use it. Zen liked bin Awg, the country's unofficial patron of the
Air Force—he had an enviable collection of Cold War aircraft
and could talk about them entertainingly for hours and hours.
Like many Bruneians, he was also generous to a fault. But his
baby daughter was sick and he had been called away on government business. Zen loved Breanna and wanted to spend as much
time as he could with her; he just would have preferred somewhere other than a beach.

A Lakers game, maybe.

It wasn't so much the fact that beaches and wheelchairs
didn't go together. Truth be told, wheelchairs didn't really fit

smoothly anywhere. Much of everyday life in the A-B world—as in "able-bodied," a term not used by the handicapped without at least a touch of sarcasm—was a succession of physical barriers and dignity-stealing obstructions. Going to the beach was probably no worse than going to the grocery store. And the fact that this beach was a private, secluded refuge meant there were no people to gawk at the geek in the wheelchair—or worse, take pity on him by "helping."

No, what bothered him was deeper than that. There just seemed to be no point, existential or otherwise, in lying on your belly and watching water lap against the sand.

"My, but you're a slowpoke," said Breanna, returning with their coolers. "Need a push?"

"No," he said stubbornly, gripping the wheels of his chair and half-sliding, half-rolling off the hard-packed pathway and onto the sand. Surprisingly, the chair wheels sank only about a quarter of an inch, and Zen was able to pull over right next to the blanket. There he started a well-practiced if inelegant lift, arch, and twist routine, sliding himself down to the ground.

"You coming in?" asked Bree, kicking off her shoes.

"Yup." Zen pulled himself up, sitting next to the cooler with the beer. He took out a Tetley's Draught—an English ale that might be the last vestige of Britain's influence on Brunei—and popped the top. A satisfying hiss and fizz followed.

" 'This can contains a floating widget,' " he read from the top of the can. "What do you think a floating widget is, Bree?"

"An excuse to charge two dollars more," said Breanna, who had complained earlier about the high price of beer. As an Islamic country, Brunei officially frowned on alcohol consumption, and between that and the fact that the beer had to be imported from a good distance, the six-pack Zen had purchased through the hotel concierge had cost over twenty-five dollars, American.

But some things were worth the price.

And others couldn't be bought for any amount of money: Zen watched as his wife stripped off her jeans and T-shirt, revealing a red one-piece bathing suit that reminded Zen there were *some* good reasons for going to the beach after all.

"Mmmm," he said.

"Don't get fresh."

"What? I'm talking about the beer."

He ducked as Breanna tossed her T-shirt at him.

DESPAIR'S BLACK HANDS TOOK HIS THROAT, AND SAHURAH NIU struggled to breathe.

The prince's wife and infant daughter had not come to the beach. His informants had been wrong.

Sahurah pushed his fists into his arms, struggling to calm himself. It was of vital importance to remain in control in front of his men.

The commander had made clear that he must complete the mission today. They had discussed the possibility of taking other hostages if necessary; clearly that was his course now.

The two people on the beach were Westerners—Australians, he thought, though Sahurah Niu was not close enough to know for certain. Undoubtedly they were guests of the prince, or they would not have been allowed here on the private beach. They would do.

One was in a wheelchair. A pity.

Sahurah was not without a sense of mercy: he would be killed rather than taken.

"What are we doing?" asked Adi, the little one. He handled the Belgian machine-gun they had obtained two months before from their brothers across the border. Despite his small size, Adi had learned to handle the weapon and his body well enough so that he could fire the gun from his hip. This was not easily done; the others and Sahurah himself preferred to fire prone, as their instructor had first taught them.

"We will go ahead with our plan," said Sahurah. "Tell the others be ready."

THE WATER FELT LIKE A MINERAL BATH, BALMY AND THICK against her skin. Breanna stroked gently across the small bay in front of the beach. The salt water tickled her cheeks, and the sun felt good on her back and shoulders. She took a few strokes parallel to the beach and looked back at Zen, who despite being crippled was a strong swimmer.

"Are you coming in or not?" Breanna yelled.

"Later," he said.

"Oh come on in!" she yelled. "The water is fantastic."

"I'll be in," he said, sipping his beer.

The shoreline was crescent-shaped and slightly off-center to the east, bordered on both sides by strips of jungle. To the west, a pile of rocks formed a small mini-peninsula about a hundred and fifty yards from the mainland. The rocks were just barely above the surface of the water, and they weren't very wide; there looked to be just about the surface area of a good-sized desk there. Still, it was a destination and Breanna turned and began doing a butterfly stroke toward it, her old high-school swim team warm-up routine popping into her brain.

Zen DUG THROUGH THE COOLER, SORTING THROUGH THE food they'd taken from the hotel, looking for something that might seem at least vaguely familiar. He took out what seemed to be a roast beef sandwich—meat stuck out from the edges—and then leaned toward the backpack to get a plate. As he did, he caught a glint of something in the trees to his right, well back in the jungle off the beach by fifty or sixty yards.

Zen put down the sandwich and opened the cooler again, pretending to fish for something else while looking surreptitiously into the jungle. He hoped he'd see a curious child, a teenager copping a cigarette or some such thing, looking at the intruders with curiosity. But instead he caught the outline of a short, squat man with a large gun.

Someone sent by the prince to protect them?

Zen closed the cooler. Sliding his arm through the strap of the backpack, he sidled to the edge of the blanket, estimating the distance to the water.

Twenty feet.

They didn't have a radio or cell phone. The Brunei air force was so ill-equipped it barely had enough survival radios for its flight crews; American cell phones didn't work here. And besides, this place was paradise—nothing ever went wrong here.

Breanna was about thirty yards out, stroking steadily for a little jetty or rock island at the edge of the cove.

"How's the water?" he shouted. Then without waiting for an

answer, he added, "Maybe I will come in. What the hell. Might as well have a quick swim before lunch."

He twisted around on his elbow, turning to drag himself toward the water.

If he'd had his legs, Zen thought to himself, he'd have confronted the son of a bitch beyond the trees, gun or no gun. But he didn't have his legs, and the worst thing he could do now was let the bastard know he saw him. He went slowly toward the water, lumbering like a turtle.

As he reached the water line, something crashed through the brush above. A strong shove brought Zen to the edge of the surf; a second got him into six inches of water.

On his third push he felt his body start to float. Salt water stung his face, pricking at his nostrils.

Something rippled near him. He heaved his body forward and dove beneath the waves.

As Breanna watched from the water, the brush behind the beach opened like a curtain. Three men came out from the trees, and then a fourth. Two had rifles.

Zen was at the water—Zen was in the water.

They were going to fire at him.

"No!" she shouted. "No!"

Sahurah Niu grabbed the tall one's arm as he fired.

"Wait," he told Abdul, first in his own Malaysian, then in Abdul's native Arabic. "Don't waste your bullets while he's in the water."

"He'll get away."

"This will not be so. He is a cripple." Sahurah Niu repeated his command not to fire so the others could hear. "Wait," he added, pointing to the horizon. "The boat is coming. Do you see it?"

Zen pushed his head up for a quick breath, then dove back down, stroking toward Breanna. The world had narrowed to a tiny funnel in front of him. He could see rocks on the bottom of the ocean, twenty or more feet below as he pushed downward.

Where was his wife? He pulled his body in the direction of the rocks she'd been heading for. In the back of his mind he heard himself yelling at his body, as if they were two separate people, coach and athlete:

You've gone further and faster than this in rehab. Push, damn it, push.

The pressure in his lungs grew and finally he came up for a gulp of air. Bree was a few yards away.

"The rocks!" he told her. "That island on my left!"

She hesitated.

"The rocks," he repeated.

"What's going on? Who are they?"

"Come on." He took hold of her, pushed her down under the water, then took a stroke away. When he was sure she was going in the right direction he dove down, following.

They reached it at the same time. The rock furthest from shore was shaped like a giant turtle shell and tottered at the top of a deep pile. Zen pushed around to the other side, opening the backpack as he did. He wedged his stomach against the side of the rock, balancing as he pulled the Ziploc bag with his service pistol out from the bottom of the knapsack.

"What the hell is going on?" Breanna asked.

"Trouble in paradise," said Zen. He heard the sound of a motorboat. Turning, he saw a black triangle approaching from the eastern horizon.

"You're going to have to go for help," he told her.

"I'm not leaving you."

"You have to," Zen told her. "Swim down the beach line to the spot where those houses we passed were. They can't be more than a half-mile."

"God, Jeff, it'll take me forever to swim a half-mile. They'll get you."

"Get going then."

"Come with me."

"If we both go, they'll just follow in the boat. Besides, I can't get ashore."

"I'll carry you."

"Just fuckin' go, Bree. Now!" He pushed her away awkwardly, holding the pistol, still in its plastic bag, up out of the water.

The look she gave him wounded him as badly as any bullet, but she ducked down beneath the water, stroking away. Zen pulled himself up against the rock, waiting to see what the men on the shore would do next.

SAHURAH PUT HIS HAND TO HIS FOREHEAD, SHADING HIS eyes. The two tourists were huddled at the edge of the cove, foolishly thinking it would protect them.

They had rehearsed this. The next steps were easy.

"Abdul, go through the trees and then to the first rock. Do not go into the water." It was necessary to tell the Yemen this because he was a very simple man. "When you see that we have them, come back and meet Fallah at the edge of the beach, there."

Sahurah pointed to the eastern edge of the protected area. "Fallah, you will guard that side, in case they attempt to swim away. You may shoot them, but only if they are more than ten meters from us. Ten meters, you understand?"

"Of course."

Adi looked at him expectantly. The motorboat was now approaching, moving toward the beach at a good clip, precisely as planned.

"You and I will go in the boat," Sahurah told the short one. "We will have to wade. Make sure the weapon does not get wet. If they do not come easily we will need it."

BREANNA PULLED THROUGH THE WATER, PROPELLED BY HER fury. She was angry at Zen for sending her away, angrier still at whomever it was who was trying to kidnap or rob them.

Brunei was a paradise; how could this happen here?

The houses they had seen were no more than a mile away: 1,600 meters. One of her events in high school.

She'd never finished higher than third in it.

Breanna continued her stroke, falling into the rhythm, willing away everything, even her anger, as she plunged through the water.

* * *

ZEN WATCHED AS THE BOAT CUT ITS ENGINES AND DRIFTED toward the shore. The thugs on the beach had rolled up their pants and started to wade out. One of them had a largish rifle, possibly a machine-gun like the M249 or Belgium Minimi, a squad-level weapon that fired 5.56-millimeter ammunition from magazines or belts, which could be held in a plastic box-like container clipped beneath the chamber area just ahead of the trigger.

They moved almost lackadaisically, obviously not seeing him as much of a threat. More than likely they didn't know he had a gun.

The closer they got, the better his chances at hitting them with the pistol. On the other hand, the closer they got, the more difficult it would be to swim away.

But that wasn't an option. They had a boat. He'd never outswim it in the open water. Nor would there be much chance of surprising them from the sea.

His goal wasn't to escape. It was to distract them long enough that Breanna could escape. He would let them get close, then take out as many of them as possible. He'd target the man with the machine-gun first.

SAHURAH PUT HIS HAND DOWN ON THE GUNWALE OF THE speedboat as it came next to him in the water, trying to steady it before he pulled himself over the side. His ancestors had been fishermen, but Sahurah himself disliked boats; no matter how big, they seemed flimsy and unprotected against the awful power of the sea.

The two men in the boat looked at him with puzzled expressions, but did not speak. Unlike the others, the men who had been selected from the boat were Indonesians with a limited command of Malaysian and no knowledge of Arabic; he had to use English so they would understand.

"There has been a change in plans," he told them, grabbing onto the back of one of the seats. "The people we have come for are there."

He pointed to the rock. One of the tourists was treading water next to it; the other must have been hiding behind him.

"There?" asked the man near the wheel of the boat.

"Yes," said Sahurah. "Take us there."

He took the machine-gun from Adi's hands, cradling it against his shirt. While it was heavier than the AK47 he had first learned to shoot as a boy, it was surprisingly small for a gun that could fire so rapidly and with so much effect. Sahurah had only a pistol himself, strapped in a holster beneath his shirt.

Adi took the gun back greedily as soon as he was in the boat.

"We will not shoot them unless it is necessary," Sahurah reminded him.

Adi frowned, but then set himself against the side of the boat in a squat, holding the weapon's barrel upward and protecting it from the spray as they turned and started toward the rock. The helmsman brought the boat around in an arc, circling around from the west.

The man at the wheel cut the engine when they were twenty meters from the rock. Sahurah reached to his shirt for his gun; he would fire a shot and then tell the tourists to surrender. He would use sweet words to make the idiots believe he meant no harm. The Westerners were, without exception, cowards, eager to believe whatever they were told.

Adi tensed beside him. Sahurah knew he was about to fire. He turned to stop him, but it was too late: the gun roared. Sahurah turned and saw Adi falling backward as the machine-gun fired—he thought the little man had been pushed back by its recoil and tried to grab him, but both Adi and the gun fell off into the water. Stunned, Sahurah reached for him when he felt something punch against him, a stone that tore into his rib. He grabbed for his weapon and found himself in the bottom of the boat, finally realizing that the man on the rocks had a gun.

ZEN'S FIRST SHOT MISSED, BUT HIS SECOND AND THIRD caught the man with the machine-gun in the head. He fired three more shots; at least one struck the man next to the gunman. The boat jerked to the left and roared away out to sea.

Zen lost his grip on the rock as the wake swelled up. He couldn't keep the gun above the water, let alone himself—he slid down and then pushed up with his left hand, clambering up on top of the rock.

The boat was headed off. Thank God, he thought to himself. Thank God.

Something ricocheted against one of the rocks about thirty feet from him. Zen threw himself into the waves, still clutching the pistol. He pushed around to the seaward side of the rock then surfaced.

There was a man on shore about fifty yards away with an AK47. Zen went down beneath the waves as the man aimed and fired again. The rocks would make it almost impossible for the gunman to hit him unless he came out on the isthmus. A second gunman stood near the brush on the eastern end of the beach; Zen paddled to his right, finding a spot where he couldn't be seen from that angle. He was safe, at least for a while.

Then he heard the motor of the speed boat revving in the distance. They were coming back.

WHEN BREANNA SAW THE OBJECT IN THE DISTANCE, SHE thought at first it was a large crocodile. She stopped mid-stroke, frozen by fear.

Then she saw that it was bobbing gently and thought it must be a raft. She started toward it, and in only a few strokes realized it was part of a dock that had been abandoned ages ago and now sat forlornly in the water. Abandoned or not, it was the first sign of civilization she had seen since setting out and she swam with all her energy, kicking and flailing so ferociously that she reached it in only a few seconds. She pulled herself against it to rest. As she did, she saw a small skiff maybe seventy-five yards away, the sort of small boat a fisherman might use to troll a quiet lagoon on a hazy afternoon. An old American-made Evinrude motor, its logo faded, sat at the stern. Breanna threw herself forward, stroking overhand in a sprint to the boat. She got to the side and pulled herself up.

The boat sat about five or six yards offshore, a line at the stern anchoring her. The shore here was lined with trees; Breanna saw a path at the right side, though it wasn't clear what was beyond it.

"Hey! Hey!" she yelled. "Help! Help!"

She couldn't see anyone. Breanna turned to the motor. It was old, possibly dating from at least the 1960s, with part of the top removed. It had a pull rope.

She grabbed the rope and yanked at it. The engine turned itself over but didn't start.

Breanna stared at the motor, which had been tinkered with and repaired for more than thirty odd years. The motor seemed to be intact, without any fancy electronic gizmos or cutoff switches; even the turn throttle seemed to work. She tried the rope again and this time the engine coughed twice and caught. The propeller growled angrily as Breanna got the hang of the jury-rigged replacement mechanism that set the old outboard properly in the water. The boat jumped and started to move forward; she just barely managed to turn it in time to keep the craft from sailing into the rocky shore. She realized she hadn't released the anchor—the boat groaned, dragging the rock along. She couldn't steer and reach the line at the same time; since she was moving forward at a decent pace she didn't bother pulling it in, concentrating instead on getting her bearings as she sped back to rescue her husband.

ZEN PUSHED HIMSELF BACKWARD FROM THE ROCK, DUCKING down under the water and swimming to the west. He stayed below for as long as he could, the pressure in his lungs building until it became unbearable. As his face hit the air he heard a cacophony of sounds—the motorboat, guns firing, a distant jet. He gulped air and ducked back, pushing again. He didn't last as long this time. When he surfaced the boat was nearly on top of him. He pushed down and waited, the wake angry but not as close as he feared.

When he resurfaced, the crack of a rifle sent him back underwater with only half a breath.

WHERE WAS THE INFIDEL BASTARD? SAHURAH LEANED against the side of the boat, searching for the tourist in the water. The man had gone beneath the waves somewhere around here; he couldn't have swum too far away.

Sahurah knew that it was the cripple who was shooting at

them. How exactly he knew that—and surely that was not the logical guess—he couldn't say, but he was sure.

So the moment of pity he had felt on the beach had been a grave mistake. A lesson.

He heard one of his men firing from shore and turned toward the east. A head bobbed and disappeared in the water nearby.

"There," shouted Sahurah, momentarily using Malaysian instead of English. "There, over there," he yelled. "Go back. Get the dog. Run him down!"

BREANNA STRETCHED FORWARD, TRYING TO GRASP THE knotted line holding the stone while still steering the boat. She was about three inches too short; finally she leaned her leg against the handle, awkwardly steadying it, and grabbed the rope, pulling it back with her as she once more took control of the motor. The anchor turned out to be a coffee can filled with concrete; she pulled it up over the side and let it roll with a thud into the bottom of the craft.

A boat circled in the distance offshore. Breanna bent down and held on, steadying herself as she made a beeline for it.

SAHURAH BROUGHT UP HIS PISTOL TO FIRE. HIS FIRST THREE shots missed far to the right. As he shifted to get a sturdier position he felt the pain in his side again; the bullet had only creased the flesh but it flamed nonetheless.

He would have revenge. He aimed again, but as he fired, the boat jerked abruptly to the north.

"What?" demanded Sahurah, turning toward the helm.

The men pointed toward the west. A second boat was coming.

For a long moment, Sahurah hesitated. He felt his anger well inside him. Unquenchable thirst—frustration—rage.

He had failed.

"Get the others," he said finally. "Get the ones on shore. Quickly."

* * *

THIS TIME THE PRESSURE TO BREATHE WAS SO FIERCE ZEN started to cough as he broke water, his throat rebelling. His body shook with the convulsions and he found himself twisting backward in the water, unsure where he was.

He'd saved Bree, at least, he thought. They might have gotten him but his wife at least was safe.

Zen heard the boat behind him. Surprised that it was there, he pushed his tired arms to turn him in that direction. But instead he slipped beneath the waves, his energy drained.

BREANNA SAW THAT THE OTHER BOAT WAS GOING IN TO THE beach. She cut the throttle back but even at its low idle setting it still pushed the boat forward. She dared not pull the ignition wire or fiddle with the eccentric controls too much; instead, she put the boat into a circle, taking some of its momentum away before approaching the rock, about two hundred yards away.

She didn't see Zen.

Did they have him already? Was that why there were going to shore?

"Zen! Zen!"

Something bobbed to the left, about thirty yards away.

"Jeff! Jeff!"

It was him. He started to swim for the boat, but he was moving in slow motion, not swimming as strongly as he normally did. She maneuvered to the left and right, but couldn't quite get close enough on the first pass and still didn't dare to turn off the motor.

"I'll circle around. Grab on!" she called. "This is as slow as I can go."

Breanna pushed against the throttle switch on the engine, managing to slow the speed a little more but still not entirely cut it as she came around. Zen grabbed the side of the boat, clamping his arms against it like a hobo pulling himself onto the side of a freight car.

"What are you doing?" he yelled as she pushed at the throttle, trying to get it to increase speed gently. "Let me get in for cryin' out loud," said Zen, pulling up against the side.

"Wait," she told him, fighting to keep the boat balanced and moving in the right direction as the engine began churning the water faster.

"They're going away," Zen told her. "It's all right."

"It's all right," she repeated, not quite ready to believe it.

Brunei International Airport, military section
1830

Mack Smith looked at his watch again and shook his head. Everyone in the damn country ran at least a half-hour late.

It was bad enough that his pilots were cavalier about reporting on time, but now even Breanna had caught the bug.

Mack paced in front of the A-37B Dragonfly he was supposed to fly for the night exercise. He was so short of trained pilots that he had to take the plane up himself. It wasn't that he didn't want to—Mack loved to fly the old Cessna, which was similar to the T-37 "Tweet" air force pilots cut their teeth on—but the fact of the matter was, as head of the air force, he should at least have had the option of assigning someone to go in his place, just in case he wanted to party or kick back a bit. He currently had only five other pilots with suitable ratings and training to fly jet aircraft, and he was training them all to handle the Megafortress as well as his four A-37Bs. Besides getting these guys up to speed, he needed to at least triple his stable of jocks before the two other Megafortresses arrived.

Hence the importance of tonight's session.

Stinking Breanna. Where was she?

Come to think of it, he didn't spend *any* time partying anymore. There was just too much to do to get this tin can air force in shape. New planes, pilots, ground people—he had a few kids who could strip a jet engine with their eyes shut and get it back together, but he needed more, more, more.

"Excuse me, Minister."

Mack turned to find one of his maintenance officers, a friendly but sad-sacked sort named Major Brown, who was descended from a nineteenth century British regent or some such thing.

"You can just call me Mack. You don't need to use my title," Mack told him for the hundredth time.

Brown's attempt at a smile looked more forlorn than his frown.

"We have only a week's worth of fuel supply left, sir. You asked me to bring it to your attention."

"Did you put through that requisition or whatever the paper-work was?"

"Yes, sir."

"Did we get it?"

"No, sir." Brown explained that simply forwarding a form into the morass that was the Brunei defensive forces purchasing system was hardly enough to elicit a yawn, let alone needed fuel supplies. Mack had heard some variation of this lecture three times a day since taking this job nearly a month ago.

"I want you to go over there tomorrow and baby-sit the damn request," said Mack. "We need a ninety-day supply of fuel at a bare minimum."

"Where?"

"Wherever you have to go. No—bypass the stinking bureau-cracy. Go to the central defense ministry office and tell the chief of staff I sent you."

Brown blanched. Things in the kingdom of Brunei were done by strict protocol. A mere major, or even a general of in-sufficient breeding, did not talk to the chief of staff, who like most people of importance was related to the sultan.

"All right," said Mack, recognizing the look. "What do you suggest?"

"If I go to the finance office, perhaps I can get an expedi-tious result."

Two weeks ago, Mack would have asked why Brown would have to go to the finance office to get something as simple as a fuel order sent up the line. Now he knew that the explanation would not clarify anything.

"Do your best," he told Brown. "We're all set for the exer-cise, right?"

"An hour ago, sir."

"You're a good man, Brown," said Mack. "Do your best on the fuel thing."

"Perhaps if you spoke to the chief of staff yourself."

"I intend on kicking his butt if I ever see it," said Mack un-der his breath.

While Mack and Brown had been talking, two other mem-bers of Mack's staff had approached. One was his administra-tive assistant, Suzanne Souzou, who had a thick wad of folders in her hand. The other was his director of operations, a Brunei of Chinese extraction named Han Chou.

"Miss Souzou first," said Mack. He smiled at Han, who was offended by the fact that a woman was given priority. "Beauty before brains."

"You need to sign these," said his secretary. "The interviews are set up."

"Which interviews?"

"The contract people to fill your temporary positions?"

"Yeah, okay. Right. Good."

"You will need to sign these or the men won't get paid."

Mack flipped through the folders; it would take him more than an hour to sign them all. He'd tried telling her two weeks ago to sign for him, but that, too, was a major breach of Brunei etiquette.

"All right. I'll leave them on your desk first thing in the morning. Good night."

Souzou flashed a big smile before turning and heading back to the car that had brought her. Mack admired her walking style before turning to Han, who bowed stiffly and handed him an envelope.

"Uh, I don't get it," said Mack, taking the envelope.

Han said nothing.

"This isn't a resignation, is it?"

Han still refused to speak.

"Yo, Han, my man. My main man—you can't leave. We're just getting going. Come on. We're going places, my friend. Going places."

It was debatable whether Mack's attempt at camaraderie would have worked in the States, where someone at least would have understood the expressions he was using. The only effect it had on Han was to confuse him. Mack opened the letter reluctantly.

"You're really leaving me?"

Han's English was heavily accented, but Mack got the gist of it. The new regime—Minister Mack—had brought too much change.

Mack waved his hand. "You're free," he told him. "Go. Hit the road."

Han bowed again. Mack simply shook his head. He was now down to four legitimate pilots, plus himself.

Breanna's SUV appeared at the far end of the road, heading toward him. Mack waited with his hands on his hips, frowning as he saw that Zen was sitting in the front seat beside her. He'd shown up unannounced yesterday, but Breanna had insisted his visit wouldn't interfere with the training schedule.

"Captain," he said as she rolled down the window. "We're running a little late."

"I'm sorry," said Breanna. "We were detained."

"I'll bet," he said, interpreting her words as a euphemism for sex.

"We were at the police ministry," she said. "We tried calling you."

"Police ministry? What'd you do? Get nailed for speeding?"

Mack listened, dumbfounded, as Breanna explained what had happened that afternoon on the beach. It seemed far-fetched. People here left their doors unlocked and keys in their cars.

"This for real, Bree?" he asked.

"Bet your ass it was real," growled Zen from the other side.

"Who were these jokers?"

"Police weren't sure," said Breanna. "Possibly guerillas from Malaysia trying to kidnap tourists. There are Muslim extremists trying to take over the Malaysian part of the island."

"Not on that beach. That's the prince's beach," said Mack.

"Maybe they missed the sign," said Zen.

"Maybe they were trying to get the prince," said Mack.

"Police said that was impossible," said Breanna.

"That's because they don't think it's possible," said Mack. "They don't think that way—they don't think like you and me."

"Listen, about the exercise tonight, we're going to have to call it off," said Breanna. "The State Department wants to interview me."

"What?" said Mack.

"They asked me to go over to see one of their intelligence people for a debriefing. I told them fine."

"Well, sure, after the exercise."

Breanna shook her head. "Sorry. We're already late. And I haven't had anything to eat, either."

Mack had enough experience with Breanna to know it was useless to argue. "How about tomorrow night?"

"Fine," said Breanna.

"Oh wait, I can't do it tomorrow night. I have some dinner with the prince."

"Blow it off," said Zen sardonically.

Mack pretended he didn't hear. "How about early the next morning, just before dawn? Say four or five?"

"Dawn?"

"Yeah, that would work," said Mack. "What do you think?"

"I don't know."

"Come on, Bree. You owe me."

"Owe you? How?"

"I got you that beach," said Mack.

"Oh there's a debt to be repaid," said Zen.

"I'll do it. We'll set it up tomorrow," said Breanna.

"Great," said Mack. "Just great."

Washington, D.C.
6 October 1997 (7 October Brunei), 0743

"Hey, Colonel," said Jed Barclay, pulling up in front of the suburban motel where Lieutenant Colonel Tecumseh "Dog" Bastian had been waiting. "Sorry I'm running a little late."

"It's okay," said Dog, aware that his voice probably suggested the opposite.

"Want to grab a coffee?" asked Barclay.

"I had breakfast."

"Yes, sir."

Barclay pulled out into the traffic. Though he looked like he belonged in college—if that—Jed was the National Security Council's assistant director for technology and the right-hand man for national security advisor Philip Freeman. He was the unofficial go-between used by the president and the NSC for directing Dreamland's "Whiplash" operations, and just about Dog's only real ally in Washington. The colonel felt bad about snapping at him, but he was in a foul mood; his daughter and son-in-law had been involved in some sort of incident in Brunei, of all places. While they were fine, the call he'd gotten a few hours ago about it had cost him the last sliver of sleep he'd been counting on before this morning's meeting with the president. Brunei and Washington were exactly twelve hours apart; when it was day there it was night here, and vice versa.

"Hotel okay?" asked Jed.

"Fine. Listen, I didn't mean to bark at you there. I just don't want to be late for the meeting."

"Well, we won't be," said Jed. "I got a heads-up. The president is running behind."

"I thought I was his first appointment."

"You were. But they slid in some domestic stuff and the chief of staff called last night to slide back the appointment. We're not on until nine-thirty. And given the way things usually go . . ."

Dog curled his hands in front of his chest. The president *was* the president, and you waited for him, not the other way around. And surely there were many important things on his plate.

But this wasn't a good sign.

"I didn't have time for breakfast myself," added Jed.

"Let's get something then," said Dog, acceding.

Jed described the restaurant as a "coffee place," but if that was true, it was the fanciest coffee place Dog had ever been in. A hostess greeted them and escorted them across a thick, plush carpet to a table covered with three layers of thick linens. Dog recognized two senators and one of the aides to the vice president at different tables along the way.

"The NSC'll pay, don't worry," said Jed before Dog opened the thick, leather-bound menu.

That prepared him, somewhat, for the prices. Dog told the waitress he just wanted coffee. She nodded, then turned to Jed. "Feta omelet. Light toast. Right?" she asked.

Jed nodded.

"You come here a lot?" said Dog.

"Uh, Mr. Freeman does. And so, because of that, I do."

"He's going to drop in on us?"

"He might," admitted Jed.

"You might have warned me," said Dog, finally understanding that Jed's delays and hunger were part of a prearranged plan.

"I am warning you," said Jed. He closed his mouth as the waitress approached, not continuing until she left. "Look, the president has already made up his mind on Brunei."

"Brunei doesn't need a fleet of fighter jets. Or Megafortresses, for that matter," said Dog.

"The president isn't going to reverse the Megafortress decision, Colonel. Not even for you. The two other planes are to go to Brunei as soon as they're ready."

"With Flighthawks?"

The Flighthawks, or U/MF-3s, were among Dreamland's most prized possessions. "U/MF" stood for "unmanned fighters." The Flighthawks were highly capable interceptors, typically launched from the wings of the Megafortress and used for a variety of tasks, from defending the big plane to attacking ground targets. About the size of a Miata sports car, they could go nearly the speed of sound and could be controlled up to twenty miles from the mother ship.

"That's still to be decided," said Jed.

"We have to protect our technology, Jed."

"I don't disagree. But it's not my call."

"You're not in favor of any of this, are you? Rewarding their cooperation in dealing with China is one thing, but giving our technology away to countries that don't need it and have their own agendas—"

"They are allies."

"For now."

"It's not my call," said Jed. "I think we'll hold the line on the Flighthawks. And probably the F-15s. But they do have a legitimate need for surveillance aircraft, and for more modern fighters. And they'll buy from the Russians if not us."

"Did you try pushing LADS?" asked Dog. "They could buy that system with the money they'll spend on jet fuel for one Megafortress over the course of a year."

"I did. State did, too. Very hard."

"That's what they need. It's low-cost, and we could work with them. It'd be useful to us as well. Let them keep the one Megafortress for sea patrols, and use LADS to guard the kingdom's borders."

"Blimps aren't sexy," said Jed. "However much they make sense."

Dog frowned, but he couldn't argue. LADS stood for Lighter-than-Air Defensive Surveillance system, and at its heart it was simply a blimp—or more accurately, a network of blimps.

Outfitted with millimeter and phased array radar as well as infrared and optical sensors, the small airships could be posted over the ocean and kept on station for weeks for about the cost of a Megafortress sortie. The system was scaleable—in other words, blimps could be added almost indefinitely, increasing the area to be covered without overly taxing the system. (The theoretical limit of inputs for the present system was 164°, far above the practical limitations that would be imposed by the coverage area itself.) The blimps could be pre-positioned to cordon off a patrol area several hundred miles wide, or deployed ahead of a mission team.

While LADS had several Dreamland-style features that made it unique, including technology that made its vehicles nearly invisible to the naked eye, it was only one of a number of lighter-than-air systems being developed by the U.S. military and defense contractors. Airships could handle tasks from cargo transport to geostationary surveillance. Relatively inexpensive and extremely dependable, the old technology had a bright future, except for one thing: blimps weren't sexy.

"I was thinking I might suggest F/A-18s if we turn down the F-15s," added Jed. "A package similar to Malaysia's."

"It's still overkill for their needs. What about selling them more A-37s?" asked Dog. "Very versatile and reliable aircraft. Perfect for their needs."

"They're pushing hard, and they have friends in Congress," said Jed. "Assuming we can stop the F-15s and the Flighthawks, do you think F/A-18s are too much?"

"A dozen F/A-18s, along with three Megafortresses, would make them a pretty potent power," said Dog. "They could threaten Malaysia and Indonesia."

"Malaysia has F/A-18s and MiG-29s already," said Jed.

"But they're on the peninsula, more than a thousand miles away. Indonesia's forces are also too far to threaten Brunei. Besides, they're all allies."

"We want a counterbalance to the Chinese, and we have to reward the sultan," said Jed. "Those are the real issues."

"That sounds a lot like your boss talking, Jed."

Jed glanced up, then held his coffee cup out for a refill as the waitress approached. Dog, sensing it was going to be a long morning, slid his over for a refill as well.

* * *

"Tᴇᴄᴜᴍsᴇʜ, ɢᴇᴛ ɪɴ ʜᴇʀᴇ!"

The walls practically shook with the president's loud greeting. Dog followed Jed and NSC advisor Freeman into the Oval Office, doing his best to guard against the schoolboy awe he inevitably felt upon meeting the president. He'd met Kevin Martindale twice since he'd been elected, and talked to him on average at least three times a month. But this did nothing to lessen the slightly giddy sensation he felt in the presence of the President of the United States.

Call it a by-product of military training, old-fashioned patriotism, or a side effect of his deep appreciation of the country's history, but Dog still felt honored—deeply honored—to shake the president's hand. He even blushed slightly as the president praised him in front of Arthur Chastain, the secretary of defense, and National Security Advisor Freeman.

"What you did in China makes you a hero ten times over," said President Martindale. "And everyone in the world knows it. A million people are alive today because of you, Tecumseh. We won't forget it."

"Yes, sir."

"I have some good news. The Pentagon has worked things out with the bean counters. The Megafortress program, the Unmanned Bomber Program, and the airborne laser arrays will all be funded. As will the next generation Flighthawk program."

"That is good news," said Dog, who hadn't expected all of the programs to survive.

"You'll have to nip and tuck here and there," added the president, "but Arthur will help you on that. Won't you, Mr. Secretary?"

"Yes, sir, of course." The defense secretary smiled at him for the first time ever.

"You're here to tell me Brunei shouldn't have Megafortresses and F-15s," said Martindale. "You're mad about it, and you wanted to talk to me in person before the deal is finalized."

"Mad would be not the right word, sir," said Dog.

"But you don't approve."

"I just feel that giving Brunei—giving anyone—our technology, is a problem."

"Let's stop right there," said Freeman, the national security advisor. "Because number one, we're not giving them anything. They're paying for the privilege. And that payment is going to help us develop the next generation of weapons and aircraft at Dreamland. It's one reason we can go ahead with your work there."

"A small reason," objected Defense Secretary Chastain.

"We're not giving them our most advanced technology," said Freeman. "The basic structure of the EB-52 is older than I am."

"But sir, with respect, that's like saying the basic structure of a newborn is older than its mother," said Dog. "The Megafortresses have been completely rebuilt. Their wings are different, the fuselage is more streamlined and stealthy, the engines, the control surfaces—a B-52 would never have made it that far into China."

"The Old Dog made it into Russia," said President Martindale. Years before Dog had joined Dreamland, a B-52 had helped avert war with the Soviet Union with a daring—and officially unauthorized—mission over the heart of Soviet defenses. Immortalized in the press as "The Flight of the Old Dog," the incident had been every bit as daring—and suicidal—as Bastian's over China. Martindale had been a governor then, but it was well known that he admired the people who had pulled off the mission; he'd told Dog he kept a copy of the book detailing their exploits on his reading table upstairs in the White House.

"You have reservations about Brunei?" President Martindale asked Dog. "Can they be trusted?"

"It's a beautiful country," said Dog. "But it's not a democracy."

"Give it time," said Freeman.

"It's not just that," said Dog. "If we give them Megafortresses and F-15s, then what do we give the Malaysians and Indonesians? They share that island. What about the Philippines?"

"Those countries haven't asked for EB-52s," said the national security advisor.

"They will," said Dog. "What do we tell them? They're not as important as Brunei? What if they ask for F-22s?"

"They're not getting F-22s. No one is," said the president.

"They're not getting F-15s, either. Not F-15Cs, or F-15Es. But if we don't give them something, they'll simply buy from the Russians. The world is becoming more complicated, Colonel. Very much more complicated."

"I appreciate that. I just don't want my weapons systems making things worse."

"Neither do I," said the president. "We'll have to work hard to see that they aren't."

Malay Negara Brunei Darussalam
7 October 1997, (local) 0802

In Zen's opinion, the official Brunei reaction to the incident on the beach was schizophrenic beyond belief. On the one hand, they clearly didn't consider it, or didn't want to consider it, as anything but an isolated and freakish incident.

On the other hand, they considered it an insult to the country, which prided itself on being the perfect host. Because of this, the authorities felt obliged to apologize in person, and therefore Breanna and Zen had been invited to breakfast at the Royal House, an exclusive club used only by very high-ranking government officials just outside of town.

Zen might not have minded it except that he was due to catch a flight home at one o'clock, which meant rather than spending the next few hours alone with his wife he had to sit stiffly through a long and formal breakfast. He even had to wear a civilian jacket and tie, purchased specially for him by the State Department liaison, due to some obscure protocol that he didn't understand.

"Oh, you look handsome. Stop complaining," said Breanna.

"I'm sorry, but it really is necessary to present the proper image," said Brenda Kelly, a state department liaison who had been sent over to help smooth the Stockards past the protocol hazards. It was at least the third time she'd apologized. "And wearing your uniform might have sent the wrong message."

"I wasn't going to wear my uniform," said Zen.

"You'll have to excuse my husband," said Breanna. "He thinks wearing a clean T-shirt is dressing up."

"I'm on vacation, Bree. It's not that advanced a concept."

"There are elaborate customs here," said Kelly. "Just as people in Brunei usually eat with their fingers—"

"Only the right hand," said Breanna in a stage whisper to remind him.

"We have to follow their lead," finished Kelly.

Zen sighed. It was no use arguing; he was stuck in a tie, without hope for parole.

"So are they going to catch these jokers or what?" asked Zen.

"Please don't ask that when the minister comes," said Ms. Kelly.

"Why not?"

"It's insulting, Jeff. Of course they'll catch them," said Breanna.

"They were probably guerillas from across the border," said Kelly. "Islamic terrorists who want to disrupt the Malaysian government. Brunei itself doesn't have an insurgent problem. There's no poverty here. Everyone's happy."

Zen thought that was incredibly naive. People didn't rebel against governments just because they were poor. The people who threw the tea into Boston Harbor weren't starving.

"I think it was a kidnapping for money," said Breanna.

"Well they tried to get the wrong people then, obviously," said Zen. "They could have saved themselves a lot of trouble by looking at our checking account."

"If they could figure it out," laughed Bree.

"I think they were going after the royal family," said Zen. "It was their beach."

"Oh, my God, I was afraid of this," said Kelly. She pushed away from the chair and rose.

Zen looked up. The sultan himself had just come into the room. He wore a white Western suit, with no outward sign of his rank, but there was no mistaking his authority; a phalanx of aides followed in his wake, and they were trailed by a dozen soldiers. He strutted confidently across the room—the gait even seemed a bit arrogant, thought Zen, but then if he were absolute ruler of an oil-rich kingdom, he'd be a little arrogant, too.

The sultan smiled at Breanna and Kelly, waving his hands at them to make them sit in their seats. Zen watched him bow to the ladies, then bowed his own head as the sultan looked at him.

"The heroes!" exclaimed the ruler.

Attendants and restaurant staff swept in behind him, one

pulling up an oversized chair and others appearing with trays of food. Zen's coffee was refilled; the ladies were given fresh tea. Breakfast meats and sweets suddenly covered every inch of the table.

"I apologize to you on behalf of the people of Brunei," said the sultan, looking at Breanna.

"Oh, an apology isn't necessary," Bree told him. "It was nothing."

The sultan shook his head. "These criminals. They are outlaws before the eyes of God."

"Who were they, exactly?" asked Zen, ignoring the evil-eye glare Kelly shot at him.

"They came over from Malaysia, we believe," said the sultan, who did not seem offended. "Or they were Chinese criminals. We will catch them."

"Good," said Zen.

The sultan turned to Breanna. "You have been training our pilots."

"Yes. They're very good students."

"Thank you," he said, bowing his head. "Your plane is a wonderful aircraft. I hope we will be able to purchase many."

"Maybe you should get more counter-insurgency aircraft, if guerillas are a problem," said Zen.

The sultan's expression gave only the slightest hint that the comment was out of line. Kelly, on the other hand, seemed to be having a heart attack.

"We have requested many aircraft to bring ourselves up to present standards," said the sultan, his tone slightly indulgent. "Fortunately, we ourselves do not have an insurgent problem. We need the aircraft to fulfill our role in ASEAN, the Asian alliance. Beyond that—well, you see for yourself. Everyone is happy here."

The sultan rose. Kelly jumped up. Zen half expected her to beckon at him to rise out of his chair.

Hey, if the sultan had any *real* power, maybe Zen would be able to.

"I apologize again, and I hope you will enjoy your stay," the sultan told Breanna. "Anything that can be done to make you happy, will be done."

Then he held out his hand for her to kiss his ring. Zen rolled his eyes, but Breanna did it, as did Kelly. Then the sultan, trailed by his entourage, strutted his way out of the room.

"YOU INSULTED HIM," KELLY SAID WHEN THEY WERE GONE.

"Relax," Zen told her. "What's he going to do? Nuke us?"

"Jeff, that's terrible," Breanna told her husband. "Really, hon. I know you're still upset. But cut the guy some slack."

"Why? He's the supreme ruler, right? He's in charge. Who else should take the heat?"

Breanna rolled her eyes. It was always obvious when he was upset—he got even crankier than normal. She turned to Kelly. "I don't think he really insulted the sultan. And he has a point about the aircraft. Megafortresses are overkill."

"The sultan was insulted," said the state department rep. "Believe me, I could tell. You don't understand this country."

"I do understand that we almost got killed," said Zen.

"Weapons procurement is none of your business."

"I know more about those weapons than the sultan ever will. And I'll tell you—Brunei doesn't need them. They do need counter-insurgency aircraft. That's what you should be selling them. Those people who attacked us yesterday are just the tip of the iceberg, I'll bet."

Kelly got up. "Please contact my office if you need anything else. Have a good flight home, Major."

"You were really rude," Breanna told him when Kelly was gone.

"Come on. Kelly forgets whose side she's on."

"She's just trying to do her job. And I meant to the sultan. He's a very nice man. Very charming."

"Aw, come on, Bree. He's a dictator. Just because he calls himself sultan, you're going to let him off?"

"He's very educated and civilized. He's a hereditary ruler."

"So was King George, the guy we kicked out of America two hundred years ago, remember?"

"I forgot your ancestors came over on the *Mayflower*."

"It was the *Guernsey*," said Zen. He wasn't joking—his relatives had come over in the 1600s, landing in Virginia.

"It wouldn't hurt you to be more diplomatic," she insisted,

taking her cup of tea. "You're going to have to be more diplomatic if you want to make colonel."

"Why? Your dad doesn't kiss ass."

Breanna put her hand out and touched his arm. "Hey," she said.

"Hey yourself."

"Let's not fight."

"Who's fighting?"

"Okay."

"Want me to cancel my flight?"

Breanna looked at him. She did, actually. Not just for this afternoon—for weeks and months. She wanted him to stay here with her, stay in paradise.

Or something less than paradise. As long as they were together.

She'd been scared yesterday, worried what she would do if she found him dead there. Breanna had faced that fear before, but that didn't make it easier—if anything, it seemed to be getting worse.

She wanted to tell him to stay. But he had a job to do. He was due back at Dreamland for a VIP demonstration.

"I do want you to cancel your flight," she admitted finally. "But you better not. I'm okay." She put her hand down on his. "We have some time left. Let's go back to the hotel."

"Sounds like a plan," he said, stroking her fingertips as if they were the soft petals of a flower.

Outside Kota Kinabalu, Malaysia
1400

Sahurah Niu waited outside the hut, trying to clear his mind of all distraction. The mission, so long in the planning, had been an utter failure. The operation—the first launched by their group against Brunei instead of Malaysia, their long-time enemy—had resulted only in their own losses. The corrupt sultan and his puppet government would now prepare themselves against further attacks, and perhaps even work in concert with the Malaysians.

There was no way to take it back now. Regrets were useless. He must face the punishment that awaited him like a man.

An aide emerged from the hut and beckoned to Sahurah. He lowered his head and stepped inside, preparing himself with a silent prayer. His head throbbed, but he sturdied himself against the pain; he would find redemption in punishment, he decided. He would accept his punishment gladly.

The Saudi visitor sat beside the imam, legs crossed on the rug covering the dirt floor. Sahurah had met the Saudi a year before at the training camp in Afghanistan; he was a devout, humble man filled with fire against the Western corruptors and devils, as holy in his way as the imam who had been the spiritual and temporal leader of the movement on Borneo island for more than a decade. Sahurah had seen him arrive yesterday, but it was clear that the Saudi did not recognize him; he said nothing then, and he said nothing now, lowering himself humbly. It was unusual that another witnessed their talks, but perhaps that was intended as part of the punishment. Sahurah bowed his head and waited.

But the imam did not berate him. He asked instead if he would like something to drink.

Sahurah declined, trying to hide his surprise. He glanced at the Saudi, but then turned his gaze back to the rug in front of him.

"The next phase of struggle has begun," said the imam. He spoke in Arabic for the benefit of their visitor, who did not speak Malaysian. "You will go to Kota Kinabalu, and carry a message. It has been arranged."

Kota Kinabalu, on the coast below them, was a stronghold of the Malaysian government. It contained a police station and a small naval base. Until now, the imam had forbidden operations there—it was considered too well guarded by the Malaysian authorities.

He was being sent to become a martyr. For the first time in months, Sahurah felt truly happy.

"You will meet with a Malaysian, and you will bring back a message," added the imam. "Specific instructions will meet you near your destination, as a precaution for your security. Do this successfully, and much glory will come to you. There will be other tasks."

Sahurah struggled to contain his disappointment. He bowed his head, then rose and left the hut.

Dreamland
7 October 1997, (local) 0432

"Dream Mover is approaching target area, preparing to launch probe units," the airborne mission commander told Danny Freah over the command circuit.

"Acknowledged," said Danny.

"Software's up and running," said Jennifer Gleason, hunched over a laptop next to Danny in the MV-22 Osprey. "Ten seconds to air launch."

"Let's get it going," whispered Danny under his breath.

"Launching One. Launching Two," said the pilot.

Two winged canisters about twelve feet long dropped off the wings of the C-17. Their bodies looked more like squashed torpedoes than aircraft, but the unpowered rectangles were a cross between gliders and dump trucks. The canisters—at the moment they did not have an official name—were the delivery end of the Automated Combat Robot or ACR system, a cutting-edge force multiplier designed to augment the fighting abilities of small combat teams operating in hostile territory. As the canisters fell from the aircraft, two mission specialists aboard the C-17 took control of them, popping out winglets and initiating a controlled descent onto Dreamland Test Range C, five miles away.

Jennifer, monitoring the software that helped the specialists steer the canisters, began pumping her keyboard furiously as the screen flashed a red warning.

"Problem?" asked Danny.

"Ehh," she said. "Sensor read won't translate quickly enough."

"Is it going to crash?"

"Hope not."

"If he crashes it, three congressmen are going to tell everyone in America the system doesn't work."

"Not everyone in America," said Jennifer, putting her nose closer to her keys.

Danny tried to relax. In his capacity as the head of the Whiplash ground team, he was responsible for the system being tested. It was his first—and so far only—program responsibility, and he shared it with two senior engineers. But as the ranking military officer on the project, he'd been the one to meet with the congressmen, the face VIPs liked to attach to a mission.

The congressmen were already in a bad mood. When they had insisted on seeing the Automated Combat Robot or ACR system in a "real live test," they apparently didn't realize that it was meant to operate at such an ungodly hour.

The event scenario was straightforward. A downed airman had just been located behind enemy lines by a search and rescue asset. Danny and two of his Whiplash troopers, aided by the robots, would rescue him from the clutches of Red, the enemy patrolling all around.

In real life, such a rescue would probably have been done with considerable force, or at least as much firepower as possible. There was basically no such thing as too much muscle in that situation, and the more boots—and guns—available, the better. But the more people in the package, the more things that could go wrong. ACR could make it possible to limit the exposure of the rescuers and increase the odds of success.

"They're in. Okay," said Jennifer. "Deployment. You're looking good, Danny."

"Ten minutes," he told his men.

Down on the ground, the two gliding canisters had landed on the scrubby desert. Their sides had fallen away, disgorging a trio of ACR robots. The units were roughly two feet in length and were propelled by articulated tractor treads at both sides, an arrangement that allowed them to get over obstacles two feet high and avoid anything larger. Besides the small infrared and video cameras studding the units, the ACR robots carried what looked like a bouquet of pipe organs atop their chassis. These were reworked M203 forty-millimeter grenade launchers, which could be equipped with a variety of grenades, making the ARC units weapons as well as scouts.

The units began fanning out to form a perimeter around the downed airman. "Deployed without a problem," reported Jennifer. "The Toasters are marching on."

Danny winced at the nickname, hoping it wouldn't catch on. He picked up his smart helmet and put it on, flipping down the visor, a display screen which could be tied into the ACR system, or any of several other sensor sets supplied through a special Dreamland system.

"Gear up," Danny told his team. Then he began flipping through the ACR screens, looking for the four members of Red who were hunting his downed airman.

SERGEANT BEN "BOSTON" ROCKLAND, THE RED COMMANDER, smiled as he heard the drone of the approaching Osprey. Though it was still a good distance off, the aircraft had a very distinctive sound.

He turned and nodded to the ranger a few feet away. They'd decided not to use their radios, figuring that the Whiplash team might be able to home in on the signal. The ranger, another member of Red, lobbed a smoke grenade at the lumbering robot that was trundling toward them twenty yards away. As the grenade exploded, Boston saw that the ruse would work even better than he had hoped—the robot began peppering the air with its own smoke grenades, and provoked the robot to the north and south of it to start firing as well. The thick layer of smoke began drifting over the test range, obscuring the robots' sensors.

"Bonzai!" yelled Boston, throwing off his vest and starting to run.

THEY USED ROPES TO GET OFF THE OSPREY QUICKLY. THE large blades of the aircraft's engines whipped up the dirt, pelting the team with a mist of rocks. Danny got to the ground and spun to his right, hustling after his two men as they sprinted the fifty yards to their "airman." One of the ACR units had engaged the Red unit to the north; from this point out it was going to be a jog in the park.

The whirling sand blocked Danny's optical image momentarily, but as it cleared he saw his man a few yards away, standing in his shirtsleeves and waving his hand. His other team members had apparently detoured to protect the perimeter, so Danny went to his airman to tap him per the exercise rules and call the Osprey in for the pickup.

Except it wasn't his airman.

"Bang bang, you're dead," grinned Boston, producing a pistol from behind his back. Its laser dot settled on Danny's bulletproof vest, officially killing him. "Gotcha, Captain. Boy, if I only had a camera right now . . ."

Off the coast of Brunei
8 October 1997, (local) 0502

The stars had begun to fade from the sky, and the ocean swelled with the mottled shadows of the approaching morn. A solitary merchant ship cruised in the darkness, heading toward the capital of Brunei, Bandar Seri Begawan, which lay upriver from the Brunei Bay on the northern coast of the island of Borneo. The ship rode low on the waves with a load of motorbikes and electric goods, along with a variety of items ranging from Korean vegetables to American-style jeans.

Arriving on the bridge from his cabin, the captain of the ship noticed a shadow on the southwest horizon. He stared at it a moment, trying to make sense of it. The dark smudge moved with incredible swiftness, riding so low against the water that it could only be a wave or some sort of optical illusion; still, the captain went to the radar himself, confirming that there was no contact. His thirty years at sea had made him wary, and it was only when he looked back and saw nothing that he reached for his customary cup of coffee. He took a sip from his cup and listened as the officer of the watch described the expected weather. A storm had been forecast but was at least several hours away; they would be safely in the harbor by then.

"It is good that we are early then," he told the others on the bridge in Spanish.

It was the last thing the captain said on this earth. For as he raised his cup of coffee to his lips, the missile that had been launched from the shadow in the distance exploded five feet behind him.

THE FRENCH-BUILT EXOCET MISSILE CARRIED A RELATIVELY small warhead at 364 pounds; while the explosion destroyed the bridge it would not by itself have been enough to sink the ship. The more damaging blow was landed by the second weapon, fired a bare second and a half after the first; this missile struck at the waterline just ahead of the exact middle of the ship.

The warhead carried through the hull before exploding; the vessel shuddered with the impact and within moments began to settle. Nearly a third of the crew had been killed or trapped by the two blasts; the others were so stunned that it would be several minutes before most even got to their proper emergency stations. By then the ship would be lost.

Five miles away, the man who had given the order to launch the missiles stood over the small video screen, watching through a long-range infrared camera as the doomed merchant ship began to sink.

The attack had been an easy one; a bare demonstration of the Malaysian navy vessel's capabilities. Named the *Barracuda,* the experimental high-speed craft was every bit the voracious predator, clothed in dark black skin made of metal and fiber-glass arranged in sharp facets to deflect radar waves. The craft used a technology known as "wing-in-surface-effect," which allowed it to skim over the water at high speed; it could reach over four hundred knots, though to fire effectively it had to slow to below one hundred, and had to go even slower in choppy seas and bad weather. A one-of-a-kind vessel built in secret as part of a concerted effort to upgrade the Malaysian military, the *Barracuda* heralded a new age for the nation that spread out over more than a thousand miles of the southeastern Pacific.

A new age, and new opportunities, thought the vessel's commander, Captain Dazhou Ti. He had great wishes for the future, and above all a lust for revenge against the family that had wronged his ancestors. The *Barracuda* would make it possible to achieve all of his goals.

Dazhou straightened, then looked around the red-lit command area of his vessel. The space was barely ten by twenty feet, and every inch was utilized. Eight men and the captain worked here; another two were assigned to the rear compartment as weapons handlers to watch over the automated equipment and, if the need arose, to work the thirty-millimeter cannon.

"A job well done," he told his men.

The crew was well disciplined, and not one man looked up from his station or said the slightest word. This pleased Dazhou greatly.

"We will return," he announced. "To your course, helm."

The vessel began picking up speed instantly, slipping into the morning mist that hugged the coastline. Dazhou returned to his station at the center of the deck, mindful that he fired but the opening salvo in a long, long war.

II
"What Is Going on Here?"

MACK SMITH BANKED HARD RIGHT, PUTTING THE A-37B Dragonfly at a right angle to the Megafortress's radar. Had the radar been an older unit, he might have succeeded in confusing it. Pulse-Doppler radars had difficulty picking up returns from objects at a ninety-degree angle; many were the pilots who had managed to escape an enemy's grip because of it. But the Megafortress unit wasn't about to be fooled; the crewman aboard the EB-52 sang out loud and clear with his bearing and speed.

Hallelujah, thought Mack to himself.

It was probably the first time in his life that he actually wanted to be caught. Mack took a hard turn north and did a quick check of his instruments. The Cessna wasn't a fancy beast, but it was sure and dependable, and the indicators showed she was in prime condition.

"Dragon One, this is *Jersey,*" said Breanna Stockard, who was aboard the EB-52. "Looks like we're through with the low-altitude hunts. What's your pleasure?"

Mack checked his watch and fuel. "Let's move out to sea and practice some sea surveillance," he answered. "That okay with Deci?"

Deci Gordon was a Dreamland radar specialist who was aboard the EB-52 helping train Mack's men.

"Good for me," answered Deci. "Your people did very well on the low-altitude stuff. A-pluses all around."

He was being kind. The two pilots who had taken stints at the stick had flown decently. But the equipment operators tasked with finding Mack while he flew at low altitude around the nearby mountains had batted only about .300—great in baseball, fatal in war.

Mack knew that working the radar involved a heck of a lot more than hitting a few keys and jiggling some toggles, but his people had a long, long way to go before they would be competent enough to find a MiG hell-bent on nailing a real target.

Two weeks before, Mack would have vented his frustration at the poor score, or at least let the crew aboard the EB-52 know that they had to step it up. He was learning, however, to be more laid back, or at least more selective with his criticism.

He had to be. The two specialists aboard *Jersey* were the last two he had. The other two had quit.

As Mack adjusted his course and started to climb through five thousand feet, he saw something flare in the right side of his windscreen. It took a moment for him to realize he was seeing a fire.

"*Jersey*, this is Brunei Dragon One. I think I see a ship on fire. Stand by."

Mack gave the throttle a shove and turned in the direction of the flames. From this distance, the fire looked more like the sparkle of a gem, glittering red. The ship itself was a gray shadow around it.

"Mack, we see it," said Breanna. "We'll have GPS coordinates in a second."

"You got a Mayday or something?" Mack asked Breanna.

"Nothing."

Mack alerted his ground controller, who staffed a combat center at the International Airport control tower back in the capital. (As in many other smaller countries around the world, the International Airport or IAP handled military as well as civilian flights.) Besides calling out the navy and local harbor patrol, Mack told the controller to contact the Malaysian air force at Labuan. The small air station there—the only other air base besides Brunei IAP on the northern side of Borneo—operated a squadron of French-built Aerospatiale SA 316B Alouette IIIs for search and rescue.

"We'll stay in the area until rescue is underway, give 'em some hope, anyway," Mack added.

Breanna reported that the ship had not answered any of their hails.

"Roger that," said Mack. He was now within two miles of the ship, and could see that the vessel had settled low in the water. "I'm going to get close and see what I can see."

Low and slow was one thing the A-37B did really well. Mack decided to pop on his landing lights, not so much because it would help him see better, but because it would show survivors he was there and help was on the way. His speed notched down steadily until finally it seemed as if he were going backward.

As he approached, it looked to him as if there were two ships on fire. He banked, hand gentle on the stick as he slipped around for another look.

The ship had broken in half somewhere around the super-structure.

Must've been one hell of an accident for it to blow up like that, thought Mack, sliding around for another pass.

THE MEGAFORTRESS PILOT HAD FORGOTTEN TO TELL THE computer that the exercise was over, and so it kept blinking a warning at him that he was outside of the programmed flight area. It was nothing more than an annoyance, since the plane wouldn't override the pilot's commands, but the flash was driving Breanna crazy. Still, she avoided the temptation to turn it off herself, or even to bring it to his attention. In a few days she wasn't going to be here to straighten him out; it was time to take the training wheels off.

But boy, it bothered her.

Finally, the pilot turned to her and announced: "I have a difficulty with the warning system."

"It just needs to be acknowledged. Tell the computer the exercise is over. You might check your course, as well," she added, noticing that he had allowed his heading to drift well to the west.

"Right. Yes," said the pilot. He was in his late thirties, older than Breanna. Even so, he seemed nervous and jumpy; he didn't have the been-there, done-that, I-remember-one-time-we-had-to-fly-backward-in-a-storm-with-one-engine calm most jocks pushing forty displayed. Not that he was a bad pilot; he just didn't seem to have the hash marks his age implied.

Something else bugged her. The crew was, well, *quiet*.

In an American plane, certainly on a Dreamland crew, the specialists would be singing out, talking about contacts and the like. But the two men at the mission stations behind her on the flight deck were silent. Breanna's copilot station allowed her to peek at their contact screens; she did so and saw that the men were refining their equipment and seemed to have a competent handle on things—they just didn't talk about it.

By now, Mack had completed a third orbit of the stricken vessel and reported that he saw no boats in the water. He switched to a different frequency and began talking to the harbor patrol, which had been alerted by their ground controller.

"Captain, what do you think of this?" asked Deci. "Hit that two scan, low resolution. I'm feeding it."

Enhanced by the computer, the image showed a dark blur in the left-hand corner of the screen, racing along the coast toward Malaysia.

"Just a ghost?" asked Breanna.

"No. There's something there," said Deci. "Moving real fast—out around three hundred knots."

"What boat goes that fast? Cigarette speed boat?"

"Never heard of one even half that fast. Has to be a plane, but according to the radar it's at three feet."

"Three feet?"

"I know it's weird," added Deci, "but it's a live contact. The computer has never seen it before."

"I'll bet." Breanna flipped into Mack's circuit. "Brunei Dragon One, we have an odd contact you might want to know about," she said. "Indications are it's a plane flying very low, but it may be a weird radar bounce off a boat of some sort. Moving to the east, northeast at a very good clip. You might want to check it out."

"Give me a vector," he snapped.

* * *

CLEAN, THROTTLE LASHED TO THE LAST STOP, AND A GOOD wind at its back, the manual said the A-37B Dragonfly could do 440 knots.

Mack had it nudging 470 as he tracked in the direction Breanna had fed him, running up the coastline. He was about thirty seconds from the spot where she'd gotten the first contact—just a hair under four miles—but he had nothing on his radar and couldn't see anything, either.

He leaned his head far forward, as if the few inches of extra distance would help his eyes filter away the shadows and mist.

"Dragon One to *Jersey*—yo, Breanna, where is this thing?"

"Stand by."

She came back again with a GPS location.

"Hey, I'm in the Stone Age, remember? I don't have a GPS locator on board."

"Sorry—you look like you're almost on top of it. Two miles."

Mack reached for the throttle, easing off on his speed. The shoreline was an irregular black haze to his right.

Sixty seconds later, Breanna announced that they had lost it. "Stand by," she added.

Stand by yourself, he thought. He had let his altitude slip to two thousand feet. He was passing just over a marina, but moving too fast to sort out what he saw.

"Pleasure boat," he said with disgust, snapping the speak button as he tucked into a bank to check it out. "Hey, Jersey girl—did you have me chase a pleasure boat? There's a marina down here."

"You know a pleasure boat that goes three hundred knots? Stand by. We're looking for it."

Mack circled around. There were at least two dozen boats in the marina, but no airplanes.

"Not a seaplane?" he asked, though he didn't see one.

"Seaplane? If so the computer couldn't find it on its index. Hold on."

Mack pulled out the large area map from his kneeboard and unfolded it, checking to see where he was.

"Dragon One, we have it twenty-five miles to your northeast, along the coast," said Breanna over the radio.

"Your sure about that, *Jersey?*"

"We're as sure as—stand by," she added, a note of disgust creeping into her voice.

Mack started a turn in the direction she had advised, but as he came to the new course Breanna told him they had lost the contact completely.

"Right," he said.

"I'm sorry," she said. "We're trying."

"I'm looking at empty ocean."

"You're right on the vector."

She added that the Brunei authorities had just reported a ship underway to rescue survivors at the stricken ship, which had now been identified as a freighter due to dock at 6 A.M. in Brunei. Mack flew about ten miles to the east-northeast, then banked into an orbit fifteen hundred feet over the waves, riding a curlicue as he looked for Breanna's contact. He began heading toward the masts of a group of fishing vessels further northward on the shore.

"Flight *Jersey* to Dragon One," said the airborne radar operator aboard the EB-52. "Report: Two Su-27s coming in your direction from the south. Report: bearing one-six-five. Report . . ."

Mack listened incredulously to the contact information. The two planes were over Malaysian territory, on a course that would take them out over Mack's position. But Malaysia didn't have any Su-27s, and all eighteen of their MiG-29s were over at Subang, a good thousand miles away. As the MiGs were the most capable planes in the region, two spies at the airport there were paid good money by the prince to keep them informed.

Two others were paid so-so money. All of the air bases operated by Indonesia and Malaysia, including the two Malaysian and one Indonesian fields on Borneo, were covered around the clock by spies. Mack surely would have known by now if these planes were operating there.

Whoever they belonged to, they were moving at a good clip—the radar operator warned that they were topping six hundred knots.

"We're sure they're not MiGs?" asked Mack.

"Yes, Minister. We're sure."

"Yeah, those are definitely Su-27s, and they're hot," confirmed Deci.

"Roger that," said Mack, pulling back on his stick and climbing off the deck.

BREANNA DID A QUICK RUN THROUGH THE SCREENS THAT showed how the Megafortress was performing, and then brought up the fuel matrix, which gave the pilots a set of calculations showing how long they could stay up with the fuel remaining in their tanks. The Megafortress computer system could make the predictions seem terribly precise—42.35 minutes if they spent it doing these orbits and then headed straight home—but in reality fuel management remained more art than science. The screen gave the pilots several sets of reasonable guesses based on stock mission profiles as well as the programmed mission. It could also make calculations based on data inputted. Breanna brought a "profile map" up at the side of the touchscreen and quickly built a scenario from it by tapping a few options. They could climb to twenty-five thousand feet, engage the two Sukhois, and then slide back home.

Just.

Not that they could actually engage the Sukhois. They weren't carrying any anti-air missiles. They didn't have any shells for the Stinger air-mine tail weapon; the shrapnel discs were in relatively short supply and weren't needed for training.

"Captain, what are your intentions regarding the Sukhois?" she asked the Megafortress pilot.

He replied that he would remain on station until Mack gave him other orders. It wasn't the *wrong* response, exactly, but it wasn't exactly the sort of answer that was going to set the world on fire.

"Should we take the initiative and ask the minister what he wants us to do?" she said, her patience starting to slip a little. "Maybe suggest we try and establish contact with the bogeys and get them to declare their intent? Maybe prepare an offensive or defensive posture?"

"By all means," answered the pilot. "But the minister may prefer to deal with them himself."

"The A-37B is a sitting duck," she said.

To her surprise, the pilot chuckled. "The minister would not lose an engagement," he said.

"He's unarmed."

The pilot chuckled again, his laughter implying that she didn't understand the laws of physics—or Mack Smith. The minister could not be shot down, and anyone foolish enough to attack him would get their comeuppance—even if they were flying cutting-edge interceptors and he was in an unarmed plane designed as a trainer.

Breanna, no longer able to contain her frustration, hit the talk button. "Dragon One, what's your call on the Sukhois?"

"I want to see what the hell they're up to and where they came from," replied Mack. "Because there are no Sukhois on Borneo. Malaysia's MiGs are way over in West Malaysia near the capital."

"Mack, I can assure you, those are Sukhois, not MiGs and not ghosts. Your people are not screwing this up. Those planes are coming hot. What are you going to do if they turn hostile?"

"Hey, relax Bree. I'm cool."

"You're a sitting duck. And they haven't answered our radio calls. If they get nasty—"

"Oh, give me a break, will you? I can handle them."

One's loonier than the other, Breanna thought.

MACK CONTINUED HIS LACKADAISICAL CLIMB, TRYING TO CON-serve his fuel while making sure the pointing-nose cowboys running for him knew he was here. They were now about eight minutes away, flying at roughly twenty thousand feet, separated by about a quarter-mile. Their radars were not yet in range to see the Dragonfly.

But given their speed and direction, it seemed highly coincidental that they were flying in his direction on a whim.

"Mack, you're in radar range of the Su-27s."

"About time," he said.

"You want us to jam them?"

"Hell no! I want to see who these guys are."

"THEY KNOW HE'S THERE," DECI TOLD BREANNA OVER THE interphone. "Altering course slightly. They should be in visual range of Mack in, uh, thirty seconds," said Deci.

"I'll pass it along," said Breanna.

"Radar—uh, they just turned on their air-to-air weapons," said Deci. "They may really want to shoot him down."

MACK CAME OUT OF HIS TURN ABOUT THREE SECONDS TOO soon, and had to push into his dive before he saw the first Sukhoi. He got a glimpse of it in his left windscreen, then heard the RWR complain that one of the fighters had switched on its targeting radar.

"I was afraid of that," he groused out loud, as if the device could do anything but whine. A second later it gave another pitched warning, indicating that the enemy's radar had locked on him and was ready to fire.

Then the unit freaked out, obviously a result of Breanna's ordering the Megafortress crew to jam the airwaves so he couldn't be shot down.

Mack sighed. A completely unnecessary order, even if her heart was in the right place. Mack pulled his plane into a tight turn and put himself right below the Su-27s as they turned. Separated by ten thousand feet and a good bit of momentum, all he caught on the gun's video camera—rigged for the training exercises—was a gray blur. He pounded the throttle but there was no hope of keeping up with the Su-27s. Within two minutes, they were beyond his radar.

And he was short on fuel.

"*Jersey*, this is Dragon One. I'm bingo on fuel, headed for home."

"We're close to our reserves, as well," replied Breanna.

"Did you get any sort of IDs on those Sukhois?"

"Negative," said Breanna. "They had old-style N001 radars. Seem to be Su-27S models."

The N001 was a competent but older radar type, and no match for the Megafortress's ECMs or electronic countermeasures. It meant the planes themselves were relatively old and had been purchased second- or even third-hand. But it didn't say who they might belong to. For the moment, at least, their identity would have to remain a mystery.

"Your seaplane didn't show up?" he asked.

"I don't think it was a seaplane."

Probably not, thought Mack to himself. More than likely, his neophyte radar operators had bungled a routine contact with a speedboat, then sent him out on a wild goose chase.

He listened as Breanna updated the rescue situation—there were now two vessels conducting a search, with no survivors located as of yet.

"Time to pack it in," he told the Jersey crew. "Head for the barn."

He snapped off the mike, then did something that would not have occurred to him a few weeks ago.

"Hey, crew of the *Jersey*—I mean, crew of Brunei Mega-fortress One," said Mack, touching his speak button. "Kick-ass job. Very, very good job. Attaboys all around."

Kota Kinabalu, Malaysia
0853

Sahurah Niu's feet trembled as he got off the motorcycle in front of the gate. The bike roared away and Sahurah was left alone. He tried to take a deep breath but the air caught in his throat and instead he began to cough.

As he recovered, a soldier walked up to him, gun drawn.

"Who are you?" demanded the soldier, pointing the pistol at him.

"I was sent," said Sahurah. The gun comforted him for a reason he couldn't have explained.

"What is your name?"

Sahurah gave the name he had been told to use—Mat Salleh, a historical figure who had led an ill-fated uprising against the British on Borneo in the nineteenth century.

The soldier frowned and gestured that he should hold his hands out at his sides to be searched.

If I were carrying a bomb, Sahurah thought to himself, I would detonate it now and be in Paradise.

But he was not carrying a bomb, nor any weapon, and the search went quickly.

"This way," said the guard, pointing to the gate. "The captain is waiting. You have a long journey ahead."

Sahurah nodded, and followed along inside.

* * *

FLUSH WITH HIS VICTORY AT SEA, DAZHOU MET THE MUSLIM fanatic in his office.

"Have a drink," he said to him, putting down a bottle on his desk. He laughed at the expression of horror on the man's face. "It's juice," he told him, "but you needn't drink it anyway."

He looked at him more closely. "You're the messenger?"

The fanatic nodded. There was no possibility of mistake— no rebel would show up here on his own. Unlike many of the rebels in the movement, Sahurah appeared to be a native of Borneo, very possibly of Malaysian extraction, though with thirty-one different ethnic groups on the large island there were many who could claim to be native here. Dazhou's own family had been on Borneo for centuries.

"You know who I am?" Dazhou asked.

The young man—he was surely in his late twenties, though his face showed the pain of someone much older—shook his head.

"That is just as well," said Dazhou. "There is a bathroom there, if you need it. We will leave in five minutes. Once we start, we will not stop."

Dreamland
7 October 1997, (local) 1630

After the botched demonstration of the robot warrior system, Danny's day became an unrelieved series of frowns and down-turned glances. He avoided breakfast with the congressmen, claiming that he had to work with the technical team recovering the devices, and managed to skip lunch by tending to his normal duties as security chief on the base. But couldn't avoid the afternoon debriefing sessions, which culminated in a show-and-tell session for the VIPs in one of the Dreamland auditoriums. Danny walked down the hallway to the room feeling like the proverbial Dead Man Walking.

The ARC robots had actually worked exactly according to spec. Unfortunately, they had been foxed by Boston, who exploited a weakness in the system to torpedo the mission. The inexpensive, off-the-shelf sensors in the units could not see very well through smoke. While the grenade that Boston's team member had launched at the unit might not have blinded it for very long, once it started firing off its canisters the entire area was for all intents and purposes shrouded in an impenetrable fog. Boston had timed his intrusion just right, racing as fast as he could eight hundred and fifty meters to the downed airman, who by the exercise rules was unarmed and couldn't hear him anyway because of the approaching Osprey. Armed with only his pistol—a rifle would have slowed him down—Boston incapacitated the airman, then waited for the rescuers.

It wouldn't have worked in real life—the grenades would have been shrapnel rather than smoke, and presumably incapacitated or killed the intruders. But that distinction seemed lost on the congressmen who were watching the video feeds in the Dreamland conference center. And the army people present for the demonstration weren't very happy about it either. The Army had supplied 90 percent of the development funding so far, and its contribution was up for review.

Danny stood gamely with the project officers and the science types as they opened the floor up to questioning. One of the congressmen started things off by asking where the man who had shown the way around the robots was.

"Sergeant Rockland is probably enjoying a well-earned rest right now," said Danny, trying to force a smile. "One of my best men. We try to train them to think outside of the box."

"Or the robot," said the congressman.

Danny did his best to laugh along with them, ignoring the dagger eyes from the army people.

Boston was waiting for him in his office when he finally made it over there two hours later.

"You were looking for me, Cap?" asked the sergeant.

Something about his sophomoric smile burned right through Danny.

"You blew the parameters of the test," Danny told him. "You screwed the whole stinking thing up."

"What do you mean?"

"Those were supposed to be shrapnel grenades. Your team would have been dead."

"No, we were far enough away. I made sure of that."

"You ran right through the smoke," said Danny. "That wouldn't have happened in real life. You would never have made it in time."

Boston shrugged.

"I don't like your attitude. Sergeant," said Freah.

"Captain—don't you preach that we ought to use our heads?"

"Go on. Dismissed. Go."

"But—"

"Out!"

Danny pretended not to see him shake his head.

Brunei
8 October 1997, (local) 0900

As Mack pulled himself out of the A-37B's cockpit, the fatigue that had been trailing him the whole flight jumped out and wrapped itself around his neck. The sun beat down on the concrete apron, and the humidity hung around him like the thick steam of a shower room. Mack had originally planned to go home and take a nap after debriefing the training session, but the morning's developments meant there would be no rest for the weary; quite the contrary. The sultan would undoubtedly be wondering what was going on and expect a personal briefing, as would Prince bin Awg. The central defense ministry—a collection of service heads and other military advisors, including Mack—would also be looking for information.

The EB-52 banked overhead, preparing to land. Mack turned back toward the runway, watching the big plane swing in. It wobbled slightly—obviously one of his people was at the stick. Still, the landing was solid. All in all, they were making progress.

Slow progress, but progress.

"'Scuse me," said a woman's voice behind him. "You Mack Smith?"

Mack turned, surprised to hear what sounded like an American accent.

"You're the minister of defense?" said the woman.

"Deputy minister of defense—air force," said Mack, giving his official title. "Such as it is."

He might not have added the last comment if the woman had

been anything other than, well, plain, though plain didn't quite cover it. She was somewhere over twenty-one and under forty, five-four, on the thin side. Her short hair had a slight curl to it, and that was the nicest thing you could say about her looks. She wore a pair of jeans and a touristy blue shirt.

"I'm McKenna," she said, thrusting out her hand.

"McKenna is who?" said Mack.

"Pilot. You were looking for contract pilots? Does it help that I can speak Malaysian?"

She reeled off a few sentences in the native language, which was shared by Brunei and its island neighbors. Mack hadn't been here long enough to understand more than a few words; he thought he recognized the phrase for "have a nice day," but that was about it.

"I think you have the wrong idea," said Mack. "I'm putting together a combat air force. The civilian airline is still on its own."

"Well no shit," said the woman. "I've flown F/A-18s for the Royal Canadian Air Force, and for the last year I've been a contract pilot for a horse's ass of an outfit trying to sell third-hand Russian-made crates of crap that I wouldn't put my worst enemy in. That light your f-ing fire?" said McKenna.

Well, she could talk like a pilot at least, thought Mack.

"I don't have any F/A-18s," he told her.

"I can fly anything," she said. "Ask Prince bin Awg. He let me fly his MiG-19 and his Sabre last year. We went at it a bit and I waxed his butt good. I'd love to get behind the wheel of one of those," she added, thumbing toward the Megafortress, which was just heading toward its parking spot in front of the hangar on the left.

"It doesn't have a wheel. It's got a stick, like a real airplane," said Mack. "They put it in when they upgraded it."

"Well kick ass then," said McKenna.

Mack started toward the hangar to change, and McKenna fell in alongside him.

"So? Am I hired?" she asked.

"Hired for what?"

"For a pilot."

"What Russian planes did you fly?"

"Anything and everything."

"MiG-29s?" asked Mack.

"Do it in my sleep."

"How about Su-27s?"

"One or two."

"You fly them around here?"

"Nah."

"Out of Labuan?"

"Are you kidding? The Malaysians don't operate jets out of there."

"Ever?"

"About six months ago we tried to sell a pair of MiG-29s," said McKenna. "We brought them to Kuching at the far south of Borneo from the peninsula to demonstrate some of the changes that extended their range. But no one was buying."

"What about the Indonesians? You fly Sukhois out here for them?"

"For the Indonesians?" McKenna laughed. "Malaysia, Indonesia—their governments aren't on Borneo," said McKenna. "You have to sell where the money is."

"You haven't flown Su-27s on Borneo at all?"

She shook her head.

"You hear of either country having them?"

"You'd know better than me, Minister."

Mack stopped. "Yeah, cut the shit. They have them?"

McKenna examined his face for a moment before answering. "Indonesia doesn't have anything newer than Northrop F-5s. The Malaysian Royal Air Force has MiG-29s and F/A-18s over in West Malaysia, near the capital of Kuala Lumpur. Most of what my boss sold was used and it's hard to buy used when you've been buying new. Her dealings with the Malaysians were mostly for ammunition and some avionics spare parts."

"I was jumped by two Su-27s this morning," said Mack.

"Get out of town."

Mack smiled sardonically. "They came up out of the south-west, from Malaysian territory, turned on their targeting gear to scare me, and took off."

"They scared you?"

"Yeah, right."

"What'd you do?"

"Gave them the finger and took their pictures," he said. "I want to figure out who they are."

"I'll look at it for you if you want."

Mack shrugged. It couldn't hurt, though most likely it wouldn't help, either.

"They could have come out of Kuching," admitted McKenna. "But it's a good hike to get up here, over five hundred miles. And your spies would have told you they were there, wouldn't they have?"

"Who says I have spies there?"

"You have spies everywhere," said McKenna. "Dragonfly, huh? You would've been dead meat."

"What, from a couple of Sukhois? Give me a break," said Mack.

"Depends on the pilot," said McKenna, her voice only a bit conciliatory. "If it were me, I'd've waxed your fanny."

"If you were in the Sukhoi?"

"Either way."

"If you fly half as good as you talk, McKenna," said Mack, resuming his stride toward the hangar, "you got yourself a job."

Brunei
1600

The time difference between the States and Brunei made it difficult for Breanna to get any information without invoking official channels, which she didn't want to do. Finally she thought of Mark Stoner, a CIA agent who'd worked with Dreamland on some recent missions and who was back east in D.C. By the time she tried him, however, it was midnight there, and when she got his machine she left a message, asking him to call "when he got a chance." Then she forgot about him until, to her great surprise, the hotel desk buzzed her room at 3 P.M. to tell her he was on the line.

"Mark—what are you doing up at 2 A.M.?" she asked.

"It's 3 A.M. here," said Stoner. "There's a twelve-hour difference. No daylight savings. We're a half-day behind you. You said you had a question."

"Couple of questions. Unofficially."

Breanna told him about the aircraft, which according to the images captured by the Dragonfly had no identifying marks.

"They came out of Malaysian territory?" Stoner asked when she had finished her summary.

"Looked like." She didn't want to be too specific, worrying that anyone listening in would be able to gather information about the targeting system's abilities—and she had to assume that might include Malaysian spies.

"There are two Malaysian air bases, auxiliaries to civilian airports. Neither field is really set up to support military jets, at least not that I know."

"Can you check?"

"Have you talked to the Department of Defense?"

"I filed a report, but no one seemed particularly interested. A pair of Sukhois doesn't really rock their world."

Stoner was silent for a moment, then he asked, "If I gave you an address, could you get to it this afternoon?"

"I think so."

"It's in Kampung Ayer. Do you know what that is?"

"The island city in the bay off the capital?"

"Write this down."

BREANNA FOUND MACK STANDING ON THE BACK OF A PICKUP truck at the edge of a cliff overlooking the ocean several miles southwest of the airport. A British-built truck sat nearby, with two Brunei air force sergeants working an old field radio in the back. Below the cliff was a narrow plateau of rocks just out of the water's reach. Several pieces of plywood were set up as targets for an A-37B.

Breanna watched as the airplane came around from the north and made a run parallel to the coastline. The rocks bubbled and one of the plywood panels split in two. The airplane then rose abruptly, its right wingtip no more than ten feet from the cliff edge.

"I have to say, pretty good," said Mack. "Tell her to nail the last target any way she wants," he shouted to the men in the truck.

Not five seconds later, the Dragonfly rolled back toward land, heading dead-on for the beach—upside down. The last piece of plywood folded in half.

Not that anybody on land had seen. They'd all ducked for cover as she blew past, maybe six feet off the ground.

"New pilot?" Breanna asked.

"Yeah. I'm pretty desperate," said Mack.

"He looks pretty good," said Breanna. "Even if he is a show-off."

"It's a she," said Mack. "And actually, her looks are, uh, not exactly on the measurable chart. But she's a helluva pilot. Why are you here?"

"I'm doing you a favor," said Breanna. "We need to go out to a place in Kampung Ayer."

"We? Listen Bree, I'm due back in the capital in an hour to explain to my fellow ministers of defense how aircraft that don't exist may very well have sunk that merchant ship. I don't have time for a boat ride."

"I called Mark Stoner and told him about your Sukhois. He told me to go out to see someone there."

"Stoner's the CIA spook who's an expert on South Asian weapons?"

"One and the same."

The A-37 buzzed back. Mack didn't duck this time.

"I hate show-offs," he said, jumping out of the truck. "Especially when they're worth watching."

KAMPUNG AYER WAS A WATER VILLAGE IN THE BAY OUTSIDE the capital. Buildings rose on stilts from the murky water, whose pungent odor matched its mud-red tint. Until today, Breanna had seen the lagoon city only from a distance. She stared at the people as she and Mack passed in their water taxi, amazed at how ingenious humans could be.

"There," said the man driving the water taxi. They pulled up against a planked walkway that led to what looked like a floating trailer. Its rusting metal roof was weighted down by satellite dishes.

"You wait, right?" said Mack, pointing at him.

"I wait," said the man.

Mack jumped up and started walking toward the house. Breanna scrambled to follow. She barely kept her balance on the bobbing boards, and had to grab Mack's arm just as she caught up to him.

"Hey," he said. "Watch it or we'll fall into that sewer water."

"Thanks, Mack."

Mack pulled open the screen door and they walked into what could have passed for a doctor's waiting room. A young Malaysian sat behind the desk, paging through a magazine.

"Mark Stoner sent us," said Breanna.

"Cheese is expecting you," said the man, gesturing toward an open doorway to his left. "Go in."

"Cheese?" said Mack.

The only light in the room came from a large-screen TV, which was tuned to CNBC. Hunched on the floor in front of a leather couch was a man pounding a keyboard. A bottle of Beefeater gin sat next to him.

"Hello," said Breanna.

The man put his hand out to shush them, then continued typing.

"You're Cheese?" asked Mack.

The man picked up the Beefeater, took a swig, then held it out to them without looking away from his laptop.

"No thanks," said Breanna.

"I'll pass," said Mack.

The man took another swig, still typing with one hand. In his thirties or early forties, he was obviously American, wearing a light blue T-shirt and a pair of cut-off jeans.

"Stoner's people, right?" he asked, still tapping his keys.

"Yes," said Breanna.

"I want to know about some airplanes," said Mack.

"I don't want to know anything. Nothing. Zero."

"Mark told me to come here," said Breanna.

"Yeah, but I don't know anything about it, okay? I have a Web link for you to look at in the other room," he said. "I typed it in already. All you have to do is hit enter."

The man typed one more thing on his laptop, then put it down and got up.

"James Milach. They call me Cheese because I made a killing in the stock market involving Kraft. No shit," said the American. He shook Mack's hand—then bent over and kissed Breanna's. "Beefeater makes me formal," he said, sweeping away into the next room.

* * *

MACK THOUGHT FOR SURE HE'D STEPPED INTO AN INSANE asylum. Stoner was a spook, and spooks knew weird people, but this character was—a character.

But then this had been a particularly perplexing day all around. The sultan had expressed some concern about the Sukhois, but discounted Mack's theory that they had been responsible for the attack on the merchant ship. The spy network, meanwhile, reported that there had been no activity at any of the airports on Borneo or even nearby Indonesia or Malaysia.

The Brunei navy's pet theory was that the ship had been sabotaged by Islamic terrorists, who had placed a bomb aboard. While Mack wouldn't rule that out, it was a convenient theory in that it kept the navy from having any responsibility. The investigation was continuing; thus far, no survivors had been found.

"You hit the button, and then you can take it from there," said Cheese, standing over a Sun Workstation. "You got it?"

"Sure," said Breanna. "This is the Web?"

Cheese smiled at her. "Not exactly. But you don't want to know too much, do you?"

Mack rolled his eyes, then hit the key and bent toward the screen. Brown and black shades slowly filled the screen. It took a few moments for Mack to realize he was looking at a satellite photo of the northern part of the island, which was Malaysian territory.

"Some sort of Russian satellite," said Breanna, pointing at the characters on the side of the screen. "You think he's tapped into their network?"

"I don't know," he told her, leaning down to squint at the screen. "But that looks like the outline of a Sukhoi on what looks like a highway in the middle of nowhere. I'm going to have to look at a map but I think that's Darvel Bay, on the eastern side of Sabah province. That whole area is just jungle. Or at least it used to be."

**Dreamland
8 October 1997, (local) 1800**

Dog hustled from the Dolphin shuttle helicopter that had dropped him off at Dreamland toward the black SUV waiting to

ferry him over to his quarters. He was surprised to find Danny
Freah behind the wheel.

"Personnel shortage?" Dog asked as he got into the passenger seat beside him.

"Wanted to have a chat."

"Fire away," said Dog, bracing himself.

"We had a problem with the demonstration this morning,"
started Danny.

Dog listened as the captain detailed what had happened. "I'm
sorry, Colonel," said Danny as they arrived in front of the small
bungalow that served as Dog's quarters here. "I'm truly sorry."

"Well, the outcome wasn't what we'd hoped, I agree," said
Dog. He wanted to sound philosophical without sounding as if
he were making light of the situation—a tough balance. "But actually it doesn't sound that bad. If the technical people explained
about the smoke grenades, I'm sure it'll be kept in perspective."

"We screwed up in front of a bunch of people who would
like to chop off our heads," said Danny.

"Congress doesn't want to chop off our heads. Just our bud-
get," said Dog.

"Yeah."

"It's all right, Captain." Dog opened the door. "I'm going to
just put this stuff inside and then head back over to my office.
Can you stay a minute and give me a lift?"

"Yes, sir."

Danny's mood was even more somber than before. Dog
pulled his bag out of the truck, searching his mind for a better
pep talk as he walked up the path to his quarters.

WHEN JENNIFER SAW DOG FINALLY COMING UP THE WALK,
she leaned against the wall, knowing she'd be just out of sight
when he came in. She listened to him fumbling with the key; as
the door creaked open she heard her heart thumping loudly. She
hesitated a second, suddenly feeling foolish for sneaking into
his apartment to surprise him.

Dog, oblivious, closed the door behind him and took a few
steps into the dimly lit cottage.

"Hey," she said, staying back by the wall rather than going to
him as she'd planned.

"Jen!"

He sound surprised, not shocked but taken off-guard, as if she were the last person in the world he'd expect here, the last person he wanted to find here.

"What are you doing?" Dog flipped on the light.

"I was surprising you," she said.

"Great," he said, but it sounded unconvincing to her.

"Do you want some wine?" she tried, struggling against her growing anxiety.

"I would but I have to get over to my office and then look after the congressional delegation. Maybe later, okay?"

"Oh."

"You all right?" He put his arms around her but somehow it felt forced and unnatural.

"I'm okay," she said.

"I do have to go. I'm sorry," he said.

Kiss me, she thought. *Kiss me.* But even when he did, she thought he was distracted, and she felt worse than before.

"Later?" he said, letting go of her.

She forced herself to nod. But then she added, "I may have to work."

"Oh. Well. Try to come over."

"I will."

Then he turned and, without bothering to change, went back out the door.

Sandakan, Malaysia (northern Borneo)
9 October 1997, 1053

The long ride across the island left Dazhou stiff and impatient, though he knew better than to show emotion, let alone physical discomfort, as he waited outside the general's office. General Udara was inside, speaking on the telephone just loudly enough to make it clear to Dazhou that he was there; this was no doubt his intention, as the commander never lost an opportunity to demonstrate his superiority to his underlings. Finally, after he had waited for nearly twenty minutes, Dazhou was shown into the office. Udara pretended to be reading some report, making a show of frowning before looking up and pointing to the paper.

"You exceeded your authority," said Udara.

"The *Barracuda* had to be tested. The target presented itself. The opportunity was taken. It coincides with our greater plans and schedule."

"You think it is all that simple," snapped Udara. "You think you can use the cover of events to indulge your psychological needs. We had to divert two aircraft to take the attention away from you."

"Why?" asked Dazhou.

"The radio reports back to the Brunei air force center showed they were pursuing a craft. We could not afford discovery."

"Which aircraft?" asked Dazhou.

"Part of our project," said the general dismissively. "You do not need to know every detail."

Dazhou held his tongue. He could easily guess that the general was referring to the Sukhois that had been brought three months ago to the base in the northern mountains; Dazhou had informers in the military who had told him how the planes had been purchased from the Ukrainians and then shipped in pieces and reassembled. They were necessary for the "project," as Udara dismissively termed it, but using them to cover the *Barracuda*'s escape had been unnecessary. Still, he knew better than to argue with the general, who commanded all Malaysian military forces on Borneo. While Dazhou had first suggested the alliance with the terrorists to achieve their common aim, it was General Udara who had made it possible, and he wielded such power that Dazhou could not cross him.

Yet.

"I expect from the reports that the vessel worked," said Udara.

"Precisely as predicted."

"You are ready to proceed?"

"Upon your order."

It was the note Udara had been waiting for. His manner changed; he smiled and leaned back in his seat.

"You are tired after your journey?" said the general.

"No."

"Something to eat?"

"No thank you, sir."

"How long will the sultan fend off the terrorists?"

"Without our help, the terrorists will struggle for weeks,"

said Dazhou. "If we help them, the sultan and his puppet government may last twelve hours."

Another smile. Udara rose. He took a few steps away from his desk, filling the room with pompous swagger. "The messenger is here?"

"He is."

"Who is he?"

"I do not know."

"The secretary said he was a child."

"He is young, but not that young. I would say in his twenties. With these fanatics, it is difficult to say sometimes."

"Does he have information about the connection to Afghanistan?"

"I thought it best not to interrogate him without your authority," said Dazhou, who in truth was not in the least interested in the Islamic crazies and their network of madmen. He wanted only to eliminate the bastard sultan of Brunei, whose family had seized his ancestors' property two generations ago, casting them into poverty. At long last, the wrong would be avenged.

"If we give the terrorists Brunei, how long do you think they will be satisfied?" the general asked.

"I do not think it would be long," said Dazhou. "And it is irrelevant."

"Yes," agreed the general. "Quite irrelevant."

Whether the terrorists would be satisfied with controlling Brunei or not, the Malaysian government would not allow the terrorists to control their neighbor for very long. On the contrary—one of the attractions of the plan was that it would allow them not only to crush the terrorists and seize oil-rich Brunei, but to receive ASEAN backing to do so. Once the sultan was kicked out and the terrorists in control, the Malaysian military would turn on its allies of convenience. Dazhou had already drawn up plans to do so.

But those operations were in the future. For now, they had to concentrate on Brunei.

Udara went back to his desk and picked up the phone. "Have our visitor fetched from the room and brought to me," he told his assistant.

* * *

SAHURAH SAT ON THE FLOOR OF THE EMPTY ROOM, TRYING TO keep his mind ready. Again and again it drifted. He saw the girl he had had in Beaufort, the other in Sandakan. Beautiful, beautiful girls—temptations from the time before his commitment, sins, and yet he couldn't banish them.

He owed the true God his complete attention, especially now, especially here on this mission. He should see himself as God's trusted messenger—for as the imam's emissary what else was he? And yet the impure thoughts haunted him, hungry ghosts clawing to be fed. The flesh was a terrible chain, an awesome torment. He would be better to be rid of it, gone to paradise.

He was a coward, a coward and a failure. That was the lesson of the miscarried plans on the beach. He should have shot the infidel devils the moment he saw them, rather than hesitating.

Sahurah was not exactly sure where on Borneo he had been taken. The men who rode with him in the jeep had blindfolded him three separate times, including the last hour. He guessed he was on the northern part of the island, in the Malaysian region known as Sabah, but in truth he could have been in the south or in Indonesian territory as well. He thought he had detected the scent of seawater on the breeze as he was led from the Jeep, but it had been fleeting.

A soldier opened the door and nodded at him. Sahurah got up and followed him down the hallway. They went up two flights of carpeted stairs, past walls made of polished stone with elaborate inlays. The walls had once been lined with sculpture, but the niches were now bare.

The soldier stopped and turned in front of a wide doorway lined with an elaborate molding. Inside, Sahurah found a young man at the desk. He gave Sahurah a disapproving frown, then picked up his phone.

"Go," the man at the desk told him in Malaysian. "And be quick about it."

Sahurah gathered his dignity and walked into the room at his most deliberate pace. He was a messenger and a representative, not to be treated without respect.

Dazhou was inside, sitting in a simple wooden chair. Behind the desk was a short, skinny man in a military uniform. He was nearly bald, his face the red color of ruby glistening in the sun. Sahurah believed that the man was either the army general who commanded Malaysian forces on Borneo, or one of his immediate underlings. He had seen the pictures some time ago and couldn't remember precisely which one he was. He stared at the man now, trying to memorize his features so he could describe them later.

"You have been sent?" said the officer.

"I have been sent."

"And?"

"I was told to come," said Sahurah.

"That's all?"

"Perhaps you should begin by paying your respects to the general," said Dazhou from the side.

Sahurah bowed his head. "I am not here on my own, or I would offer profound apologies." The words came slowly at first, but as he found the formula they began to flow. "I am not worthy of the people who have sent me. They, however, are your equals, and should be treated with the respect due. As I am their representative, then I must also be accorded respect."

"Please, little puppy, don't lecture me," said the general.

He glared at Sahurah. The general's hostility stiffened Sahurah's resolve—he was here not on his own but as the representative of his imam, of men who had the word of the Prophet deep in their soul and could pass it to others. He would not disgrace them.

"I am not here on my own," repeated Sahurah.

DAZHOU FOUND THE MUSLIM MADMAN'S IMPERTINENCE rather amusing, though of course he did not laugh in front of Udara. The terrorist was showing commendable backbone. Of course, there was always the danger that would provoke Udara into having him bound and taken to the basement; whatever amusements that provided, it would set back their plans several years, if not derail them completely. And so he decided finally to interrupt and move things to their conclusions.

"No one is insulting your masters," said Dazhou. "The fact that you were brought into the general's presence rather than being shot on the street—as any rebel is apt to be—proves that the general holds them in very high esteem."

Dazhou glanced over at Udara. The general's cheeks were a

shade of bright red, and beads of perspiration were now arranged in a row on his forehead. Dazhou decided to proceed quickly.

"Were you told to say anything?" he asked the messenger.

"Nothing."

"Then your master understands the gravity of the situation, and the generous concessions that the general has made to him."

Dazhou turned and once more looked at Udara. For a moment, he feared all was lost, and decided he would have his revenge against Udara as well as the terrorist. But then the general spoke very calmly.

"Tell him to proceed on the third day after your arrival," he told Sahurah. "The third day. Do you understand?"

The messenger might have been insulted—Dazhou surely would have been had the tone been used toward him—but all he did was bow his head.

"Very good," said Udara, addressing Dazhou. "Let us have some lunch."

Though he had not planned to stay, Dazhou thought it wise to agree.

Brunei, Office of the Defense Ministry
1100

Mack fought hard to control his temper, knowing from experience that displaying any emotion would only bring smiles to the lips of the others in the room. To a man, the other ministers hated him and would seize on any excuse to stab him in the back somehow.

There were fourteen different ministers and "realm advisors" here, along with members of their staffs, crowded into a conference room that might make a good-sized closet back home. The air-conditioning didn't work very well, and more than one of the gray faces around the table looked as if it were about to nod off into oblivion. The chief of staff—officially the sultan's personal counselor for matters of defense—sat at the head of the table, eyes gazing at the ceiling fan. One of the navy ministers was explaining, for the third time, how it was impossible for the ship that sank to have been attacked by a ship.

The minister was speaking in Malaysian. A translator sat

behind Mack, whispering the words in English. Everyone in the room could speak English perfectly; Mack suspected that they conducted the meetings in Malaysian simply to emphasize that he was an outsider.

When the navy minister stopped speaking, Mack put up his finger, though he knew from experience that he would not be recognized. Sure enough, the floor went to one of the army people, who began explaining why the Sukhois Mack had encountered did not exist.

That was it. "I've had enough," said Mack, standing up. "Enough."

The translator looked at him, awe-struck. He thought he heard snickers as he walked out the door, but didn't give them the satisfaction of looking back.

PRINCE BIN AWG WAS SOMEWHAT MORE SYMPATHETIC THAN the ministers, or at least polite.

"The Sukhois have to be dealt with," Mack told him over lunch at the prince's palace a few miles from the capital. "It's possible that they attacked the ship."

"I think a bomb planted aboard remains the most likely possibility," said the prince. "It would account for the total destruction. And your aircraft did not detect the attack."

Mack couldn't argue with that. It was possible that his crew, only rudimentarily trained, had missed it. But given the course and location of the aircraft when they were detected, it seemed to him unlikely that they were responsible for the attack. But perhaps they were part of a larger attack package, or a reconnaissance flight. In any event, they were still a threat.

"The question in my mind," said Mack, "is why did Malaysia bring them onto the island secretly? What are they up to? How are the planes equipped?"

"Very good questions," said the prince. "But you are assuming they are Malaysian. If so, where would they have flown from? I have checked with our sources myself—there are no jet fighters at any of the bases on the island."

"I think they built a strip near Kalabakan, as part of a highway," said Mack "I want to fly over it and find out."

"Kalabakan?"

"That's my theory," said Mack. He'd decided it was best not to share the source of his information unless absolutely necessary—the back door might come in handy in the future.

"Flying that far over Malaysian territory—it's very far. It may be seen as provocative," said bin Awg.

"I'll take the Megafortress," said Mack. "They won't see us."

"I don't know, Mack. I will have to talk to the sultan personally."

"Okay," said Mack. "When?"

"Tonight. Or perhaps in the morning. The timing needs to be right."

"Look, we have to deal with this, and we have to deal with it now," said Mack. "Even if they didn't sink that ship, why are they sneaking interceptors onto the island?"

"Perhaps they see the Megafortress as provocative," offered bin Awg.

Before Mack could respond, the prince raised his hand and signaled to the servant at the far end of the room. The man came over with two bottles of European mineral water, refilling their glasses.

"The Sukhois were older models," said Mack. "They may have been purchased from Ivana Keptrova."

"No," said bin Awg.

"No?" said Mack, surprised by how quickly he had responded.

"I asked her, and she gave me her word of honor."

An arms dealer who gave her word of honor—Mack couldn't decide whether that was quaint or naive. Ivana was a semi-official representative of the Russian government—she claimed to work for the Kremlin but seemed to be under no one's direct control—and had arranged for several sales of naval equipment to Brunei. She'd also helped bin Awg buy old Cold War hardware and parts. McKenna, who'd worked for her, thought it unlikely she had supplied the Sukhois, but Mack refused to rule it out.

"Maybe we can use this with Washington to get the F-15s," he said. "Their main argument was that there was no threat, right? Well, with a couple of Su-27s next door, you can shoot that argument down right away."

"The F-15s are going to be denied," said bin Awg.

Mack felt as if two of the legs of his chair had just been sawed off.

"We have heard unofficially," added the prince. "The sultan is rethinking our arrangements."

"Totally denied?" asked Mack.

"We may be able to get F/A-18s. But now there are questions about the fiscal outlay."

"What do you mean?" asked Mack.

"They are very expensive."

"Are you saying we're not adding aircraft?"

"Oh, no, no, no, Mr. Minister. I'm not saying that at all. We of course are adding aircraft. Of course. Two more Megafortresses, some interceptors as well, as soon as it can be arranged. But the F/A-18s are not free, and the air force requires a great deal. I'm sure you agree."

"We need planes."

"Yes," said bin Awg. "We will get them. Eventually."

"Eventually better be pretty soon," said Mack.

"Time moves more slowly in Brunei than in America, Mack. You must learn to relax."

"I'll keep that in mind," said Mack, picking at his lunch.

THERE WERE MORE PROBLEMS TO DEAL WITH WHEN MACK got back to his office in the capital: the maintenance section had used its last spare part for the A-37B radios; the next one that broke would be out of action until replacement parts arrived in six to eight weeks.

"You can't just cannibalize them?" Mack asked Brown, the officer in charge of the aircraft. "We have four that are stuck in the hangars permanently."

"We already have," said Brown.

"What parts are you talking about?" asked McKenna, who'd been standing near the door to Mack's office waiting to come in to see him.

Brown explained, adding that he had been working on getting the parts ordered for weeks. McKenna waved her hand.

"There's a shop in Manila where you can get the radios if you want. Frankly, you can upgrade the whole avionics suite for just about the same price," she said.

Brown stammered something about protocols. McKenna shrugged.

"You have anything else, Brown?" Mack asked.

He shook his head.

"Good. We get the jet fuel?"

"Working on it."

"Well, work harder," said Mack.

Brown nodded, apologized, then left.

"Why don't we just buy off the civilian suppliers?" asked McKenna.

"Damned if I know," confessed Mack. "There's a whole bureaucracy dedicated to making sure I can't get what I need."

"The civilian suppliers are cheaper than the fuel Brown's been getting."

"How do you know?"

She smiled. "It's coming through the government, right?"

"Yeah, we have some sort of contract or something."

"You're pretty naive, Mack."

"What do you mean?"

McKenna explained that certain citizens have interests in certain businesses, which the old administration of the air force had been involved with.

"Not crooked, exactly," she said. "Just a lot of backslapping."

"So they want to be paid off now, is that it?" Mack asked.

McKenna laughed. "What they want is for you to leave. You're an outsider, Mack. They want you out of here. They'll do what they can to make you look bad."

Mack felt his face getting hot. "That's a pretty dumb game. Dangerous."

McKenna shrugged. "You can take care of most of them."

"How?"

"Cut their balls off."

"Thanks."

"It's easier than you think," she said. She pulled up a chair.

"What do I do?"

"Find another supplier. Then suddenly they'll have plenty of fuel for sale."

"You know of one?"

"I might be able to find some fuel, if you're not too particular about where it comes from."

"All I'm particular about is if it works."

"It'll work."

"That why you came in?"

"Actually, no. I had an idea on how to flush those Sukhois out, if they're there."

"I'm listening."

"Requires practicing some air-to-air refueling between the Dragonflies and EB-52."

"Forget it, then. None of these guys are good enough to fly an A-37 Dragonfly behind the Megafortress. It kicks off some very wicked wind shears. It took a while for the computers to figure out how to do it with a Flighthawk."

"I could do it. If someone who knew what he was doing was flying the Megafortress."

Mack listened as she detailed the plan. It involved a fly-around of the island by a Megafortress and two escorts two or three days in a row to establish a basic pattern. On the third or fourth day, one of the A-37Bs would pretend to have an air emergency. As it recovered, it would fly close enough to the airstrip to get a good look at it. An aerial reconnaissance pod under one of the wings would snap some pictures and they'd be set.

"That airstrip is eighteen miles inland," said Mack. "You're talking about overflying their territorial waters and then running in there—I don't know. Those planes come up, you're cooked."

"If you can handle them, I can."

"Too risky."

"Well, if you're too chicken—"

"I'm not too chicken," snapped Mack. Then he smiled at her, and laughed at himself.

A little.

"Don't do that, McKenna," he told her. "Don't try to out-macho me. Okay? Just be straight. No head games. You don't need them."

She shrugged, not particularly remorseful.

"I'll take it under advisement," said Mack. "That it?"

"Breanna Stockard tells me she goes home Tuesday. What are the odds of me doing some time in the pilot's seat before she leaves?"

"Go for it."

McKenna smiled, and got up.

"There's a tanker sailing to the Philippines with some jet fuel that's supposed to be sold to a private investor there," said McKenna. "I may be able to find a phone number so you could put in a counter offer."

"That private investor wouldn't be your ex-boss, Ivana Keptrova, would it?"

McKenna shrugged. She might not be much to look at, Mack thought, but she was one hell of an operator.

Just the sort of person he needed around here.

"Do it," said Mack. "Buy it."

"How much?"

"The whole thing. The ship if you have to. There's this guy named Chia in the Finance Ministry—"

"That's Gia," said McKenna. "Gee-uh."

"You know him?"

"I've heard of him."

"Yeah. He has this line of credit for us, operating money we can spend, but getting him on the phone is next to impossible so you have to go over there and see him in his office, buttonhole him, you know what I mean? And then on our side there's Braduski—"

"Bradushi. Like sushi. He's the guy who cuts the checks for you. I had to talk to him to get paid. He has a mother who needs an operation in Manila."

"Oh?"

"He was on the phone when I came into his office," said McKenna.

"Well, we can help him, right?" said Mack, catching on. "We make sure we fly her over there, he makes sure we have our fuel."

She just smiled.

"You just got yourself a raise and a promotion, McKenna," said Mack. "Air Commodore McKenna, second in command."

She started to laugh.

"Hey, if I'm a minister, second in command can be a commodore," he told her. "Play your cards right and you'll be 'Air Marshal' at the end of the week. Take that office with the windows down the hall. You want a secretary? Take one of mine. The pretty one."

"No way. She can't type and she can't figure out the phone,

let alone the computer. I want somebody who can do some work."

"How do you know she can't type?"

McKenna rolled her eyes. "If I want something good to look at, I'll get one of those buff boys pulling security in front of the office."

"They're eighteen years old," said Mack.

"And?"

"Kick butt, Commodore."

"I intend to," she said, marching out.

With McKenna gone and his biggest logistical problem on its way to being solved, Mack began tackling the paperwork, signing his name with abandon. He was about a quarter of the way through the pile when the phone rang. Mack picked up the line quickly, only to find himself speaking to a woman with a thick Russian accent.

"Mr. Minister Smith, good afternoon; I am so glad to have this opportunity to speak to you," said the woman.

"I didn't quite catch your name," said Mack.

"Ivana Keptrova. You have heard of me? I work with friends in the president's office. The Russian president," she added.

"Just the person I wanted to speak to," said Mack.

"And I you. It appears you have hired an employee of mine."

"Problem?"

"Not a problem perhaps," said Ivana. "An opportunity maybe. But I would watch her."

"Oh, I intend on it. Why are you calling?"

"You are in the market for aircraft, are you not?"

"I'm looking for a squadron of F-15s," said Mack. "You have any?"

"You're making fun. But if you were more serious, we could speak of the Sukhoi, a very excellent plane," she said. "With some adjustments here and there, they are twice the plane the Eagle is."

"Right," said Mack.

"I can arrange a demonstration."

"I've flown Sukhois," said Mack.

"Then the sale will be easy."

Mack wondered if the encounter had been meant as a sales demonstration. There was only one way to find out.

"Maybe we can talk in person," he suggested.

"Of course. How about lunch tomorrow?"

"Lunch?"

"You don't mind mixing a little pleasure with business, do you Mr. Minister?"

"What time?" he asked.

Washington, D.C.
8 October 1997, 2300

Jed Barclay was almost to the Metro stop when his beeper vibrated. He stopped, hung his head, and without bothering to check the number walked back to his office in the White House basement. He'd learned from experience that, whatever other virtues his boss had—and he did have many—understanding that his aides needed sleep was not one of them.

But it wasn't Freeman who had called him. It was Mark Stoner, who'd sent a message to the NSC duty officer asking that Jed contact him immediately.

"I think you want to get a look at something that's going on in Borneo," said Stoner when Jed reached him at the apartment he was renting outside the city. "I've been looking at this all day with some of our guys."

"Borneo? I think maybe Fred would be better," Jed told him, referring to a staffer who handled Southeast Asian matters.

"It may complicate that airplane deal the White House is pushing with Brunei," said Stoner. "And you have some Dreamland people over there."

Jed sighed. "Should I meet you at Langley?"

"I'd rather do this at your office," said Stoner. "And I'm supposed to leave town in the morning. Pretty early."

"Well, I'm here," said Jed, pulling off his coat.

Stoner showed up a half-hour later. He had a day and a half's worth of stubble on his face. Deeply tanned, he'd lost considerable weight since Jed had last seen him. If not quite gaunt, he looked more like a bleached-out castaway than a hardened former SEAL and CIA agent.

"I got an off-the-record phone call the other night from someone in Brunei," he told Jed, starting right off without even bothering to say hello. "It didn't make a lot of sense. So I hooked the person up with somebody there I met. And did some checking myself."

"Okay," said Jed, not quite following along.

"You have some satellite images from Dreamland's deployment at Brunei. The images may include the northern part of the island, around on the eastern shore in Malaysian territory, south of Darvel Bay."

Jed turned to his computer and tapped into one of the databases. During the operations in the South China Sea, the U.S. had moved its satellites to provide extensive coverage of the region. They had also conducted surveillance with a variety of systems, gathering electronic signals and other information to compile a profile of activity. But most of the effort had been focused on China and India. America did not yet have the capability of observing every square inch of the globe twenty-four hours a day, seven days a week. Doing so with satellites was not only absurdly expensive but technically unfeasible given present limits in technology. Improvements were steadily being made, but the day when someone could sit in a bunker in Omaha and read license plates around the clock in Beijing—let alone a less important place like Borneo—was still a good way off.

Jed paged through some images, which had been filed as part of a routine series covering the Whiplash deployment. Borneo was a large island shared by three different countries. Brunei territory formed a misshapen W on the northern coast. Sabah, the Malaysian province on the northern part of the island, wrapped itself around Brunei. Below it was the Indonesian territory, Kalimantan.

"What are we looking for?" he asked.

"Piece of road that could be used as an airstrip. About three thousand meters."

Jed hunted through the images, which mostly showed desolate rock or impenetrable jungle. "This?" he said finally, pointing at what looked like a thickened pencil line near Rataugktan.

"Compare that to an image a year ago," said Stoner.

The only picture Jed could find was from two years before. The road seemed narrower and ended in a T, which no longer seemed to be there.

"What I think they did was widen and flatten a road that was there, making it into more of a highway. The photo interpreter

I talked to says the concrete is pretty new," said Stoner. "And that what looks like a gully on the northern end there is actually painted on. It's fairly clever, and if you weren't looking for it, you might not catch it."

"So what's going on?"

"I don't know," said Stoner. "But if you can tap into the Russian network and look at their archives, there are two photos that show aircraft on the strip. I came across it by accident when your person called. They were looking for a way to get an image of the island, and I knew someone who would have access to the mirror site that the Greenpeace hackers set up when they broke in a few months ago."

"Someone?" asked Jed.

"Just someone," said Stoner. "Private guy. Thrives on information. He probably can get into the Russian system on his own, but I didn't ask."

Jed couldn't get into either the Russian or Greenpeace systems from his computer, since doing so would potentially leave a trail and therefore represent a security breach. He could have any of a number of people do it for him, however.

"What sort of planes?" he asked.

"I'm not sure," said Stoner. "The interpreter thought they were Sukhois."

"Breanna Stockard reported that the Brunei air force encountered Sukhois," said Jed.

"Two plus two," Stoner deadpanned.

"I could see having a base for counter insurgency there," said Jed. "The guerillas are operating throughout that entire area. But why would you put interceptors there? Those are pretty useless against terrorists."

"I don't know," said Stoner. "There was a ship that was blown up, right?"

"They're still investigating. No one thinks it was sunk by a plane."

"Maybe no one's right, then," said Stoner.

Jed turned back to his computer, tapping into SpyNet—the informal name for the intelligence community's intranet featuring briefings and information from around the world. The CIA was tentatively agreeing with the unofficial Brunei assessment—a terrorist bomb had been planted in the ship.

"This your assessment?" Jed asked.

"No."

"You agree with it?"

Stoner said nothing. Obviously he didn't, Jed realized—that was his whole point in coming over.

"What about a submarine?" asked Jed.

"Australians keep track of the Malaysian subs, as do the Chinese," said Stoner. "Very unlikely."

"Okay," said Jed. "But why would the Malaysians want to attack a Brunei ship?"

"I don't know," said Stoner. "Maybe they're trying to help the guerillas."

"Are you still working on this?"

"I'm not working on anything at all," said Stoner. "I'm being parked."

"Parked where?"

Stoner made a face that was halfway between a grimace and a smile. "I'm going to be an adjunct history professor at a college up in Poughkeepsie."

Jed listened as Stoner explained that his supervisors had decided, for his own good, to give him a kind of working vacation, arranging for him to go to the college as part of procedure to build a cover for a future mission. Or at least, that was the story they told him. The reality, as both Jed and Stoner knew without it being laid out, was that the CIA powers had lost confidence in Stoner for some reason, or more likely were preparing to lay the blame for certain agency failures on him. Stoner had been in charge of developing information about several Indian weapons, and had in fact been in the middle of doing that when he nearly got killed from the fallout. At the same time, his section had missed the development of two small tactical nuclear weapons and their delivery system by a private company in Taiwan. It looked to Stoner like the skids were being greased for him to tacitly take the fall. He'd never be accused of screwing up; people would just know he was "parked" and assume the worst.

"Maybe I'm just paranoid," he said.

"You want to teach history?" asked Jed.

Stoner shrugged.

"Why don't you come work for us?"

"Let me think about it," said Stoner. He got up. "Sorry, but I got to work on a lesson plan. I missed the first couple of weeks of class."

Brunei International Airport, military area, Megafortress hangar
9 October 1997, 1311

Breanna had just finished running through the last simulated flight session of the day when one of the air force liaison officers poked his head up onto the *Jersey*'s flightdeck.

"Madame Captain," said the man, "a Mr. Jed Barclay wishes to speak to you without delay."

While it was the rule rather than the exception, Breanna found the formal politeness an unending source of amusement, and it wasn't until she reached the phone in the small office at the side of the hangar that she realized it must be one o'clock in the morning back in Washington.

"Jed, what's up?" she asked.

"I need you to go to a secure phone," he told her. "Can you get to the embassy? It's at Teck Guan Plaza in the city."

"I guess. This about the planes?"

"I'll call you there in a half-hour."

"Give me an hour."

"Okay."

"THEY WERE DEFINITELY SU-27S," BREANNA TOLD JED WHEN she reached the embassy. "But beyond that I don't know anything else. They were over Malaysian air space the entire time, and the standing orders for *Jersey*'s training flights are that they be conducted either over Brunei or over international waters."

"Would an American crew have picked them up if they took off from that airstrip you found?" Jed asked.

"I don't know. Deci thinks so, but the routines we were running had us pretty low at a couple of points, and I think they would have been missed."

"Could they have hit the freighter?"

"No way. Just no way. We might not have caught them at the precise moment of attack, but we sure would have seen them earlier. Besides, I doubt they would have returned after an attack. To get back around—no way."

Jed asked her questions about the Brunei air force and the defense ministry in general. It was Breanna's opinion that, the purchase of the Megafortresses and the hiring of Mack notwithstanding, the Brunei air force remained at best a paper tiger.

"Their attitudes—they're not very serious," she explained. "Not even about counter-insurgency. They have trouble getting fuel and supplies. I think that the sultan is trying to turn things around, and certainly Mack is, but there are a lot of other people who are more interested in other things."

"Yeah, okay," said Jed. She could hear him stifling a yawn.

"What's going on, do you think?" she asked. "Were the planes and the attack on the merchant ship related?"

"I don't know. So far it doesn't fit together. The Malaysians have a pretty serious insurgency problem. Islamic terrorists have been trying to overthrow the government for years. But Brunei hasn't been targeted by the terrorists, at least not seriously. Their base of operations has been too far away."

"The people who tried to kidnap Zen and I a few days ago were supposedly terrorists," said Breanna. "So maybe they're coming into Brunei now. That incident, the ship—maybe they're looking for easier targets here."

"Could be," said Jed.

"I'm due to leave for Dreamland in a couple of days. You want me to put together a brief on the military situation here when I get back?"

"Be a good idea," said Jed in between another yawn. "If you come up with anything in the meantime, let me know."

"Will do. Now get some sleep."

Kota Kinabalu, Malaysia
2011

Sahurah waited for nearly an hour before he was picked up. Two scooters drove up and stopped; the man on the first turned to him and nodded his head. Sahurah took that as the signal to get on and he did so without comment. He held on as the bike whipped through the city streets, turning down alleyways and then doubling back, carefully eliminating any possibility of being followed. Finally it stopped in the middle of a street four blocks from the spot where he had started. As Sahurah slipped off, a battered Toyota drove up behind him. For a moment, Sahurah feared that the government had decided to arrest him.

The window on the car rolled down an inch. "Come," said the man.

Sahurah walked slowly to the vehicle, opened the door, and got inside. There was another man sitting next to him, middle-aged, someone he had never seen or met before. The car began to move, driving along the narrow road out of town and then climbing up the hill to the cliffside highway. Even at night, the view of the ocean as it spread out north was spectacular, an inspirational hint of God's expansive universe, but Sahurah did not take the chance to glance toward it.

"What happened?" asked the man.

"The imam is the only one I will address. He instructed me."

Sahurah pressed his fingers together so they would not tremble. Only a few weeks ago he would have felt anger rather than fear at being tested this way. How weak he had grown in such a short time.

The man took a pistol from his pocket. "What if I shoot you?"

That would be a great relief, Sahurah thought to himself. But he said nothing.

The man nodded and put his weapon away. "I was told you were a brave man, brother. I am impressed."

ROUGHLY AN HOUR LATER, THE CAR PULLED OFF THE SHOULDER of another road overlooking the sea. Within a few minutes, three cars passed, then two pickups with men in the rear. Finally, a battered black taxi pulled next to them. The imam sat in the back seat; the Saudi visitor sat next to him. Sahurah was told to sit next to the driver, and did so without comment. They drove for a while, taking a dirt road that tucked through the jungle and then doubled back to a promontory over the water. The driver stopped and got out of the car.

"Report now," said the imam.

Sahurah told him everything that had occurred.

The Saudi murmured something Sahurah could not hear. The imam answered, and then both men were silent.

"You have done very well," said the imam finally.

He leaned forward. Sahurah felt something press him in the side. He turned and looked down, and saw that there was a small pistol in the imam's hand.

"Take it," said the imam.

Sahurah reached across his body with his right hand and took the pistol. It was a small, lightweight gun, a semi-automatic that fit easily in the palm of his hand. It occurred to Sahurah that he might take the gun and hold it to his head.

"Kill yourself," said the imam.

Surely he had willed his leader to say that.

"Sahurah? Did you hear me?"

"To shoot myself?" he asked. "Will I be denied Paradise?"

"To die as a soldier of jihad is to be made a martyr, if you are under orders," said the imam. "No matter the circumstances."

Sahurah knew that suicide was a sin, but he also knew that there were conditions when death was not considered suicide. He had done nothing to prepare himself, however—his body was not clean or properly prepared, and he worried that perhaps he would not find Paradise if he complied.

But he must obey. More importantly, he wanted to. He wanted to be finished with this tiresome, trying world, where he could not cleanse himself of evil thoughts and failures. He wanted to be beyond weakness and lust.

"Are you afraid, Sahurah?" asked the imam.

Sahurah put the gun to his mouth and pulled the trigger. When nothing happened, he realized he had pushed too lightly, and pressed again.

And again.

He felt the imam's hand on his shoulder. "You are our bravest soldier, Sahurah," said the imam gently. "Give me back the gun. From this moment on, you are to be honored with the title of Commander. How does that make you feel?"

Sahurah stared at the weapon in his hands. He felt cheated, but he could not say that. A finger of pain began clawing up the back of his neck.

"Your future is the future of us all," added the Saudi in Arabic. "You will bring great glory to the soldiers of God."

Dreamland
9 October 1997, (local) 0830

Zen was working now. Sweat poured down his back, drenching his undershirt beneath the flight suit. A crowd of onlookers—including three congressmen and their staffs, along with some Pentagon and army VIPs—were watching from only a few feet away as he worked his Flighthawks through an exercise designed to demonstrate the future direction of aerial warfare. It was an all robot engagement—Lieutenant Kirk "Starship" Andrews and Lieutenant James "Kick" Colby were at the sticks of their own U/MF-3 Flighthawks, trying to keep Zen's Hawk One and Hawk Two from getting past them on the test range to the northwest. They were doing a reasonably good job of it, too; Kick's Hawk Three was closing in on Hawk Two, with Starship's Hawk Four right behind. A large flat screen directly behind Zen showed the positions of all of the Flighthawks, and even provided a score as calculated by the computer.

"The Super Bowl of the sky," joked one congressman. He and the others were eating it up.

Starship and Kick were aboard the Megafortress *Raven* which was flying overhead. Zen sat down on the tarmac beneath a specially rigged tarp, the center of attention. There was just enough wind and crowd noise around to interfere with the boom mike, prompting the computer to ask him to repeat every third or fourth voice command.

Zen squeezed the throttle slide on the back of the joystick controller, pushing Hawk One to accelerate past the two Flighthawks trying to close in on him. He got past Kick, but Starship was very much on his game today—he anticipated what Zen would do and managed to get right on his tail.

It took Starship another ten seconds or so to finally lock Hawk Two in his gun sights and take him down. It was a little longer than Zen had hoped—hey, these guys *were* his star pupils—but all in all, it was a respectable show.

Unfortunately for his pupils, Zen had suckered them into that encounter so he could sneak Hawk One to the target. He let the computer take over Hawk Two and concentrated on bringing Hawk One up the deck and nailing the target aircraft. He now had a clear path; the other planes were too far to interfere.

Except that he couldn't find his target, which should be dead ahead at two thousand feet.

The computer beeped at him. He was being tracked by a ground radar near the target aircraft. If he didn't confuse the radar within five seconds, the defensive system would fire a pair of improved Patriot missiles and nail him.

"Jam it," he told the computer.

While the computer filled the air with electronic static, Zen threw the Flighthawk into a hard turn, firing off chaff and flares, as well. He actually only needed the chaff, which was composed of shards of metal that confused the radars, but the flares made for a good show. He heard a few *oohs* and *ahs* behind him.

Zen's speed had dropped below three hundred knots, and he was now vulnerable to a fresh hazard—a pair of Razor anti-aircraft lasers, which were using a new optical sighting system that could not be foxed by standard ECMs, chaff, or flares. Zen leaned forward, waiting until the lasers began to revolve in his direction before starting a series of sharp evasive maneuvers, literally zigzagging back and forth across the sky. The laser system was a half-step too slow to hit the Flighthawk at very close range, but Zen knew he couldn't do this all day; he really needed to find his target, and now.

The computer beeped at him, but it wasn't marking an X on the target board—it was warning him that he was about to be pounded from above. Zen slapped his stick and dove away as Starship flailed down in a desperate attack, followed not more than two seconds later by Kick.

In anything other than an exercise, the laser would have destroyed their Flighthawks, but it had been programmed to look only for Zen's aircraft, and they flew through the air untouched. Zen shook them with a flick of his wrist, but he'd not only lost time but his orientation on the battlefield. He started to turn right, then caught a glint of something on his left.

Bingo. The target.

"Computer, target," he said, designating it with his hand. The screen changed instantly, putting up a blinking yellow triangle that boxed the spec he had pointed at.

Yellow meant not yet.

The computer warned that he was being tracked by the Patriot radar. He fired everything he had—flares, chaff, prayers.

Red.

"Gotcha," he said, pressing the trigger.

The screen blinked, then went blank.

The computer had taken over. He'd been shot down by the Razor laser.

Zen, exhausted, threw himself back in the chair. There was a gasp from the crowd, then a loud round of applause.

Dog slapped him on the back. "Take a bow, Major."

Zen looked up and gave the colonel a sardonic smile.

"I think the computer scored it as a tie," said Dog.

The others were now gathering around his station. Zen reached over for his coffee, which was propped on a small table near his wheelchair.

"That was some performance," said Congresswoman Sue Kelly, a Republican from New York. "You really had those computers going."

"Thanks," said Zen.

"And you almost got the blimp," she added enthusiastically.

"Almost," said Zen.

Of course, "almost" meant he'd lost the exercise, though that didn't seem to matter to them. And it certainly didn't bother Dog, who would now use the exhibition to talk up his favorite ugly-duck weapons system, the LADS blimp.

The blimp's shape and structure were not terribly different from the basic design airships had used since roughly 1910. It was a fattish sausage, with its inner skeleton made of carbon-fiber material that helped keep it light. The engine was a hydrogen-cell powered propeller shielded within a baffled area at the lower end of the rear. It could do fifty knots or so—not particularly fast but respectable for a lighter-than-air vehicle. The sensors employed by the unit were housed in a flat pod that hung at the bottom of the bag. The pod, and two-thirds of the blimp, were covered by a lightweight plastic panel and an array of advanced LEDs, or light emitting diodes, which were powered by the engine and a strip of solar electric cells at the top of the craft. In simple terms, the LEDs—considerably more advanced than the ones used in consumer products, though the basic principles behind their functioning remained the same—tinting reflected light to create an optical illusion. The system was optimized for daylight skies—not only would it not blend well against a forest, for example, but it also had some difficulty at dusk. Even during the day, if someone were to stare at the vehicle for a long time, they would probably realize that there was something not quite right about that part of the sky. But at a distance to a casual observer, the LED system was the closest thing to a magician's magic cloak of invisibility ever invented. Once problems with voltage spikes and the infrared signature were worked out, the system was likely to represent as big a revolution in warfare and surveillance as the first-generation Stealth Fighter had.

The blimps were visible on radar, and by very finely tuned infrared systems. The radar problem could be taken care of—as it had been in the demonstration—by placing jammer units close to the blimp but not actually in it, preventing an attacker from homing in on them. The IR problem was more difficult to overcome, but even the sensors in the Flighthawk could not pick up the blimp until the aircraft was within roughly two miles.

"Now remember, there's a lot of work to do yet," Dog told the crowd as the airship rode toward them. "You can see, though, how it comes in steadily even though there's a good wind today out of the west. High winds have been a problem for lighter-than-air ships since their invention."

"Is that a problem at thirty thousand feet?" asked one of the congressmen.

The airships' ability to fly that high—it actually had been taken to over forty, and larger ships could go much higher—was classified. Dog made a show of acting perplexed, then answered.

"I thought I heard a question about altitude. I can only say we fly very high around here. And our altitude at the moment would be limited by sensor abilities to something oh, just out of the range of normal anti-aircraft guns. But no, that's not a problem."

There were some nods and appreciative winks. Zen shook his head, admiring the way the colonel handled the VIPs. For a guy who didn't like politics and Washington BS, he sure could play the bigwigs when he had to.

Dog continued, waxing poetic about the system. The colonel was totally sold on blimps—with or without cloaking LEDs—as a low-cost way of providing radar and other sensor coverage over remote areas in the future. Much larger blimps were also being studied as low-cost equipment movers, and to hear Dog tell it, the day of the lighter-than-air vehicle was just around the corner.

The VIPs started drifting away toward the LADS landing area, watching the six-foot aircraft slide downward. Zen snickered as the aircraft's controllers—it was flown entirely from the ground—pulled one last trick out of their hats: the LED system flashed, making the airship disappear into the background for a moment. Then the crowd of onlookers seemed to appear in the sky; as they settled down, they were replaced by a message: "Welcome to Dreamland."

The VIPs applauded heartily.

"Everything's PR," said Zen, shaking his head.

"Yes," said Ray Rubeo. Rubeo was the head scientist at the base, and its resident cynic.

"You should be happy, Ray," Zen told the scientist. "Your computer beat me."

"A draw is not a victory," said Rubeo. He put his hand to his ear, squeezing the tiny gold earring there. "You flew well, and probably were only held off because your two students cheated."

"Want to go for two out of three?"

"Another time, Major," said the scientist, walking away.

DOG SPOTTED JENNIFER WALKING TOWARD ZEN'S STATION AS the blimp dropped into a hover. He turned to Major Natalie Catsman, his second in command, and asked her to take over for him. She nodded.

"I have to tie up a few things, but I'll meet everyone for lunch," he announced. Then he walked swiftly toward Jennifer.

She was wearing a pair of faded jeans and a light blue T-shirt. Even in those simple clothes, even with her hair military-short, she was beautiful, ravishingly beautiful.

And she was angry with him, though he wasn't exactly sure why.

Dog waited while Jennifer and Zen discussed the parameters of the exercise they'd just flown. Zen started to laugh.

"Good morning, Jen," said Dog, finally breaking in. He saw her whole body stiffen, inexplicably tensing up. Dog ignored it, turning to Zen. "You flew very well, Major. Your guys did a good job, too."

"I almost got your blimp," Zen said.

"Either way, we would have looked good," said Dog. "You going to be at lunch? The congresspeople can't get enough of you."

"I'll do my bit for the team."

"I appreciate it." Dog turned to Jennifer. "You have a second, Doc?"

She shrugged, then followed as he walked toward the hangar.

"Are you mad at me?" he asked.

"No," she said.

"You weren't at the apartment when I came back."

"I had to work."

"I'm sorry I had to leave. I know you were trying to make it a surprise. I just . . ."

The words stopped coming. He wanted to tell her—what, exactly?

That he loved her, damn it. But he couldn't get that to come out of his mouth. Maybe it was because he was her boss, maybe it was because he was a good decade—well, decade and a half— older than her.

Maybe it was because the sun glinted off her hair and made her look like an angel. He just couldn't say anything worthwhile. And so he said nothing.

"I've got some work," she said. Her hand reached to her shoulder, as if to flick back her hair. It was an old habit, one she hadn't completely erased. Something flashed into her face—pain maybe, a grimace of recognition.

"Dinner later, you think?" suggested Dog.

"I don't know," she said, turning.

He watched her walk away, feeling as impotent as he ever had in his life.

Brunei, near the capital
10 October 1997, 0600

Sahurah saw him as he walked from the house.

How young he is, thought Sahurah. Sixteen or seventeen.

The boy turned and went up the path. Sahurah waited a moment longer, then began pedaling his bicycle in the opposite direction, riding away from the small, well-kept house where the recruit lived with his mother and father and five sisters.

An only son in heaven. The parents would be proud.

Sahurah reached the intersection and turned right, pedaling more slowly now. The center of town was on the right. He took the turn and continued past the mosque, not daring to raise his eyes as he turned up the drive of an office building and pedaled around the dirt lot. There were no cars, and Sahurah saw no one. He rode back to the road, saw that the string was still tied to the post—a sign from the two men he had posted as lookouts that all was well. Then he turned right again and went to the end of the street, turning into the driveway of the last house and riding into the back.

The property had not been occupied for some time—it belonged to the mosque—and the jungle had begun to reclaim the yard, pushing close with large trees and brush. Sahurah put his bicycle down in the weeds where it could not be seen, then walked up the back steps into the house.

The recruit was in the back room as instructed, sitting in the middle of the floor.

He was smoking a cigarette. Incensed, Sahurah went to the young man and grabbed it from his mouth, throwing it against the wall.

"Where did you get that?" Sahurah demanded in Malaysian.

The recruit was so terrified he could not speak. Sahurah looked down at his face and again thought to himself, he is young.

Too young.

And yet some might have said that of Sahurah himself only a few years before.

"Stand, and let me look at you," Sahurah said roughly.

The recruit rose and turned around. How old was he? Sixteen? Fourteen? Old enough to be a soldier in jihad?

But this was not Sahurah's concern. The imam had already decided, and his own job was simple. He did not even need to know the boy's name.

"Come with me," he told the recruit, walking to the next room. He knelt at the side of the floor and removed two boards, then pulled up a small case. He unsnapped the lock and opened it. A small weapon sat inside.

The gun was an INDEP Lusa submachine gun. Made in Romania, the weapon fired nine-millimeter bullets. It measured only seventeen inches with its stock folded, and weighed barely five and a half pounds. The barrel could be removed to make it lighter and shorter, even easier to hide; Sahurah decided to do this.

He had three magazines. Two would be used for training.

"Come," he told the recruit. "We have much to do, and only a short time."

New Lebanon, Nevada
9 October 1997, 2005

"So when are you coming home?" Zen asked Breanna when she called the apartment. It was just past 8 P.M. in Nevada; over in Brunei it was a little after eleven o'clock in the morning.

"Supposed to leave tomorrow," she told him. "But it looks like I'm going to have to take a commercial flight to Japan. Since I'm going to be there anyway, I was thinking of staying in Tokyo for a day or two."

"Why?" asked Zen.

"Because it's *Tokyo*," she said.

"Well, yeah, *Tokyo*."

"Zen, sometimes I think you are the most boring person in the world. It's Tokyo! There are temples there, museums, restaurants, sights—I'd even like to ride on the trains."

"Like a sardine?"

"You wouldn't want to look around Tokyo if you had a few days off?"

"Oh sure, if Godzilla was around."

"What would you do?"

"Besides rushing home to the arms of my darling wife?" He took a sip of his beer.

"Don't be a wise guy."

"I'm not being a wise guy. If I were in Tokyo—I know what I'd do. I'd check out the Tokyo Giants. Supposed to be a great baseball team."

"Zen."

"Well, not compared to American baseball, of course. But good for Japan."

Zen laughed as his wife made a flustered sound.

"All right, they could probably beat, say, the Cincinnati Reds. But not the Dodgers," he added.

"Be serious."

Speaking of baseball, the Dodgers should be on by now. He put his beer between his legs on his lap and bent his head to hold the phone on his shoulder as he rolled his wheelchair into the living room.

"So, I've been thinking," Breanna continued. "What do you think about what we were talking about in Brunei?"

"What do I think about what?" he asked, stalling as he looked for the television remote. He knew what she was referring to. The game came on. The Dodgers were ahead of the New York Mets, two to zero, bottom of the second.

"I meant, about a family," said Breanna.

They had spoken about a "family"—a euphemism for having a baby—for all of ten minutes in the car going over to the beach.

"I'm sorry, I was fiddling with the TV. What are you talking about?"

"Never mind. We'll go over it when I get home."

There was a certain tone in her voice that Zen called the "husband can't win" tone.

"Maybe we should talk about it when you get home," he said.

"We should," she answered, a little too forcibly.

"So if you play tourist in Tokyo, when will you be back?"

"I don't know."

"I vote for straight home. I miss you," he said.

"I miss you, too."

"But if you want to stay," he added, "I understand."

"I'll think about it, babe. You take care of yourself."

"I always do." Zen smiled at her, though she couldn't see him. "You take care, too. They figure out what those Sukhois were all about?"

"They're still pretty baffled. Same with the ship. Jed seems to think the Islamic guerillas who have been fighting in Malaysia are looking for easier targets."

"I could see that," said Zen. He was glad she was getting the hell out of there, but saying that he was actually worried about her somehow seemed out of bounds. "How's Mack doing? Come on to you yet today?"

"I told you, he hasn't at all since I've been here," said Breanna.

"Yeah, right."

"No. He's—you won't believe this, but he's changed. He's more—I don't know. More mature."

Zen laughed so hard he nearly spilled his beer. "Right. Mack Smith, mature. What a concept."

"I'm not kidding."

"You've been sitting in the sun too long, babe. Mack Smith?" He laughed even harder.

"All right, all right. Maybe I'm wrong. I'll try to call before the plane takes off. It'll be early afternoon your time."

"Sounds good," he told her, hanging up.

Mack Smith? Mature? Changed?

Mack Smith!

Zen began to laugh so hard tears formed in the corners of his eyes.

Brunei
10 October 1997, 1310

She was beautiful, he had to give her that. Mack watched Ivana Keptrova turn heads as she walked across the restaurant toward his table. Tall and thin, with dark features and a simple strand of pearls as her only jewelry, she had a regal appearance. She wore a black business suit, with a skirt that stopped just at the knee; on someone else it might have seemed boring, even dowdy, but on Ivana Keptrova it seemed as sexy as a piece of lingerie.

Mack rose and took her hand. She swept down into her chair, smiling at the waiter, who faded toward the back for a moment and then reappeared with a bottle of champagne.

"It's the only thing worth drinking while discussing business," she told Mack, holding her glass up for a toast. "Or for pleasure."

Mack played along, very careful about taking minute sips of wine. He listened to her talk about Prince bin Awg and the sultan as if they were all close personal friends; he feigned interest in her talk about the navy, which she was apparently supplying with new patrol boats.

"What I'm interested in are fighters," he told her finally. "Sukhoi Su-27s."

"A very good airplane," she said. "The newer models especially. We have upgraded the avionics to a point where they rival the F-15s."

"The ones I'm interested in are older," said Mack. "They're used."

She made a show of confusion. "We can always find inexpensive alternatives," said Ivana. "But I was under the impression that the sultan wanted frontline equipment."

"I'm talking about two aircraft that Malaysia's operating on Borneo."

"Malaysia?"

He had to admit, she was good. Mack had no idea if she was bluffing or truly ignorant.

"Malaysia or Indonesia," said Mack.

"Neither country has purchased new Sukhois from Russia," said Ivana.

"What about used?"

"I don't believe so, darling."

"So, you don't know anything about them?"

"Quite honestly, no. Sukhois to Indonesia? They haven't the funds."

"My theory is Malaysia," said Mack.

"Well, perhaps they purchased some surplus weapons from another country. Have you considered the Ukraine?"

"I've considered many things," said Mack, bluffing himself.

"Well, I might be able to make inquiries for you, if you are truly interested," said Ivana. "But in the meantime it occurs to me—this is a threat you must meet."

"I don't disagree."

"Even the older model of the Su-27 is formidable, especially against your Dragonflies. Now, a dozen Su-30MKIs, with full support, associated weapons . . ." She let the sentence drift out of her mouth as if she were reading the bullet line from the front cover of a sales brochure. "And you know, there is a side-by-side attack version being planned, better than your F-15E."

"How much money are we talking?" said Mack.

Ivana pouted. "We do not discuss numbers at lunch," she told him. "Drink your champagne. How is Miss McKenna?"

"She's fine. Sends her regards."

Ivana smiled. "You are not a very good liar, Minister Smith.

Truth suits you better. Miss McKenna and I had an unfortunate misunderstanding over money. A commitment was not fulfilled at the proper time and—but these things happen. I would gladly take her back."

"Yeah, well, she works for me now," said Mack. "You don't know anything about those Su-27s?"

She patted his hand indulgently. "I'll find out for you. I have done good business with the sultan's navy. There's no reason we can't be friends and do business together."

"We might be friends," said Mack, "if I knew how Malaysia got those Sukhois."

"I will find out," she said. "Come. You haven't even ordered your lunch yet. Here is our waiter."

As Mack looked up, something on the other side of the room caught his eye. He turned toward it and saw a short, thin young man entering the room, clearly out of place. He had a black garbage bag with him.

"Death to the sultan!" yelled the kid. The bag started to fall away. As it did, Mack saw that there was a gun behind it, a small weapon barely bigger than a pistol.

"Down!" yelled Mack. He threw over the table, knocking Ivana to the ground. The tart pop of the submachine gun echoed over the screams of the people.

Mack reached beneath his jacket and pulled out his Beretta. The kid turned the weapon toward his side of the room. Mack rose and fired, both hands on the pistol. The first two bullets caught the kid in the stomach and chest, pushing him backward. The machine-pistol he had been firing fell to the ground; the young man seemed to crumple against the wall.

Someone tried to push Mack down.

"Leave me the hell alone, damn it," Mack yelled at him. He took a step forward, then saw that the terrorist was still writhing on the floor.

He fired two more shots into the man's body, then realized belatedly that the terrorist had been wearing a vest of explosives. By now others were reacting, bodyguards springing forward belatedly, guests cowering on the floor. The person who had been trying to push Mack down was his driver and bodyguard; Mack turned and saw his face had blanched white with shock. Two policemen came in from the front door; another came up behind them.

Ivana lay face up on the floor. One of the madman's bullets had caught her in the side of the head.

"What the hell is going on in this damn country?" said Mack, holstering his pistol. "This is supposed to be paradise, for christsake."

III
World Gone Mad

Washington, D.C.
10 October 1997, 0700

WHEN HE FIRST READ THE ALERT ON THE MORNING BRIEFING, Jed couldn't believe it. According to the Associated Press, a lone gunman had shot up a restaurant in the capital of Brunei. Two people had been killed and several more injured, but the casualty list could have been considerably longer if a lucky shot had not severed the wire on the man's explosive vest.

Terrorists in Brunei? It seemed inconceivable.

It was incredibly inconvenient, since the president was due to announce the sale of three Megafortresses to the kingdom today. Dreamland had already been ordered to have the aircraft ready for delivery within two weeks.

Jed glanced at his watch. It was a bit early to call his boss, but he knew he'd better get some bulletins out on this right away.

Brunei Air Force Headquarters
10 October 1997, 2100

Breanna listened as Mack recounted the incident in the restaurant, and the oddly detached reaction of the government officials afterward.

"So they think he's just a nutcase?" she said, finally.

"They don't want to deal with reality," said Mack. "That kid had a Romanian submachine gun. That's pretty rare in Brunei."

"You think he's tied in with what happened to Zen and me on the beach?"

"Has to be," said Mack. "I think there's a whole network of extremists running around. But as soon as I ask any serious questions, all I get are dumb-ass smiles from my fellow defense ministers." He said the title as if it were a slur.

"Maybe it's time for you to get out."

Mack frowned but said nothing.

"You want me to hang around for a few days longer?" she asked.

Mack shrugged. "Nah. My guys are probably about as up to speed as they're going to get."

"Don't be too hard on them, Mack. They're not terrible pilots. They just need more flight time. Same with the equipment ops. Deci'll work with them for a few more days. They'll get it together."

"Yeah. The whole country is not very serious about the military here. That's the problem," said Mack.

"Well you're turning it around." She meant the compliment; Mack was working hard at straightening out the air force—surely harder than she would have thought. "McKenna's working at it, too."

"She's good," said Mack. "Maybe I ought to send over to Canada for more contract pilots." He got up. "Listen, Bree, I appreciate everything you've done."

"Don't mention it," she told him.

"I'd buy you a drink but I have a pile of things to go through."

"It's all right. I have to get up early tomorrow for my flight. It leaves at 4 A.M. If I miss it, I'll be here until Tuesday."

"You stopping over in Japan?"

She shook her head. "I was thinking of it, but I want to get home."

"Don't blame you," he said, his voice almost wistful.

Dreamland
10 October 1997, 1310

Dog realized that things between him and Jennifer had been derailed for reasons unknown—at least to him. Rather than spending a lot of time analyzing why, he decided to go on the offensive. Big time.

He made sure all of his work was squared away early Friday afternoon, skipping both breakfast and lunch to get his various duties finished. Chief Master Sergeant Terrence "Ax" Gibbs, who functioned as a combination right-hand man and ward healer in the stripped-down Dreamland hierarchy, ran interference for him. He also facilitated the first strike in the operation, helping Dog arrange for a dozen roses to be delivered to Jennifer's lab first thing in the morning.

The roses sat in a makeshift vase—a sawed-down Coke bottle—on one of the tables near the entrance to the computer lab. As Dog came into the lab, Ray Rubeo had just gotten down on his knees next to Jennifer, seemingly praying over something on the computer.

"You never struck me as the religious type," said Dog.

"Colonel. Hmmph," said Rubeo, giving Dog his usual scowl. "Problem?"

"Just the usual avalanche," said Rubeo. "We need more personnel, Colonel. I need coders. Real coders."

Rubeo made a similar plea at least once a week, and usually Dog would cut him off after a few words. But today the colonel let the scientist go on, using the opportunity to watch Jennifer working over the nearby computer. She pounded the directional keys, repeating numbers to herself as she stared at the screen.

Beautiful. Absolutely beautiful.

"So when do we get more personnel?" asked Rubeo finally.

"We may be able to get some extra heads as part of the Megafortress program," Dog told him.

"The Megafortress? Why?"

"Because we're selling three to Brunei."

"Piffle," said the scientist.

"Piffle? In what way?" Dog continued to watch Jennifer, who was absorbed in the screen.

"Piffle in that they're about as useful to Brunei as a toaster is on the Australian outback," said Rubeo. "And we shouldn't even be wasting our resources on the EB-52. The unmanned bomber and satellite stations are much more important—they're the future, Colonel."

"Ray, sometimes you're just too much to take," said Dog. He looked over at Jennifer, still staring at the screen. "But I love you anyway."

"More piffle," said the scientist, muttering to himself as he left the room.

Finally alone, Dog put his hand on Jennifer's shoulder. "Hey," he said.

"Mmmmm."

He ran his fingers along the back of her neck, tickling the light down that grew there. "Come on. You're taking the rest of the day off. And the weekend."

"I am?"

"Yes you are. I cleared it with the base commander."

"Ax?"

"Very funny."

"And what am I doing with this time off?"

"It's a surprise," he said.

"I really have to work."

"No, as your commanding officer, I order you to take the weekend off."

"I think that's a violation of military law."

"I think you're right," said Dog, gently coaxing her to her feet so he could kiss her.

"Do I have to pack?"

"Your suitcase is already in the car."

JENNIFER LEANED BACK IN THE SEAT AND CLOSED HER EYES, letting the sound of the tires on the pavement soak through her body. The steady hum hypnotized her the way a rocking chair did.

Dog was trying, really trying. Roses, a weekend away—she had to admit he was really trying.

Did she still love him?

That was a difficult question, one she couldn't answer right now.

Maybe Monday.

The car began to slow. Jennifer opened her eyes just as Dog turned off the highway onto a narrow, dusty back road. She had no idea where they were; she wasn't even sure if it was still in Nevada.

A plane engine roared nearby and a shadow passed over the car. Dog turned left and a trio of small airplane hangars, each not much larger than a garage, appeared across a chained entrance.

"You have a plane here?" she asked.

"Borrowing it from a friend," said Dog.

"Really? You can fly a light plane?"

He started to laugh and she felt embarrassed, realizing how silly the question was.

"It does take more adjustment than you'd think," Dog told her. "Not that I'd ever admit it to anyone but you."

He put the car in gear, driving past the small chain separating the road from the airport lane. He got back out and rechained it—there was something charming in the informality of it all, even if it wasn't exactly the most secure facility in the world. The small airstrip was all about informality—Dog rolled down the window before driving any further and stuck his head out.

"Have to make sure no one's trying to land," he told her.

It wasn't a joke: just after they crossed the apron to the hangars, a small Cherokee came in, passing within twenty or thirty yards of the car. A short, balding man wearing a grease-stained flannel shirt appeared from the side of the hangar as Dog parked the car.

"Hey, Colonel!" he yelled. "Been waitin' all day for you."

"Traffic was tough," said Dog, winking at Jennifer.

"And hello to you," said the man, bending low to Jennifer.

Dog introduced the man as William T. Goat.

"Billy. Get it?" said Goat, who owned the tiny airfield as well as the services connected to it. Goat had been in the air force, working as a maintainer, or aircraft technician. The air operation, land and all, had been in his family for four generations.

"Great-grandfather was a barnstormer," said Goat, showing them to their plane. "Supposed to have flown under the Brooklyn Bridge upside down."

Goat went over some details of the aircraft quickly with Dog. Jennifer climbed in; within a few minutes Dog had joined her in the cabin, worked through a checklist on a laminated card, and started up the engine.

"You know, I've never been in a plane this small," said Jennifer as they taxied out to the head of the runway—a grand total of forty yards away.

"Nothing to it," said Dog. "All you do is sit and relax."

The engine's growl turned into a loud whine, and the plane bolted forward.

"I think—" she started, but before she could finish the sentence the plane lurched upward. Jennifer felt her lungs bump into her stomach.

"Oh boy," she said when she finally got her breath back. "Oh boy."

Off the coast of Brunei
11 October 1997, 0500

The target sat at the lower left-hand corner of the screen. Dazhou Ti stared at the green and black shadows, waiting for the indicator at the center to show they were in range of the missile.

Dazhou had once marveled at the *Barracuda*'s technology, not simply the propulsion system but the gear that allowed his small crew to run the boat: the global positioning locator, the different screens for passive infrared detection, and the radar receiver, which showed if others were looking for them. The faceted sides of the vessel made it as difficult to see on radar as its low-slung profile and black paint made it hard to spot with the naked eye. The passive detectors and burst radar targeting system allowed them to operate nearly invisibly, minimizing the electronic signals that indicated a conventional warship's presence as surely as a searchlight on an otherwise darkened deck. But now, barely six weeks since his first trial voyage, Dazhou took it all for granted.

"Captain, we are within range," said the weapons officer. "Speed stablilizing at eighty knots."

"Prepare the missiles."

The weapons officer touched two buttons on his panel. The metal grate below Dazhou's feet vibrated as the hatchway above the missile launcher separated. Information on the target—a large oil tank at the center of a tank farm near Muara on the northern coast of Brunei—was downloaded into the guidance system of the missile.

"Missile ready," replied the crewman.

"Fire," said Dazhou.

There was a snarl on the rear area of the *Barracuda* as the Exocet took off. The French-made anti-ship missile accelerated upward, approaching the speed of sound. After a few seconds, its nose tilted slightly downward and it began skimming along the waves, making it very difficult to track, let alone intercept. When it came within ten kilometers it would activate its own radar and use it to close in on the tank.

"On course," reported the weapons officer, tracking the missile's progress.

"Unknown contact bearing one-zero-eight, at thirty kilometers, making ten knots," said the radarman. "Appears to be a patrol vessel. Brunei. One of their new Russian craft. Not close enough for positive identification."

"Does it see us?"

"Negative."

Dazhou was tempted to destroy the patrol ship, one of two recently purchased by the sultan to equip his paltry navy. But his orders from the general were to avoid engagements if possible. Striking the patrol ship, as tempting as it might be, might prematurely alert the enemy to the existence of his ship.

Turning back now meant there would be no chance of seeing the fire his missile would cause. But vanity was not among Dazhou's weaknesses. The more difficult decision involved whether to proceed away at high speed or not. Taking the turn at high speed involved a tilt maneuver that made the craft visible by sophisticated radars, including the one aboard the Brunei ship. A slow turn, which for the *Barracuda* meant roughly twenty knots or a little less, kept the ship's profile low in the water and almost surely invisible. But dropping the speed to turn would mean he'd lose the flight effect; he would be turning the *Barracuda* back into a "normal" ship. Not only would he lose his momentum, but he would have to wait until he was a good distance from the Brunei ships to pop up. The "takeoff regime"—the word they used for initiating the effect—could not be made radar efficient. And besides, achieving the thrust necessary taxed the cooling capabilities of the ceramic baffles at the rear; he would be visible on infrared. Dazhou had to decide: remain unseen but go slow, thereby increasing the length of the mission, or go fast and hope the men on the Brunei ship didn't believe their sensors.

Throughout his career, he had taken the risky path, preferring its quick rewards. But there were no rewards in this case; he wanted to keep the ship secret for as long as possible.

"Rig for full stealth mode," he told his crew. "Return to base as planned. Remain on passive detectors only."

The men moved silently to comply.

Brunei
11 October 1997, 0530

Mack Smith groaned as the phone rang, then reached over to the side of the bed and picked up the receiver.

"Yeah?" he said.

"Mack, McKenna. We got some sort of terrorist thing going over at Muara. Looks like the navy's screwing everything up. You want me to get the Dragonflies up?"

"Hold on a second." Mack pulled himself upright, trying to will himself back to full consciousness. He hadn't had more than four hours of sleep in weeks. "What exactly is going on?"

"Terrorists attacked a tank farm out near Muara, where petrol is stored before it's picked up by tankers," said McKenna. "Navy has a patrol boat in the area but they're coming up empty. I want to launch Dragonflies to patrol the area."

"What sort of attack?"

"I don't have all the details yet. May have been some sort of missile or mortar rounds."

"Missile? From terrorists? More likely they snuck in there and planted a bomb."

"Could be. Should we get up in the air or not?"

"We have fuel?"

"We have fuel."

"All right. Send up a two-plane patrol and have another stand by. You lead the first flight; report in when you know the situation. Get the Megafortress ready."

"Done and done," said McKenna.

"I may marry you yet, McKenna."

For the first time since they'd met, she didn't have a snappy comeback. "Coffee'll be waiting at the hangar," she said.

AS HE GOT DRESSED, MACK DECIDED HE WOULD TAKE Breanna up on her offer to hang around for a few more days; he could use an aggressive pilot in the cockpit of the EB-52.

Then he realized that her flight home would have left an hour ago.

So he decided he'd take the plane up himself.

While Mack respected the capabilities of the EB-52, he'd never been particularly enamored with the plane. Early on during his stay at Dreamland, he had gone through the familiarization courses and did well enough to have been offered a pilot's slot in the program. But for all the sleek modifications and sophisticated upgrades, the big jet was still a big jet, a lumbering bomb truck, a B-52. Mack Smith flew pointy-nose go-fast jets, not big ugly fat fellas.

But you did what you had to do. By the time he got to the airport, the ground crew was fueling the plane. Mack stopped at the tower where his ground operations center was coordinating mission information and getting updates from the other services. McKenna's flight had taken off twenty minutes before and was patrolling over the tank farm, twenty miles away. Meanwhile, other guerilla attacks were reported on the outskirts of the capital.

Security at the airport was primarily provided by the army, but Mack had a small force of his own soldiers; after checking over at the hangar to make sure the Megafortress was nearly ready to go, he turned his attention to his ground force. He saw the apprehension in their eyes when he told them they were authorized to shoot to kill.

"But that won't be necessary, Mr. Minister," said the captain in charge of the detail, trying to reassure the men.

"It damn well may be necessary," said Mack. "Anyone comes up to that gate and doesn't stop when you challenge them, you shoot them. Make sure we have patrols around the whole perimeter, and double-check with the army. Tell them this is serious shit. Got me?"

The captain looked as if he had swallowed his lips. Mack looked at his soldiers—all eight of them, none older than twenty-three. They were well trained, thanks largely to the British, who had supplied instructors from the Special Air Service or SAS, the British inspiration for America's Delta Force. Still, these were kids who had never had to fire their weapons in anger before; there was no telling how they would do until things were really on the line. Mack sensed that he should tell them something, leave them on a high note. Colonel Bastian did that sort of thing all the time, not so much with a speech but with his voice. Mack tried it now, making himself sound a hell of a lot more confident than he felt.

"Your job is to keep this place safe," he said. "I'm counting on you."

"Yes, sir," said the captain.

"Good," said Mack. He snapped off a salute, then walked back toward the hangar, wishing he could have come up with something more eloquent.

The Megafortress crew had arrived at the hangar and was suiting up. Mack called the two pilots over and told them he was coming aboard as commander and would fly, but both men were needed in the aircraft. The scheduled pilot looked relieved—which bothered Mack quite a bit, since in his mind that meant the man wasn't aggressive enough. He himself would have thrown a fit if he were replaced, even by Dog himself.

Mack got his gear and went to check with the acting head of the ground crew. They were just topping off the tanks, moving a little awkwardly, both because of the hour and the fact that the plane and its systems were still unfamiliar. Mack longed for the snap of the air force's Dreamland maintainers—God protect the airman, let alone a sergeant, who wasn't in exactly the right place when Chief Master Sergeant "Greasy Hands" Parsons was scrambling to get one of his aircraft ready. But you didn't really appreciate the job Chief Parsons and his people did until they weren't there to do it.

Mack went over to the crew with the idea of telling them to move faster. As he approached, a look of horror spread over the face of the sergeant supervising the fueling operation.

Yelling at the man wasn't going to get the job done any faster or better, Mack realized as he opened his mouth. Once more, Dog popped into his head as a model. He changed his message to something he hoped was encouraging—"Let's do it, boys"—and gave them a thumbs-up.

Whether that worked or not, Mack couldn't tell. He walked under the big aircraft and went up the fold-down steps into the belly, landing on the stripped-out Flighthawk deck. Then he climbed up to the flight deck, where he was surprised to find

Deci Gordon, the Dreamland radar expert, at one of the operator stations.

"Deci, you coming with us?" said Mack.

"Figured you'd want me to."

"Yeah," said Mack. He started toward the pilot's seat, then stopped, realizing from Deci's frown that he'd somehow managed to say the wrong thing.

How would Colonel Bastian handle it? Mack asked himself.

Just like that, or even simpler, with a nod. But somehow, what worked for Bastian didn't work for Mack. Mack turned and saw Deci frowning at him.

"Listen, I'd appreciate it if you came with us," said Mack. "I really would."

Deci looked at him, as if expecting a trick. Not sure what else to do, Mack nodded and climbed into the pilot's seat.

They were off the runway in twenty minutes, which would have been a decent time for a scrambling Dreamland crew, Mack thought. McKenna checked in a few minutes after Mack cleaned the landing gear and began a wide patrol orbit, climbing up through fifteen thousand feet, en route to thirty-five thousand.

"Dragon One to *Jersey*," said McKenna. "We came up negative on our search. No speedboat, no nothing."

"Roger that," said Mack. His patrol circuit took him over the ocean; Deci and the radar operator handling the surface contacts ID'd a freighter approaching from the west about ten miles away; it was the only sizeable ship except for Brunei coastal patrols in the area.

"Say, Mack, I think I have the Sukhoi again," said Deci. "Planes we picked up the other day. Coming up toward the coast."

"Feed me a vector," said Mack.

San Francisco
10 October 1997, 1810

Dog had planned it all out so well that the cab was just pulling up to the flight service building as he shut down the aircraft after their flight from Nevada. They got in, and arrived just in time for their reservation at Il Cenacolo, an Italian restaurant a few miles northwest of the city, which Jennifer had mentioned once during a date. The host greeted them by name; Jennifer seemed to float across the room, and Dog thought to himself that things could not be going more perfectly.

It was at that moment that he heard the voice from across the room.

"Tecumseh Bastian, what are you doing in San Francisco?"

He closed his eyes, but he knew it was useless. His ex-wife had somehow managed to ruin the one perfect romantic moment of his life.

"Karen, how are you?" said Dog, turning in the direction of the voice.

Dr. Karen Melenger was sitting with three other women at a table near the side of the room. She rose, came over, and made a show of kissing his cheek. Dog stepped back and, with as much politeness as he could muster, introduced Jennifer.

"Your girlfriend?" said Karen. She held out her hand as if she were the Queen Mother and expected it to be kissed.

Dog thought he saw a smirk in the corner of Jennifer's mouth. She said hello, declining the handshake without calling attention to it, and said how nice it was to meet a person Dog spoke so highly of.

It was a remarkably smooth lie, thought Dog, and even Karen seemed taken in. But Jennifer then made the mistake of suggesting that they all get together for a drink sometime.

Dog cringed, knowing Karen would accept—sooner, rather than later.

"Tomorrow night would be perfect," she said. "The convention ends in the afternoon, but I'm not flying back to Las Vegas until Sunday afternoon."

"How lucky," said Dog, nudging Jennifer away.

"Where are you staying?" Karen asked.

"At a hotel," said Dog. "We'll call you."

"We'll I'm at the Max," said Karen. It was naturally one of the most expensive hotels in the area. "You won't forget?"

"No."

"Jennifer, make sure he doesn't forget."

"Tecumseh is definitely responsible for his own actions."

"Yes, he is, isn't he?" said Karen.

Brunei
11 October 1997, 1013

"They're still over Malaysian territory," Deci told Mack as he turned the Megafortress in the direction of the Sukhois. "No indication they see us. Range is one hundred and fifty miles. They're doing about five hundred knots, still at twenty-two thousand and twenty thousand feet, respectively."

"You have that on your screen, Jalan?" Mack asked the copilot.

"Yes, sir."

"All right. What we're going to do is run as close to them as we can but still stay over Brunei territory. It's going to take us one loop down at the south before they're in range to pick us up."

"You want them to pick us up?" asked Jalan.

"I want them to attack us," said Mack.

"You think they'll attack?" Jalan didn't sound worried so much as surprised.

"Probably not," said Mack. "But if they do, we want to be ready for them. And if they come over our border, we'll have justification to follow them. I'd like to find out for sure where they're operating from."

"Yes, sir."

One thing in Jalan's favor, thought Mack: he didn't point out that the only weapon the Meagfortress carried was the Stinger air-mine dispenser in the tail, which was designed to work against pursuing aircraft at close range.

"Be ready with the ECMs if we get close," Mack told his copilot. The ECMs disrupted the guidance systems of enemy missiles, rendering them useless. "The computer can blind that sucker and any missile he's carrying, don't worry. These planes have done it a dozen times. It knows those avionics systems better than we know our names."

"Yes, sir."

If the Sukhois were operating from the base Mack had seen on the satellite images, he'd have to fly fairly far from Brunei territory to get the proof he wanted. It was a calculated risk, given that he didn't know whether or not there might be more aircraft. But he would have to take some risks to find out what the Sukhois were up to; ignorance was much more dangerous in the long run.

Mack checked back with his controller at the airport to see what the situation was. The controller had double-checked with the spy network to find out if there had been activity at any of the other airfields on Borneo; a few helicopters were missing from Kuching in the southwest, but otherwise the situation seemed to be status quo.

The situation with the terrorists, however, was anything but. The Royal Brunei Police Force now reported several disturbances and attacks throughout the kingdom; Mack told the liaison officer to call over to the headquarters and see if any of the units needed assistance.

"Already have. They've declined."

"Call the regional offices, as well," said Mack. "Let's see if they have a different opinion."

"Yes, sir, Mr. Minister."

The Brunei border ran parallel to his flight path about five miles off his left wing; it extended only about fifty miles south. Doing roughly four hundred knots, they would have to turn in six or seven minutes if they were going to stay over their part of the island.

"Sukhois are changing course, Mack," said Deci.

"Where are they going?"

"Not clear at the moment. Heading . . ." Deci hesitated. "They're coming west, picking up speed, uh, angling down a bit."

The Sukhois had made a sharp left turn and started to descend from twenty thousand feet. The two Malaysian planes were now flying a course that would take them directly over the border. According to Deci, they hadn't seen the Megafortress—they were not using their radars, a sign to Mack that they didn't want to be detected. They had also selected their afterburners for a burst of speed as they dropped down closer to the mountain tops.

"Setting up for a bombing raid?" Mack asked Deci.

"Too soon to tell."

"Get on with the liaison and have him send an alert."

"Got it."

Mack continued southward for another minute and a half, trying to visualize what the Malaysian jets were up to. They continued to descend, passing through seventeen thousand feet en route to sixteen; it wasn't a rapid descent but by the same token they showed no sign of leveling off. They'd backed off the afterburners but were still moving very quickly, up around five hundred and fifty knots.

"There guerilla camps in that direction?" Mack asked.

He meant the question for Deci but Jalan answered.

"There are guerillas along the mountain sides, yes, Minister, but on the south side, not north," said the copilot.

"One thing I'd point out, this model Su-27 ordinarily wouldn't be carrying air-to-ground weapons," said Deci.

"Yeah," said Mack. The early Su-27s were intended primarily as interceptors, but they did have some capability to drop bombs, and in any event might have been upgraded to do so. "You talk to ground?"

"Passed it along. Entire army is already on alert."

"Minister, two helicopters approaching Brunei territory southwest of Labi," said one of his operators. It was the first time the crewmen had called out a contact on their own.

"Good work," said Mack. He clicked into McKenna's frequency. "Yo, Dragon One, I got a job for you. Stand by for a brief."

MCKENNA ACKNOWLEDGED THE INFORMATION ABOUT THE helicopters and snapped onto the new course, her hand slapping the throttle to full military power. Her wingman, Captain Yayasan, acknowledged tersely when she called over to make sure he was following along.

"Pedal to the metal," she told him. "Look sharp, eh?"

"Yes, ma'am."

The Bruneians didn't particularly like taking orders from women, and McKenna could hear the resentment in her wingman's voice.

Have to kick his butt when we get down, she thought to herself.

"Make sure your cannon is ready and keep your head in the game," she told Yayasan. Not expecting a response, McKenna leaned forward against her restraints, urging the A-37B to get a move on. At roughly one hundred miles away, it would take just under eight minutes for them to get there.

By then it might be too late.

THE SUKHOIS TOOK ANOTHER SHARP TURN TO THE NORTH-west, now at five thousand feet over the Limbang River Valley. They were still over Malaysian territory.

"I think they're aiming for one of the guerilla camps at the southwest side of the river," said Deci.

"What do we have near there?" Mack asked.

"Police barracks on the other side of the border," said Jalan.

Mack punched up the map on his left-hand display screen, studying the border area. He was just over three minutes away.

"Deci, can we jam the Sukhois?"

"Uh, you mean screw up their bombs with ECMs?"

"Exactly."

"No way. Unless it's an air-to-ground missile working off a GPS system, and even then it'd have an internal backup."

"Then I guess we'll just have to get in their faces," said Mack.

"Minister, are you sure they're going to attack our barracks?" asked Jalan.

"Not at all," said Mack. "But I don't intend on giving them the chance."

He reached to the throttle slide at the side of his seat, coaxing more power from the EB-52's four engines.

"It's going to get a bit twisty at the end," he told his crew. "The pilot has put on the no-smoking sign. Please fasten your seatbelts. Remember to keep yours hands inside the car at all times."

He pitched the plane onto her wing, sliding down in a three-dimensional pirouette as he got the Megafortress's nose turned toward the border post. The EB-52 growled at him as the G-forces shot up exponentially, but it complied nonetheless, speed increasing as he dove down toward the border. The copilot began reading off the altitude as the altimeter ladder revolved downward. Meanwhile, the Sukhois had not altered course.

"Try getting them on the radio," Mack told Jalan. "Tell them they better not go over the border."

Jalan broadcast on the Malaysian air-force frequencies, but got no response.

"They're sixty seconds from the border," said Deci.

"There they are!" said Jalan. His voice lost its professional calm and he jerked his hand toward the windscreen, pointing out the window toward the two airplanes, black blurs in the lower left-hand quadrant of the glass. "Motherfuckers."

It was the first curse—in English at least—Mack had heard from a member of his crew.

"You're starting to get the hang of this piloting thing, Jalan," he said. "I'm proud of you."

"Computer's optical system confirms they're carrying bombs beneath their wings," said Deci. "Something in the 250-pound range."

Mack held to his course to the last possible second, then pulled sharply on the stick, sending the EB-52 into a controlled skid across the sky in front of the two Sukhois.

"Where are we? Our territory or theirs?" he said as gravity slapped his head and chest back against the ejection seat.

"Ours!" managed Jalan.

"Stinger," Mack told the computer. "Track one."

"Target tracked. Target locked," replied the computer. A bracket had appeared on his HUD, boxing the lead Sukhoi.

"Fire."

Six airmines flashed from the rear of the Megafortress. The airmines were essentially unaimed canisters of metal shards which exploded behind the rear of the Megafortress, producing a cloud of engine-killing shrapnel. The Malaysian jets, belatedly realizing they were in trouble, dove violently away, then escaped to the north. The computer recorded a minor hit on its target, but not enough to take it down.

"They dropped their bombs in the jungle," said Deci. "They definitely missed the border post—they may have landed on in their side of the border."

"Great," said Mack, wrestling his wings level and preparing for the inevitable counterattack. "ECMs. Full suite—play every song in the jukebox."

The Sukhois' weapons radars tried desperately to poke through the electronic fuzz kicked out by the Megafortress's countermeasures. The radar warning detector indicated that the planes were carrying R-27Rs, known to NATO as AA-10 Alamo-As. These were radar-guided anti-air missiles, efficient killers but easily confused by the Megafortress. One of the Malaysian pilots fired anyway; the ECMs blew out its brain circuitry and sent it sailing off to the west.

Mack cut sharply east then back south, and found himself head-on toward the two jets, only two thousand feet above them and separated by roughly five miles. The position in theory favored the interceptors, who could easily turn and get behind him, where they would be in a good position to fire heat-seeking missiles.

It was what Mack wanted them to do; he intended on suckering one close enough to dish out the airmines as he used flares to knock out the heat-seekers. But they didn't play along. Instead, one aircraft broke east and began to climb, possibly trying to position himself for a front-quarter attack from above. The other Sukhoi turned and dropped down on the deck.

If Mack wanted to escape, all he had to do was hold the stick steady. But instead he put his wing down, intending at first to tack back west; just as he started to turn he came up with a better idea and rolled the plane into a loop to change direction.

It would have been a great idea if he had been flying an F-22 or F-15, much smaller planes designed to challenge Newton's laws with some regularity. The Megafortress reacted by pushing her nose sideways and drooping her Y-shaped tail. The spine of the aircraft began to bend, and the computer belatedly screamed at its pilot for exceeding all reasonable bounds of stress and strain. Mack could feel the pressure himself—his head felt as if it were being pummeled from every direction. He managed to get the aircraft upright and straighten her wings— just in time to narrowly miss getting clipped by the thoroughly confused Sukhoi pilot, who sailed over his wing.

"Stinger. Track one. Fire when locked."

"Target tracked. Target locked," replied the computer. *"Firing."*

Mack had no time to check this barrage—the second Sukhoi was diving on his tail from four miles.

"Minister—"

"I see him, Jalan. Relax. Stinger. Track." Mack pointed at the touchscreen where the plane was painted by the EB-52's radar.

The computer replied that it was out of range.

"Stay with him, baby," Mack said.

The computer complained that it did not understand the command.

"Range, three miles," said Jalan. "He's launching missiles."

"Flares," said Mack calmly.

"Target tracked. Target locked," said the computer.

"Fire."

As the airmines dished out behind them, Mack pushed hard on the stick, initiating a series of hard zigs to avoid the missile that had just been launched. It turned out to be unnecessary—one of the airmines immolated the missile. The Sukhoi, unscathed, broke off.

"Enemy is accelerating north," said Jalan.

"He's going to run out of fuel," said Mack. "Let's encourage that." He twisted around to follow.

THE HELICOPTERS WERE SA 330 F PUMAS, FRENCH-MADE military helicopters that could carry sixteen troops as well as weapons to support them. The helicopters were unloading men via ropes as McKenna approached in her Dragonfly; they refused to answer her hails.

They were also clearly in Brunei territory.

"Mine's the one on the right," she told her wingman.

"Shouldn't we consult with the minister before opening the engagement?" replied Captain Yayasan.

"He's busy," said McKenna as she swooped into the attack. The Cessna's sturdy frame shrugged off the four and a half Gs she threw at it, twisting into a dive that put its nose head-on for the side of the lead chopper. The Dragonfly's nose gun was aimed through an optical sight; McKenna leaned forward and tilted her head, steadying her focus as she moved her plane into the sweet spot of her target. She juiced the trigger and a stream of 7.62-millimeter shells flew from the minigun.

The first wave of bullets spit downward and to the left of the helicopter. McKenna eased the pressure on her stick and fired again, managing to get a few dozen rounds into the lower portion of the helicopter's fuselage before losing her angle on the chopper. She stomped the throttle and roared overhead, spinning on her wing as she angled for a second approach.

The helicopter shot upward, jinking back and forth as it tried to get away. McKenna couldn't line up her plane quickly enough for another shot as she crossed back. She growled at herself, slapping her knee as if she were an animal that had tried to enter the wrong paddock on her family's farm. She took this turn wider, coming around a bit more slowly and more consciously taking her time, aware of the adrenaline rush threatening to scramble her brain. She angled slightly to the right of the helo and about two thousand feet above it as it skimmed down close to the vegetation, desperate to get away. McKenna tilted her body with the plane's and gave the gun a tentative tickle. She had the range down; as the first bullets sailed into the rotor she stomped her rudder pedal and nailed the trigger down, walking a stream of lead back and forth across the engine housing. Wisps of black smoke appeared at the side, but the helicopter did not go down.

"Dragon Two, how are you coming with that helicopter?" she asked her wingmate, climbing over Malaysian territory. She banked around for another run on the helicopter, figuring it would take one more pass to put it down; the 7.62-millimeter gun in the Dragonfly's nose was a very light weapon by aircraft standards, and while being on the receiving end was no fun, its bullets did not have the sheer oomph of larger weapons like the twenty-millimeter and thirty-millimeter cannons carried by most frontline interceptors. But the helicopter had begun a hard tilt to the left, its tail rising. It flew onward for a few hundred meters, a duck winged by a hunter's shotgun shell. Then it plunged into the hillside, flames erupting in a stream behind it.

"Two, what are we doing?" McKenna barked as she started south. She saw the other Dragonfly about a mile and a half away, on her left, above her by at least three thousand feet. She leveled out, not sure of the situation.

"Two? Two?" she snapped.

When her wingman still didn't respond, McKenna began to fear that he had been hit. She had already started in his direction when she saw the shadow of a helicopter fleeing to her right. Cursing, she turned to pursue, but the helicopter had jinked down and managed to get behind a row of trees. By the time she finally saw it, it was scooting past a small town, flying deep into Malaysian territory. As McKenna checked her position in the sky she saw puffs of black cotton swirling off her left wing and realized for the first time that she was being fired at.

Time to call it a day.

"Two, what's your situation? Please advise," she said.

McKenna did a quick instrument check, knowing her fuel was getting low—it was actually a bit better than she thought, not quite hitting her reserves.

"Two? Is your radio out or what?" asked McKenna again.

"Two," said the other pilot finally. She could see Yayasan's aircraft, well over hers and a tiny black dot in the sky.

"Were you hit?"

"Negative."

While McKenna was sincerely concerned for the safety of her fellow pilots, and especially those on her wing, that wasn't the best response, given the circumstances.

"Get back to the airbase," she told him.

"Two," he said, wisely guessing there was no sense in doing anything more than acknowledging.

MACK HAD NO HOPE OF KEEPING UP WITH THE SUKHOIS AS they pumped dinosaurs into their afterburners. The dual Saturn Al-31FMs pumped out over thirty thousand pounds of thrust, taking the Sukhois up over Mach 2, at least for a brief moment.

Mack plotted a course toward the area where he thought their airfield was. But as he started to pursue, the ground controller relayed a request from the police for assistance at Badas, a small city in the south-central portion of the country. They claimed they were under attack by helicopters.

"Not on our screen," said Deci.

Nonetheless, Mack felt obligated to check it out at close range. They overflew Badas, taking a pass below a thousand feet. Whether that had any effect or not, the police reported that the attackers had fled.

A few minutes later, another request came from the authorities in Muara, north of the capital. Mack directed his second flight of Dragonflies into the area, orbiting with the Megafortress overhead. But even the low-flying A-37Bs couldn't be of much help as the situation unfolded; two terrorists were holed up in a residential area at the eastern end of the city. After a thirty-minute gun battle, the men immolated themselves, destroying the shanty they had holed up in as well as the two on either side.

With the Sukhois gone for the moment and no fresh helicopter attacks—real or bogus—reported, Mack decided to take the opportunity to refuel the Megafortress and give the crew a rest. He also wanted to see if he could come up with some air-to-air missiles for the aircraft, and needed to check on the Dragonfly pilots.

Mack had Jalan land; the copilot came in a little fast, but the vast runway gave him plenty of margin for error. All in all, the crew had performed pretty well, and Mack made sure to give them attaboys as they shut down. He unsnapped his restraints and went down to the runway, planning to change and then shoot over to the tactical center at the tower.

Prince bin Awg's car was sitting in front of the hangar. Mack walked over to the car, but instead of the prince he found a staff member from the central defense ministry.

"Prince bin Awg needs to see you right away," said the man.

"I'll be right with him once I get out of these duds and check with my people," said Mack.

"The prince's orders were to bring you directly to town."

"Yeah, very good," said Mack, starting to walk away.

The aide got out of the car. He was about six-two, with shoulders that looked like they could bounce a cement truck.

"The prince gave his orders," said the man.

"No shit," said Mack, annoyed. "Have a seat, asshole, I'll be right with you."

Two of Mack's security people came out from the hangar. Maybe because of that, the aide stayed back by the car. Meanwhile, Mack went into the life-support shop, a small area at the side used for maintaining and changing into flight gear. The two women in charge of the shop began clucking at Mack as soon as he walked in.

"One at a time," said Mack. He had trouble with their accents when they weren't excited.

"Miss McKenna under arrest," blurted one of the women. "They took her away."

"What?"

The women explained that six soldiers had come to the gate demanding to see McKenna soon after she landed; mindful of his orders, the security team had denied them access—and then been threatened with being shot. McKenna was called over and apparently agreed to go with the men.

"Why are you saying she was arrested?" asked Mack.

"They said that."

"The whole world's gone mad," said Mack. He left his flight suit on but took a moment to make sure his pistol was loaded. Brown, his maintenance officer, appeared near the doorway.

"Minister, we have difficulties—"

"Can the minister crap and spit it out, Brown," said Mack. "What's up?"

"We—our fuel is gone."

"Send the trucks over to the civilian side of the airport and take what we need," said Mack.

"But—"

"Give them a chit or whatever paperwork you want. Get the fuel."

"Yes, sir, Minister."

"What's our weapons situation?"

Brown stuttered but managed to report that they had four five-hundred-pound bombs and exactly two dozen smaller 250-pounders, along with some rockets and flares.

"What happened to our request for Sidewinders and AM-RAAMs?" Mack asked.

"You made it only last week, Minister."

"We need those weapons now. Why did they take McKenna?"

"Commodore McKenna? Who took her?" Brown's face blanched.

"Look, Brown, here's the situation. Whether the sultan likes it or not, whether Brunei likes it or not, some serious assholes have decided to shoot up the country. I think Malaysia's helping them. We're going to need everything and anything we can get our hands on."

"Yes, sir."

"Look, if you're not up to this, you tell me now, because I'm relying on you here," said Mack. "I need that Megafortress ready to fly as soon as possible. The same with the Dragonflies. Can you do it?"

Brown nodded. "Yes, Minister."

"They're trying to take over your country, Brown. I'm telling you. That's what this is about. We're not going to let them, right?"

Finally, he'd struck the nerve.

"No, Minister," said Brown, his face flushing with anger now. "No, we will not."

"Damn straight, Jack."

"Damn straight, Jack," repeated Brown.

Mack almost smiled. Two members of his security team were standing near the aircraft.

"Yo!" he called to them. "Get over here."

The two men, neither older than nineteen, double-timed across the concrete.

"You locked and loaded?" Mack asked.

The men looked at each other.

"Jesus, even I know you look at the gun for the answer, not each other, damn it!"

The two men snapped to, holding their rifles at the ready.

"That's what we want. Come on," said Mack. "Let's go see the prince."

Dreamland
0200

Every fifth weekend, Danny Freah took a turn in the rotation as the duty officer in the Dreamland command center, an important though not exciting responsibility. Not that it was particularly onerous. It entailed staying on base from 4 P.M. Friday afternoon until 8 A.M. the following Monday. He had to periodically check in with the command center, which was a high-tech situation room linked to similar facilities at the various military commands, the Pentagon, and the White House. It also had high-speed satellite links to deployed Dreamland units.

Danny generally spent his time catching up on his official reading and, nearly as important, his sleep, sacking out in one of the small "ready rooms" located off the corridor of the center. The rooms were more like mini-dorm rooms; each had a bunk bed, a small television that had cable TV access, and a computer loaded up with games. Because they were located in a subbasement away from any machinery, the rooms were dark and quiet, and in Danny's opinion by far the best places to catch real rest on the base.

Assuming no one woke you up.

"Sir!" shouted a voice somewhere in the blackness beyond his dreams. "Sir!"

"Boston, is that you?"

"Sir! An alert from Washington, D.C."

Danny started to curse and roll out from under the blanket. As he did, the lights snapped on. The room was not locked and the standing orders called for the officer to be awakened personally.

"Center is requesting your presence," said Boston, much louder than Danny thought necessary.

"Yeah, I'm coming, Sergeant. Relax."

Danny stood up and pulled on his shirt. He slept in his pants, belt and all; he figured it was easier and saved potential embarrassment when the night people were women, which was occasionally the case.

Danny walked out to the command center, hoping whoever was on duty there had a full pot of coffee going. Unfortunately, that was not the case. He went over to the main communications console, typed in his password, and squinted into the retina scanner. The machine hesitated for a second, and Danny wondered if his fatigue might confuse it.

It didn't, at least not fatally. The screen blinked, allowing the connection.

"Freah," said Danny, picking up the secure phone.

"Captain, this is Jed Barclay over at the White House."

"Jed? What's up?"

"We've been tracking developments at Brunei and the national security advisor was wondering, uh, hoping he could get a direct report from your people there."

"Right, yeah," said Danny. "Uh, Breanna Stockard is on her way back to the States."

"Can you locate her?"

"Yes, sir," said Danny.

"Are there other personnel there now?"

He thought they had at least one technical expert there. Danny bent to the keyboard of the computer at his right, hunting and pecking his way to the information.

"Deci Gordon. He's a wizzo—a radar intercept officer who handles the gear in the AWACS versions of the EB-52s," said Danny. "We had some maintainer types over there until last week," he added.

"We'd like to talk to anyone who might be able to give us on-the-spot insight," said Jed.

"Zen was there," said Danny. "He's at home right now."

"I know the number," said Jed. "Can you get a hold of Mr. Gordon?"

"Will do. And I'll track down Breanna, if I can."

"Thanks. We'll be waiting."

Bandar Seri Begawan (capital of Brunei)
11 October 1997, 1710

"Mack, I agree this is a difficult situation, but we must use patience." Prince bin Awg paced the length of his office in the modern-high rise overlooking the bay, the soles of his Italian shoes squeaking softly on the polished marble floor. "But it is a time for diplomacy, a delicate time."

"Look, Prince, you know airplanes pretty well," said Mack. "You've got a great collection of Cold War hardware over in your hangars. Those aren't just pretty planes. The Russians and the Americans—the reason there wasn't a nuclear war was that we were both matching each other. Those were serious war machines, and both sides had to be careful of the other."

"What's your point, Mack?" asked the prince.

"It means you have to show your resolve, not just to these terrorist punks, but to the Malaysians."

"The Malaysians say they weren't involved," said bin Awg. "The helicopters were on a routine training mission."

"Aw, that's bullshit and you know it. They were clearly in our territory. And their Sukhois would have hit the police station if we didn't stop them. You have to help me clear the red tape away so we can get missiles to shoot them down," said Mack. "And we need F-15s. Or something. Hell, I'll settle for the Sukhois Ivana Keptrova was peddling."

"The sultan does not want to upset the current equilibrium," said bin Awg. "He's put all our purchases on hold for the time being."

"He better change his mind damn quick," said Mack. "Or he'll be the ex-sultan. Now where's my pilot?"

"She was taken over to the central ministry to be interviewed. I'm sure she'll be released after a few hours."

Mack had already spun around and headed for the door.

"Mack!" said the prince.

Against his better judgment, Mack stopped.

Confusion and fear mixed in equal parts of the prince's face. Bin Awg had not impressed Mack as a great statesman; it was clear he was used to the finer things in life and was a bit too fond of pleasure to make the personal sacrifices you needed to make to be a great leader, even in peacetime. But neither had he thought he was a coward or fool.

"Mack, listen," said the prince, his voice firmer than it had been earlier. "I want you to succeed. Take the steps necessary, and I will do what I can. But there are procedures that we all must follow, even myself."

Mack glanced at bin Awg's hands, curled together in tight fists. He wants to be brave, Mack thought to himself, and he knows he has to be. But he's used to having things laid out for him, and letting other people do the dirty work.

At least his heart is in the right place. That's going to have to be enough.

"Just back me up, okay?" said Mack.

Bin Awg hesitated, then nodded.

"I'll keep you informed."

THE FACT THAT MCKENNA WAS AT THE CENTRAL DEFENSE ministry allowed Mack to kill two birds with one stone. He and his two security men, weapons ready, marched up the steps and through the reception area, pausing at the desk where two Brunei policemen looked at them with jaws just about on the floor.

"Your country is under attack," Mack told them. "And we're kicking butt to protect it. I need more security people. So if you get tired of this bullshit desk job, you come see me. We'll pay twice what they pay you here, and you'll be patriots besides."

Mack then spun and walked up the grand stairway before either man could manage to gather his wits. He marched to the office of the central minister, in theory his boss; the man was gone for the day.

Just as well, thought Mack, who then proceeded back downstairs, this time to the basement where McKenna was being interviewed about the helicopter incident. As they came down, one of the young men who had been in the lobby began tagging along. Mack looked at him for a moment, saw the man nod, and nodded back.

A guard stood outside the interrogation room. Mack walked up to him.

"Soldier, you're at war. At a minimum, your sidearm should be ready to be used," said Mack, pointing at the buttoned holster. "If you want to see real action, you join us at the airport."

He slapped the door open and walked into the room, where McKenna sat behind a long table across from two white-haired officers.

"About freakin' time, Mack," said McKenna, pushing up.

The two officers looked at Mack in disbelief. One of them started to say something, but stopped as Mack's soldiers came in behind him.

"Come on, McKenna, we got a ton of work to do," said Mack, spinning around. "Can't have you lolling around on your pretty butt all day."

"Pretty butt? I think that's sexual harassment," said McKenna, hustling to keep up with him as he strode out of the room.

New Lebanon, Nevada
0400

Though he would have flown past a dozen anti-aircraft batteries in a Sopwith Camel before admitting it, Zen slept very poorly when his wife was away. In fact, he hardly slept at all most nights. He was watching *ESPN SportsCenter* when the phone rang, and he snagged it on the first ring.

"Yeah?"

"Zen, it's Jed. Hey, you awake?"

"Well no, I'm sitting here talking to you in my sleep, cousin. What's the story?"

Jed brought him up to date on the situation in Brunei, where there had been somewhere around a dozen terrorist attacks over the course of the day. Zen flipped over to CNN as they talked, hitting the mute; there was no mention of the attacks.

"I'll tell you, that place is a lot more dangerous than people think," Zen told his cousin. "And something's going on with Malaysia. Bree said they picked up two Sukhois the other day that supposedly don't exist."

"Yeah, we've been looking into that. We think the Malaysian government may have purchased them from the Ukraine roughly a year ago, then had them shipped into the country. I won't know for sure for a while."

"You think they're working with the terrorists?"

"I don't know. There's no evidence. As a fellow member of ASEAN, they should be allies."

"Being allies hasn't stopped people from going to war before," said Zen.

"Agreed. If we had evidence that they were cooperating, we might be able to pressure them to stop."

Good luck, thought Zen. He glanced over at the clock on the night table, hoping Breanna was long gone from there.

Brunei
1910

The back of Sahurah's head continued to pound as he got out of the car and walked slowly to the house. The pain had been with him since yesterday evening, a dull throb that receded at times, but never fully lifted.

A woman with her face covered met Sahurah at the door, staring at him a moment before removing the chain to open it fully. She had a machine pistol in her hand, similar to the one Sahurah had given the boy yesterday. Sahurah frowned at the weapon as he passed into the house. Women were useful in some situations, he believed, and certainly the faithful might follow the dictates of the Prophet, but to arm them was close to folly, and to depend on them at a moment of stress surely desperation.

The two young brothers at the end of the foyer, both equipped with AK47s, were much more reassuring. Sahurah recognized one—he had been in the boat for the beach mission—and nodded before passing by them to go upstairs to the room he had been given. Inside, he closed the door and lay down on the wide bed. He spread his arms out as if supplicating the angels for relief of his headache and tried to sink into the mattress beneath his back.

Just as the pain began to ebb, a sharp knock on the door brought it crashing back.

"Commander Sahurah?" said a voice he did not recognize.

"Yes."

"Commander Besar wishes to discuss the day's events with you."

Sahurah opened his eyes and stared at the ceiling another moment, then closed them again. He pushed his right leg down so that it bent to the floor, and rolled his body to its side, rising like a wounded animal struggling to its feet. He went to the door, and was surprised to see that the messenger was a man nearly three times his age, with hair whiter than bleached cotton.

Sahurah followed him back down the stairs, through a pair of empty rooms, into a hallway that led to a suite at the back of the house. There was a pool and a patio to the left; the old man led him outside through a pair of French doors, gesturing to the semicircle of chairs just beneath the roof.

Besar sat with his back to him, flanked by a pair of women in Western-style bathing suits. The women were of Chinese extraction—no Muslim would dress so outrageously, surely. They sipped from tall glasses of liquor, both of them obviously drunk.

Pain poked into the side of his head, a hot spear breaking through the bone into the soft flesh.

"Commander Sahurah, sit, sit," said Besar. He gestured and the women rose. Sahurah closed his eyes and they were gone.

"Besar," he said, still standing where he had been.

"You don't look well. And yet your operations have had exceptional results. Sit. Sit. Rest yourself."

Sahurah managed to slide over to a nearby chair. He had the exact opposite opinion of his missions. The attack on the restaurant had killed only a few people, since the boy had not managed to ignite the bomb before being killed. He had helped plan other operations, including two attacks today on police stations that had demolished both buildings, but to take credit for their success when he himself had not expended any effort would be a great sin.

"Relax, my young friend. Relax. Have a drink." Besar

pushed a glass into his hands. Sahurah, suddenly thirsty, brought it to his lips, then smelled the bitterness of the liquid. He threw the glass to the ground.

Besar laughed. "Never to be tempted."

Sahurah's head pounded or he would have yelled at Besar, who was always playing such tricks. Besar snapped his fingers, and someone walked toward them. Sahurah, his eyes still closed because of the pain, heard liquid being poured.

"Tea only, my friend, iced tea from China. A soothing drink," said Besar.

Sahurah was not sure whether to trust him or not. He opened his eyes and saw the glass being held out to him. The young man with the glass trembled slightly.

"Is it tea?" Sahurah asked.

"Yes, Commander."

"I will kill you if it's not." Sahurah took the glass. It contained only tea.

"You really have to relax," said Besar. "And remember the teaching—our sins are being cleansed by our actions."

"Forgiveness is not a license to sin."

"Life without sin is not possible," said the other guerilla leader. "We are men, not angels. Even an ayatollah sins. The imam himself is not without fault; he has said so himself. You are not holier than a holy man, are you?"

Sahurah did not answer. Soon this would all be over, he told himself. He would soon receive the order from the imam to join his brothers in heaven. Sahurah prayed for that day; he prayed for release from the throb at the top of his head.

"Five hundred brothers from the Malaysian territory will join us by daybreak," said Besar. "We will storm the sultan's palace at eight, after the council arrives."

"Five hundred?" said Sahurah. The number seemed incredible.

"Too little, you think?" For the first time, Besar's voice was contrite, even concerned.

"I could do it with twenty," said Sahurah, who had planned such a mission several months before.

Besar laughed lightly, then reached over and patted his knee. "You are thinking too conservatively now, Sahurah. We have the entire country to take over. Capturing the sultan is a priority."

"How will we feed five hundred men?"

"From the sultan's own kitchen," said Besar, sliding back in his chair.

San Francisco
0430

Dog's weight against her side felt reassuring, and as she stared into the dimly lit hotel room Jennifer realized she felt safe for the first time in weeks.

What was safety? Being comfortable? Being immune to attack? She'd been on combat deployments and in test aircraft and not felt vulnerable. It was when she'd been accused of being a traitor to her country—that was when she had felt vulnerable.

Why? Because people didn't believe in her? Or because she didn't believe in herself?

Was she afraid that she might be a traitor? That she might not truly believe in all the things she professed to believe?

That her father, dead before she was born, might think of her as an unworthy daughter?

Dog rolled away onto his side. Jennifer slid over, pushing her hand up across his arm and then over his chest, clutching him from behind.

Tecumseh believed in her. He loved her. She could feel it like a physical thing, a coat she could wear. He was inattentive at times, maddeningly so. But he had many concerns, and the same could easily be said of her. His love, however, couldn't be questioned.

She pressed her breasts against the muscles of his back, starting to drift back to sleep.

And then the phone rang.

"Rrrrr," said Dog, the sound more like a snore than a word.

"Phone?" she muttered.

"Yeah." He reached toward it, dragging the receiver to his ear. "Bastian," he said.

Jennifer already knew that it would be Dreamland—and that it inevitably meant it was time to get up. She sighed, then swung out of bed to take a quick shower before dressing.

Brunei
1930

"We have to get missiles for the Megafortress," Mack told McKenna as he drove back to the airport. "I'll try calling around and see if I can break through the paperwork crap. Maybe I can beg some out of Dreamland."

"What do we need?"

"Sidewinders, AMRAAM-pluses. We could use older AM-RAAMs if we had to."

"How about Sparrows?"

"AIM-7s? I don't know. I think the Megafortress can fire them off the rotating dispenser in the bomb bay, but I'm not sure," said Mack. "I don't know what sort of avionics link they need or if it was hardwired into the computer or what."

"Well, find out."

"Well, no shit." Mack saw her scowl and laughed. "But assuming I find out, what difference is it going to make?"

"I know where we can buy some."

"Sparrow missiles? How?"

"Ask me no questions, I'll tell you no lies," said McKenna. "But we can have them in a few hours, assuming we go to pick them up ourselves."

"Where?"

"Philippines."

"Shit," said Mack. "Is this legal?"

"Legal for who?"

Mack snorted. "Okay. What about air-to-ground weapons? Smart bombs?"

"How about early model Mavericks?"

"I don't know," said Mack. "I can check though."

"Well, check."

The Maverick—officially known as the AGM-65—was an American air-to-ground missile developed at the end of the 1960s and into the early 1970s. It came in a variety of flavors, guided by infrared and video. Though old, it was an effective weapon, especially against tanks and other hardened targets.

"We need more small bombs for the A-37s," Mack told her. "Can you get some?"

"We may be able to get all of this from the Philippines," said McKenna. "There are some people there that Ivana knew. They're a lot further down the food chain, though, and they're going to be expensive."

"Sultan's just going to have to pay through the nose if that's what it takes," said Mack, slowing down as he approached the gate at the airport. A pair of army soldiers stood near the main gate; Mack got ready to stop but they didn't challenge him, or the car behind them carrying his soldiers and the new recruits who had joined him from the defense ministry.

"They still aren't taking this seriously," complained Mack as they rolled through.

"They've been fat too long," said McKenna.

"Ain't that the truth." Mack sped toward the tower, where the army and police guard had been augmented by his own air force people. "I want to rotate the Dragonfly crews so we have airplanes in the air at all times. Yayasan can take the first flight with you in the morning—"

"I fired him."

"What are you talking about? He's one of our best pilots."

"He was flying wing with me this morning. He lost his guts when I went after the helicopter."

"You just fired him?"

"Soon as we landed. What good is a pilot who loses his nerve? He's chicken."

Mack might have said the same thing himself a few weeks before. But now he saw that there were many more jobs in the air force than flying planes. He could have found something for Yayasan to do.

"Okay," said Mack. "You gotta do what you gotta do. But from now on, I do the hiring and firing, all right? We might have been able to use him on the ground."

She pursed her lips for a second as if she were going to pout, but then said, "Sir, yes, sir."

"Fuck you, McKenna."

"Any time, Mr. Minister. Anytime."

Off the coast of Brunei
2200

Dazhou Ti leaned forward over the weapons officer's shoulder, looking at the screen. When they had drawn up the mission, they had not dared to hope for such luck—both of the Brunei navy's new patrol vessels were sailing together in the direction of the oil platforms west of the Bay. The two ships were separated by less than a hundred yards.

The only question was whether to use his last Exocets on them, or to close in with his torpedoes and cannon.

Dazhou wanted to reserve the precious French-made missiles; he had only four, and there was no telling when or even if he might obtain replacements. But the two Russian-made Nanuchka-class ships were capable enemies. They had powerful surface-search radars, and as stealthy as the *Barracuda* was, it could not count on escaping detection once it began firing its cannon.

"Range is twenty kilometers on target one," said the weapons officer.

"Prepare to fire."

Dazhou turned toward the helmsman, who was holding to a steady course. Dazhou could see the speed sliding below two hundred knots on the screen, pushing down toward one hundred. While the engineers claimed that a launch speed of one hundred was optimum, Dazhou had concluded from their earlier missions that anything faster than eighty knots increased the margin of error unacceptably; the missile they had launched this morning had actually struck a storage tank beyond the one they were aiming at. The trick was to hold the craft steady at that speed, as it began to settle around eighty-five, losing the benefits of its stubby wings.

"Target is locked," said the weapons officer.

"Speed?"

"One-ten."

"Steady."

"Ninety-five knots. Eighty-five."

"Fire missile one."

"Firing."

"Fire missile two."

"Firing."

"Target two is changing course!" said the radar operator.

Dazhou looked across the deck at his screen. The second patrol vessel was turning eastward toward them.

"Prepare missiles three and four."

"Ready to fire, sir."

"Missile in the air!" warned the radar operator.

For a split second, Dazhou felt his breath catch deep in his chest. The Brunei navy vessel had fired one of its SS-N-9 Siren anti-ship missiles. The missile's warhead carried roughly 6,600 pounds of explosives—more than four times the weight of the Exocet.

"Prepare for evasive maneuvers," he said. Then he turned to the weapons officer. "Are we locked on the target?"

"Yes, sir."

"Fire. Both missiles."

The ship rumbled with the launch as the slender French missiles jumped from their tubes behind the bridge area. The *Barracuda* then abruptly settled into the water. Dazhou's decision to fire had cost him the wing in surface effect, making it almost impossible to race away.

But he had no intention of doing so.

"Evasive maneuvers. Chaff and ECMs," said Dazhou.

The *Barracuda* lurched sideways as the helmsman tried to duck the incoming missile. A quartet of small mortars pumped shards of aluminum, copper, and tin into the air, creating a fog for them to disappear behind.

"Still tracking us," reported the defensive weapons officer.

"Continue evasive maneuvers," said Dazhou calmly.

He stood over the radar operator's station, watching the display.

"Still tracking," reported the defensive weapons officer.

"ECMs are on?"

"Affirmative, sir."

"Target one hit. Hit on target one," said the offensive weapons operator.

Dazhou struggled to keep his head clear. The missile was still tracking them. He'd thought it would be easier to duck in stealth mode.

Should he have run?

"More chaff," he said. "And flares as it closes."

"Ninety seconds," reported the radar operator.

"Strike on two! Strike on two!"

Yes, thought, Dazhou, we have sunk both. But that will be of small consolation if they hit us as well.

The *Barracuda* slapped left and right, then left again. The enemy missile continued to home in on them.

Dazhou went to the weapons station. They could use the small cannon as a last-ditch weapon and try and shoot the missile down from the sky. The twenty-millimeter gun was an excellent weapon and the SS-N-9 relatively slow moving, but still, they would have only a few seconds to hit it. The gun was in the nose of the ship and the craft would have to be turned to fire. They would also have to kill their engines to increase the odds of success.

"Come around so we can bring the small cannon to bear," Dazhou told the helmsman.

"Aye, sir," he said, already starting the turn.

"Still coming!" warned the radar operator.

It's looking at our radar, Dazhou realized. The Russians had sold Brunei a radar homing device, and they had been smart enough to use it.

"Turn off the radar," said Dazhou quickly. "Fire more chaff. Helm, resume evasive pattern."

The mortars with the chaff roared at the back. The *Barracuda* hunkered down as her helmsman, worried that turning too sharply would tip them over disastrously, shunted left vaguely, then back right.

"Harder, helm," said Dazhou. He reached to the control wheel, placing his hand on his crewman's. He was not showing the man that he didn't lack confidence in him—he was taking responsibility for the brash maneuver.

The *Barracuda* roared and shot left, nearly pirouetting around on its wing and flipping over as it tried to follow the harsh jerks on its controls. Dazhou barely stayed upright as they jinked across the ocean left, left then right and right again, left, right, left.

"Chaff!" he called again. "And flares."

The diversionary weapons exploded from the rear.

Dazhou pulled his arm up. For a second, two seconds, he did not breathe.

And then he knew they were safe.

"Very good," he told the helmsman, even before the defensive weapons operator and the radarman reported that they had lost track of the enemy missile.

"Head back toward our targets," Dazhou said calmly. "Let's make sure they don't need to be finished off. Remain in stealth mode. Do not activate radar except on my command," he added.

Within seconds, they were pointed back toward the two Brunei patrol ships. Both were on fire, one clearly taking water. A distress signal came over the radio band.

"Go no closer than ten kilometers," Dazhou told his helmsman.

"Aye-aye, captain."

His crew had performed well. He himself, however, might have realized why the SS-N-9 had stayed on them much sooner than he had. In truth, the earlier attacks had made him far too cocky; he should have approached without his radar as he had before.

An important lesson. He would remember to apply it tomorrow, when the stakes would be even higher.

IV
High Stakes

MACK CHECKED HIS GPS READING AS HE APPROACHED THE dark island, making sure he was in the right place before taking the Megafortress down through the storm. Jalan, his copilot, seemed calmer than he had been yesterday; maybe the fact that the man had had very little sleep before being roused for the mission had calmed him somehow.

"Infrared still blocked," said the copilot as Mack pushed the Megafortress downward.

"Yeah, the rain's going to play havoc with our sensors," Mack told him, speaking over the interphone. "I want you to watch our altitude and that little lump of sugar guarding the approach."

"Yes, Minister."

The "lump of sugar" was a mountaintop 1,335 meters above sea level which Mack had to skirt to get onto the runway. As an added bonus, the runway would have no lights and be wet besides. But then again this was probably the perfect weather for arms smugglers.

McKenna's contact had promised eight Sparrow missiles, two Sidewinders, and a dozen five-hundred-pound bombs. To pay for this windfall, Mack had emptied the air force treasury of the hard currency kept in the safe for operational emergencies—essentially petty cash, though fifty thousand American dollars was hardly petty. The cash was just the down payment; he had had to authorize wire transfers from a number of accounts, including his own. All together, the black marketeer had demanded $265,000 for the weapons. That was a veritable bargain, as the U.S. air force reckoned the cost of one Sparrow missile at $225,700, but then again, these guys didn't have the same overhead costs.

"There, Minister," said Jalar, pointing to the peak, a shadowy lump of danger materializing in the right half of the windscreen.

Mack was closer to the mountain than he'd thought. He nudged the stick slightly, blowing a wad of air from his lungs. The computer helping him fly the plane now came into its own; he selected the synthetic landing assist module and a ghost of the unlit airfield appeared at the top of a small square on his HUD. Mack had programmed the destination into the computer before takeoff; the silicon brain was able to find the airfield in its extensive database even though it had been abandoned by the U.S. and Filipinos a decade before. As they approached, the Megafortress used its sensors—in this case its radar and GPS—to verify the preloaded image, confirming that there was an air base there. Mack could proceed in as if the airfield were broadcasting a set of guidance signals the same way a commercial airport system would show an airliner how to land in inclement weather.

Almost. Mack was not only landing completely in the dark, but there was no way to know whether someone with an antiaircraft cannon was waiting on the nearby hillsides.

"Landing gear down," confirmed the copilot as they worked through their routine.

The Megafortress's wheels hit the end of the slick runway hard as a burst of wind pushed Mack down a split-second sooner than he anticipated. Computer or no, the nearly 350,000 pounds of aircraft, fuel, and men represented a massive amount of energy trying to go in several different directions at once. Mack broke into a serious sweat as he worked to keep the plane moving in a straight line toward the end of the runway, applying brakes and going to reverse thrusters all on cue from the computer. As they came to a stop, Mack spotted a tiny pinprick of light on his left. It blinked twice, the signal they had agreed on. Mack was supposed to kill his lights to confirm that they'd seen the signal.

It seemed a bit superfluous—how many other big jets would be landing on this runway tonight? But he did so, bringing them back on as he found the small apron on the right and turned the aircraft around, trundling back gingerly on the narrow ramp to the point where he had landed.

The rain was now an intermittent drizzle, but it still made it difficult for the IR gear to see anything. Mack switched over to the low-light video, making sure Jalan would be able to monitor what was going on once they were outside.

"Keep the motor runnin'," he told the copilot, undoing his restraints.

"Yes, Minister," said Jalan.

Mack pulled off his helmet and survival vest, exchanging them for a com set, flak vest, and small radio. The two soldiers who'd been sitting on the flight deck had already gotten up and were checking their weapons. Brown got up somewhat shakily from the jumpseat at the rear. He'd spent the flight memorizing the instructions from the computer library on how to work the AIM-7s into the Megafortress weapons controller.

Mack went to the weapons locker at the far end of the deck and retrieved his own weapon, an MP5 submachine gun, as well as an attaché case with the cash.

"Let's do it, boys," he shouted over the loud hush of the Megafortress's idling engines. He tossed the attaché case to Brown and started down the ladder.

Two other soldiers had ridden on the Flighthawk deck; the four men fanned out behind Mack as he walked forward along the edge of the concrete, striding toward the edge of the white-yellow halo thrown off by the Megafortress's landing lights. His heart pounded; he moved his finger away from the trigger of the MP5, aware that his adrenaline level was off the board.

"Yo, assholes, let's get this show on the road. I don't have all night," he yelled to the darkness.

A set of truck lights switched on in the distance. Mack stopped.

"Fan out, men," he told the soldiers accompanying him. "Don't shoot the bastards unless I say so. Jalan, what's coming at us?"

"Pickup truck, two men I think," said Jalan. "Empty."

"All right, be cool," said Mack. He had expected the weapons dealers to show some caution, but was nonetheless disappointed that they were coming forward in a truck that obviously didn't have the goods.

The pickup stopped about thirty feet from Mack. It left its high beams on; he took two steps to the right, avoiding the worst of the glare.

"Minister Smith?" said a voice that sounded more Hispanic than Filipino.

"In the flesh. Where are my missiles?"

The truck door opened. Mack's men snapped their weapons up behind him—a nice little flourish, thought Mack—but the man proceeded across the concrete calmly. Something red flared in front of his face: he was smoking a short, monstrously fat cigar.

"Minister Smith," said the man, sticking out his hand. "Allow me to introduce myself. José Cadero, purveyor of goods."

"Where are mine?" said Mack, not taking the man's hand.

"Ah, Minister, first we make sure we have the money, then we complete the exchange."

"No goods, no money," said Mack.

"Ah, no one is trustworthy these days. But, as you are a new customer, this is understandable."

He turned around and started to reach into his pocket. Mack slapped his hand on the man's arm.

Despite his small size, Cadero had a large and hardened bicep; it felt like a boulder in Mack's grip.

"I just have to give a signal," said the man mildly.

Mack let go. Cadero took out a small walkie talkie, pressed the transmit button, and said "Sí." Another truck, this one with a loud, unmuffled engine, started in the distance.

"Cigar?" Cadero asked.

"Not right now," said Mack.

Cadero smiled and took a big puff. "I must say, an impressive aircraft."

"You don't know how impressive," said Mack.

"Oh, I have seen reports. It is a superplane. Did you bring Flighthawks?"

"They're overhead," lied Mack.

"Impressive," said Cadero, looking upward. "I understand they fly by remote control and fire thirty-millimeter cannons?"

"Twenty millimeter. Similar to the M61 in F-16s and F-15s."

Cadero smiled. "I can get shells."

"Let's focus on the Sparrows and bombs for now."

An ancient American six-wheeled truck rolled slowly down the runway. It had a flatbed at the back; several boxes were stacked atop of it.

"Six people, all with M16s alongside the truck," said Jalan.

"Thanks," said Mack. "Don't blow them up unless I tell you to."

"Were you talking to me?" asked Cadero.

"Just my crew," said Mack. "They're a little jumpy in the plane. You understand. Long flight and all. They want to stretch their trigger fingers."

Cadero smiled, but seemed somewhat less easy than before. When the truck stopped, Mack walked to it and climbed up with Cadero. The air-to-air missiles were in long wooden crates marked "bicycles" in English, a rather half-hearted attempt at camouflage. Two of Cadero's men took a box down and opened it for Mack; the long, finned body of an AIM-7E sat in a bed of wood shavings.

Mack jumped down to the ground and took the attaché case from Brown.

"Check them all," he told him. "Then get them loaded."

"Yes," said Cadero. "The bombs are in the smaller boxes at the front," he added, pointing at the truck bed. "You must be careful of the fuses. As I told Commodore McKenna, we can guarantee the explosives only; the fuses I do not vouch for."

"She told me," said Mack.

"She drives a hard bargain," added Cadero. "But she said you would perhaps be interested in future purchases?"

"We definitely would," said Mack. "Better air-to-air missiles, air-to-ground—"

"Better air-to-air? Than the AIM-7? Very difficult," said Cadero.

"Aw, come on, you can't steal AMRAAMs?"

Cadero became indignant. "These weapons were not stolen. They were purchased."

"Not a problem," said Mack.

"That is for me?" asked Cadero.

Mack handed the attaché case over. Cadero turned without opening it.

"Not so fast," said Mack. "You don't leave until I'm sure those weapons work."

"But how will you be sure?"

"I'm going to fire one from the air."

"But that could take hours."

"Only ninety minutes if Brown here does everything I've told him to do. Right, Brown?"

"Ninety minutes, Minister."

"Come on. You can sit on the flightdeck. It'll be the thrill of a lifetime."

"Well, thank you, but—"

"If you don't, my people in the plane will kill you all. Which seems kind of a rotten way to start a business relationship."

Cadero took a puff from his cigar. Mack realized they were both acting; the question was, who was better?

"It is an impressive aircraft," said Cadero finally. "And perhaps if I see it up close I will be able to make more recommendations for sales."

"That would be welcome," said Mack.

"But your man—he knows how to arm the missiles and arrange for them to be fired?"

"You better hope he does," Mack told the Filipino. "Because if he doesn't, you're going out the hatch."

Brunei
0600

McKenna gunned the Dragonfly off the runway, stowing her landing gear and climbing up over the Pacific. The Brunei navy had lost its two crown jewels overnight—a pair of brand new patrol ships purchased from the Russians through Ivana. The ships could only have been sunk by a missile attack, which meant the Malaysians had to be involved, but the reports were very confusing. The Brunei government was in deep disarray, several of its ministers still refusing to admit that the Islamic fundamentalist guerillas had declared total war on them.

Her wingman, Captain Seyed, checked in as she crossed over the water. Both planes were carrying bombs as well as full loads for the minigun.

"Dragon One acknowledges," she told him. "We'll go out toward the ships as planned, then circle back."

"Roger that," said the wingman. While Seyed's flying skills

were as yet unrefined, the pilot had a gung-ho grin and a forward-leaning gait—no substitute for experience or ability, she realized, but positive attributes nonetheless.

The charred hull of one of the patrol ships floated on its side a few miles away, surrounded by small boats that were continuing to search for survivors. The ship carried a complement of sixty men; according to the morning brief, thirteen had been recovered.

Exactly none had been rescued from the other craft, which was somewhere beneath the oil slick further north. A set of oil derricks sat to the west, lonesome and uneasy sentries.

"Dragon One, this is AF Control," said the ground controller back at their war room.

"Dragon One acknowledges, AF Control," said McKenna. "Do you have information for me?"

"We have an urgent request—the palace is under attack," said the controller.

"The palace?"

"Police units are responding."

"Get a forward-air-controller over there on the double," McKenna told him, changing course. "Have him contact me directly and tell me what's going on."

Dreamland
11 October 1997, (local) 1730

Dog stood in the center of the command room, waiting for the feed to come through from the White House situation room. Finally, the screen blinked, and Jed Barclay's pimple-studded face appeared.

"Colonel Bastian?"

"Hi, Jed."

"President wants to speak to you, sir."

The screen blinked, and Kevin Martindale appeared at the front of the room.

"Tecumseh, thanks for cutting short your weekend," said Martindale.

"Yes, sir."

"We've just had a National Security meeting discussing the situation in Brunei. Terrorists have launched a concerted attack against the entire country. There are rumors, which no one has been able to prove yet, that Malaysia may be involved as well. ASEAN is having an emergency session this evening, our time, to discuss the matter. In the meantime, it may be necessary to evacuate American nationals. The nearest carrier group was up north watching China and it's going to be some time before they can get there in force, but they're en route. Because your people are somewhat familiar with the sultan, I'd like you to stand by to offer assistance if necessary."

"Yes, sir," said Dog.

"I want someone I can trust to talk to the sultan," said Martindale.

"Yes, sir."

"We promised them two Megafortresses. Can they be delivered?"

"We do have two aircraft, but they're not ready for them to take possession," said Dog. "They still have Flighthawk apparatus."

"What if we get them into the area, then prepare on the ground once they're in place?"

"My crews would have to operate them in the meantime," said Dog.

"How soon can they get there?" asked the president.

"They can take off tonight, along with transports to assist any evacuation, if needed. And security."

"Do it."

"Sir, I've received an informal request from their air force defense minister for weapons," Dog added.

"What sort?"

Dog hesitated for a moment. Mack had spoken to Danny earlier, asking for "anything and everything." It was a highly unorthodox request; even if Dreamland had been a "normal" air force command, U.S. units weren't in the habit of loaning out missiles.

"They're looking for air-to-air and air-to-ground missiles," said Dog. "The Megafortress that we provided to them under the first phase of the demonstration project was equipped with Stinger airmines only."

Someone stepped close to the president, and Dog saw an aide giving him advice.

"We'll have to look into the request," said the president finally. "There are treaty implications. But in the meantime, any Dreamland assets that are in the area must be equipped to defend themselves. Is that understood?"

"Amply, sir."

"This is a Whiplash order," added the president, making the deployment official. "You get with Jed if you need anything else."

"Yes, sir," said Dog as the screen went blank.

He looked over at the lieutenant on the communications desk.

"Tell Danny Freah it's official. We're deploying tonight. Get Zen as well. Is Breanna still on Brunei?"

"I believe she may be en route back home."

"See if you can locate her. You better call Major Catsman as well."

"She's on her way, sir. Chief Gibbs also called a little while ago to alert you that he would be in."

"Ax called you?"

"Yes, sir."

Dog thought of something else. He picked up the base phone and called over to Jennifer's apartment.

"Hey," he said when she answered.

"Well, hey yourself. Are we having dinner?"

"Maybe," he said, glancing at his watch. "If you come over to my office with it."

She hesitated a second but then said, "All right."

"Where's Ray Rubeo about now, do you think?" Dog asked.

"Uh, well, this being Saturday night . . ."

"You're not going to tell me something I don't want to know, are you?"

"Well, that depends on you, doesn't it?"

RAY RUBEO PUT HIS LIPS AGAINST THE SILVER PIPE, HESITATing for just a moment. He felt the muscles in his neck tense slightly as he pursed his lips; he tried to relax them, took a breath, then began to blow.

The beeper on his belt buzzed just as the first notes came out from the flute.

"It figures," said the scientist.

His flute teacher looked up at him through her thick glasses.

"I'm sorry," he told her. "I'm afraid I'm going to have to cut my session short."

"Go ahead, young man," she told him. "Your family is more important."

Rubeo, bound by his agreements with the government not to divulge anything about his activities to outsiders, growled to himself but did not correct her.

THE MAN IN CHARGE OF THE KITCHEN AT DREAMLAND'S RED Room—officially an all-ranks mess but closer in practice to a civilian-style grill—was an air force staff-sergeant who not only looked younger than Jennifer but was twice as skinny. How Sergeant Jorge Boca stayed thin was undoubtedly a classified military secret, but one bite of his food cleared up any doubt how he had achieved his rank at such a young age: he had surely been promoted on merit.

Sergeant Boca could prepare anything from killer barbe-cue to grilled tuna with chipotle chili sauce. Dreamland might be the only military base in the country where seafood crepes were a regular feature on the lunch menu. And his blue-cheese burgers were worth marching twenty miles through the desert for.

It was his potato salad that Jennifer sought now. The wizard himself was on duty, dicing carrots as he oversaw his staff.

"Ms. Gleason of the wonderful long hair," he said as she snuck in the back.

"Not any more," said Jennifer.

"Have to come up with a new name," said Boca, sliding his carrots aside. "What can we do you for?"

"A little picnic dinner?"

Sergeant Boca waved his knife in the air as if it were a baton. "For tomorrow?"

"For ten minutes ago."

"Jennifer, Jennifer, Jennifer."

"Cold chicken?"

"Tuna niçoise salad," he answered, veering toward the re-frigerator.

* * *

"I HAVE NO DOUBT ABOUT THE SENSOR COVERAGE," SAID Rubeo, frowning at the map of Borneo Dog had spread over his conference room table a half hour later. "Deploying the blimps is another matter entirely. They have to be launched from the ground."

"My guys can handle it in an afternoon," said Danny Freah. "We just helicopter in to these six spots and we're set. Once they're in, we can add the others as we go."

"You're assuming the Bruneians are going to remain in control of things there," said Rubeo.

"You don't think they will?" Dog asked.

The scientist merely frowned.

The alternative involved launching the blimps from the rear of a cargo plane at twenty-two thousand feet. It had been done twice during trials at Dreamland, using Dreamland's MC-17D/W, a special version of the C-17 cargo aircraft. The results had been mixed.

"I think worse case scenario, we can still set them up," said Danny. "We bring them into an area via helicopter, inflate them, and launch."

"Really, Colonel, I think you're pushing the development envelope here," said Rubeo.

"Oh, come on, Doc, they've passed all the preliminary tests," said Dog. "They'll provide round-the-clock coverage without us having to fly a Megafortress twenty-four/seven."

"If they work."

There was a knock on the door.

"Come," said Dog.

"Am I interrupting?" Jennifer asked.

"Hopefully," said Rubeo.

"I brought some dinner," she said.

"Great!" said Danny, helping her with the cooler.

"I didn't realize it was a party," she said. "Or I would have brought more."

Dog saw the disappointment she was hiding behind her smile.

I'm going to marry her, he thought. If she'll have me.

"Jennifer, as an uninterested bystander," said Rubeo, "is LADS ready to be deployed?"

Dog held his tongue.

"I don't see why not. The technology is all off-the-shelf, with the exception of the airships themselves. Where?"

"Brunei," said Rubeo.

"When are we leaving?"

"You're not," said Dog.

"Why not? I hear it's a great place."

"Until a few days ago," said Danny. "There's some sort of revolt or religious uprising going on."

Jennifer looked at Dog. Part of him wanted her along. The other part wanted her far from harm's way.

"LADS isn't your system," he told her.

"Technical people will have to be along," she said. "Who's going to supervise the engineering team? Ray?"

"Hardly necessary," said Rubeo.

Dog looked at her. "We're deploying tonight. I wasn't planning on bringing a technical team. Danny's people have already trained on the equipment."

"You need a technical team. And maintainers."

"For blimps?" said Rubeo.

"As a follow-on, sure," said Dog. "After we assess the situation."

"It should deploy with the weapons system." Jennifer crossed her hands in front of her chest, the way she always did when she knew she was right. "And there should be an evaluation team as well, headed by a senior scientist."

"Probably as a follow-on," said Dog. "Depending on the situation. It's volatile."

"It is," said Danny, who was munching on a chicken leg. "We're setting up camp at an oil platform, Jen. It's not going to be a picnic."

"I was in Iraq, remember?"

"We'll bring the support team in once the situation has been assessed," said Dog. "And an evaluation team."

"I'll be ready to take off in two hours," said Jennifer, starting to leave.

"You won't be needed until tomorrow afternoon at the earliest," said Dog, pulling over the food. "Stay and have some dinner."

Brunei
12 October 1997, (local) 0640

McKenna took a low pass over the palace compound. She saw a few figures moving near the building, but was moving far too fast to get a good read on what she was seeing.

"Dragon One to control—you have that forward-air-controller down there yet?" she asked as she pulled off. She wanted to get a handle on the ground situation and make sure she didn't hit any of their own people.

"We're working on it, Dragon One."

"Well work harder," she snapped. She watched her wing-mate come over the palace on the side near the sea. It didn't appear as if anyone on the ground fired at him.

"Two, I'm going to take a real slow pass back over the dome," she said. "Hang back and see if anyone fires at me. I want to get this sorted out."

The little Cessna poked her nose down toward the ground, settling down to a brisk walk over the compound at treetop level. This time McKenna saw several knots of men in what looked like white pajamas near the walls. These were obviously the guerillas.

Three bodies in plainclothes lay sprawled near the building. A green British Land Rover sat near the gate on the far side of the compound. McKenna saw a grenade explode near the vehicle. From this altitude, the shock of smoke appeared harmless, though she realized it was anything but. She saw a pair of vans parked on a side street, a large group of men in white near it.

The forward-air-controller finally came on over the police frequency. It was one of the security people who had been with Mack yesterday when he rescued her from the ministry. The man had received training in directing aircraft for attack, but it still took a few exchanges for her to work out where he was and vice versa.

"I'm going to hit those vans," she told him once it was clear the government troops were not nearby. "Tell the officer in charge there."

"Yes, yes, he says do it."

McKenna tipped forward in her seat, pushing against the re-straints as the ground flew through the optical sighting panel

ahead of her. The wind was minimal, and as she came in from the
water side she had a clear run at the vans. Still, the close quarters
and her low altitude made the bombing run dangerous as well
as complicated; for the first time since she'd arrived she saw trac-
ers arcing in her directions. She hunched her body around the
stick, ignoring them, ignoring everything but the slowly changing
view and pipper marks in front of her eyes. The vans jerked into
her crosshairs and she pickled, loosing all four bombs as she
pulled back on the stick. Heavy flak erupted just off her left wing
as she climbed. McKenna coaxed the Cessna upward as the air
began percolating and rumbling with the exploding shells. She
cleared right into the open air and saw her wingmate about a
thousand feet above her and a quarter mile to the south.

"Two, where was that flak coming from?"

"Tank mounted weapon," said the other pilot.

"One of ours?"

"Looks like."

The weapon was apparently a Brunei army vehicle that had
been stolen from its base. A Panhard M3 VDA, the French-built
twenty-millimeter cannon had radar guidance but was apparently being operated by sight—otherwise McKenna would have
been perforated. The gun was now being used to chew up the
area in front of the highway at the entrance to the palace compound; guerillas were moving behind it.

"Two, can you get that gun?" McKenna asked.

"Roger that," said the copilot.

"I'm going to cover your butt and clean up after your pass,"
she added, working the A-37B around.

IT HAD GONE BETTER THAN SAHURAH HAD DARED IMAGINE.
Besar, though clearly a degenerate, had pulled off the impossible and stolen the self-propelled cannon from under the noses
of the army. Their main force was now in control of two of the
four sides of the palace perimeter; inside, they were engaged in
a battle with forces in the main ministry building. Once they
took care of those forces, they could move on to the palace itself, using the roof of the ministry to lay down gunfire.

Two jets danced overhead. Sahurah looked up from his position as one of the planes dropped its bombs on the city-side and

the Panhard anti-aircraft gun began firing. He wasn't sure what the target was; Besar had a command station in that area but from where Sahurah stood he could see nothing.

One of his squad leaders motioned from the corner of the building. Sahurah ducked his head and ran forward, sliding down as he neared the man. The headache that had haunted him yesterday was gone and he had fresh hope—perhaps he would die today and become a martyr.

"Commander, the enemy has a machine-gun inside the building," said the squad leader.

"Bring up the rocket-propelled grenades," said Sahurah.

Another jet passed overhead. Sahurah flinched, then felt himself flush with shame at his momentary cowardice.

Human, perhaps, but a failing before the eyes of God.

He grabbed the rifle from one of the men nearby and stepped out as another aircraft passed, emptying the magazine.

MCKENNA WATCHED HER WINGMAN'S BOMBS FALL ON TARGET and took her plane further east, where a fresh clump of white-pajamas ran for the wall. She pressed the trigger and the Dragonfly's gat began spinning, drawing a red line through the scattering sea of white-clad fanatics. She stayed on the trigger a bit too long, and pulled off into a thick cloud of smoke; she completely lost track of where she was.

By the time she cleared she had flown out of the capital and was now over the lagoon-city in the bay. She regrouped with her wingman, who sounded as if he were hyperventilating after his successful bomb run.

The situation in the palace was growing desperate. Several hundred guerillas had attacked the compound; there were less than fifty army defenders, along with some plainclothes security and a dozen or so policemen. Reinforcements were engaged in a fierce fight at a guard post outside the city; it was unlikely they could reach the palace to prevent its being taken.

The sultan had strapped a gun on his side and was with the army commander inside.

McKenna started back toward the compound. The guerillas were clumped at one end of the water beyond the highway, but did not yet control the roadway.

"Get a helicopter over here on the double and get the sultan the hell out," McKenna told her controller back at the airport. "We'll cover the approach."

"Helicopter is forty minutes away."

"Forty minutes!"

"It's coming up from Tutong," said the controller.

Smoke began pouring out of the side of the ministry building.

"Can you get some sort of boat in to make a rescue?" McKenna asked.

"The navy is working on that."

That wasn't going to do. White-pajamas were swarming all over the place. McKenna tipped downward and spit shells at them, but she barely made a dent. The Dragonfly rocked as it took a few bullets in the right wing.

"Yo, ground FAC, what's your situation?" she asked as she recovered on the city side of the compound.

"Under fire."

"The sultan there?"

"Yes. We're going to retreat to the south."

"Negative! Negative!" she said, catching sight of three pickup trucks filled with white-pajamas. "No, listen, can you get out to the highway near the main entrance?"

"Maybe."

"Get the sultan there." She spun back around, sizing up the roadway. It was straight, relatively flat, and unobstructed— if you didn't count the two burning cars about thirty yards from the palace gate. "Push the cars off to the side and wait," she said.

"For what?"

"Just get those cars out of the way."

South of the Philippines
0653

Mack turned the helm over to his copilot and undid his restraints, stretching as he got out of the pilot's seat. One advantage the Megafortress had over an F-15—a working galley at the rear of the flightdeck.

Not to mention a microwave and a convenience area, otherwise known as a john. All the amenities of modern life.

The Sparrow had worked well enough for Mack to set the arms dealer down in one piece—and to order another dozen, as well as some heavier arms for his ground soldiers. The first variants of the Sparrow had seen action in Vietnam, where they had proved rather disappointing. The latter versions, however, were considerably more successful.

Unfortunately, the ones they had just bought were early models. Mack knew that some of the failures were due to pilot training—Naval aviators had been behind the triggers, 'nuf said in his book. But even an air force jock with an oversized ego like Mack Smith had to admit that the hardware wasn't quite on par with the AMRAAM, let alone Dreamland's improved version of the AMRAAM, the AMRAAM-plus, also known as the Scorpion.

On the other hand, they were better than no arrows at all.

Mack had a drink of water and went and checked with his men downstairs, giving them all a thumbs-up for a job well done.

"How we looking, Jalan?" he asked his copilot when he returned to the flightdeck.

"On course, sir. Estimated time of arrival is now two hours and three minutes."

Mack brought up the course screen on the configurable display at the left side of his dash. The wall of instruments that constituted his "office" was infinitely configurable, constructed from a thick layer of touch-sensitive chips. Nearly every Megafortress pilot found it easiest to use a preset one, which divided the dash into large panels of multi-use and devoted displays. Mack had a little trouble with the course module, and it took a minute to get the large-area map he wanted, showing the large island of Borneo and the surrounding water. He then double tapped the compass icon with his finger, and drew the course he wanted.

"Compute," he told the computer, and a window opened in the screen showing what it would take to patrol the eastern portion of the island where the Sukhois were.

It was a detour, but a strategic detour. He'd have plenty of fuel—as long as he cut over Malaysian territory to get home.

"Jalan, we have a new course," said Mack.

"Yes, sir," said the copilot, who brought it up on his own screen. He studied it for a moment. "Minister, should I alert Ground to the changes?"

"I don't believe we're in range to notify Ground," said Mack.

"Sir?"

"Let's stay silent com for a while," said Mack. "We're only going to add about an hour to our flight plan, maybe even a little less," he added, putting his hand to the throttle bar.

Brunei
0654

The men who had put pencil to paper and designed the Cessna Dragonfly some forty years before had set out to accomplish some deceptively modest goals. They wanted to create a sturdy, predictable aircraft that didn't cost all that much to operate, and yet could provide a novice pilot with a suitable learning environment, one that would help him transition to the hot jets at the time. They surely did not envision that their aircraft—beefed up, to be sure, but still the same basic design—would not only be flying as the century came to a close but would be doing so in combat situations.

And surely they never envisioned doing what McKenna intended as she dropped low toward the highway that spanned the waterfront outside the palace.

The A-37B's wings were just a hair under thirty-six feet wide—short maybe for an airplane, but a bit wide for this roadway. But McKenna judged that she could make it as long as she stuck to the left side of the road as she came in.

Problem was, that was where they were pushing the wrecked cars.

Something flashed at the right side of the aircraft as she approached. The explosion was a good distance away but McKenna realized she couldn't afford the luxury of a second approach; she might make it down only to be swarmed by the guerillas.

"FAC, where's the sultan?" she asked.

"Ready! Ready!"

"Push that other car out of there, way off the road!" she said. "And get down. I'm coming in."

McKenna gave the throttle a light tap for luck then pushed in for her landing. She touched down slightly right of where she wanted to, but still had enough clearance to get by the light poles. The men pushing the car ahead saw her coming and gave the vehicle one last shove before throwing themselves out of the way; her wing cleared the fender by perhaps three feet, which as far as she was concerned was a country mile.

As the Dragonfly rolled to a stop, McKenna popped the top; she pushed her feet up and saw three men in suits running toward her. The sultan, a trim man in his early sixties, athletic and with a movie star's face, appeared at the side of the aircraft. He said something, but although the A-37 had many assets, quiet engines were not one of them. McKenna shouted at him to get in; he pulled himself over the side and practically fell into place as she got the plane moving again. Bullets were exploding against the concrete nearby; she saw the shadow of her wingman pass overhead, suppressing some of the ground fire from the seawall on the left. The ground began to shake with explosions; McKenna reasoned that they were either very large or very close, or both.

There was no question of turning around to take off into the wind. The way in front of her was clear, though short.

Could she make it?

The Dragonfly was made for short field operations and this one was light on fuel, with hardly much of a load. More importantly, McKenna was desperate. She gunned the engines, revving the J85s to the red line.

"Yee-haw!" she shouted as they cleared the wall at the edge of the highway by a good two inches. "Brunei Dragon One is off the ground and looking for permission to land," she told her controller.

"Negative, negative—we're under attack!" said the controller. "Airport is not secure! Airport is not secure!"

McKenna turned toward the sultan. He didn't have a headset.

"We can't land at the airport," she shouted to him. "But I'll take care of you, Your Majesty. Don't fret."

Whether he understood what she said or even heard it all, he gave her a thumbs-up.

Aboard Brunei Air Force EB-52 1 (*Jersey*), over the Sulu Sea (northeast of Borneo)
0720

Mack studied the radar warning screen, which showed the range of the radar covering the northeast tip of Malaysian territory. The Megafortress was well out of range of the radar, but what was interesting to Mack was the type of radars that had been detected—a large-band system identified as a Russian P-37 Bar Lock, and a shorter-range P-15 Flat Face. Malaysia was not known to possess either, and Mack hadn't encountered them on Borneo before. The P-15 Flat Face was especially troubling, since it was designed to work with surface-to-air missiles—SA-3s or more capable SA-6s and SA-8s. Any of those missiles could splash an A-37B without breaking a sweat, and even a Megafortress couldn't afford to completely ignore SA-6s or SA-8s.

"We're abreast of Sandakan," reported Jalan, as they reached one of the waypoints programmed for a course change.

They brought the Megafortress onto the new course heading, still skirting Malaysian territory. Mack checked with his radar operators; with the exception of a commercial flight far to the south, they were the only plane in the air.

"Sixty seconds to Darvel Bay," noted Jalan.

"All right, boys, this is for keeps now," said Mack. "I need everybody on their game. We're going to be over hostile territory for thirty minutes. Ready?"

He spoke to each crew member, more in hopes of giving them a boost than making sure they were ready.

Did it work? Did telling Jalan he was going to "kick butt" make the copilot handle his instrument screens any faster, or make his hand more assured on the stick? Did the radar operators click through their panels quicker?

There was no way of knowing; Mack realized he was going to have to take it on faith that it *did* help somehow. They took the Megafortress to three thousand feet, enough to see . . . and be seen.

"Patrol ship is trying to lock on us with his radar," reported Jalan as they crossed over land. "He's—we're out of range."

Mack concentrated on his course, nudging the stick slightly at their next waypoint, flying on a diagonal toward the mountains at the center of the island. The air in front of him gave no clue of the danger; a few wispy clouds hugged the far side of the mountains but the rest of the sky was clear and bright.

"Anti-aircraft radar operating," said Jalan, noting a ZSU-23-4 emplacement off their left wing. This low they were easy targets, but Mack had the element of surprise on his side, and was beyond the flak dealer's range before it could fire. In the meantime, they mapped the small army base protected by the weapons, finding six helicopters out in the open and possibly more in a hangar. The helicopters, identified as American Hueys or similar civilian models by the computer system, did not appear on any of the force estimates of the Malaysian army. The computer recorded all of the data they collected, allowing it to be analyzed later.

"P-15 Flat Face," said Jalan, repeating an alert just now flashing onto Mack's warning screen, accompanied by an audible buzz. "Should I go to ECMs?"

"Hang off a second," said Mack. "We got a location?"

The radar unit was near Kalabakon, a small city a few miles from the coast.

"Airfield, Mr. Minister!" said one of the operators. "I have it on the video."

As Mack reached to bring the image onto his screen, the RWR barked out a warning that they were now fat in the target pipper of the missile system connected to the Flat Face radar. A J-band radar had begun tracking them, indicating that the system was ready to fire.

"ECMs," said Mack.

Before Jalan could even punch the buttons the Malaysians launched two SA-8 missiles. The missiles had an effective range of roughly sixteen miles, but they had been launched near the edge of that envelope and within seconds the Megafortress had disrupted the ground link, obliterating the I-band guidance radar and persuading the missiles to veer off course.

"Good," said Mack as the missiles detonated several miles to the south. "Hang on, now—let's get some close-ups of that airfield, shall we?"

He wheeled the big plane over in the sky and put her nose on a line to the airfield they'd seen, pulling upwards of eight Gs briefly as he twisted in the sky. He felt himself being pushed and pulled by gravity as the plane whipped toward the earth, its momentum shifting abruptly. The Megafortress wasn't a fighter jet, but damn, she could get out of her own way when she had to.

"ECMs—give 'em the whole symphony," said Mack as the warnings sounded again.

There were more SA-8s, as well as anti-aircraft cannons and

a battery of very short-range IR seekers, ID'd by the computer after analyzing the video feed. Mack had the airstrip fat in the left part of his windscreen—it had been shaded to make it look like a pair of different roads, and to the naked eye there looked like there was a hill about midway down and a ditch at the western end. The camouflage had undoubtedly been meant to fool satellites or high-altitude spy planes. Mack saw a missile battery on the right side—it was an SA-8 launcher, a large amphibious vehicle with what looked like a tray of missiles on top. The back of the tray exploded; one of the missiles took off, fired pointblank toward the Megafortress.

Mack threw the plane left, firing off defensive chaff and flares while Jalan stayed on the ECMs. The SA-8 had been launched "blind," its radar guidance completely blitzed by the Megafortress's ECMs. The missile sailed high over the right wing, climbing to forty thousand feet before imploding.

More dangerous were the two missiles with infrared guidance launched just as the Megafortress passed. These were M48A1 Chaparrals—very short-range heat-seekers that were essentially ground-launched versions of the AIM-9D Sidewinder. Mack's maneuvers had cost him some speed, and one of the missiles ignited less than a hundred yards from his right wing sending a spray of shrapnel into the back of the fuselage. But the damage was minor, and they climbed through the neighboring mountain valley without a problem.

"Did you locate the Su-27s?" Mack asked the radar operator.

"Negative," said the man. "No hangars visible."

"Well they have to be there somewhere," said Mack. "All right, one more pass."

This time, Mack went low—very low, as in twenty feet from the ground, covering his approach with a salvo of flares and chaff as well as the active electronic countermeasures. The ground defenders were either confused, out of arrows, or both, and the Megafortress passed unscathed.

They found the hangar, a dug-in bunker on the south side of a hill facing away from the runway, reached by a short dirt road.

"Got to give them points for ingenuity," he told Jalan. "We'll work up some sort of attack on the base when we get home. We can drop some of those five-hundred-pound bombs and put a big crater about midway down that runway, and keep them quiet for a while, but we're going to need air-to-ground missiles to do anything about the hangar."

"Striking the defenses would also be a good idea," said the copilot.

"They were pretty inept."

"They were caught off guard," said Jalan. "They won't be next time."

As they climbed over the mountains in the direction of home, the ops detected a number of Malaysian helicopters flying near the Brunei border to the west, flitting in and out of radar coverage as they skimmed through the mountains. They were undoubtedly supporting guerillas, Mack thought, though he suspected the Malaysians would claim they were fighting them.

The sultan better put the bastards on notice that allies were supposed to help legitimate governments, not homicidal maniacs, Mack thought. He had the computer calculate a flight path to the area where the helicopters were operating, toying with the idea of unleashing one or two of the Sparrows at them; there were five left on the rotating dispenser in the rear bay. Before he could decide, Jalan relayed a warning that one of the Sukhois was taking off from the airfield they'd buzzed.

"That was fast," said Mack.

"They must've been standing by in the hangar," said Jalan. "Or they have a better hide near the field we didn't spot."

There was no doubt in Mack's mind that he was taking on the Sukhois; the only question was where.

He decided he'd lead them out to sea before turning to tango. That way he'd avoid any nasty surprises like Malaysian ground-to-air defenses that he hadn't spotted. He'd also have a quicker route home; his fuel gauges were trending toward empty.

"What it'll look like to them is a big sitting ducking trying to foolishly outrun them," Mack explained to Jalan as he laid in the course to the computer. "They'll figure they have us nailed. We'll fire two Sparrows at each plane once we have them flat-footed."

"What if they're carrying radar-guided missiles as they were the other day?"

"Oh, they definitely will be. You'll just confuse the hell out of them with your ECMs," Mack said. "I'll handle the Sparrows."

They had about a five minute lead on the two Malaysian

planes as they reached the coast. Mack used some of it to climb to thirty-five thousand feet, then told Jalan to open the bomb bay door, preparing the Sparrows for firing. As their air speed dropped, the Sukhois came charging at them. The interceptors were spread nearly three miles apart, much more wary than they had been the other day; they'd thought about their encounter and tried to learn from it.

Which he was counting on.

"We're going to make it look like we want to get them with the Stinger, turn, and then turn again," he told his crew. "If you have to puke, do it now."

One of the ops laughed and Mack smiled to himself—he was finally getting through to these guys.

"We're spiked," said Jalan, meaning that the targeting radar in the lead Su-27 had locked onto them.

That was the signal Mack had been waiting for.

"Break it," he said calmly. Then he put *Jersey* into a wide turn to the north.

The lead Su-27 started to turn as well, planning to parallel his course while his partner came around and cut him off. As the Sukhoi tried to get close enough for heat-seekers or maybe a cannon shot, Mack pushed his stick harder and tucked the plane due south. The plane seemed to skid in midair as if she were a massive motorcycle pulling a one-eighty. It took a few seconds to get the wings back level; by that time the Su-27 pilot had tightened his own turn as well. Mack now twisted south and then back, snaking through the sky in a series of feints until the Sukhoi finally bit on one of his fakes. The enemy pilot shot off to Mack's right, realized it had been fooled, and tried to dive away.

"Locked," said the computer. *"Range five miles."*

"Fire Sparrow One," said Mack.

"Missile is launched."

"Fire Sparrow Two," said Mack, seeing the diamond in the targeting screen close around the target.

"Target is locked. Launching."

With the missile away, Mack immediately turned back to the east, looking for the second Sukhoi. He expected the first to take a head-on approach, but found him flying parallel five miles ahead, and actually moving more than fifty knots slower than the Megafortress.

"Computer, lock target two."

"Locked. Range five miles."

"Fire Sparrow Three."

"Missile is launched."

Mack was about to launch another Sparrow when Jalan warned that a radar had locked on them. Mack, surprised, fired off chaff and took two quick cuts in the air. He had no idea which radar could be tracking them.

"Score one Sparrow!" said Jalan excitedly.

"What about that radar?"

"Still tracking us."

Paranoia surged through Mack as he continued to have trouble picking up the opposing fighter. Just as he felt convinced— absolutely convinced—that the Su-27 was locked on his butt, he finally spotted the red dagger at the right corner of his screen. He started to pull the Megafortress around but Jalan yelled a warning over the interphone.

"Missiles! Missiles!"

Mack flailed back east, unable to sort the situation out in his head. He had one Sukhoi down, but must have missed the second one somehow. He blew a hard breath into his oxygen mask, trying to concentrate on what he needed to do, not on what he'd missed. Jalan and the computer ID'd the missile as a radar-guided R-27R. Mack flailed desperately in the air, zigging and zagging and dispensing the last of his chaff. The missile avoided the tinsel and hung with the Megafortress until it was about three hundred yards away; finally, the ECMs managed to shake it off. Desperate, a little angry at being jilted, the missile immolated itself as soon as it realized its date wasn't showing up. Part of the warhead flew through the Megafortress's number four engine, outboard on the right wing. The engine instantly lost power; Mack felt the wing tug downward before the computer helped him trim the plane to compensate.

"Jalan, we've lost engine four," said Mack calmly.

"Yes, Mr. Minister," said the copilot, already double-checking the computer's automated safety programs.

Meanwhile, Mack spotted the remaining Sukhoi beginning a turn toward him from ten miles away; the computer announced that it had once more locked on the target.

"Fire Sparrow Four," said Mack.

The missile clunked off the rotating launcher in the rear. Mack once more changed direction, but this time the Sukhoi pilot didn't have a chance to target him.

"Score Sukhoi number two!" said Jalan.

They could see this explosion, a black puff in the distance at just about their altitude. Mack felt his shoulders sag; he'd been flying for hours without much sleep, and however good it felt to nail two enemy planes there was no way to put off fatigue forever.

"All right," he told the crew. "Let's take a deep breath."

He and the copilot ran through the computer's screens, double-checking the damage. Besides the engine, there had been some light damage to the control surfaces on the right wing. But it wasn't too severe; the plane remained eminently controllable and they were climbing at a decent pace.

"Time to head back for the barn," Mack told his tired crew. But as he brought up the screen to plot a course home, they reported an odd contact on the surface of the water, heading at high speed toward the Brunei oil derricks.

"Range, twenty miles, almost directly ahead," said Jalan. "Computer can't identify it, but it's doing at least fifty knots."

It was almost directly ahead.

"Let's have a look," said Mack.

Off the coast of Brunei
0844

Dazhou Ti folded his arms as they approached the oil platforms. He planned on drawing to within a mile before firing. The target was unarmed, and destroying it would be child's play. The fact that the shells from the *Barracuda*'s gun were only twenty-five millimeters meant that they would have slightly more time to practice their marksmanship.

"Sixty seconds to firing point," announced the weapons officer.

"Steady," said Dazhou Ti.

"Captain, the aircraft we noted earlier is tracking us," said the radar operator.

"How can that be?" Dazhou moved over to the radar station, where the indicator showed that they were indeed visible on the airplane's radar. It was the American Megafortress that had been given to the enemy.

General Udara had promised that their spies and radar would keep track of the aircraft, and that if necessary the Malaysian air force's two Sukhoi Su-27s would distract it—or, if the opportunity presented itself, shoot it down. But obviously the Megafortress had managed to slip by them.

Imbeciles.

"Prepare the anti-aircraft missiles," said Dazhou Ti. "Stay on the course but lower our speed. If they come close enough, we will make them very sorry."

Aboard *Jersey,* off the coast of Brunei
0848

The ship—if that's what it was—looked like a black triangle with wings on the surface of the ocean ahead, a metal loon that was aimed like an arrow at the Brunei oil field. And it moved incredibly fast—around a hundred knots.

"I'll bet that's what sunk the merchant ship the other day," Mack told Jalan. "Probably hit the oil tank as well."

"I can alert the navy," said Jalan.

"Yeah," said Mack, looking at the image in the enhanced video. He wasn't much of an expert on naval architecture, but the craft looked as if it used something similar to wing-in-ground effect, skimming over the surface of the water like an airplane at very high speed. The sharp, odd angles would also make it hard to spot for most radars, even the EB-52s, except at close range. The black paint made it hard to see.

During the nighttime, that is. They must be feeling their oats to operate during the day.

The nearest oil platform was only a few miles away. It'd be easy pickings for a missile or even a gun attack.

"Not getting an acknowledgment from the navy," said Jalan.

"Get our ground control and give them the coordinates," said Mack. "See who's on alert—Dragonflies could probably take out that piece of tin with a couple of 250-pound bombs."

"Minister—the vessel is targeting us with its radar," said Jalan. "Its roof is opening."

Mack cursed as he realized what the strange craft was up to. By the time he leaned on the throttle the ship had launched two missiles at them. Mack fired off the last of his flares and poured on the dinosaurs, his heart pounding as the flat-footed Mega-fortress tried to pick up momentum against the SA-14s, small Russian heat-seekers similar to the American Stinger shoulder-launched anti-air missile. The weapons had a very limited range and small warheads; even so, the Megafortress's tail caught some shrapnel as one of the warheads exploded.

Which *really* pissed Mack off.

As he banked back, he told Jalan to open up the bomb bay.

"Minister?"

"Do it, Jalan."

"Yes, sir."

"Give me the air-to-ground attack mode, standard bomb program one."

The Megafortress's computer hadn't complained about firing the Sparrow missiles; while it had been designed to operate with the more advanced weapons, the system's designers had realized there might be an emergency in the field and made sure the system was backward-compatible with earlier weapons. But now the computer refused to recognize that the missile was on its sling, even as Jalan and Brown tried the different air-to-ground attack modes.

"What about as a JDAM?" Mack asked, suggesting that the copilot tell the computer the missile was actually a guided bomb known as a JDAM or Joint Direct Attack Munition. The weapon was a modern version of an iron bomb, with a guidance system that could use either GPS coordinates or an internal guidance system to hit a precise point from relatively close range, usually no more than ten kilometers.

"Negative."

And then Mack realized he was being far too clever.

"Reset the program back to the Sparrow parameters."

Once the computer was ready, he brought up the targeting panel and told the weapons system that he had a bogey at low altitude.

Very, very low altitude.

The computer didn't even hesitate.

"Target locked."

"Fire at the motherfucker."

"Unknown command."

"Fire Sparrow."

"Launching."

Off the coast of Brunei
0851

Too late, Dazhou realized he had misjudged his enemy. The big aircraft quickly ducked his missiles and locked its radar on him.

"Evasive maneuvers," the captain said calmly, moving to the helm. "Active and passive countermeasures. Everything we have." He gave the order to increase speed to maximum power.

The *Barracuda* slammed hard to the left and then the right. They thundered over the waves, tucking back to the south and picking up speed.

They were just touching two hundred when the missile struck the rear quarter of the craft.

Aboard *Jersey,* off the coast of Brunei
0854

"Missile struck the target," said Jalan. "Starboard side at the rear."

Mack put the Megafortress into a shallow dive, still wary. The ship was so strange that it could easily have some other trick up its sleeve—a laser anti-aircraft weapon, perhaps.

"He's dead in the water," reported Jalan as Mack banked a mile and a half from it. "Stern is settling. I think he's taking on water."

If he had had another missile loaded, Mack would have finished the stinker off. He debated getting in close and firing the airmines at it, but the weapon was designed to shred jet engines moving at high speed; it wasn't particularly good at punching holes in anything thicker than an airplane fuselage.

And besides, he was down to three engines, had wing damage, and his fuel tanks contained a heck of a lot more fumes than liquid.

"Tell the navy where that thing is," Mack told Jalan. "We're going home."

"Yes, Minister."

"And one other thing, Jalan."

"Yes, sir?"

"You can call me Mack from now on. You've earned it."

"Yes, sir. Thank you, Mr. Minister."

Off the coast of Brunei
0856

The disadvantage of a small crew became clear as Dazhou struggled to deal with the damage to the vessel. Automated pumps began bailing the compartments in the damaged section, and there seemed no question of sinking, but some of the control lines had been severed and even with its redundancies the *Barracuda* could no longer be steered. Two men crawled out through the access tunnel and began replacing burned out circuits and breakers. Dazhou and another of his men went topside to survey the physical damage, walking gingerly along the recessed decking at the top. The winglets were intact but one of the engines had been destroyed; the top of the exhaust outlet seemed charred, as if it had been on fire. The ship sat with its stern in the waves, and some of the large panels were buckled from the explosion. Fortunately, the *Barracuda* had been moving away from the missile when its proximity fuse exploded the warhead; the blow had been more of an angled, glancing shot than a piercing direct hit.

That was small consolation at the moment. Dazhou had no option now except to call for help.

At least the Megafortress was gone.

Fools, thought Dazhou. They would meet again—and this time, he would be much better prepared.

Aboard *Jersey,* approaching Brunei IAP
0902

"This is Mack Smith aboard Brunei EB-52 One, *Jersey.* We are declaring a fuel emergency," Mack repeated for the fifth or sixth time as he approached the airfield. "Repeat. I have a fuel emergency. I'm landing."

"Still no answer from the tower," said Jalan. "Maybe our radio was damaged in one of the attacks, because I'm not getting anything—no response at all."

"All right," said Mack. He had enough fuel to take one pass if he saw someone in the way, but that was it. The radar showed the air was clear, at least. He steadied into the approach, the airfield coming into view.

"Looks clear," said Jalan.

"Yeah, okay."

Mack kept expecting something to appear at the last second, even as the wheels hit the concrete. He didn't relax until they were just about at the end of the long runway.

As they approached their hangar, he realized he didn't see any of his security teams nearby, or even the maintenance people. In fact, the area looked deserted—none of the Dragonflies was on the ground.

As soon as they stopped, Mack left Jalan and the others to secure the aircraft. He hopped down the ladder, pausing on the Flighthawk deck, where his security team had spent a rather restless flight.

"All right, guys, let's get the stuff unloaded and see what the situation is," Mack shouted. One of the men looked a little green around the gills—and had a paper bag in his hand.

Poor guy, Mack thought to himself, lowering the ladder to the runway. He felt a surge of adrenaline, anxious to tell McKenna about his mission.

Too bad she wasn't much of a looker, he thought as his feet touched the concrete. Hell, she was perfect in every other respect: maybe he should just close his eyes.

"That's far enough," said a voice behind him.

Mack, startled, started to turn.

The barrel of an AK47 caught him in the side of the face. A moment later, something hit him hard in the back of the legs. He cursed and reached for his gun.

Then something smacked him on the top of the head. His arms and legs fell limp. He tried to breathe, and found he couldn't; in the next moment he felt himself falling, the black sky descending over him.

V

Resistance

JED BARCLAY PUT THE PHONE DOWN AND STARED AT THE desk. He felt a little like a diver who'd come up from a great depth a touch too quickly; the events unfolding in Brunei had left him slightly disoriented. Islamic rebels were in control of the capital and at least two other cities; the sultan was missing, the military was in disarray. The Brunei navy's two new patrol ships, purchased from Russia within the last six months, had been sunk overnight. There was no word on the whereabouts of the Brunei's Megafortress. Officially, Malaysia claimed that it had not helped the guerilla forces, but that seemed highly un-likely.

The CIA was preparing a brief on the Islamic terrorists, cit-ing evidence of a new organization involved behind the scenes known as al Qaeda. Funded by a Saudi millionaire, the group was closely connected with the government of Afghanistan, where it had established training camps for terrorists. The head of the group was a man named Osama bin Laden, a fanatic mil-lionaire dedicated to wiping out the Great Satan—America, of course.

Jed had heard of al Qaeda before, of course, and even knew that it had connections with Islamic extremists in Indonesia and Malaysia, but the collapse of Brunei had been nothing short of remarkable. It seemed impossible that a relatively small band of outsiders, no more than ten thousand according to the CIA estimate, had taken over the country. And yet they appeared to have done just that, perhaps succeeding largely because the idea was so outlandish that it didn't appear possible.

"Jed? Are you ready?"

Jed looked up and saw his boss, Philip Freeman, standing in the doorway.

"Yeah," said Jed, standing. "I have the latest from Brunei. It's pretty ugly."

"How ugly?"

"Capital has definitely fallen. Sultan is missing," said Jed.

"Sultan is dead?"

"Unsure. Just missing, at this point."

"Where's the Megafortress?"

"Not clear. We'll have a satellite over the country in about thirty-five minutes. The NSA is working on some intercepts as well."

Freeman nodded grimly. "Come along."

Jed followed the national security advisor as they walked over to the White House situation room, where the president had asked his military and national security advisors to meet. President Martindale had not yet arrived, and Jed started talking to some of the Pentagon staffers who were standing along the back wall. He quickly realized that he had much more up-to-date information than they did, and one or two had only a vague notion of where the tiny nation was located. Brunei had been far down on nearly everyone's priority list until today.

"Gentlemen, ladies, thank you for coming at such an ungodly hour," said the president as he strode abruptly into the room. "I realize I've destroyed the weekend for most of you and I apologize. Let's get started."

Brenda Kelly, a State Department aide who had just flown back from Brunei, gave a brief overview of the situation there. Several times she emphasized the kingdom's importance as an oil producer. Jed took over with details about the government's collapse, finishing with the fact that an ASEAN emergency meeting scheduled for the next morning Brunei time had been postponed an hour ago because of the rapidly changing situation.

"The question is, do we care about Brunei?" said Arthur Chastain, the secretary of defense. Chastain could be blunt, but the comment was brutal even for him. "Brunei is a minor country in a small corner of the world, certainly not worth the expenditure of our blood."

"You're wrong," blurted Jed. "Aside from its importance as an oil producer, it's important b-both strategically and as a sy-symbol," said Jed. His stutter had a habit of appearing at the worst possible times; he sped on, knowing the best strategy for dealing with it was to ignore it. "Brunei helps balance Malaysia and Indonesia in the region. It provided a base during the operations against China. It's been a more stable ally than the Ph-Ph-Philippines, all things considered. And also, these terrorists have to be taken seriously. This is just the start for them. We have to beat them here."

"They're just poor rabble-rousers," said Chastain. "Poverty's the problem with all of these people."

"No one is poor in Brunei," said Kelly.

"And they have the Megafortress," added Jed. "It is not a weapon we'd want in terrorists' hands."

"Absolutely not," said the president. "At the minimum, we want to take it back or destroy it."

"And the maximum?" asked Chastain.

"The maximum is what we're here to discuss," the president told him.

Dreamland
11 October 1997, 2203

The new orders came just as they were boarding the planes. Dog pulled Danny aside on the apron near the hangar a few feet from the MC-17. Danny's men—along with two small scout helicopters and Dreamland's mobile command trailer—were already aboard Dreamland's version of the versatile McDonnell Douglas cargo plane.

"Brunei's going all to hell," Dog told him. "The Megafortress is at the International Airport in the capital. Mack Smith can't be located at the moment. The president wants to make sure the terrorists don't operate the aircraft."

"We going to blow it up?" asked Danny.

"It may come to that, depending on the situation," said Dog. "There's been some contact with Prince bin Awg, who's asked for the aircraft to be preserved if not recovered. The president wants us to scope out the situation and destroy the plane only if necessary. I'd like to see exactly what's going on."

"What about Deci Gordon?"

"He's hiding with some people outside the capital. He called into our center a while ago. He seems okay for now. I've spoken to Breanna by phone," Dog added. "She's in Tokyo. She'll be joining us in the Philippines."

Dog explained that, rather than going to Brunei International Airport as they had planned, the Megafortresses and MC-17 would land at a Philippines airfield, using it as a temporary base.

"I'll take *Pennsylvania* and do a survey of Brunei as soon as we arrive," continued Dog. "We'll check the oil platform we were going to use as the LADS base, double-checking that it's okay. If possible, we'll operate the helicopters out of there."

"I don't know if that's going to work," said Danny. "The platform doesn't have a dedicated helipad."

"Then we may have to improvise. You told me the structure of the building had been designed for a landing deck, it just wasn't installed."

"The plans say that. We'll have to get in and check it before we can land."

"Then that's what we'll do."

"If we're going to get people off the island, we should land directly at the airfield," said Danny.

"Not until we know what the situation is," Dog told him. "And I doubt we could hold it with just the Whiplash team."

"Where's the navy?" asked Danny.

"There's a carrier group several days away. They won't be offshore and in a position to conduct operations until the end of next week. This has caught everyone by surprise, including us.

"We'll get some satellite intelligence over to the MC-17 via the Dreamland network," added Dog. "It's daytime over there right now. By the time we get over there with the travel time and time change, it'll be late at night."

"Understood," said Danny. "We'll try to sleep on the flight over."

Dog was piloting *Pennsylvania,* an AWACS-equipped radar version of the EB-52, which was also carrying two Flighthawk U/MF-3s strapped to her wings. The robot planes would be piloted by Zen, who was already in his specially adapted seat on the Flighthawk control deck on the Megafortress's lower level. The area had once been used by the B-52's offensive team; Zen sat roughly where the navigator would have had his post before the aircraft was overhauled.

Kevin McNamara, Dog's copilot, was going through the preflight checklists with the help of the computer when Dog slipped into the driver's seat next to him.

"Welcome aboard, Colonel," said McNamara. "We're just about ready to give these turbines a twist and see what they can do."

Across from the *Pennsylvania* sat the *Indianapolis*, getting a last minute check from the ground crew. The *"Indy"*—like the *"Penn,"* named after a famous battleship—was an almost mirror image of the *Pennsylvania*, with a long snout and a slight bulge for her radar gear about midship. *Indy* had not yet seen action, but the man at the helm, Major Merce Alou, was a veteran of several Dreamland deployments. The two Flighthawk pilots—Starship and Kick, who would each control one U/MF-3—had done themselves proud over the South China Sea and Taiwan barely a month before.

Dog glanced across at the other plane's lit cockpit and saw Major Alou. He gave him a thumbs-up and got one in return.

"Let's get this show on the road," he told McNamara, punching up the computer screen that controlled the engine start.

Brunei
12 October 1997, 1408

Sahurah watched quietly as the brothers brought the limp bodies to the shaded area at the side of the sultan's compound, composing them respectfully.

Commander Besar was brought up last. The blast that had killed him had struck him in the back and neck, nearly severing his head from his body. The men who set him down were grim-faced; one appeared to be near tears. Sahurah considered scolding them, for surely Besar was now at bliss in Paradise.

If so great a sinner as Besar could find peace, why could Sahurah not?

"Cars!" said one of the men near the front of the compound, relaying the word from a lookout.

Sahurah left the others to care for the bodies and went out to the front. Three vehicles came up the drive. The first and last were filled with heavily armed men, crammed four across, front and back.

The middle car contained the imam and the Saudi. The imam pushed open the door and got out with a smile. "You have done well, Sahurah. So well!" he shouted, and he clasped Sahurah to his chest.

"The brothers have done their duty," said Sahurah.

"And you remain humble!"

The imam seemed to be chiding him. But did the Prophet not direct a believer to know his proper place, to master overweening pride? If the great patriarchs, if the rulers and teachers had not boasted, how could such as Sahurah?

"We have not found the sultan," reported Sahurah. "He escaped from the compound during the fighting."

"A small matter in the context," said the imam, waving his hand. "The capital is ours. Within a few days, we will control the entire country. The future is great, Sahurah."

"Yes."

"More work remains," said the imam. "But we must give praise to Allah for the triumphs so far."

"Yes." Sahurah saw now that he had denied the Lord his just thanks, and felt ashamed.

"I have heard that an American was taken prisoner at the airport," said the commander.

"I was not aware of that," said Sahurah. "My work has been here."

"Yes. It would be good if you were to take charge of him. He may prove valuable in the future. He was the head of the sultan's air force."

"I will look into it immediately."

"There are anti-aircraft missiles there," added the commander. "A crew has been sent from Malaysia to train our people to use them. You should select some of your best men to learn. There may be a counter-attack."

"Understood."

"We will have control of the nation very shortly," said the commander. "Very shortly."

"For the glory of Allah," said Sahurah.

The imam smiled and got back into the car.

Brunei, near the Malaysian border
12 October 1997, 1708

McKenna crouched amid the rocks as the speedboat cut its engine and coasted toward the shoreline. The two Brunei policemen with her started to rise.

"No," she said sharply. "Wait until we're sure of them."

The men immediately dropped back into a crouch. McKenna picked up her binoculars as the speedboat turned parallel to the shoreline, drifting for a moment. There were five men in it, all armed with large guns—machine-guns, she thought, something on the order of Minimis, the Belgian weapons known in the U.S. as M249s.

The man at the wheel was bin Awg.

"All right," she told the two policemen. "Carefully."

As the men moved down to the water, McKenna worked her glasses up and down the shoreline, making sure no one had managed to sneak past the guards she'd posted. Two dozen members of the Brunei police force had rallied to the small camp at the very tip of the country. McKenna's wingman had recommended the old airfield when it became clear they couldn't land at the airport; until today it had mostly been used by helicopters and very light aircraft. The strip was barely wide enough for the A-37Bs. It was long, at least, and, if you ignored two mud holes at the right side about a quarter of the way from the northern end, smooth and solid. She thought she could get the Dragonflies off it with a full or nearly full load of fuel and weapons. Of course, to do that, she'd need jet fuel.

Ammunition would be nice, as well.

McKenna waited until Prince bin Awg was ashore before going down to greet him.

"The sultan is here?" asked the prince.

"He's fine."

"He must leave now," said bin Awg. "I've arranged safe haven in the Philippines."

"Why?" said McKenna. She headed for the trail back to the camp.

"You don't understand. He's in great danger."

"Of course I understand. But his duty is to liberate his kingdom and protect his people," said McKenna.

"His duty is to preserve himself while we do that," said bin Awg. His strides lengthened as he found the trail.

"I disagree," said McKenna.

"It's not up to you."

"Or you."

THE PRINCE ARGUED WITH HIS UNCLE FOR MORE THAN A HALF hour, but the sultan would not be convinced. The only concession he made was that he would not personally use a rifle unless desperate measures were called for.

McKenna—who heard the argument through the thin walls of the office they had taken as their headquarters—wasn't sure whether those conditions might not be met at any moment. They were getting different reports from the radio and the one telephone line that remained working. Guerillas—Islamic terrorists who had been operating against Malaysia until a few days before—had taken over the capital and much of the northern portion of the country. While a good number of Brunei policemen and soldiers had fought bravely, the country had largely been taken by surprise. Sadly, a number of government officials had been less than brave, fleeing their posts at the first alarm.

Brunei was by nature a land of peace. That was its greatest problem now—when the unthinkable came, it was difficult to respond.

McKenna worried about Mack Smith and the Megafortress. She assumed that he had turned around once he saw the airport had been taken over, but in the confusion there was no way to know.

The sultan came to the door of the small room he had adopted as his headquarters and called in McKenna, along with the local police chief, who had rallied his men to the camp.

"The prince and I have discussed his request, but I am staying with my people where I belong," announced the sultan in Malaysian.

"Good," said McKenna.

Bin Awg frowned but told the others what he knew of the situation in the rest of the country. Small army and police units were continuing to resist in the area south of the capital. Many men had gone underground and were said to be loyal, waiting only for leadership. The army's third brigade had been untouched by the first wave of the attacks, and had set up a defensive perimeter around Medit in the southern part of the country, where it had been conducting maneuvers. It had armored personnel carriers and reconnaissance vehicles. Additional units were in control of Sukang, but were under heavy fire.

The navy had lost its two Russian patrol ships as well as two other smaller coastal patrol boats. Some of the remaining vessels had rendezvoused in the South China Sea under command of the assistant defense minister for the navy.

The prince recommended that the sultan join up with the main army group, which was roughly fifty miles away across a rough jungle.

"We may be able to bring in a helicopter at nightfall," said the prince.

"How about getting some fuel for my airplanes?" said McKenna. "We can support the troops there."

"I don't know if we can find any. Fuel is hard to come by."

McKenna told him about the tanker filled with jet fuel that Mack had arranged; it should be nearly offshore by now. In the meantime, fuel could be purchased from the Indonesians in the south.

"Get it up here by boat. We'll carry it up to the airfield. Or better yet, use those helicopters you have. Get us some ammunition for the guns and we're in business."

Prince bin Awg started to speak, but the sultan cut him off.

"Make it so," he said.

The prince bowed his head.

Brunei International Airport
12 October 1997, 2100

Mack Smith folded his arms and pushed his back against the chair in the small room in the basement of the civilian terminal building. The side of his face had swelled where he'd been hit earlier; his lower lip sagged and his nose felt like it had been broken. But he was otherwise physically okay.

His pride sure hurt like hell. Taken by surprise on the tarmac by jerks in white pajamas with beach towels on their hair—how the *hell* was he ever going to live that embarrassment down?

Mack had been interviewed twice; in both cases the interviewers' English was so poor that he hardly understood them when they asked his name, let alone their other questions. The men ended up shouting at him, but seemed under some restraint not to hit him. He'd simply waited them out until they left.

Mack figured that eventually the sultan would rally his troops and retake the airport. The question was how to survive in the meantime. He'd been a prisoner before—and in fact, had been captured by *real* Islamic madmen and transported all the way from Somalia to Libya. These guys were amateurs in comparison.

The hallway outside the room was carpeted, and Mack had no warning that someone was approaching until the door opened. A thin man in his mid- or late twenties entered the room. Unlike the others, he wore khaki fatigues and had on a bulletproof vest. He seemed confident, his step deliberate. Two of the pajamaboys with submachine guns came in behind him, standing by the door and pointing their weapons at Mack.

"You are an American," said the man. His English had an accent that sounded similar to the accents the Brunei officials Mack dealt with had; it was polished, and vaguely British.

"That's right," said Mack. "What are you?"

"I am Commander Sahurah Niu," said the man. It was a simple declaration, not a brag. "Your name is what?"

"Mack Smith."

"Smith is a very common name."

Mack shrugged. "That's what I'm told."

"You are a pilot?"

"Sure."

"You flew the large aircraft?"

"Yup." There was no use lying about that.

"Yup?"

"Means yes," said Mack.

Sahurah's eyes seemed to search Mack's face, as if he were trying to look for clues that his prisoner could be trusted.

Yeah, trust me, Mack thought to himself. *Trust me so I can screw you big time.*

Once I come up with a plan.

"The big aircraft—it is a bomber?" asked the man.

"No," said Mack. He wasn't sure how much information Jalan or the other pilots would give the guerillas, so he had to be careful with his lies. But he wanted to steer them away from the possibility of using the aircraft as an offensive weapon.

On the other hand, if they thought it might be useful, maybe they'd put him in the cockpit. A few high-g maneuvers and he'd be free.

"It's a radar plane," said Mack. "It, uh—the radar searches for other aircraft. It's like an early warning system. It can be very useful when you're under attack."

"It contains no weapons?"

"Defensive weapons," said Mack. "It can defend itself."

Sahurah changed direction, asking how long Mack had been in the country.

"Couple of weeks," he said.

"Where did the sultan go?"

"Couldn't tell you."

"We control the city. We will find him. When will the Americans come?"

"Which Americans?" Mack asked.

"Your marines," said Sahurah.

"Any second," said Mack.

Sahurah turned to one of the men at the door and said something in Malaysian. The man nodded and left.

"You will be fed," he told Mack. "A cot will be brought. If you are mistreated, the man who does so will be punished."

"That's awful nice of you," said Mack, unable to control his sarcasm.

"No, it is merely the way the law directs a prisoner be treated," said Sahurah, interpreting the words, not the tone. "I remind you that if you attempt to escape, you will be executed."

"That's the law, too?"

"Yes," said Sahurah. He bowed his head slightly, then turned and left the room.

* * *

THE PAIN IN HIS HEAD WAS SO INTENSE THAT SAHURAH HAD to pause in the hallway and rub the sides of his temples in an effort to get it to stop. He had much to do and could not afford to stop now, even for such pain. He needed to find men who could tell him about the aircraft here; he needed to survey weapons, to prepare defenses for a counterattack, to make sure all of the brothers were being fed, to find a way to welcome the new recruits who were sure to pour in to their lines now that the decadent order had been swept away.

The Brunei pilot and the others who had been with Smith had been shot in the cockpit unwisely by the brothers who took the plane. Apparently one of the soldiers who had followed Smith down the ladder had started to fire, and from that point on there had been little discipline among the attackers. It was a miracle that the American had been spared, though Sahurah did not know what exactly was to be done with him; surely he could not be trusted in the aircraft.

"Commander, the Malaysians who were sent to man the antiaircraft weapons are complaining about their air-conditioning."

The voice sounded as if it came from the opposite end of the hallway, but when Sahurah turned he found the man who had spoken just a few feet away.

"What is their complaint?" asked Sahurah.

"The air-conditioning needs to function or their equipment will not," said the man.

"Find Salem the Yemen and tell him that a technician is needed to repair it."

"Yes, Commander," said the man, spinning away immediately.

Sahurah once more closed his eyes. He wanted to rest. But God did not want him to, not yet. And he must accept the wishes of his Lord. He took a breath that filled his chest, then resumed his inspection of the airport.

Aboard EB-52 *"Penn,"* approaching Brunei
13 October 1997, 0428

Zen waited as the computer that helped him fly the U/MF-3 Flighthawk counted down the time to launch from its mothership, the EB-52 *Pennsylvania*. Numbers drained in the main control screen, which replaced the visor in Zen's helmet. The projections helped make it seem as if he were inside the small aircraft, and in fact he generally felt as if he were, as he flew. The screen was divided in half; the top showed a video supplied by one of three Flighthawk sensors at the front of the airplane, usually an optical feed, though he could select an infrared or synthetic radar view instead. The panel below this main screen was divided into three different views. The one at the right showed his instruments, or rather a summary of those important at any given moment. The one in the middle was a "sit rep," or a situation representation, a kind of God's-eye view that showed the Flighthawk, its mother ship, and anything else within fifty miles. The data was actually provided by a link with the EB-52, constantly checked and updated by the Flighthawk communications and control computer, dubbed C³. At the far left, Zen had a view synthesized from the long-distance radar feed from *Penn*'s AWACS-style radar, also presented as a God's-eye view. He could change the displays as needed, but preferred this arrangement when he was just flying one aircraft.

The Megafortress tilted its nose downward, beginning a shallow dive that helped increase the separation forces on the robot aircraft, making it easier to launch. The computer hit zero and Zen felt his body shifting exactly as if he were sitting in the tiny little bird that rushed from the wing. The engine flared and he nudged his stick forward and slightly to the left, diving into an arc that would take him toward the oil platform they had to survey.

"Hawk One is away," he told Dog, who was piloting the mothership.

"*Penn* acknowledges."

"Platform at ten miles. Approaching as planned."

Zen put his finger against the throttle slide, notching down his power as he approached the platform. The structure had a pair of exposed decks about twenty feet from the waves. The decks ran around three sides. At the rear of the platform sat what amounted to a prefab ranch house at the top. The platform was smaller than those Zen had seen in the Gulf of Mexico, and a bit less elaborate—there was only one satellite dish, for instance, and no helipad. The flat roof of the trailer was just big enough for the Quick Bird helicopters the Whiplash team was riding in.

There were no ships or boats nearby. Zen took the Flighthawk through an orbit about seven thousand feet over the platform, descending gradually to allow the infrared camera in the Flighthawk to get a good look.

"Clean so far," Zen told Dog.

"We copy," said Dog, who was looking at the feed on his own display.

Two more passes and he saw nothing.

"I'm going to clear Danny in," said Dog. "Let's head over toward Brunei International Airport and have a look at the Megafortress."

"Roger that," said Zen, starting to climb away from the ocean.

Brunei, near the Malaysian border
0430

The helicopter brought enough fuel for only one Dragonfly. McKenna decided she would use it to scout the jungle, then escort the helicopter to the stronghold. Assuming things went well, she'd take a run over the southern part of the kingdom and scout out positions for the army people at Medit and Sukang, where the last report had the army under constant fire.

The sultan gave her a tired but nonetheless enthusiastic smile as she headed for her plane. "I owe you a great deal, Miss McKenna."

"Don't worry about it," she said.

"She's a rough one, but a tough one," the sultan commented in Malaysian to one of his aides, apparently forgetting she spoke it. "We need more of that."

McKenna snorted to herself, then went to her aircraft at the end of the runway. Just as important as the fuel, Prince bin Awg had managed to find two mechanics to tend to the aircraft; they brought enough tools and parts with them that McKenna thought they could build one of the Dragonflies from scratch.

One thing about operating on a shoestring out of a jungle camp—there wasn't a lot of hassle with the control tower. McKenna started her engines, checked her thrust, made sure the control surfaces moved in the right directions, and let it rip. The plane bucked as the wheels hit one of the mud holes—unavoidable because of the narrow path—but picked her nose up without a problem well before the trees.

McKenna tucked her wing toward the Belait River, which

ran a crazy pattern up the southern Brunei countryside from the South China Sea. Both the river and the nearby roads, what little she could see of them, were deserted.

"Good to go," she told the helicopter pilot. "Let's do it quick."

"Brunei One," acknowledged a familiar voice. The sultan, an experienced pilot, had taken the controls himself.

Brunei International Airport
0430

Mack felt the cold hand grab his throat. He jerked nearly straight up and practically fell off the cot.

"I apologize if I startled you," said the man who had interrogated him last night, Commander Sahurah Niu. "I trust you have rested."

"Oh, yeah. Hell of a sleep. Thanks for the cot."

"Put on your shoes and come with me," said Sahurah.

"Come where?"

"I wish you to show me the aircraft."

Mack frowned as if he were reluctant to do so, hesitating just long enough for Sahurah to tell him that, while prisoners had to be treated with respect, that commandment applied only to those who were obedient.

"All right," said Mack, pulling his shoes on. He ran his hand over his jaw, scratching the nearly two-days-worth of growth there. "Can I get some coffee at least?"

Sahurah said something to one of the men at the door.

"The coffee will be brought to the plane. I wish to complete my tour before dawn."

"I'll take you wherever you want," said Mack, hopeful now that he'd be free inside a few hours.

Aboard EB-52 *"Penn,"* approaching Brunei
International Airport
0502

Dog kept his eyes on the image displayed by the Flighthawk as he flew the Megafortress in a double-eight pattern about ten miles from the runway. He could see the Megafortress sitting in front of the hangar as he rode the Flighthawk in toward the large hangar in the military half of the complex. He couldn't help but think about his daughter Breanna. A few days earlier and she would have been captured along with Mack.

Assuming he'd been captured. No one had heard from him, and it was possible that, like Deci Gordon, he had managed to escape and was simply hiding out.

Though that didn't quite seem like Mack's style.

"Any radars?" Dog asked his copilot, Kevin McNamara.

"Negative."

"Hawkins, how are the radar sweeps looking?"

"Clean," replied Lieutenant Jesse Hawkins, one of the two radar operators who had stations just behind him on the extended flight deck. "Quick Bird helicopters are approaching the platform. They're running slightly ahead of schedule."

"Good."

"They have two guards on the road, no one close to the aircraft," Zen told Dog. He nudged the Flighthawk down through four thousand feet, taking a slow turn above the hangar and parking area. Several Dragonflies were lined up near the hangar; Zen had been told during his visit that all of the aircraft were inoperable because of serious maintenance issues. Another Dragonfly sat wrecked near the end of the runway. The two helicopters used by the air force were missing, as were the three other operational Dragonflies; they knew from earlier reports that at least one of them had crashed after being hit by small arms fire yesterday.

Over on the civilian side of the vast complex, a 757 sat next to the terminal building and another aircraft sat alone at the far end of the parking area. That airplane looked like a 707; its nose slumped downward and Zen guessed that its front gear had been disabled.

Two Hawk anti-aircraft batteries guarded the airport, along with four Panhard M3 VDA anti-aircraft weapons. The American-made surface-to-air Hawk missiles were old models, though still deemed reliable by the Pentagon briefers. While they were potent weapons, they required a highly trained crew; Zen could tell from his radar warning receiver that their associated radars had not been activated. The Panhards were armored cars with a pair of twenty-millimeter cannons mounted on top; these could be fired by radar or manually sighted and as a practical matter were likely to be more of a hazard. But they, too, seemed silent.

"Have some activity near the terminal area," said Zen, spotting it as he came back around. "Looks like there's a gun emplacement on the road in, machine guns I think. That wasn't there when I was here. I'm going to take a pass at rooftop level. Hold on—looks like somebody's heading toward the Mega-fortress."

"Target the Megafortress," Dog told his copilot. "Get ready to take it out."

Brunei International Airport
0505

Mack recognized the low hush of the Flighthawk engine as it approached from the north.

Zen and his stinky, lousy timing, he thought to himself. He froze on the tarmac.

"What?" demanded Sahurah.

"Down," hissed Mack as the Flighthawk buzzed down less than a dozen yards away.

Aboard EB-52 *"Penn,"* approaching Brunei
International Airport
0506

Dog swung the Megafortress out of its orbit, lining her up for a direct shot at the airport.

"I have the Megafortress," said McNamara. "It's far enough from the civilian side of the airport that we shouldn't cause any collateral damage there, but the hangar in front of it will be wiped out, along with most of the apron. If it's fueled, it'll be a hell of a fire."

"Understood," said Dog.

"Range is ten miles," said the copilot.

"Bay," Dog told him, giving the order to open the bomb-bay door. A GPS-guided smart bomb rotated to the bottom of the launcher, ready to fire.

"I could be mistaken," Zen said over the interphone. "But I think that's Mack near the plane. I'll go back through the video freeze-frame images in a second. That might even have been Deci with him, wearing a flak jacket."

Dog immediately started to level the plane, breaking off his attack.

"Colonel?" asked McNamara.

"Let's see if we can figure out what's going on down there," Dog told him. "I'd prefer not to have to kill our people."

"Yes, sir."

IT WAS HIS WALK THAT HAD GIVEN HIM AWAY—ZEN WOULD recognize that strut anywhere. And sure enough, the enlarged image in the screen had the familiar buzz cut and crooked smile that said Mack Smith had an ego so large most days he didn't need an airplane to get off the ground.

"You sure it's Mack?" asked Dog.

"Looks like him. The flight suit looks like his, and there aren't too many six-foot Anglos around here. His cowboy boots, I think."

The boots, made from alligator, cinched it for Zen.

As Zen swung the Flighthawk over the airport again, he told the computer to push the infrared sensor settings to their maximum setting. The Megafortress was a dull brown in the screen—the engines weren't on.

"I don't think she's fueled," he told Colonel Bastian. "Nobody aboard."

"You think we could land and pick them up?"

Zen was just about to tell him that was too crazy an idea when McNamara broke in.

"Radar up!" warned the copilot. "One of the Hawk missile batteries."

Zen mashed the throttle as the radar-warning indicator showed that he was being targeted.

"Out of there, Zen," Dog said. "Everybody hang on."

"Missiles in the air!" shouted McNamara.

Off the coast of Brunei
0515

Danny Freah could see the shadow of the derrick in the distance, rising up over the platform a few miles away. The Dreamland Quick Birds had made good time getting here.

A good thing, too. The helicopters were many things—fast, reliable, heavily armed—but comfortable they were not. Their seats had about as much padding as a metal washboard.

Danny pulled on his smart helmet, which allowed him to communicate with the rest of his team and the helicopter pilots. The helmet's visor included a panel that could be used to display feeds from video and infrared cameras at the top of the helmet, as well as images from other team members and an array of sensors.

"All right, we do this the way we drew it up," Danny told them. "Team one rappels down, then team two. We secure the facility, make sure the roof can take the helicopters' weight, then land. Questions?"

Danny waited for Boston's wisecrack. He was almost disappointed when it didn't come.

"Sergeant Liu, we ready?" he asked Liu, who was heading team two in the second chopper.

"Ready, sir."

"All right, pilots, your move."

Unlike conventional helicopters, which used tail rotors to help them maneuver and remain stable in flight, the Quick Birds used a system similar to the "Notar" McDonnell Douglas had developed for the MD 530N version of the basic design. The innovative design made the small helicopter even more maneuverable, and the pilot was able to swing in close to the large metal framework as he and Danny gave it the once-over.

"Let's do it," said Danny.

The three men who'd been sitting in the rear compartment had already readied their ropes, anxious to get out of the cramped quarters of the scout. Danny was the last one down, his boots clunking on the metal roof of the small building that sat above the double deck of the platform. Just as he let go of the rope he lost his balance; he managed to pitch back and fall on his butt—undignified, but far better than falling on his face, and light-years ahead of going off the side.

"First deck is secure," said Sergeant Geraldo Hernandez. "Bison, where are you?"

"Yo, right behind you," answered Sergeant Kevin "Smokes" Bison.

"Going downstairs."

Danny felt the rush of wind from the second helicopter overhead as he jumped down off the roof. He checked the time on the status bar at the bottom of his smart. They had about ten more minutes to decide whether the helicopters were staying or not; after that, the mission plan dictated that the choppers head back to the Philippines and return later in the day. Even the Dreamland helos couldn't carry enough fuel to linger very long.

The door to the enclosed office and rest area was locked. Danny drew his pistol, and fired once point-blank at the lock. The bullet had a specially designed metal slug as its payload; it worked like a sledgehammer, removing the lock.

MP5 ready, Danny sprung the door open with his foot, staying back in case there was a reaction. After a few seconds, Sergeant Jack "Pretty Boy" Floyd inserted a telescoping wand with a fish-eye camera into the open space; it fed a shadowy image into their smart helmets.

"Clear," said Pretty Boy.

Danny moved quickly into the large room, still on edge. A beach chair sat on the far wall; a bag of clothes or linens was nearby it. There were two open doorways on Danny's right. The smart helmet sensors couldn't see very far into the rooms.

"Right first," said Danny. Pretty Boy checked both rooms with the telescoping eye; both were clear, as was a shower and restroom area inside the second room.

The rest of the team, meanwhile, landed. Sergeant Liu had begun inspecting the interior of the building.

"Bad news, Cap—this'll never hold the helicopters. There's supposed to be braces here," said Liu, pointing at the wall area. "This is just Sheetrock through here. We're lucky this held us."

Danny went over to it. The plans that he had seen showed a trio of thick girders running across the center of the building area, and the plan notes had indicated that the roof was strong enough to brace an additional deck or helipad.

"Guess they don't believe in building inspectors in this part of town," quipped Boston.

"Shit," said Danny. He glanced at his watch—three more minutes. "I'm going to check that dock area we saw," he told Liu.

"Want me to watch your back?" asked Boston.

"Secure the two decks and see if you can figure out the electric situation. That generator is supposed to be on the first floor somewhere."

Aboard EB-52 *"Penn,"* over Brunei International Airport 0516

Dog instinctively threw the Megafortress into a hard zag as soon as the missile warning sounded.

"Tracking us," said McNamara.

"ECMs. Break it."

"Trying."

The HAWK MIM-23 was an excellent anti-aircraft missile, but it was an American weapon and in theory it should be easy for the electronic counter measure system to confuse. Theory and practice weren't quite the same thing, however. McNamara reported that one of the missiles was continuing toward them, its speed closing in on Mach 2.5.

"Hang on," shouted Dog, and he put the Megafortress onto her wing, just barely ducking the missile. The computer complained that he had exceeded flight parameters and tried balancing the different forces, working hard because of the second Flighthawk that was still attached to the right wing. The Hawk exploded off the right wing and the Megafortress slipped into a spin, her momentum corkscrewing around, and the aircraft's wings lost her grip on the sky. A second missile exploded nearly a half-mile away, but now gravity and momentum were much more worrisome enemies.

Dog had learned to recover from spins very early in his training as a pilot, but the sharp smack of gravity multiplied by the harsh twist of surprise made his hand slow to respond. His head felt as if it were being forced to the left; he fought it at first, concentrating on his skull rather than the aircraft. It was only a moment's hesitation, but had they been much lower, it might have been fatal. Finally Dog's instincts and training came through; he stopped worrying about his head and was able to move with the plane, willing it under control and pulling up as the altimeter dipped down just below a thousand feet.

"Shit," managed McNamara as they started to climb. Dog looked right; his copilot was holding his left arm, which he'd smacked up during the plummet. "I think I broke my arm."

"Target the HAWK control van," Dog told him.

"There's a backup."

"Both of them."

"If we do that, we won't have any bombs left for the plane on this run," said McNamara.

"Target the HAWK vans."

"Yes, sir." The copilot groaned.

"You okay, McNamara?" asked Dog, ready to bring up the targeting screen himself.

"No," he said. "But I'll nail those mothers with my toes if I have to."

As the Megafortress slapped downward, Zen struggled to keep his Flighthawk straight and level. He had to fight against his instincts to do this; his stomach told his head they were in a spin, and his head wanted to move his hand and legs to get them out of it.

His legs.

The idea taunted him, a devil just out of reach as he held the stick steady. A black cloud began to rise around him; Zen felt himself choke, and waited to hear the Megafortress's alarm indicate that they were on fire.

He coughed again. The cloud started to recede.

The Flighthawk was nearly head-on for the HAWK missile battery.

"Targeting screen," Zen told the computer. A pipper appeared in a shaded area before his eyes. "Dish," he said, telling the computer what he was aiming at. The pipper immediately turned from gray to yellow, indicating that he was close but not quite on target.

Zen moved his hand slowly toward the screen. The pipper began to blink yellow, then changed to red.

He pushed down on the trigger and bullets streamed from the front of the robot plane. He moved the stick very gently left and right, cutting an oval pattern through the metal before pulling off.

"Zen, we're taking out the HAWK batteries with our bombs," said Dog.

"Hawk leader," he acknowledged, pulling the Flighthawk up and away from the airport.

Brunei International Airport
0520

Mack crouched on the cement, watching as the black shadow of the Flighthawk darted across the empty field to the south, going after the radar dish that guided the anti-air missiles. The front of the tiny aircraft blossomed red; a moment later he heard the quick stutter of the plane's cannon. By the time the sound died the wedge-shaped aircraft had flickered upward, from this angle seeming to rise straight up, a puppet pulled by the strings of heaven.

"Out of here," Mack yelled. "Away from the military side of the airport." He got up, saw Sahurah still on the ground near the Megafortress, then reached back and grabbed the back of his shirt, pulling him to his feet.

They'd gotten about thirty yards when the first bomb exploded. The target was a good distance away, but the shock of the five-hundred-pound warhead threw Mack abruptly toward the pavement. He got his left arm out, skidding across the concrete. Cursing, he stumbled back to his feet just as another bomb hit. He saw a geyser of smoke rising over the area near the HAWK trailers.

Something grabbed at Mack; he turned and found Sahurah clutching him. Blood ran down his hands. Mack instinctively picked him up, hauling him over his back and starting to run toward the terminal building. After a few steps his pace slowed to a walk.

He heard the whine of an approaching Flighthawk and threw himself down as it passed. Sahurah's weight pressed against his upper body and made him slam his chin against the concrete. Mack cursed, rolled over to his back, and edged up on his elbows, dazed and unsure now where the hell he was.

Off the coast of Brunei
0526

Danny surveyed the dock area from the ladder, using the range-finder in the smart helmet as a measuring tool. The dock was eight feet wide, which would make it a precarious perch for the helicopters. Nor did the sections look particularly stable or long. There was no way they were getting the helicopters down here.

"Freah to Quick Bird One. Jack, you guys better head back," he told the pilot. "We'll do an assessment on that roof. In the meantime, come up with a plan to shore it up. Worst case, you can fly the grid in overnight."

The grid was a portable landing area that could be set up over either the deck or the housing area.

"I was thinking we could land on derrick two," replied the pilot. "The backup platform."

"Negative," said Danny. It was more than a mile away and they'd have no way of getting back and forth until the MC-17 dropped their zodiacs along with additional supplies. "Let's just do this the way we drew it up."

"You got it. We'll be back."

The helicopters banked low, saying good-bye before heading off. The Whiplash team would be on its own for the next several hours.

Danny came up the ladder and joined Liu on the lower deck, where they had found a generator and a barrel of diesel that the sergeant estimated would last at least forty-eight hours. The motor balked at first, but within a few minutes they had it up and running, and the interior lights came on in the building area and around the platform. A floodlight came on below, illuminating the dock area; Danny went back to look for a switch; he found one inside a metal box near the hatchway to the area below. The switch was stuck, and when he tried prodding it with his knife the handle broke off, leaving no easy way to turn the light off. Frustrated, he decided to climb back down and see if he could unscrew the light; if not he'd just shoot the damn thing out.

Danny had to get down to the dock and then climb up a nearby support beam, but once he did he found another switch box with a control inside that was considerably easier to use and the light snapped off. He shimmied back down to the dock and started to go back to his men. As he did, he noticed a thick black shadow about a hundred yards from the southwestern leg. His first thought was that it was an oil slick, but the edges seemed too linear. Then he thought it must be some sort of optical illusion, a shadow cast by the platform in the dim predawn light. He took a step up and then down, trying to puzzle out how it was formed.

And then, as he watched, the shadow began to move.

"Liu," he said softly, "come down to the dock area real, real quiet. I'm on the ladder. Take one other person with you. Everybody else, hold your positions and be real quiet."

Aboard EB-52 *"Penn,"* over Brunei International Airport 0527

"No way that was anything but an unguided, lucky shot," said McNamara, talking about the missile that had nearly clocked them. "They may have gone to the K-band range-only-radar when we jammed but I'd bet they had a general direction and just launched."

Dog, completing the system check with the computer, didn't respond. Lucky shot or no, the HAWK anti-aircraft system wasn't something you could operate merely by throwing a switch. These weren't raw kids they were dealing with. Whoever had been in the guidance trailers knew what they were doing.

They were also now dead. Both GBU-30s—also known as JDAM or Joint Direct Attack Munitions, bombs that steered themselves to specific GPS points—had struck their targets dead-on. The five-hundred-pound warheads had obliterated the guidance trailers and everything nearby.

"What's the situation down there, Zen?" Dog asked.

"The trailers are fried. More missiles on the launcher at the south side. First launcher fired all three I think. Couple of gun batteries but they haven't done anything. Hang on," added the pilot, turning his small craft around for another survey.

"What about the Megafortress on the ground?" Dog asked.

"Same as before. The people who were going toward it ran back for the terminal. One of them was definitely Mack, but I think the person with him was a local, or maybe one of the guerillas. There are a bunch of guys in white clothes near them. I had an idea," he added.

"What's that?"

"Why don't we eliminate the fuel trucks so the Megafortress can't be refueled," said Zen. "Keep it grounded for a while without doing any damage. Brunei Air Force only has one tanker. That was one of Mack's big gripes. There are six over on the civilian side but they're all parked by an auxiliary building. I can shoot up the pumping apparatus as well, but I'm not sure if there's a backup."

"They'll just bring another truck in," said Dog.

"At some point, maybe. But if you're looking to keep them on the ground without taking apart the plane completely, that might work."

It was a temporary measure to be sure, but it would be adequate for now. If the militants made any move to fuel it, they could still use the Flighthawk to disable it. Dog also could have *Indy* take a shot at cratering the ramp area from the military side of the airport.

"Let's do it," he told Zen.

"I'd like to launch Hawk Two," added Zen, referring to the second Flighthawk.

"I don't think we can," said McNamara. "I have a fault on the program screen."

"Nothing here," said Zen.

"Can you do it with just Hawk One?"

"Not a problem."

"Go."

Off the coast of Brunei
0530

Dazhou Ti turned the optical viewer to the left, making sure that the helicopter had gone. The viewer, similar to the periscope on a submarine, allowed him to survey the area without using his detectable sensors. Its field of vision was limited, however; he could see only a small swatch of the ocean or sky at a time.

The helicopter had left two or three men at the platform, but who they were wasn't clear. He suspected either Australians or Americans, since he had not recognized the aircraft type as Malaysian—or Bruneian, for that matter.

It was hardly an academic point. A tug was due to meet him within an hour here. Despite considerable work by his crew, they had been unable to restart their main engines. Their emergency backup power was supplied by an electric generator. They had manually rerouted it to provide power to the in-port maneuvering system, but could make no more than two or three knots, and even that required shutting down the rest of the electrical systems. The power arrangements meant they could only use the cannon. It would have to be aimed and operated manually, and even then there were doubts about what effect the power drain would have on the rest of the ships' systems. It was unlikely they could destroy the platform before the men there called for reinforcements.

Still, it was not in Dazhou's nature to do nothing. All his life he had seen boldness rewarded.

"We will move to the east side of the platform," he told his crew. "When we arrive, we will send a boarding party. I will lead the party myself," he added on the spur of the moment. "There are no more than three men on the platform; they should be easy to overcome."

Brunei International Airport
0535

"They're blowing up the fuel trucks," said Mack as the Flighthawk tucked left and lit its cannon on the other side of the civilian terminal. He crouched down though he was several hundred yards away.

He had to hand it to Zen—he was an efficient SOB. Anyone else would have taken two or three passes. But here the pilot had gone for the trifecta, swooshing three trucks in the space of maybe ten seconds.

"Why are they doing that?" said Sahurah next to him.

Mack shrugged, though he knew the answer—they didn't want the EB-52 to take off, but had decided for some reason to hold off on blowing it up.

Lucky for him.

"You saved my life," said Sahurah as the Flighthawk swooped upward. "Why?"

Good question, thought Mack.

"Why did you save me, or not try to escape?" asked Sahurah when he didn't answer.

"Just stupid, I guess," said Mack, watching as the Flighthawk made another pass and another fuel truck erupted in flames.

* * *

WHY HAD THE INFIDEL SAVED HIS LIFE? WONDERED SAHURAH.

Had God moved him to do so?

Or had the devil?

What if neither had? What if he had acted solely on his own?

Sahurah put his hand on his hip over his holster, contemplating what had happened. He had been taught that Westerners, Americans especially, were thoroughly corrupt and without virtue. He'd seen ample examples of this during his life.

And yet the actions of his prisoner, surely meant to save him, were against every expectation. It was one thing for the man to be strong and brave—these were things he expected, considering that Mack Smith had an important position. But his actions were beyond that.

"Commander!" shouted one of his men, running toward him. Four other brothers, all with AK47s, trotted behind him. "Are you okay?"

"Yes," said Sahurah. "Take Mr. Smith back to the building where he was held. Treat him with the greatest respect." He turned to Mack. "Remember, you are a prisoner."

"Hard to forget," replied Mack, following them toward the building.

Over western Brunei, near Sukut
0540

McKenna banked her Dragonfly low over the river, giving the tops of the nearby trees a good look at her belly. The Brunei army had fortified positions on the northern side of the bridge that led to Sukut, and had only a few scouts on the south. She couldn't see them because of the thick jungle canopy, nor could she tell if there were rebels there.

"You have a truck moving on the road," she told the Brunei army unit on the ground. "Pickup type truck. Rear is, uh, looks empty."

The army sergeant on the other end of the line thanked her. Unlike yesterday, the responses were sharp and very focused.

McKenna flew over the road and then banked north, looking for any concentration of militants. The citizens of Sukut had rallied to the small army and police force there, swelling their ranks with volunteers. Reinforcements were due soon from Medit.

"This is Dreamland EB-52 Pennsylvania to unidentified aircraft operating near Sukut. Identify yourself," crackled the radio.

"Who the hell are you calling unidentified?" snapped McKenna. "Why are you using Brunei Air Force communications frequencies?"

"Identify yourself," responded the voice.

"Just like an American," answered the pilot. "Dreamland EB-full-of-yourself-52, this is Brunei-Air-Force-kick-your-butt-and-spit-in-your-eye A-37B Dragonfly Dragon One. You are in sovereign Brunei territory," she added. "State your purpose and position."

There was a brief pause. McKenna began climbing and made sure her radar was in long-range scan. The scope was clear, though she knew the Megafortress's stealthy characteristics meant it could be as close as ten miles away.

"Dragon One, this is *Pennsylvania*," said another, older voice over the radio. "We are here to assess the situation."

"Well, that's damn American of you," responded McKenna. "A day late and I'm going to guess a dollar short. What's your location?"

"We've just finished eliminating the ground-to-air defenses at Brunei International Airport and disabled their fueling capacity."

"What about our EB-52?" she asked.

"We haven't touched it," said the American. "It's near your hangar at the base."

McKenna felt a stab of pain in her ribs—she had hoped that Mack had been warned off and gone back to the Philippines.

"Is the plane under the militants' control?" added the voice.

"Unknown at this time."

"The airport is clearly in militant control, as is the rest of the capital," said the voice. "Do you have information to the contrary?"

Hopes, but not information, she thought to herself.

"Not at this time," she answered. "Who are you?"

"Lt. Colonel Tecumseh Bastian. Who are you?"

"Brunei Air Commodore McKenna."

McKenna filled the Americans in on the situation as she knew it, without identifying the base she was operating from. She guessed that they were here primarily to make sure that Brunei's Megafortress didn't fall into the militants' hands.

"Are you offering to help the sultan, who is the rightful and lawful ruler of this country?" she asked finally.

"We're here to assess the situation," answered the American.

"Well don't take too long to choose up sides," she told him. "Or there may be only one left."

Off the coast of Brunei
0540

"Some sort of ship," Liu told Danny over the communications circuit. He was standing a few feet away on the dock, using binoculars to examine the shadowy vessel. "Stealthy. Those triangular wings on the side allow it to skim over the water. Marines were talking about something like that to move troops in, but they're a bit bigger."

Whatever it was, it was moving, albeit very, very slowly, to the east of the platform. It remained several hundred yards away.

"Who does it belong to, Captain?" asked Boston, who was back by the ladder.

"Good question," said Danny. "I'll alert Dreamland Command. For the time being, Boston, Bison, you guys keep it under surveillance from the lower deck. The rest of us will continue searching the platform. Weapons locker would be particularly handy right now."

"Gotcha, Cap," said Bison.

Danny climbed back to the housing area, where Pretty Boy had set up the satellite communications gear. Danny's helmet plugged in via an infrared link, and he found himself talking to Major Catsman in the command center. The vessel—or whatever it was—didn't appear on any of the force listings or any of the intelligence briefings that she could find.

"It's not an optical illusion," said Danny. "I can replay the image I recorded with the helmet. It's moving in the water. Pretty slowly, but it's moving."

"We'd like to see it," said Catsman. "I'll ask Colonel Bastian to overfly it. They're over the southern portion of the country right now."

Before Danny could reply, Boston broke in over the team circuit.

"Captain, there's a boat coming out of the back of it. Looks like there's a boarding party."

"Be right there," said Danny.

Aboard *"Penn,"* over Brunei
0550

"I see where she's heading," said Lieutenant Hawkins, working one of the radar boards on the Dreamland EB-52. "Small strip, tiny—surprised she can get out of there."

The lieutenant forwarded a map image with the strip marked out on it to Dog's station. Dog zoomed out, getting a better idea of the location, and then brought up a satellite image from the library. The base was indeed tiny, but it was also near the coast and protected by rough terrain from neighboring Malaysia.

"Zen, let's get an overflight of that area," Dog said. "Get an idea of what they've got there and whether their defenses can withstand an attack."

"Sure she won't try shooting me down?" said Zen.

"She may just take you on," Dog told him. The pilot— McKenna—reminded him a bit of his own daughter. "But if you don't think you can outfly an A-37B . . ."

"I can handle a Tweet, thanks," snapped Zen, using the somewhat derogatory slang term for the aircraft's trainer version, the T-37.

If the base seemed secure, Dog thought he might be able to air-drop supplies in. That would be exceeding his orders—but it was the right thing to do, as long as he could find a way to do it.

"Dreamland Command to *Penn*," crackled the radio. "Colonel, Danny's reporting an unidentified vessel in the water near his position."

"On our way," said Dog, immediately changing his plans.

Off the coast of Brunei
0551

It didn't take more than a few seconds to see that the boat was definitely headed for the platform. Danny came down to the lower deck, watching as the rubber boat came toward them. There were four men, paddling steadily. The team looked extremely disciplined—so much so that they reminded Danny of the SEAL team he had spent an exhilarating and exhausting week training with a year before.

"Dreamland, are you sure these aren't our forces?" Danny asked, punching the back of his helmet to connect via the satellite. "These guys remind me of SEALs."

"Not to our knowledge."

"Cap, what do you think of going down to the dock? They can't see the ladder from where they are."

"Hold off, Boston." The last thing he wanted to do was kill four of his countrymen. "Dreamland—have we checked with the navy?"

"That's negative, but to our knowledge, they're not navy."

He was authorized to protect himself. If these guys were SEALs, they were in the wrong place at the wrong time.

That wasn't going to be good enough if he was wrong, though.

"Liu, you got that high-powered telescope trained on these guys?"

"Still working on it, Captain."

The vessel they had come from was definitely not American; it didn't appear on any listing of U.S. forces that Danny knew of or that Dreamland could access. Then again, most of Dreamland's equipment didn't either. Whiplash itself was to be found nowhere, except as an insignificant security detail attached to a nonexistent unit at Edwards Air Force Base.

The boat was fifty yards away.

"Captain?" asked Boston.

"They have MP5Ns," said Liu.

The same type of submachine gun SEALs used.

"Russian RPG in the bottom of the boat."

"Fire!" said Danny.

SOMEHOW DAZHOU TI SENSED THAT THEY WERE UNDER FIRE before he heard or saw the gunfire. He immediately reached to the motor of the boat—they'd kept it off so they could make a silent approach—and started the engine. The four-stroke pancake motor, adapted from a motorcycle design, was located completely underwater, except for the air intake and exhaust. It coughed then caught with a roar, lifting the prow of the rubber assault boat forward in a rush. As it did, one of Dazhou's men fell back against him; the captain pushed him back upright but the man slumped to the left, his face and arm riddled with bullets.

"There," shouted one of the others, pointing. The guns began popping, the loud staccato competing with the roar of the engine. A stream of lead ripped against the wall of the boat, puncturing some of the cells but not enough to threaten its buoyancy. Another of Dazhou's men leaned to the side, then fell into the water; Dazhou kept his sight fastened on the dock area ahead.

He'd thought there were no more than three people here, but obviously there were.

Something roared behind him, and part of the platform crumpled and fell into the water—the *Barracuda* began to fire its cannon.

THE FIRST SHELL LANDED ON THE DECK BELOW THEM, RUM-bling through the metal framework with a groaning screech. The cannon flashed several times again, apparently without hitting the platform.

Meanwhile, the boat was continuing toward them. Danny emptied his magazine, then slapped in a fresh box.

"Liu, put a grenade on it if it gets close enough," he told the sergeant as he ran in the direction of the ladder down to the dock. As he reached it, the enemy ship's gun found its target once more and the platform rocked with three blows from the cannon. Danny fell near the railing; he looked over and saw Boston down below emptying his M4, a shortened version of the M16.

"What the hell are you doing down there? Get up, get up," yelled Danny. Machine-gun fire peppered the dock near his man, and at least two slugs bounced off Boston's carbon-boron vest. Danny couldn't find the boat for a second; finally he saw it at the far end of the dock area. He fired his MP5 submachine gun, the bullets rattling out from the weapon, his whole body shaking. Someone in the boat began to fire back and Danny pushed back, out of the line of fire, and reloaded.

"Boston where the hell are you?"

He, didn't answer. Danny pushed back to the edge of the deck area as the platform rocked violently with fresh salvos from the enemy ship. He thought he could get a grenade into the boat but didn't want to with Boston exposed somewhere below.

"Boston, where the hell are you?" he said again, firing a short burst in the direction of the boat.

Aboard *"Penn,"* heading toward the Brunei coast
0553

Zen saw the flashes in the right side of his screen even though the radar was having the devil of a time picking up the low-lying ship near the oil platform. He changed the input to only optical and saw what looked like a Civil War-era Confederate ironclad with stubby, sharply angled wings on either side. A cannon was firing at the oil platform from what looked like an open porch at the top of the hull.

Zen pushed left, moving to get the Flighthawk's nose on the cannon. The pipper blinked red then went solid; he waited a half second and then started to fire. His stream of bullets punctured the side of the ship immediately behind the cannon. He pushed his stick left, trying to run the slugs into it.

And then the targeting screen abruptly disappeared. He was out of ammunition.

Off the coast of Brunei
0554

The ladder down to the dock extended from an open hatchway on the lower deck. It was completely exposed to fire from the water. Further down at the end of the deck a pair of close-set girders dropped to the edge of the platform; Danny thought he could climb down them and be protected from gunfire by their bulk.

He half-crawled, half-ran to the railing there, moving his large frame gingerly into the open space. His right hand started to slip as he swung around; his left boot missed the strut that ran between the two pier pieces. Danny clamped the hand to the metal, trying to somehow rub it dry without actually losing his grip. For a moment he dangled freely against the side, his weight supported by only one hand. A thick bolt extended from the girder in front of him; he was able to grab it with his left hand, the submachine gun falling and hanging by its targeting wire to his smart helmet. He managed to get a foothold as a fresh salvo of cannonfire rocked the platform. The vibrations tingled in his hands and knees, but his grip was tight. Danny managed to work his way down, slapping his knee hard against the steel. He climbed toward the waves, able to peek through the space but not seeing much of anything.

"Boston!" he yelled as he neared the platform.

He heard a squelch or something over the circuit, but no answer. Danny pulled his gun to his right hand, then swung around to the dock. The boat had pushed against the far side; he could see people in front of it.

"Boston?" he yelled, but still there was no answer.

VANITY HAD BROUGHT DAZHOU TI TO THIS POINT, AND VANITY now kept him from retreating. One of his men was dead, another overboard.

"Captain?" shouted his other crewman.

Dazhou didn't answer. He knew he had made a grave mistake. They'd made it to the docking area, but there was no sense now going aboard; the *Barracuda* was pummeling it with shells.

And yet he wouldn't throw the vessel into reverse.

Something moved in the water to the left of the dock and platform area. As he raised his gun to fire, a fresh round of bullets rained down from above. Dazhou turned his rifle upward abruptly and raked the spot; he continued to press the trigger even as the magazine was exhausted.

"All right," he said in a whisper to himself. He reached for the motor, reengaging it. "All right."

Aboard *"Penn,"* heading toward the Brunei coast
0557

Dog came out over the water just as Zen announced that he had run out of ammo for his cannon.

"Bring up one of the AMRAAM-pluses," Dog told McNamara.

"Uh, Colonel? An AMRAAM against a ship?"

"You have a problem with that?"

"Uh, no, sir, if I can get the computer to allow it."

"Use the manual setting if you have to."

"Yes, sir."

McNamara busied himself with the targeting screen. Though they were less than fifteen miles from the vessel, the radar had difficulty locating it, let alone getting a lock. Dog could see the vessel in the enhanced video screen. The gun had stopped firing, and smoke seeped from the opposite side.

"Got a lock," said McNamara finally.

"Fire."

Off the coast of Brunei
0558

Dazhou had just pulled the small boat around to retreat when the missile or bomb struck the side of the ship. It plowed right through without igniting. Dazhou stared in disbelief, the sun glinting into his eyes.

It couldn't have happened, he thought. He couldn't have seen it.

And then the *Barracuda*'s stern slid down to the port side, bobbed upward, and then down, disappearing. The nose of his ship—his great, wonderful ship—rose from the water like the mouth of a shark getting ready to clamp on its prey. It stayed upright for a moment, locked in his stare, then slowly slipped away.

"No!" he shouted. Dazhou took his fist and began pounding the side of his head viciously. His mistakes had killed his men—his mistakes had killed his ship.

"No!" he shouted. "No!"

DANNY COULDN'T SEE BOSTON ANYWHERE. HE CROUCHED at the side, unsure exactly what was going on.

The boat that had tried to land at the oil platform was gone. The enemy ship had stopped firing.

A Flighthawk buzzed overhead, spinning around the derrick at the top of the platform like a midget racer completing a test lap. Danny went to the edge of the dock just in time to see the enemy ship put its bow up into the air and slide down to a watery grave.

But where the hell was Boston? Had he been taken prisoner by the men in the boat?

Something moved in the water to his right. Danny spun quickly, pointing his submachine gun.

A boat.

Danny aimed but stopped himself from firing only at the last second.

It was Boston, in a small aluminum skiff.

Danny pulled off his helmet and yelled at him. "Boston, why the hell didn't you answer me?"

"I been answering you!" the sergeant shouted back. "I told you I found the boat and was trying to fire at the rubber raft. Everybody's been trying to tell you. Your radio's out or something."

Danny nearly threw the offending helmet into the water. He turned and went back up the dock, looking in the direction of the ship that had been sunk. Another ship had appeared in the distance.

"I found this boat and thought I could flank 'em," said Boston, coming up on the dock. "It's a little aluminum thing. We used to use them for fishing on the lake."

"Yeah," said Danny. "All right. There's another ship coming. Let's get upstairs."

Aboard *"Penn,"* heading toward the Brunei coast
0615

"They claim they're a Malaysian salvage tug," McNamara told Dog after he was able to raise the approaching ship on the maritime radio bands. "Damn nervous, too. They say they're civilians, answering an emergency call from a Malaysian naval vessel."

"Tell them they can recover the people in that small boat, but if they go within five hundred yards of that platform, we'll sink them."

"Yes, sir."

"How you looking, Zen?"

"Could use a refuel."

"Now's as good time as any," said Dog. He started to climb, laying out a track where he could have the computer fly the Megafortress while the Flighthawk took fuel through the special boom below her tail. "Meet you at eighteen thousand feet."

"Hawk leader."

Dog checked in with Danny on the platform. His men had been bruised a bit, but none of the enemy's bullets had penetrated

their carbon-boron vests or helmets, and the cannon had done little damage to the platform. That tracked with U.S. navy experience during the Iran tanker war and the Gulf War, when some of
the better-built platforms sustained hundreds and even thousands
of rounds before being destroyed. Partly it was a function of the
design of the platforms and their superstructure, and partly it was
a function of the size of the bullets being fired—twenty or
twenty-five millimeters just didn't measure up to the mammoth
shells *Penn*'s namesake had once dished out.

Dog clicked into the Dreamland Command frequency.
"Dreamland, this is Colonel Bastian. Ask Major Alou if he can
push up his schedule in *Indy;* we're out of ammo. Then see if
you can locate Jed Barclay and get him in touch with me. I have
some information he's going to find very important, diplomatic
type information."

"Right away, Colonel," said Major Catsman.

Brunei International Airport
0800

They gave Mack a breakfast of some sort of fruit and then
left him alone in a basement room of the terminal. He spent the
time stewing, berating himself for saving Sahurah rather than
sending the idiot to the fuel trucks where he could have had the
fiery death a terrorist deserved.

The concrete had scraped the palms of his hands and little
specks of blood dotted the flesh; he had cut up the side of his
face as well and could feel it swelling. Tired, he lay down on the
floor next to the wall—there were no chairs or other furniture in
the room—staring at the ceiling but not sleeping. He was still
there when the door opened and two men came in.

"Mr. Mack Smith, you are to come with us," said one of the
men. He held a Beretta in his hand; Mack noticed that the gun
shook slightly.

"Okay," said Mack. He pulled himself up slowly. The other
man stood back by the door with some sort of rifle; the gun had
a folding metal stock and looked as if it had been cut down.
Though both were in their thirties, the men were clearly nervous, and Mack moved as deliberately as possible, aware that
their fear was probably twice as dangerous as their weapons.

The light in the hallway hurt his eyes; he held his hand over his head as he walked to the stairway. The two men stayed behind him, and Mack thought of making a break for it when he reached the top. But there were other guards there, younger but just as jumpy, their bodies visually twitching as he approached.

The Brunei airport would never make a ranking of the busiest airports in the world or even Asia, but it looked positively forlorn now, an empty plain of concrete and roadways. Only two vehicles were in the parking lots as Mack was led from the building. One was a burned out Toyota that sat in a black heap near the main entrance to the terminal. The other was a white pickup truck, also a Toyota, idling near the access road a few hundred yards away. The men led Mack to it, then made him get up into the back.

This'll be easy, he thought, envisioning jumping off the side. But then two other men approached with chains and manacles. They locked his hands and then chained his leg to the back of the truck with several sets of combination locks. Mack settled against the side, sweating in the sun until the truck set out.

Zamboanga International Airport (Andrews Air Base), Philippines
0805

Breanna stepped out of the Beechjet, finally deposited on Philippine territory after what seemed like a marathon of short-hop plane rides. Dreamland had set up shop on a small corner of the airport, and the U.S. air force jet—actually a multi-jet trainer borrowed temporarily as a taxi—had deposited her about fifty yards from their hangar area; she could see the tips of a Megafortress V-shaped tail sitting over the building to her right. She passed through the double line of security—Filipino and regular U.S. air force, but no Whiplashers—and walked around to the back of the building, where the Dreamland Command trailer had been set up as a temporary headquarters on the tarmac. Inside, she found Major Alou getting ready for his mission to relieve the flight currently patrolling over Brunei.

"Just in time," Alou said as Breanna walked in the door. "I can use a copilot. Russ's stomach is acting up. He's in the bathroom stinking it up."

Breanna bristled at being made copilot—she had trained

Alou on the Megafortress—but protocol and manners called for her to smile. Besides, she was eager to get into the action—whatever it was. "Sure," she told him.

Alou recapped the situation—*Jersey* had been located at the airport; it was out in the open and an easy target. But at the moment it wasn't fueled and didn't seem likely to be used. Their orders directed them to preserve it for the sultan unless the terrorists made an overt attempt to use it as a weapon. They would patrol over the island and destroy it if any attempt was made.

Danny Freah and his Whiplash team had taken up a post on a platform offshore, which they intended to use as a base while deploying the LADS system. They had just fended off an attack by a high-tech Malaysian boat with the help of the other Megafortress. Their Quick Birds were being outfitted for a return flight; the MC-17 had left a short while ago with supplies that would be parachuted nearby, allowing them to shore up the platform so the choppers could land there. The team had found a small boat which they would use to recover their Zodiacs; once the boats were inflated and operational, the rest of the material could be easily plucked from its floating containers. *Indy*'s job would be merely to watch and make sure no one came back for another go at them.

"Kick and Starship have the Flighthawks," Alou added. "We may be able to share some of the video input with the Brunei army."

He pointed to a large map of Borneo that showed the areas of Brunei where the guerillas had taken over. Strongholds of loyalist troops were shaded in blue in the south of the country.

"The sultan has joined up with the army and is organizing a counter-offensive," added Alou. "We're not exactly sure what form it will take, but it looks as if they're moving north."

"Are we authorized to help them?" asked Breanna.

"Not at this time. Our only mission is to make sure the Megafortress is not used by the rebels. We blow it up if it takes off. And we can protect our own people on the platform."

The sound of a C-17 rumbling nearby shook the small trailer.

"That'll be more of our technical people," said Alou. "I'm going to have to see them; we want one of the engineers to go over in the helicopters and inspect the landing area before they set down."

"What's he going to do, jump?" asked Starship.

"He may if he doesn't know how to rappel," said Alou.

THE HEAT AND HUMIDITY ALMOST KNOCKED JENNIFER GLEAson down as she walked off the ramp of the big C-17, carrying a briefcase with two laptops and a backpack with extra clothes. The airplane had left from Dreamland several hours ahead of schedule, partly because the situation seemed more dire as news of the guerilla attacks came in, and partly because the Dreamland people couldn't see the point in hanging around twiddling their thumbs once they were ready to go. Jennifer had spent the flight brushing up on the LADS technology, learning about the lighter-than-air vessels. While she knew a bit about the computer systems already, she wasn't familiar with their operating procedures. The skins of the aircraft were made of a high-tech fabric containing LED matrices and what might be called a flexible plastic lens; the system made the airships almost invisible from a distance. The engines were also extremely efficient, thanks largely to recent inventions. But the rest of the airship design was hardly revolutionary, and materials aside, the small bag of air and its semirigid interior spine could have been designed fifty years before. Its simplicity was among its assets.

The blimps were controlled by a central ground station, which communicated with them via satellite. At present, the design allowed only one "live" receiver, which meant that the images from the system had to be uploaded back to Dreamland through a slightly kludgy arrangement that used Dreamland's regular com channels. Turning over control of the blimps to another remote station, or to Dreamland for that matter, was a similarly laborious affair; the system had been designed with the idea that it would have its own dedicated command and control network for security purposes, and the present arrangement was actually a hack around those safeguards.

Jennifer spotted Major Alou near the C-17, talking with the loadmasters.

"Have we deployed LADS yet?" she asked after he said hello.

"Whiplash is in the process of launching two of the airships from the platform to cover the city. The helicopters will be bringing additional units with them as soon as they leave." He glanced at his watch. "Which ought to be any second now."

"Great. Where are the helicopters?"

"Over beyond the second building on the right. Why?"

"Because I have to oversee the LADS technical operation."

"You mean you want to go out to the platform?"

"How else would I do it?"

"And stay there?"

"How else would I do it?"

Alou gave the men a look and then motioned with his head toward the side. Jennifer followed him.

"You can't stay out on the platform," said Alou.

"Why the hell not?"

"Because it's dangerous. They've already been attacked."

"Do we have other people there?"

"Well, the Whiplash team."

"If they deployed LADS from there, that's where I have to be."

"No."

Jennifer put her hands on her hips. "I'm sorry, Major. But I have a job to do. And you can't tell me not to do it."

"I'm in charge of the deployment."

"No, you're not," she said. Jennifer felt her cheeks starting to burn.

"I mean—listen."

"I've been on deployments before," she said, turning and heading for the helicopters.

Washington, D.C.
12 October 1997, (local) 2100

Jed took the information Colonel Bastian had given him, double-checking what he could against the last CIA briefing and compiling it into a briefing paper and a PowerPoint slide presentation. His boss, Philip Freeman, had told him to bring it down to the White House situation room as soon as possible; Jed pulled the paper copies of the briefing page by page from the printer, barely making sure they were in order before starting for the secure area on a dead run. When he burst into the conference room a few minutes later, President Kevin Martindale was on the phone; Freeman motioned for Jed to come forward and give him the paper version of the briefing. Jed slid it over, and Freeman spun it around and separated the pages, showing one copy to the president and the other to the secretary of state, whose gray face turned even darker.

"Interesting," the president told whomever he was speaking with. He leaned back in his chair and gave Jed a thumbs-up. He seemed somewhat tired, though as usual his voice was so calm he might have been chatting at a cocktail party.

"Well, perhaps you can explain then how one of your ships came to be firing upon an oil platform off the Brunei coast?" the president said finally to the person on the other end of the line. "Seems to have had some bad luck there."

Jed started up the laptop presentation and then slid it over toward the president. A wry smile came over the president's face; he looked a bit like a poker player about to reveal a hand filled with aces.

"I'm looking at an image of it in the water right now. Very interesting craft," President Martindale said. He leaned forward to read the notes in the pop-up window on the screen. "What does this use? Surface effect technology? No—wing-in-ground effect? Wing-in-wave? Very impressive."

The president looked at Jed. One of the CIA technology experts believed that the ship might have been built for Malaysia by China, but Jed had his own theory—the U.S. had experimented with some of the technology, and used parts built by a South Korean firm. He thought it possible that the plans were stolen somewhere along the way through industrial espionage; heads were going to roll if that was the case.

"Well, as prime minister, you're in a position to do something about it, aren't you?" said Martindale. He sat up straight, figuratively laying his cards on the table. "I expect to see concrete steps toward cooperation with Brunei forces within twelve hours. In the meantime, I've dispatched some of my own units to keep an eye on the situation. It would be very good if we could use one of your bases."

The president listened, nodding as the Malaysian prime minister spoke. Jed slid out one of the sheets from his report, placing it so the president could see.

"Well that's very good," the president said finally. "I'm told you had some troubles at that secret base in the hills above

Meruta where you were operating Su-27s until the other day. Rumor has it you bought those from the Ukraine—odd that the purchase wouldn't have been announced, or shared with other members of ASEAN."

The president smiled as he listened to the Malaysian leader's continued excuses. After a minute or so, he interrupted.

"With all due respect, you have treaty obligations to honor. If you don't honor them, I think you'll find your position in the world community very, very tenuous."

The president handed the phone to the secretary of state, who listened for a few more moments, said "Great," and then hung up.

"They'll cooperate," the secretary announced. "We can use any of their facilities we want."

"Dreamland preferred the, uh, hidden base," said Jed. "Because it's location is more isolated. Less chance for spies to see them coming and going. There are some security issues—we're very short of personnel."

"The Malaysians promised assistance," said the secretary of state. "I think they're sincere."

"I doubt they're sincere," said President Martindale. "But I think they'll go along with us for the time being. We've just given them carte blanche to attack the terrorists wherever they find them. I imagine they'll use it to justify all manner of things. But for the moment, these terrorists are a bigger problem. Imagine what they'd do if they controlled a country like Brunei, with all its oil revenue. Jed, give Colonel Bastian the heads up. Get the Pentagon to send them more security personnel, Special Forces, whatever they need. Then you go get some sleep young man. You look as tired as I feel."

VI
Snakes in the Jungle

DANNY FREAH TIGHTENED HIS HAND ON THE SIDE OF THE
seat as the Quick Bird thundered over the Brunei Jungle, heading for the last launch point for the LADS system. He'd given
up his usual spot in the front of the helo to Jennifer Gleason,
who had hooked one of her laptops into the blimps' command
system. Jennifer had modified some of the programming en
route, allowing them to activate the sensors on the fly as each
blimp was launched. Though the system was scalable (meaning
units could be added without major hassle), before her alter-
ations it had to be shut down and rebooted, a lengthy process,
each time a new unit came on line.

Who said scientists weren't useful? And this one, even in a
carbon-boron vest, was damn easy on the eyes.

"Thirty seconds to touchdown, Captain," announced the pilot. "Hawk Three says we're clear."

"Good," said Danny. He stamped his foot up and down, trying to knock away the pins and needles.

"Problem, Cap?" asked Boston, who was sitting next to him.

"I'm all right."

"Foot fell asleep, huh?" Boston laughed.

"My leg," said Danny.

"My grandmamma had an ol' recipe to fix that."

"Your grandmamma, huh?" said Sergeant Garcia. "Did it in-
volve castor oil?"

"Mighta. She put castor oil into anything, including the stew."

Danny's grandmother had actually done the same thing. But he wasn't about to encourage Boston, who'd find some way to make another joke out of it.

"Here we go," said the pilot, tipping the helicopter downward.

Danny and Garcia jumped from the helicopter just as it set down on the wide highway. They ran in opposite directions, scouting the dark terrain around them with their helmet sensors. Once they were sure the area was clear, Danny had Boston and Jennifer unstrap the small LADS vehicle kit from the side of the helicopter. The helicopter cleared out to scout the area as they began inflating the lighter-than-air vehicle.

"Cap, got something moving down off the road," said Garcia.

Danny spun around and ran down the highway. The long day and steamy weather were starting to take their toll, and he was huffing before Garcia came into view, crouched at the side and looking down a long curve.

"Too far away to get a good view," said Garcia, pointing along the ravine. "Two bodies, but I can't tell if they're people or what."

Even at maximum magnification, Danny couldn't see anything.

"Whiplash team to Quick Bird, I want you to stay clear of the area south of us," Danny told the helicopter pilot. "We have something moving. I'm going to get the Flighthawk to take a look."

Aboard EB-52 *Indianapolis* (*"Indy"*), over Brunei 2312

Lieutenant Kirk "Starship" Andrews acknowledged the request from Captain Freah for a close-up of the area to the southeast of the LADS deployment team and turned his Flighthawk back in that direction.

Lieutenant James "Kick" Colby sat next to him on the Flighthawk deck of the *Indy,* controlling Hawk Four. Kick had just taken his plane up for a refuel, leaving Starship to handle the reconnaissance request on his own.

Not that he didn't prefer it that way.

The U/MF-3 slid through five thousand feet, descending toward a blur of vegetation. Starship rode the plane over the right shoulder of the road for about a mile and a half, then started his turn to bank in the direction of the area Whiplash had pointed out. The sensors in the belly of the Flighthawk scoured the ground as he flew; the computer gave him two frozen frames as he pulled up.

"Hawk Three to Whiplash ground team. Captain, we got some blurs on that pass. Computer ID'd two people, but there may be more. I'm taking another run. I'll feed you the video from the sensors," he added, reaching with his left hand to the one-switch toggle that allowed the data to flow through the Dreamland network. "Thick canopy," he added, meaning that the trees and vegetation would limit the sensors' ability to see.

"Whiplash leader," acknowledged Danny.

Starship banked Hawk Three well south of the target area and lined up again, practically walking over the area. He came around and found himself barely fifty feet higher than the rock outcropping on the opposite end of the highway. He'd been so intent on flying the airplane that he was surprised when Danny asked if he could give him another view of the troops.

"Sorry Whiplash, I lost that," he told the captain on the ground.

"Take another run," said Danny. "I couldn't tell if they were rebels or regular troops."

Starship banked around and began another pass. As he did, he got two warnings from the computer—one because he was drifting too far from the Megafortress to control the Flighthawk properly, and the other because he was into his fuel reserves.

"I can manage one more pass," he told Danny, "but then I have to refuel. Hawk Four is en route to take over."

"Give me a good one then."

Near Labi, southern Brunei
2318

"I can't tell who they are," Danny told Garcia after the third pass failed to show anything definitive. "We're just going to have to wait and see if they get close."

"Yeah," said Garcia.

Danny ran back to Jennifer and Boston. They had not yet begun to inflate the blimp.

"We have some people moving up about a mile and a half from here, in the jungle," he told them. "We can't tell if they're good guys or bad guys. How long is it going to take to get that bag up in the air?"

"Another five minutes before we can start the inflation," said Jennifer. "Then about ten minutes on top of that."

Once inflated and launched, it would take the blimp at least ten minutes to climb up and out of easy range. The engine was fairly quiet, but could be heard when the craft was at ground level.

"All right," Danny told her. "Move as quickly as you can. "Boston, you're the last line of defense here. Garcia and I are going to go down into the jungle off the road. This way if that patrol comes up in your direction we can cut them off before they get close enough to do any damage. We'll hold them off long enough to get the LADS vehicle launched and you guys out."

"We're not leaving without you," said Jennifer.

"Yeah, Captain, no way."

"It won't come to that," said Danny, turning and running back to Garcia.

Aboard EB-52 *Indianapolis* ("*Indy*"), over Brunei
2320

Kick finished the refuel and ducked away from the Megafortress, gliding back to the southwest. He could see the Quick Bird that had deposited the LADS team off on his right as he descended toward the jungle to update the Whiplash people on the situation.

"Hawk Four to Whiplash leader. Looking for you," said Kick, trying to orient himself. He banked and got the road on his right. He had two people at the top of his screen—the LADS team, getting ready to inflate the lighter-than-air vehicle.

The response from the ground was garbled and partly overrun as Major Alou gave an update on *Indy*'s position, flying north so it could cover one of the government's strongholds as well as the Whiplash operation. Kick double-checked his Flighthawk's position to confirm for Alou that he would remain in communication range. He lost his bearings again; as he banked he temporarily lost sight of the road. He came westward and realized he was completely disoriented, now nearly two miles south of the team's position. He found the road again and flew along it, following the curve back in the direction of the LADS unit, which had just activated a radio beacon as part of its start-up.

Some figures moved through the brush a few hundred yards south of the launch point.

The soldiers threatening the team.

His heart thumped as he put the Flighthawk into a wide turn so he could position himself for a run back at the enemy. The Flighthawk cut a lollipop in the sky, its altitude dropping as he came around.

"I have two, three figures, in the jungle, near the road, very close to the team, in a threatening position," he said. "Can't see them too well."

"Make sure they're not our guys," said Starship over the plane's interphone circuit.

"No shit." He clicked back into the Dreamland channel. "Ground, we got somebody just about on top of your guys."

"Where?"

"Northwest." Kick activated his weapons screen and pushed his nose down, running toward the road area in a diagonal from the northeast. Something moved on the left but he was going too fast to get a view, much less fire; he cursed and pulled off, try-ing to wing back and get another angle from the south. The geometry just wouldn't work and he cursed himself again as he came out of the turn far too fast. He could feel his chest starting to pump with his quick, shallow breaths, and tried to force him-self to breathe more slowly.

Zen had told him that the trick to flying the small aircraft in combat was to relax and keep your adrenaline level down. It was only by remaining relatively calm that you could process the information being given to you, and punch the right buttons.

"Let the computer do the frenetic stuff," Zen had advised. *"You're like the CEO, checking off the options."*

"Northwest?" asked Danny on the ground.

"Looking at them—I have one blur. They're in range of your people."

He brought the Flighthawk around, putting the road on his left wing. He couldn't see anything for a moment. Finally he got a target. His heart jumped, and his body moved reflexively to nail down the targeting pipper.

The computer didn't let him. In the next second he realized he was looking at the Whiplash team. Fortunately, the signals from the smart helmets had registered in the computer system and the safeties wouldn't have permitted him to fire without an override.

If I'd been piloting an A-10A, Kick thought to himself, I might have splashed my own guys.

Shit.

"Hawk Four to ground team. All right, I have it all sorted out now. There are five, six men, uh, three hundred yards from where you are." Even though he hadn't done anything wrong, Kick's hand began to tremble. "I can take them out."

"Negative," responded Danny. "Hold off. We're still not sure if they're friendly or not. Just hold your position."

"Yes, sir," he said, banking around.

Near Labi, southern Brunei
2330

Danny studied the blurry infrared in the left-hand side of his helmet's visor, still trying to figure out if the people coming toward him were terrorists or government troops on patrol.

Since they were off the road, was it a reasonable assumption that they were terrorists?

"Getting closer, Captain," said Garcia, who was crouched about ten yards to his left.

"Can you see their weapons?"

"I can't tell."

"How we doing back there, Boston?"

"Two more minutes. We're doing the pre-launch countdown while we're still inflating. This girl's a whiz."

"Good."

"Two hundred yards," said Garcia. "They heard the Flight-hawk that time—they stopped when it came around."

"Hawk Four, this is Freah. Can you take a really loud pass at them?"

"Not sure what you mean, Captain."

"I'm trying to get more time. When you cross overhead they

stop. If they hear you again, we'll get the last few seconds we need to launch the blimp."

"Uh, I'll give it my best. You want me to fire my cannon?"

"Negative for now."

Danny could hear the Flighthawk come overhead. Sure enough, the patrol stopped.

"We're launched," said Boston. "I'm setting out the radar disrupters right now."

The disrupters were small, backpack-sized units that jammed radars in the vicinity of the blimp.

"Garcia, let's move back up toward the road," said Danny. "Swing up through that gully to your left."

He waited until his sergeant had reached it before he started up himself. "We need another pass, Flighthawk."

"Hawk Four."

Danny moved slowly, climbing over several tree trunks as the Flighthawk took another run. His foot slid down into the muck as he got over the last tree; as he leaned back and pulled his leg out he heard a shout.

"Shit," said someone over the Dreamland circuit.

Then the jungle lit up with gunfire.

JENNIFER TAPPED THE ARROW KEYS ON THE LAPTOP, STEER-ing the small airship to the north, away from the gunfire. She had the power set low so it would be very quiet; unfortunately, that made its speed slower than a person walking.

As the bullets continued to fly, she moved the throttle command to max. Even so, the blimp couldn't move very quickly; it walked rather than ran away.

"Come on," said Boston, pushing on her shoulder. "Let's get across the road to some cover."

"I can't leave the unit right now," said Jennifer.

"I'll carry the transmitter," said Boston. He started to reach for the antenna, which looked like a small satellite dish with a rectangular collection of tubes at the center.

"No," she told him, grabbing him. "It's not meant to be portable. I don't know what'll happen if we change the transmitting location. The blimp has to be above a thousand feet before it'll go on auto-guide."

"Well I know what'll happen if we get shot," said Boston.

"We're not going to get shot. Danny has it under control."

"He's not Superman," said Boston, but he let go of the antenna and instead went and crouched between her and the area that the firing was coming from.

Aboard EB-52 *Indianapolis* ("*Indy*"), over Brunei
2335

Starship came off the refuel early and winged back toward the Whiplash team. The ground action was a mishmash, and while he had a general idea of what was going on, the two sides were so close together it was difficult to figure out exactly who was who.

"Get up to the highway and we'll pepper the tree line," Kick told the ground team.

Starship didn't catch the acknowledgment—he was too busy ducking out of the way of the blimp as it rose to the north of the team. He banked back and came down just over the road, identifying the four members of the Whiplash ground unit and turning his nose just to the side of the highway as he lit his cannon. His forward air speed dropped and he had to break off; as he did there was a flash on the ground and he got a warning that a shoulder-launched SAM had been fired. He unleashed decoy flares and tightened his turn. The missile sniffed one of the flares and flew north, exploding about three-quarters of a mile away.

Near Labi, southern Brunei
2340

Danny and Garcia pulled back toward the blimp launch point as a second Flighthawk made a run at the enemy position, splashing it with cannonfire.

"Yo, get into the trees on the other side," Danny yelled as he ran toward them.

"We're almost ready," replied Jennifer. "I'll be able to transfer control to the central unit in another minute or two."

"Put it in auto mode," said Danny.

"I can't until it's at a thousand feet."

"Just let it go."

"Sixty seconds," protested the scientist.

"Boston," said Danny. "Move her."

"Um, yes, sir, if you say so."

The sergeant physically picked up the scientist and began dragging her off the road.

"EB-52 *Indianapolis* to Whiplash leader," said Major Alou. "Danny, if you can put more distance between you and them I can launch a five-hundred-pound bomb."

"We're working on it," said Danny. "We're going to go off the road to the northeast and get across that ravine there."

But as they started, gunfire raked the highway and the ridge. The guerillas were now on both sides of the road; Danny and his small band retreated along the pavement. Reinforcements were coming up from the southwest; another twenty had made it to the road about a mile and a half away and were trotting toward them. If the nearby group managed to bog them down, the Whiplashers might be overrun.

"I don't know if we're going to make it to that ravine," Danny told Alou.

"Acknowledged. Hold on," added Alou.

Danny's helmet included a laser-dot pointer showing where his MP5 was aimed. He fired as three figures came up the road, hitting one and sending the others scurrying back.

"Danny, the Brunei air force is two minutes from your location," said Alou. "They have napalm and want to know if they can help out."

"Sounds like a great idea if you can get them into the right location," Danny told him. "Maybe we can sneak the helicopter in at the same time."

"That's what I was thinking."

In the air, approaching Labi
2344

McKenna spotted the tail end of the little Flighthawk three hundred yards to her left as she approached the target area. The moonlight wasn't strong enough for her to see more than a smudge, but the smudge was enough to get her on course.

"You see that?" she asked Captain Seyed, who was flying as her wingman.

"Yes, ma'am."

"All right. Follow him into the target. Once the flare ignites I'll come in and give them a good thrashing."

Lacking high-tech night-vision gear and GPS locators, McKenna had fallen back on a strategy dating to World War II. Seyed, following the Flighthawk to the area where the American unit was under fire, launched a large parachute flare called an LUU-2 just as he passed overhead. Descending by parachute, the flare illuminated the darkness, a giant candle that descended slowly because of the heat of the flame. An old method—but highly effective.

McKenna swooped downward, nose at a thirty-degree angle as she cleared the narrow roadway. She saw four or five guerillas ducking behind the tree line, pushed them into her bomb screen, and dropped two of the napalm canisters. The bombs—which were probably nearly as old as her tactics—dropped down and ignited. McKenna didn't stop to admire her handiwork; as soon as she pulled up she spun the Dragonfly back and dumped two 250-pound bombs behind the conflagration. Her right wing sagged as she started to recover; she'd been peppered with gunfire and one or more of the bullets had damaged the ailerons, elevator, and her rudder. She had to fight a bit, arm wrestling the wind gods to get the plane level.

"Commander, you're on fire," said Seyed.

Shit, thought McKenna. She started to climb to the north, trying to both get away from the terrorists and to get her plane high enough to bail out if she had to.

The helicopter, meanwhile, had swooped in about a half-mile away to pick up the Whiplash ground team. As she passed by it, she saw the shadow of the mountain rising quickly in front of her. McKenna pulled the stick back and slapped the throttle against the last stop, but the Dragonfly wouldn't put her nose up. Realizing she wasn't going to clear, she muscled the aircraft right. The controls began to buck, the stick jerking in her hand as if an elephant were jumping up and down on the control cables. McKenna glanced at the instrument panel and saw one of the oil pressure gauges spinning, as if it had decided to unscrew itself from the panel.

"Listen, Seyed, I don't know that I'm going to make it very far from here," she told her wingman.

"You're on fire!"

"I don't doubt it," she said as another mountain loomed ahead.

DANNY COULD SEE THE AIRCRAFT FLAMING IN THE SKY AS their helicopter took off.

"We better follow her," he told the pilot. "See if we can pick her up."

STARSHIP WATCHED AS THE FRONT OF THE DRAGONFLY CAME apart. It didn't look like an explosion—it was more like a sneeze and then a disintegration, with the plane separating into large chunks. He steadied the Flighthawk and waited, watching the sky nearby.

"Got a chute!" he said finally. "Got a chute. Good chute. I'll feed you a GPS coordinate."

FOR ALL HER EXPERIENCE, MCKENNA HAD NEVER ACTUALLY hit the silk from the pilot's seat. She had taken a grand total of six jumps for training purposes, including two jumps at night; none compared in any way to this.

The seat pushed her out of the doomed plane with the loudest sound she had ever heard in her life, except for the time her cousin exploded a cherry bomb in her aunt's bathroom. She flew straight into the darkness, soaring into the black night on what seemed like an unending trip. And then, just as she thought she'd reach orbit, something grabbed the top of her chest and yanked her backward, pulling her along as if from the back of a freight train.

Whoa, she thought. This might be pretty cool if it weren't so dark and weird.

Somewhere in the back corner of her brain was a long lecture on the intricacies of a night-time ejection, instructions on the importance of checking the chute to make sure it had opened properly, tips on controlling the descent, some pointers on how to hold your body and the pros and cons of giving yourself a pep talk as you fell. But McKenna's brain cells were so awash in the adrenaline of the moment that they didn't have the patience to search for any of that information. She felt herself tipping forward and to the right; somehow she managed to get her body situated perpendicular to the ground just as a large shadow came up to meet her. She tried to get her legs ready to hit the ground. As she did, something smacked her from behind and she lurched to the right—she was falling into a large tree. McKenna grabbed for a branch, tumbling and twisting around as she skidded downward. When she finally stopped she was hanging upside down, suspended several feet from the ground. Her arms and face burned with the scrapes.

"Well, that was fun," she said to herself, reaching for her knife.

THE LADS GOT A GOOD IMAGE OF THE PARACHUTE TWISTED around the top of the trees, beaming it back through the Dreamland network and down via satellite to Danny's smart helmet. Jennifer had stalled just long enough to get the blimp operational, and while Danny felt he couldn't condone the fact that she had exposed herself to the bullets, he was grateful for the result. He spotted a clearing a hundred or so yards from the trees, up a rocky slope.

"There's a spot where you can put us down over there," Danny told the pilot, pointing to the clearing.

"Terrain's rough back to that tree," said the pilot. "If you have to take her out with a stretcher you're going to have a hell of a time."

"Maybe we can take her out somewhere else," said Danny. "If we go east a little."

They looped around the area, looking for a better spot. There didn't appear to be one, at least not nearby.

"Let's see what the situation is," said Danny. "We'll just have to work it out on the ground."

The helicopter tipped toward the trees, the pilot weaving back toward the clearing. He eased the Quick Bird into a hover about twelve feet from the ground and Danny and Boston quick-roped down.

The slope was more severe than Danny had thought from the air, and he slipped against one of the rocks before he'd taken more than a step. He tumbled down, bouncing against a boulder.

A pair of hands grabbed him from behind and helped him to his feet.

"That little helicopter's going to carry all three of us?" asked a woman, shouting at his face.

Danny flipped up the visor on his helmet. "You're McKenna?"

"Brunei Air Force Air Commodore McKenna, thank you very much. You know, you look like a *Star Wars* space trooper in that armor. Very impressive." She put her hands on her hips. "So, we getting out of here or what?"

Southeastern Brunei
Exact location and time unknown

By the time the truck finally stopped it had been nighttime for hours and Mack had fallen into a fitful sleep. The guards shook him awake, unlocking the chain that had kept him attached to the truck bed and prodding him out. His neck and the back of his head were sore, the muscles mangled by the awkward posture of his body.

They put a blindfold on him, and then removed the manacles from his hands. Mack, cold and stiff, lost his balance as he was led off the truck and fell against one of his captors. He felt, or thought he felt, the metal of a pistol near his side, but before he could grab for it he was yanked to his feet.

"Hey!" he said. "Don't push. I can't see where the hell I'm going. And my legs are all screwed up."

A set of hands took him by the shoulders and steered him to the right. Mack's feet kicked against some stones and he nearly tripped again. Another hand pushed him from the left side; he found himself walking over a smooth path. After twenty paces he was stopped. He heard a lock being turned and then felt something, probably a rifle barrel, prodding his legs to step upward. He made it up some steps and into a building, where he was led down a hallway. His captors left him in the middle of a room; Mack waited a few seconds before reaching for his blindfold and peeking out.

The room had a small mattress on the floor near the corner.

There was a window at the left side of the room, covered with a simple curtain.

Mack slipped back to the door, sidling next to it to listen; there were people in the hallway, talking softly. He walked quietly back across the room to the window; he couldn't see anything through it. He tried tugging at it to see if it would open; when it didn't give way easily he gave up for the moment and sat down on the mat.

Mack rubbed at his wrists where the manacles had been, then began kneading the back of his neck, trying to work out some of the cramps. When he heard the truck drive off, he got back up and went back to the door. This time he didn't hear anything, and so he put his hand on the doorknob and slowly twisted it open. His heart began thumping wildly. He sensed that his captors had gone off and left him. Cracking open the door, he peeked out but saw no one in the hall.

Mack pulled open the door and took a step out of the room—only to find an AK47 in his face.

A man shouted at him in Malaysian or some other language. Mack couldn't decipher the words but the intent was pretty clear—he threw his hands out at his side.

"I have to take a leak," he claimed. "Bathroom. Bathroom."

The voice repeated whatever it had said.

"I don't understand."

Once again the words were repeated, this time slow enough for Mack to realize they were English.

"Step outside the room," said the voice in his thick accent, "and you will be shot."

"I have to pee," insisted Mack.

"There is a can in the room for you."

"Gee, thanks," he said, finally retreating.

Aboard *"Penn,"* approaching Malaysian Air Base, north of Meruta
14 October 1997, 0600

Dog borrowed— "shanghaied" was probably more accurate a word—two Air Force Special Tactics Squadron members from a unit in Korea and flew them south to the Philippines to help the Dreamland team set up operations at the secret Malaysian air base near Borneo's southern coast. The men, adept at creating airfields out of strobe lights and chewing gum, parachuted off Dreamland's MC-17 and helped guide the Megafortress in. The airstrip was just barely long enough for the EB-52, but Dog figured the risk was worth it; it would cut nearly two hours off each way as they patrolled from the Philippines but also allowed for rapid response to any developing situation.

And situations were developing. The sultan's army had retaken two posts on the southern border with Malaysia and now seemed in firm control of the southwestern third of the country. Police units in the towns on the northern coast that had not fallen to militants had rallied over the course of the day. A number of telephone and power lines that had been cut had been restored. Loyal forces had won a major battle with guerillas near Kapit, killing over a hundred. Neither LADS nor the patrolling Megafortresses had detected any Malaysian army units assisting the terrorists, and in at least one instance a Malaysian army unit had helped the Brunei police force pursuing a group of rebels over the northeastern border.

On the other hand, the militants had spent the preceding day tightening their grip on the area around the capital. They controlled the shoreline and had appropriated at least two small patrol boats, operating them on the river.

The LADS system provided low-powered radar coverage of much of the kingdom. It also provided video coverage of much of the capital and several major road and waterways, along with the entrance to the harbor and the platform where Whiplash was. Two more units were en route from Dreamland; one was intended for the Malaysian air base, and the other would be used as a roving sentry. Twice as long as the others, the sentry carried better resolution cameras and could be flown higher and faster. It did not, however, include the LED technology that made the others almost impossible to see from the ground.

Dog steadied Penn into her final approach for the runway, fighting the optical illusions that made it appear as if it were two different roads, a ravine, and a set of boulders. The men on the ground had cleared the obstructions and assured him that it was solid concrete covered by paint; Dog focused on the landing cues in his HUD and settled perfectly onto the runway.

"And for our next trick, we land in downtown Las Vegas," joked McNamara, his copilot, as they spotted one of the Special Tactics controllers playing traffic cop near the end of the runway. He had them turn on an apron to an access ramp at the side; from the sky it had appeared to be a pond, though up close the camouflage didn't work nearly as well, making it seem more like an abstract painting by Mark Rothko. The trees bordering the ramp were real enough, as was a collection of jagged rocks; the path was too narrow for the Megafortress and so Dog had to park the plane there.

Dog had picked up a three-man U.S. Army Special Forces team in the Philippines; the men had worked with the Malaysian military in the past and would assist with setting up security, which was to be provided by the local Malaysian forces for the time being.

"All right, let's get the plane squared away and assess the situation," he told the crew and the soldiers below as they shut down the engines. "McNamara, you find out what the status of the C-17 is with our tech people and maintainers while I go talk with the locals. Don't anybody go too far away," he added. "I hear the snakes in the jungle can be pretty vicious."

Kota Kinabalu, Malaysia
0800

Dazhou Ti felt as if the terrace he was standing on had given way and he was now falling toward the sea. The smokestack of the tug that had brought him to the seaside town loomed below, a black whirlpool sucking him toward that abyss.

General Udara had traveled to the seaside town to speak to Dazhou personally: not to berate him for losing the *Barracuda*, but to tell him that the war was over. The sultan was to be allowed to regain his kingdom.

"Impossible," said Dazhou, who had only finished notifying the kin of his dead crewmen an hour before. "Impossible."

"The president has decided," said Udara.

"No. No. My men have died." The general was not a man to argue with, but Dazhou could not help himself. "No," he repeated. "This cannot be. There is so much to be done—the Americans, we can defeat them. They're paper tigers."

"You of all people should know they're not," said Udara. "They proved it in their encounter with your ship. This all helps us in the long run," added the general, trying to remain upbeat. "Because the guerillas will be taken care of by the Americans. Leaving the maggot sultan and his family alone is a small price for ridding ourselves of the fanatics. Kuala Lumpur has spoken," he said. He referred to the central command, not the prime minister, and meant that the matter was closed.

"No," said Dazhou.

Udara's patience was now exhausted. His face flushed, its brownish tint becoming nearly purple with his rage.

"You will accept your orders, Chinaman!" he thundered. "You will do as you are told!"

"My men," Dazhou said. "They must be revenged."

"You will do as you are told. You are lucky, Dazhou, that I remember the contributions you have made, and your own glory under fire. Because otherwise I would pummel you with these two fists."

Their faces were so close that Dazhou felt the heat of the general's rising blood. He knew that the proper action now—no matter what he really intended—was to feign submission, to pretend to be willing to go along with his orders. But he could not control his emotions sufficiently to make an accommodating gesture, even a small one. The best he could do was keep himself from yelling back at the general.

"Do you understand me, Dazhou?" said Udara.

"I have no ship," he managed finally.

The general took a step away. "Then the matter is settled."

Dazhou didn't respond. Udara had not berated him for losing the *Barracuda,* but this was completely in character for the general. Since he had nothing to do with its creation or operations, Udara looked on it as just another weapon, little more than a jeep or armored car that could go to sea.

Kuala Lumpur would have a considerably different view.

Dazhou's options were clear. Either he ran, or he sought revenge.

"Do you understand me?" Udara said, once more master of his emotions.

"I have no ship," Dazhou repeated. "And no men."

Udara nodded grimly. "War is a difficult thing."

Somehow, Dazhou managed to nod, rather than telling the general what he really thought of his easy cliché.

Bandar Seri Begawan (capital of Brunei)
1000

Sahurah's head throbbed constantly, a sharp thump at the top and right side, God's drumbeat calling him to task for his failures.

How could he doubt the wisdom of his teachers?

How could he think that the devil American was as honorable and holy as he?

Sahurah tried to set the questions aside, tried to ignore his transgressions, his many failings. He had to concentrate on his duties. Brothers were streaming into the city, each one willing to do what needed to be done, but each needing to be shown his responsibilities step by step. Sahurah had selected several deputies, but they still turned to him for orders. He had become the most important person in the capital, after the imam.

Success had been incredibly swift; not even in his dreams would Sahurah have thought things would go so well. And yet, when he thought of this, when he saw the obvious sign that Allah had blessed them, his head pounded even more. He wanted—what did he want?

His place in Paradise. Nothing beyond that.

One of his lieutenants, a young man named Dato, appeared at the door and was searched by the two bodyguards who had attached themselves to him since the attack at the airport. Dato had come from near Djakarta, and a slight accent of the poorer districts around the Indonesian city lingered on his tongue when he spoke.

"Fifty more brothers have come to watch the road to the south," said Dato in Malaysian. "We need weapons."

"What about those at the police station?"

"The weapons there have been given out."

"The armory?" asked Sahurah.

"What wasn't blown up by the nonbelievers is so antiquated we have no ammunition for it," explained Dato.

The pain in Sahurah's head subsided as he focused on the

problem. "We can give them trucks, and the supplies taken from Tutong. Deliveries have been promised from our allies. But we cannot wait; send the men while you search for weapons. I would expect a counterattack soon."

Another of Sahurah's men came to the door. This was Paduka, a native of the capital who had proven invaluable in finding sympathetic friends.

"Two pilots," announced Paduka triumphantly. "Including one who worked for Air Defense Minister Smith."

"Who?"

"His name is Captain Yayasan. He's in the hallway."

"Is he a sincere believer?"

"We have spoken many times before today," said Paduka. He told him of an encounter the pilot had had at the start of the offensive when he had feigned cowardice to avoid shooting at a unit of brothers.

"He would have done better to have shot down the other plane," said Sahurah at the end of the story. "Bring him in. Let me talk to him."

"Just him? Or both men?"

"Just him."

Sahurah turned to the table where a map of the area had been laid out. He showed Dato where the brothers were to be deployed. A network of reinforcements had to be established. They had machine-guns mounted in several pickup trucks; they could bring firepower within a few minutes if attacked.

They lacked heavy weapons; Sahurah was hardly a military strategist, but he understood that this was a great weakness.

Paduka and the pilot Yayasan stood silently as they finished. Sahurah turned to them. Yayasan was a short man, no taller than five-three; his face had sharp, tight angles.

"You believe?" Sahurah asked.

"I—I do," said Yayasan.

The hesitation reassured Sahurah. He glanced at the pilot's hands. His fingers moved as if they were on fire.

Sahurah recognized that the man would crumble under pressure, and that as much as his faith may have accounted for his decision not to fire on the brothers the other day. He could be used, but very carefully.

"Could you teach the other pilots how to fly the large American plane?"

"My lord, of course."

The top of Sahurah's head pummeled him. "I am not a lord. I am nothing but a servant. Address me as 'Commander'."

"Pardons, Commander." The pilot's fingers vibrated ever more violently.

"What do we need?" asked Sahurah.

"I would have to examine the aircraft, Commander."

Sahurah nodded, then looked at Paduka. "There is a man at the terminal, he piloted a 747. He told me last night he would be able to fly the large aircraft. Yayasan will teach him. And the other man you found."

"Yes, Commander."

The guards at the door snapped to attention. Sahurah turned to see the imam and the Saudi. An entourage of bodyguards and others flooded into the room behind them. Though the room was fair-sized, it now seemed crowded.

"Imam," he said, bowing his head.

The imam gave him a tired smile and touched his shoulder. "Sahurah, my young friend, you have done well."

Sahurah felt himself blush. "The Americans have formed an alliance with the Malaysians," said the Saudi, speaking in Arabic. "It was not unexpected. But now will come the test."

Sahurah turned to him. This was the first time that the older man had addressed him directly. His voice seemed thin, almost frail, and yet his eyes were steely. Their gaze held Sahurah, and for a moment his pain retreated.

"We will triumph because Allah is on our side," said Sahurah. "It is a holy war, and our cause is just."

The Saudi said nothing. He did not smile, and his eyes did not blink.

This is what faith looks like, Sahurah thought. These are Allah's eyes, shining through his holy servant. If only I were worthy of such a gaze.

The imam tapped his shoulder gently. "Prepare then, son," he said. "Prepare well."

Sahurah bowed, and for a moment everything else in the world receded. When he put his head back up, the imam and the Saudi, along with their entourage, had gone.

Southeastern Brunei
Exact location and time unknown

One thing he had to say for captivity: it sure made him hungry. Mack had eaten all of the slop they'd given him for breakfast—or lunch or dinner, whatever meal it was.

He could tell from the window that it was daytime outside, but he'd fallen asleep earlier and couldn't be sure how long he'd slept. The window had been nailed shut from the outside; now that there was light he could see one of the nails at the very top where it had come through the casing. The glass panes and wood between them would undoubtedly give way if he hit them hard enough. But the sound would undoubtedly alert the guard near his door, and there was no telling how many others were posted around on the outside. He couldn't see anything out the window except for vegetation.

Paper covered the walls, which were constructed of wooden boards nailed up against studs. The paper had buckled near the mat that served as his bed. The bubble ran along one of the boards, as if the air had squeezed in from the outside. Mack glanced at it several times as he walked back and forth, trying to come up with a plan to escape. Finally he went to the wall and poked at it with his finger. The material, though thick with paint, was pretty brittle, and he was able to punch a slight hole by jabbing with his thumb. He started tearing the paper, and exposed a jagged strip about six inches wide and two feet long, where two of the boards were joined together. A bit of sunlight poked through at the corner.

If he had a crowbar, or something he could use for one, he thought he'd be able to dismantle the panels easily. Mack stepped back from the wall, reexamining the room for something he could use as a tool, though he'd been over every inch earlier. He flipped the mat and ran his hands over the material, thinking there might be a spring inside.

Just as he concluded there were none, the door opened. Mack looked up from his knees at the large man who came in. The man, dressed in loose-fitting white pants and a long white tunic, seemed perplexed; Mack, on his knees, realized that the militant thought he had found him praying.

"What?" Mack snapped.

The man said something he couldn't understand, then glanced around the room. He finally spied what he was looking for: the piss bucket. He walked to the corner and took it.

Mack got up, walking slowly to the doorway. A guard stood just outside; he had an AK47 in his hand. Unlike the man who had come for the can, he was short, and in Mack's opinion easily overpowered. As Mack stared at him the idea of rushing the man began to percolate in his brain. His adrenaline began screaming at him, blood and hormones rushing together.

Then he heard more footsteps. The man who had taken the can returned with it, empty. He glanced at him but said nothing.

My chance, thought Mack. Rush the kid and grab for the gun.

But by the time the idea formed in his head the man was closing the door.

Aboard *"Indy,"* approaching Malaysian Air Base 1100

Breanna swung the EB-52 over the southeastern tip of Borneo, checking her location as she got ready to land at the scratch air base. With the rest of the crew starting to drag after a long patrol and return to the Philippines to refuel, Bree had done almost all the piloting.

"Pretty country," said Major Alou.

"Yeah. It's paradise down there, I'll tell you," she said. "If you ignore the madmen with the guns."

She hit the last waypoint and turned, spotting the airport in her windscreen. The other EB-52 and the C-17 that had brought the tech people sat at the far end of the strip. The airfield was narrow and the camouflage a bit disorienting, but Breanna had landed under much worse conditions; the wheels didn't even chirp as she touched down.

"Hey, stranger," said her husband when she came down the ladder ten minutes later.

"Hey," she said. She leaned over and grabbed him, felt his strong arms clutching her back.

"I missed you," he whispered.

"I missed you, too."

She felt tears coming to her eyes, then running down her

cheeks. She pressed her head against the side of his head for another few seconds, then slowly, reluctantly, straightened.

"Boring flight?" asked Zen.

"Boring flight."

"Good," he told her. "So I hear you're first officer now."

"Don't rub it in, Zen."

"Want to see our digs?"

"Nice?"

"Sure," said her husband, wheeling himself away from the plane. "If you like concrete and spit."

THE MALAYSIAN COMMANDER ASSURED DOG THAT HIS twelve men were more than enough to secure the base. The terrorists in the area had fled a month before.

"You think he's right about the terrorists?" Dog asked the Special Forces soldiers when they left the Malaysian commander's post.

"I doubt it," said one of the soldiers. "The Malaysians were always underestimating them."

"You guys better look over the defenses and see what you need to beef them up," said Dog. He paused, watching as a Hummer descended from the MC-17 with the Dreamland trailer in tow. The MC-17 was to take off as soon as it was unloaded, flying back to the Philippines for supplies. And Dog had plans for the Hummer.

"That trailer will be our headquarters," Dog told the SF men. "Make a list of what you need and we'll try to get it."

"Battalion of troops wouldn't be bad," said one of the sergeants, Tommy Lang.

"If you can find one, let me know," said Dog.

He walked over to Zen, who was overseeing the deployment of the command trailer. "How we looking?"

"Should be up and running in a few minutes," said Zen. "Can't wait for the AC."

"Bree okay?"

"She went to look for a shower," said Zen. "I tried to warn her."

Dog smirked. "I have to go down to the village south of here and meet the lieutenant governor for the area. He's expecting me sometime today and I'd like to get that over with. The Malaysian commander said we need to truck more water in no later than tomorrow. Hold down the fort while I'm gone."

"I'll do my best," said Zen, swiveling his wheelchair around momentarily. Dog realized he'd gotten so used to Zen being in the wheelchair that he now simply took it for granted, not even considering whether it might be a factor in his doing his job.

"You're not going by yourself, are you?" Lang asked him.

Dog shrugged. "I don't think I need a translator."

"Two of us ought to go for security," said another of the SF sergeants.

"Fine with me, as long as one of you stays and figures out what we need for security here," said Dog, heading for the Hummer.

THE CAPITAL OF THE TINY REGION WAS A SMALL VILLAGE FIVE miles from the base. The road through the jungle was paved and easy to travel. Once they reached the village, however, they found that the main street was no wider than a sidewalk back home; they had to leave the Humvee near a pack of small houses and walk in on foot. Dog and the two soldiers got about ten feet before they were surrounded by a mob of children. The Army men had come prepared—they pulled pieces of candy from their pockets, making sure the kids got a good look at them before tossing them to the side. But there were so many children that the way remained clogged.

Dog tried to push them aside as gently as possible. One kid held onto his leg, and the only way to dislodge him was to pick him up. This actually helped clear the way for some reason, the other kids stepping back to get a better glimpse of their friends in the stranger's arms.

"Here we go, Colonel," said one of the sergeants, pointing to a white-washed three-story building made of masonry block. It had no sign but it was clearly the most substantial building on the block.

Dog made it to the threshold, still holding the child. He turned around awkwardly, then settled the tyke on the ground.

"Sheesh," he said.

"Yeah," said Sergeant Lang. "Almost enough to make you get a vasectomy."

Dog roared with laughter.

The meeting lasted only a few minutes. Dog thanked the Malaysian region's lieutenant governor with some stock phrases a State Department official had suggested. The Malaysian, who spoke impeccable English, assured him that his country was a "steadfast ally" and would provide any hospitality possible.

"A truckload of water would be greatly appreciated," said Dog, adding that the Malaysian base commander had said the arrangements were already in place.

The lieutenant governor knew about this and said it would be arranged. And then he suggested that they have something to eat. This could not be refused without giving offense, and Dog and the soldiers went inside to an office that had been hastily made over into an impromptu banquet hall.

The soldiers were familiar with the local cuisine. Even better, they were extremely hungry, and while his rank demanded that Dog take the first bite, he had no trouble letting his companions consume most of the food. They raved about the satay; Dog nodded and picked strategically at his plate, making sure to sample and praise everything while ingesting as little as possible.

After forty-five minutes of lunch, he used another State Department supplied formula to excuse himself. The Malaysian protested; he apologized and excused himself again; they protested once more, though less profusely, and Dog repeated the formula. The procedure took ten whole minutes to complete. Finally outside, he and his two escorts made it about halfway up the block before the children appeared again. Once more Dog found his way blocked by a two-year-old. He hoisted the kid to his chest, then scooped up another and made it to the Humvee.

"You could run for mayor, Colonel," said Lang as they eased the Hummer back onto the highway.

"Yeah."

"You got kids?" asked the other soldier, who was driving.

Dog laughed. "Yeah. One. She's a captain in the Air Force. Matter of fact, she should be on the ground back at our little base by now."

The sergeant did a double take. Dog decided that he would recommend the man for a decoration for his diplomatic tact.

"I got a two-year-old," said the sergeant. "Smartest little kid you ever saw."

"I'll bet," said Dog.

"Then he sure can't be related to you, huh?" said Lang.

"Always busting my chops," said the soldier.

As he spoke, the Humvee ran over a mine that had been planted in the road. It exploded under the left front wheel, killing the driver and throwing Dog and the other sergeant out of the vehicle into the brush beyond the shoulder of the highway.

Off the coast of Brunei
1200

Danny Freah hunched over the table in the first room of the oil platform building, looking down at the satellite photos of Brunei Airport spread on its surface. The civilian portion of the airport sat at the right; the military base was beyond, to the left. At the very bottom of the map was a narrow access ramp through a boggy area which led to a trio of large hangars.

The hangars were owned by His Royal Highness Pehin bin Awg; he used them to house his impeccable collection of Cold War aircraft, including the MiG-19 that Brunei Air Commodore McKenna wanted to commandeer.

"That section of the airport is completely isolated," McKenna told him. "There's a fuel truck in the hangar on the extreme left; we blow the lock, hot-wire the truck, and we're in business."

Danny got up and went over to the table where the LADS field control units were set up. Blimp Four was directly over the airport; the three hangars were unguarded and in fact there were no more than a handful of people at the airport.

"Drop me off, I take the MiG," said McKenna. "Simple as one-two-three."

"Risky operation to retrieve one aircraft," Danny said.

"Well, I'd take more if I could." She laughed and hooked her thumbs into her belt loops, looking a bit like a Canadian cowboy. "You find me some more pilots. I've flown that MiG-19, though, and I know I can operate it off my strip. As long as the parachute at the rear works."

"What else is in there?"

"A very nice but temperamental F-86, a large Tu-16 Badger C—Mack Smith's claim to fame—and a Hawker Hunter. I don't know what model Hunter it is, but it dates from the fifties. Everything else he has doesn't fly, at least not reliably."

"I'd rather blow them up than steal them."

"Seems like a waste of good hardware," she told him. "None of the planes are going anywhere without good pilots. And trust me, there aren't too many of them on the island. But go ahead—blow them up right after I take the MiG."

"How are you going to maintain the MiG if you take it?"

"Two of bin Awg's men are back at my base. Think of it this way, Captain: You say you can't spare either of your helicopters to transport me back to my airbase at least until tomorrow night. This way, not only do I get back to my base, but you take out a potential threat. You trash the hangars and they'll be out of business."

"I can order an air strike by the Megafortress," said Danny. "Less risky."

"Where's the fun in that?"

Danny frowned at her. "This isn't fun and games."

"Yeah, no shit," she said. "Look, taking that plane out of there helps everybody and it's easier than hell. I see by your blimp video thing no one's around. The approach is isolated from the rest of the airport—it'll be bodaciously easier than what it took for you to launch that bag of air down south."

"I don't know."

"If you don't help me do it, I'll swim ashore and find my own way to the hangar."

"Hey, Cap," said Bison, monitoring the LADS images. "We got movement going into the airport. One vehicle. No—two, a car and a fuel truck."

"They heading toward the Megafortress or the civilian plane?"

Bison waited a second, watching. "Looks like the Megafortress."

North of Meruta
1209

As Dog started to get up from the dirt he smacked his head against the side of a tree or a rock and rebounded to the side, rolling into a thick clump of brush. He pulled his head back, got his arms under him, and looked up, disoriented and not completely sure what the hell was going on. Something fell against him, a green blur—it was one of the Special Forces soldiers, scrambling back toward the road. Dog pushed after him, then threw himself down as an automatic weapon began popping somewhere to the right. The SF soldier did the same; Dog crawled up next to him and saw that the soldier had recovered his rifle, a small, lightweight version of the M16 favored by special operations troops and known as the M4.

"Got at least two shooters, up over there," said the soldier. It was Lang. He pointed to the right. "Must've planted some sort of mine in the road, detonated it when we got close."

The Humvee, its front end torn up, sat upside down on the opposite shoulder. One of its tires had been ripped off by the impact and landed in the middle of the road.

"Where's your partner?" Dog asked.

"Don't know."

A burst of bullets slashed through the vegetation. Dog took out his Beretta, but neither he nor Lang fired; it wasn't clear where the gunners were.

"You cover me while I go to the truck," said Dog.

Lang started to object, but to Dog it was a no-brainer.

"I'd guess you're a better shot with that gun than I'll ever dream of being," he explained. "If I can get over there and get our radio, we can get all sorts of help. Otherwise those assholes'll pick us off eventually."

"Yeah, okay, that makes sense," said Lang. "You wait until I lay down some fire, okay? When I yell 'go,' you just scoot right across. Save your pistol until you have a damn close target."

"Will do."

The soldier crawled forward, then fired a short burst, which was immediately answered by at least two enemy soldiers, who fired long, poorly aimed bursts from their weapons, draining their magazines. Lang held his fire until the shooting died down. When it did, he jumped up, shouted "Go!" and began blasting the area where the gunfire had come from.

Dog threw himself toward the Humvee, leaping headlong across the road. He ran several miles every day, but the five or six yards he ran now felt like a marathon. By the time Dog slid down behind the wrecked Humvee, he was out of breath. He rolled onto his belly and crawled along the side of the truck, watching the vegetation on his left.

The driver's body had been pitched in the tall grass just at the edge of the shoulder. Dog crawled over to him. As soon as he got there he realized the man was dead; his leg had been sheered off and his left arm was a blackened stub. Dog turned away, pushing back to the truck as more gunfire erupted.

The SF men had carried an A/PSC-5 (V), a lightweight but very powerful radio that could use both satellite and UHF frequencies. Dog hunted for it but couldn't find it in the jumble of the truck. He did see his pack, however. Besides extra ammunition for his pistol, a survival knife, and a small first-air kit, he had a PRC-90 radio there, an old emergency radio from his flight gear that he habitually carried as a backup.

The pack was wedged against the crushed windshield, next to an M4 rifle. Dog pushed in through the side of the truck, making his way in like a gopher exploring a new hole. As he reached for the pack he saw that his hand was covered with blood; three long, jagged scrapes had been torn along the flesh. He grasped the bag, expecting to have to fight to free it. But it came out easily, and so did the gun. He searched once more for the Special Forces' radio but couldn't find it. He got out of the truck and looked around the nearby jungle but saw nothing; finally he went back to the vehicle to look again. As he did, the Humvee began to shake and he heard gunfire in the distance.

They must have some sort of damn mortar in the hills that they're firing nearby, Dog thought, not realizing at first that the vehicle was shaking because it was being pummeled by bullets. By the time he finally saw he was the target, he was out of the truck and in the shallow ravine. Dog pulled the M4 up, hunched over it, and put his finger on the trigger, aiming in the direction of the gunfire. He braced himself and pulled the trigger, but nothing happened. He looked down at the gun, made sure it was loaded, and then looked at his hand, double-checking to make sure he had his finger positioned against the trigger. But still nothing happened when he tried to fire.

Dog stuck the barrel of the rifle into his pack, took out his pistol, then crawled forward along the side of the road. The enemy gunfire had stopped, but Lang waved at him to stay there from across the road. Dog scouted the area for the soldiers' radio before scrambling back behind the Hummer, where he took the PRC-90 radio from the pack.

While the PRC-90 was still used by some aircrews, it had been superseded by newer models long ago and had a number of drawbacks as a general-purpose radio, not the least of which in this case was its limited range. It had an auto-beacon mode which sent out special distress signals, as well as a voice mode, but it could only communicate effectively with another radio in line-of-sight, and given the terrain there was no hope of being able to contact the Dreamland Command trailer directly. But Dog hoped that its signal might be picked up by one of the LADS units or perhaps an aircraft operating nearby. In any event, it was all they had.

Something caught his eye in the brush about thirty yards away. He pushed the radio transmit switch to "auto beacon," then tossed it down and pulled out his Beretta. When the shadow moved again he fired twice; the pistol jumped in his hand and his second bullet hit the leaves high above.

Lang yelled something to him, then started firing. As he did, the Humvee was peppered with gunfire. Dog flattened himself, then pulled his pistol into firing position, both hands properly on the weapon this time. He sighted into the brush, waited until he saw something move, then fired. The recoil didn't seem nearly as bad this time.

"They're all over the place. Get back here!" Lang yelled.

"Good idea," shouted Dog. He slipped the radio into the pack and backed up, still moving on his stomach. As bullets began ripping into the ravine, Dog scooped up his knapsack and ran for it, crossing in two bounds and diving head-first into the bushes. Guns popped everywhere. Dog waited for the burn and catch in his stomach and chest, sure he'd been hit. When they didn't come he turned himself over and crawled on his hands and knees to Lang, pushing the rifle to him and then retrieving the PRC-90.

He made a broadcast. He didn't get a response but he hadn't really expected one; he tried twice more, then put the unit back on beacon. The radio was small enough to slide into the pocket on his bullet proof vest.

"I couldn't find your radio," Dog told the other man. "This unit has pretty limited range. It may be a while before someone hears mine."

"I don't think it matters at the moment," said the soldier. "We're on our own here."

"They'll send somebody for us."

"They don't have anybody to send," said the soldier. "At least not right away."

Dog reached back into his pack for his first-aid kit. "Your face is cut up," he told the soldier. "I have some antibacterial ointment that'll keep it from getting infected."

"Save it for yourself."

"I'm not cut," he said.

The soldier looked at him as if he were out of his mind.

"I'm cut?" said Dog. Then he remembered that he had gashed his hand and arm. He looked down at it, and saw that much of his uniform was torn and covered with blood. "This is nothing," he told Lang.

Despite their predicament, the soldier laughed. "That's the spirit, Colonel. Keep thinking positive."

Southeastern Brunei
Exact location and time unknown

This time, Mack was ready when the door opened. He'd filled the can with urine and was poised near the door, balanced on his haunches and ready to spring.

He hit the big man full in the face with the urine; as the terrorist reeled backward, Mack bolted through the open space, aiming to flatten the man in the hallway who stood guard with the rifle. He caught him in the neck with his fist, then felt himself tumbling across his body, the AK47 in his hands.

How he got it turned around, much less how he managed to aim it or make sure it was ready to fire, Mack didn't know. It seemed to him that one second he was smacking his left shoulder against the wall and the next he was standing over the two dead Muslims, the AK47 smoking. The hallway became a cave filled with smoke. Mack saw the door at the end of the hall in front of him and ran for it, sure that flames were roaring behind him.

Someone shouted as he flew through the door. He turned left and right, firing from his hip and not stopping, never stopping as he ran for the road. As he reached it he heard the pop-pop-pop of an assault rifle behind him; the next second he fell nearly straight down. He threw his hands out, realizing he'd slipped onto an embankment, but there was nothing to grip, and he tumbled wildly down a deep ravine, sliding past a thin strip of vegetation to dirt and stone and then mud. He crashed into a wide, deep stream, flailing in the water that bit at him and pushed him wildly backward in its current. At first Mack was content just to get away. Then he realized the rushing water represented a danger all its own. He tried to grab something, anything, and stop himself from being carried away. Finally, at least a mile if not more from where he had gone in, Mack crashed into a log and managed to hold on.

Water rushed all around. He spit and coughed as he worked himself up the log toward the stream's bank. He kicked against something solid; thinking he could stand he tried to get his feet under him, only to lose his balance and nearly his grip on the log.

When Mack finally got to the side, he crawled up over a small, narrow bed of sand into the bushes. There, exhausted, he lost consciousness.

Dreamland command trailer, Malaysian air base
1220

Zen had just finished showing Starship how to work the communications board in the command trailer when Danny checked in from the platform.

"We have movement at the airport near the Megafortress," said Danny. "I'm going to knock it out of action with the helicopters as planned. We're just about to board the choppers."

"Okay, do it."

Danny hesitated a moment. "I have this other proposal—

request, really. From the Brunei air force. They want to liberate one of their planes."

"At the airport?"

"There's apparently a section owned by a prince that has older aircraft, which could be used."

"We're talking about Prince bin Awg?"

"Yeah. We've examined the airport with the LADS blimps. There are no forces in that section, and we can cut off their access pretty easily once we disable the Megafortress."

"I'd say go for it. Just don't take any unnecessary risks."

"Yeah. Dog's not around?"

"Went to pay a courtesy call on the locals. He's due back any minute. I'll have him get a hold of you when he's back if you want."

"All right. I'm going to move ahead."

"I'll have him get in touch, one way or another," said Zen.

A peal of thunder rumbled in the distance as Zen signed off. Zen looked over at Starship, who glanced toward the nearby window. There wasn't a cloud in the sky.

A second clap came so close that the trailer vibrated up and down.

"Was that thunder?" asked Starship.

The door to the trailer jerked open. "Incoming!" yelled Major Merce Alou. "We're being shelled!"

"Shit. The planes," said Zen, wheeling back. "We have to get the Megafortresses up. They're sitting ducks."

"Right," shouted Alou, disappearing back outside.

"We'll never get off the ground," said Breanna.

"We have to," said Zen, pushing his wheelchair for the door.

Off the coast of Brunei
1228

Jennifer took over the LADS system for Sergeant Liu as he left to join the assault team. Jennifer made sure the feed for the airport was directly available to Danny's team via the Dreamland network, then began switching through the others. The images were also being monitored back at Dreamland. The command center there was also receiving some of the operating data from the blimps, but could not control them unless the takeover command was specifically ordered from the field terminal. The satellite link used up a large portion of the available bandwidth, and was somewhat kludgy; it was generally considered easier to operate them directly from the field.

It had been a while since Jennifer had spoken to Dog, and she couldn't resist the temptation to check in with him at the Malaysian base under the guise of seeing if the two additional LADS blimps had arrived there yet.

"Dreamland command trailer, this is Whiplash base," she said. "Looking for an update on the new units. What's their situation?"

There was no answer. Jennifer glanced at the communications board, making sure that she had it set properly.

"Dreamland command trailer—are you receiving me?" she asked.

"We're under attack," blurted Starship over the radio. "We're taking mortar fire."

"Mortar fire, copy," she said. "Do you need assistance?"

There was no answer. Jennifer looked at the screen showing where the LADS units were located; the nearest blimp was monitoring the Brunei-Malaysian border about a hundred and seventy-five miles away from them—much too far to see them.

"Do you need assistance?" she asked again, but there was still no answer.

"Dreamland command, this is Whiplash base," said Jennifer, switching over to the direct channel back home. "The team with the Megafortresses in Malaysia is under fire."

"Copy. We're working on getting some local support," responded Major Catsman, who was on duty in the center.

"Okay," said Jennifer, her voice so soft it was nearly a whisper.

What could she do? Sending one of the LADS units there seemed like a futile gesture; even at maximum speed it would take the blimp close to four hours to arrive.

But she had to do something. She selected the control screen for unit eight and cursored into the target area, setting the course. Then she enabled the unit's auto-pilot; the blimp would fly its course on its own without needing to be checked, and then politely buzz its minders when it was within ten minutes of its destination.

"Whiplash Leader, are you hearing me?" she asked Danny.

"Roger base. We have the Megafortress in sight on the ground at Brunei International Airport. We're preparing to disable it via TOW missiles."

"Dreamland team is under fire at their site," she told him.

Danny didn't respond. Jennifer suddenly felt foolish for giving him the useless information; all she was doing was sharing her anxiety.

"I'm sending a blimp for observation," she added. "They've called local support."

"Understood," said Danny finally. "Keep me informed."

"Roger that."

Malaysian air base
1232

Zen cursed the wheelchair, cursed the Brunei kingdom, cursed the Malaysians, cursed the Islamic madmen, and cursed his no-good legs as he pushed himself along the cement as fast as he could go toward the EB-52, determined to help get it in the air. The short field—and certainly the situation—demanded that the Flighthawks be used as boosters, helping the plane rocket off the runway.

The ground shook as a shell landed about a hundred yards away.

Shit, he thought to himself. This is crazy. But he pushed harder, determined to get the big planes off the ground.

And then launch the Flighthawks to pound the daylights out of whoever was firing at them.

Zen felt the veins in his face and chest straining as he wheeled onto the roadway. A geyser burst somewhere behind him, close enough to throw dust against the back of his head.

Something grabbed the back of his wheelchair and he felt himself jetting forward.

"Hey, Major, figured you wouldn't mind a push," yelled Starship in his ear.

"I'm in *Penn*," shouted Zen. "See if you can get into *Indy*. They need the assist off the Flighthawks."

"Yes, sir."

If Starship thought it was crazy to try and take off under

such circumstances, he kept his opinion to himself. Zen twisted around. "Where's Kick?"

"I think he's already aboard with Major Alou, there," shouted Starship.

Another shell landed, this one in the jungle to the left. The Air Force Special Tactics people started yelling as they hustled to the aircraft. Zen couldn't hear what they were saying though it wasn't particularly hard to guess.

"You can let go," Zen told Starship as Penn's engines kicked to life. "I'll take it from here."

"Talk to you upstairs," said the lieutenant, giving him a push and then hustling for *Indy*, whose engines also wound into action.

Zen had to twist the wheelchair around and back into the ladder, which had a special clamp for his chair. He hooked the metal into the side, then looked down to make sure the wheels were locked. Set, he arched his back and shoved hard, as if trying to pop a wheelie. The abrupt pressure activated a microswitch, which turned the ladder into a primitive elevator, hoisting Zen up. As he lifted up, yet another shell landed, this one on the runway; the wheelchair abruptly stopped, sagging against the metal pipe that held it.

"Come on, damn it," cursed Zen. He leaned backward, trying to see how far he was from the hold. Just as he had concluded he was going to have to twist around and drag himself up the stinking ladder and into the ship, the chairlift caught again and he moved up into the hold.

Hell of a time to be a cripple, he thought.

BREANNA BROUGHT ALL FOUR ENGINES UP IN QUICK SUCCESsion. The screens flew by on the glass cockpit wall, the indicators flashing green as the computer ran through its system checks. She'd grabbed a helmet from the rack at the back of the flightdeck, and pulled it on, connecting into the communications system. But she hadn't had time for the rest of the flight gear.

"Override checklist," she told the computer.

The screen beeped at her, telling her the override was not allowed.

"Override, authorization BreeOne."

"Overridden!" flashed on the screen.

"Who's with me?" she said over the com system.

"You and me, kid," said Zen from below. "I need power to the Flighthawks if you want to get out of here."

"Take too long," she said. "I'll jettison them and run down to the other end of the field."

"All I need is sixty seconds," said Zen. "And you'll have enough thrust to take off from here."

A shell landed close enough to rock the plane. "Do it in thirty," she said, pounding the command sequence on the screen that authorized the Flighthawks' engine ignition while they were still on the wings.

"I'm on it."

Starship found Kick already running through the Flighthawk checklists with the computer when he reached his station.

"Hey!" he yelled, sliding into his seat.

"Hey," said Kick. "Major Alou wants a quick start—he's got the engines up. Flighthawks are cycling."

"Yeah, no shit," said Starship.

"We have to give him a thirty-second burn on his signal," said Kick. "Zen says just ramp it up and hold on. As long as we go together, we'll get up in a shot."

"Zen would know," said Starship.

The airplane bucked as something landed nearby.

Hope we get the hell out here quick, Starship thought.

"Yeah, me, too," said Kick over the interphone.

North of Meruta, Malaysia
1232

Dog could see the three men who had them pinned down. They formed a semicircle in the jungle; they'd crossed the road and moved in about ten yards.

"We pick the weak link on one of the flanks, and take him out," said Lang. He'd torn a piece of his uniform off and tied it around his leg, which had been cut pretty badly.

"What if they have other people on the flank, watching their backs?" asked Dog.

"We deal with that when it happens." Lang winced as he shifted his weight. "Can you do this?"

"Yeah, I can do it."

The sergeant handed him one of the M4s.

"You better show me how to get it to fire," said Dog. "I couldn't before."

Lang took the gun back and slid his thumb against the selector on the side above the trigger area. The weapon had been safed. As he watched him Dog realized he hadn't even thought of checking.

"Brace yourself as best you can when you fire. You get three shot bursts," said Lang, handing the weapon back. "You'll probably tend to fire too high. Keep that in mind."

"I will."

"We're going to go after the guy on this side," said the sergeant, gesturing to the left, "because if we get past him, we're clear back to the village."

"Okay," said Dog. "Hold on a second, Sergeant," he added as the soldier started to the left.

Lang gave him an intense stare.

"I'm sorry, but I forgot your first name."

"Tommy," said the sergeant, scowling.

"Sorry I forgot. I'm Dog."

"Yeah, I know, Colonel. Let's do it, okay?"

Brunei International Airport
1232

Danny leaned forward in his seat in the helicopter as they settled into a hover a little less than a thousand yards from the Megafortress. The terrorists who had driven the tanker in from the city got out of the cab.

"They're going to shoot at us," he said calmly as the pilot stabilized the aircraft.

"Firing," said the pilot.

A TOW missile leapt from the side of the small chopper. The six-inch warhead hit the right stabilizer at the rear of the aircraft, carrying through the structure and exploding next to the left fin. A second missile, fired at the rear section of the plane, struck a few seconds later, obliterating the back portion of the aircraft.

"All right," yelled Danny. "Phase two, phase two."

The helicopter whipped to the side, spinning back around over the civilian terminal. The other helicopter had already started in toward bin Awg's three hangars. The video feed from the LADS that showed there were no terrorists nearby but Danny wouldn't trust it; the helicopters did a quick circuit to make sure the ground was clear before depositing the Whiplash team on the ground.

"McKenna, you got twenty minutes," Danny said over the com circuit. "If you can get that plane launched by then, it's yours."

"I only need fifteen," she shot back.

Malaysian air base
1238

Breanna brought the EB-52's engines to full military power, the thrust rippling through the muscles of the big jet as it was held in place by its brakes.

"Ready?" she asked Zen.

"Ignition in three," he said.

They counted down together. At two, Breanna slapped off the brakes and the big jet leapt forward, propelled by nearly a quarter of a million pounds of thrust from its four P&W engines. A second later the Flighthawks added their thrust. Within a blink the plane's speed passed a hundred miles an hour. Bree started back on the stick and the aircraft rushed upward, springing off the pavement as if its landing gear were pogo sticks.

A black streak flew across the right side of her windscreen; by the time Breanna realized it was a mortar shell she was far beyond it. The impact of the explosion was lost in the turbulence behind the aircraft; if it affected the plane at all the computer controls compensated without Breanna noticing. She held the Megafortress steady as the plane rose over the runway and out of danger.

*   *   *

STARSHIP GLANCED AT KICK AS THEY COUNTED DOWN TO-
gether with Major Alou and the computer. The EB-52 vibrated
madly, and the noise of the revving engines leaked past the
noise-canceling headgear, a steady hum in the back of his head.

"Two," they said, and the Megafortress began to roll, cued
by Major Alou up on the flightdeck.

"Three," they said, and the Flighthawk engines whipped on.
Starship felt himself pushed back in his seat as the Megafortress burst ahead in quick-takeoff mode. His view screen
played a feed from the nose of the Flighthawk; he could see the
tail of the other Megafortress disappearing to the right. The
strip and surrounding jungle slid by, the EB-52's speed ramping
quickly. He could feel the plane starting to lift, gravity beginning to tilt his body back like the gentle rock of a cradle.

And then the plane sagged left. Something popped in Starship's ear. A red emergency light blinked, and as Starship
reached his hand to the screen control, a cold curtain of darkness descended around him and he fell unconscious.

ZEN SHUT DOWN THE FLIGHTHAWK ENGINES AND BEGAN CY-
cling fuel into Hawk One, replacing what they had used to get
off the runway.

"*Indy* was hit," Breanna told him. "They didn't get off the
runway."

Zen felt his throat tighten. Trying to take off had been fool-
hardy, a ridiculous gamble. He was responsible for the men
who'd been in that plane.

He glanced at the instrument screen on his left—he was using the auxiliary controls, since there hadn't been time even to
get his helmet—double-checking that he had enough fuel to
launch.

"Ready to launch Hawk One in sixty seconds," he told Breanna.

WHEN STARSHIP OPENED HIS EYES, HE WAS AT THE STICK OF
an F-15E. The altimeter ladder in his heads-up display showed
that he had just notched up over forty thousand feet, and he was
still climbing, winging upward like an angel called to heaven.

The blue void of the atmosphere thinned as he rose, the color paling into white and then becoming almost black. The black deepened, and still he climbed, over a hundred thousand feet now, the altimeter calmly notching it off. One-ten, one-twenty, one-fifty, two hundred . . .

"I can't go this high," said Starship. "Not in a Strike Eagle."

With that thought, the blackness turned red and he felt his body twisting hard against his restraints. His arm smacked against something hard and he heard a scream coming from the middle of his chest.

"I got to get the hell out of here," said Starship, and by instinct he reached for the ejection handle, but he couldn't find it. He managed to get his head down and look, then realized he couldn't eject—they were too low, too low—

No, they were on the ground, and the seats hadn't been properly prepared besides.

He saw one of the emergency lights blinking on a panel and realized they had crash-landed at the end of the runway.

"Out, out, out!" he yelled, and started to jump from his station. He couldn't move and for a moment he despaired, thought he'd been crippled like Zen.

He'd kill himself before he lived like that, as much as he admired the older pilot.

And then he realized he was still buckled into his seat. A wave of relief powered into his legs and arms as he threw off the restraints, bolted upright, and started for the exit. He remembered Kick, turned and saw that he was still back in his seat. Starship shook him, then when he didn't respond reached down and unsnapped the buckles, helped him up—more like picked him up—and dragged him behind him to the hatchway. The motor that worked the ladder growled as the lower door started to open. Something in the mechanism snapped and it stopped after moving only an inch or so. Starship pounded on the control, but it didn't move. He swung around and tried kicking at the hatchway, first gently and then with all his weight, but nothing budged.

"Upstairs," he told Kick, who was crouched over where he'd left him.

Starship grabbed his friend and tried pushing him up the ladder which led to the flight deck, but Kick was so out of it that he finally draped him over his side and back and pulled him up with him, crawling onto the rear of the long cockpit area.

"Major Alou! Merce! Merce!" he yelled to Alou.

The pilot sat at his station, head slumped over, hand on the throttle slide. As Starship came close, he saw that the front wind panel and some of the aircraft structure around it had been shattered. A piece of metal twice the size of Starship's hand had embedded itself in the side of Alou's head. Blood covered everything around the pilot.

"We got to get the hell out of here," he told Kick. He started to go back down, thinking they could use the emergency hatchways at the forward part of the Flighthawk compartment. But then he realized it would be quicker to use the emergency roof hatches above the ejection seats, which could be blown out by the computer or by hand.

He squeezed past the center console, trying not to look at Alou. The consoles were still lit.

Starship got up on the seat, balancing awkwardly as he struggled with the hatchway. He fumbled with the large red bar that had to be pushed back to override the computer's emergency system and access the controls directly. Once that was out of the way, he hit the thick, square button at the top of the panel, which blew all of the upper hatchways off at once.

"Up we go, up we go!" he yelled to Kick.

He put his head out of the hatchway, breathing a whiff of the hot, humid jungle air. A machine-gun started to fire in the distance.

Starship ducked back down. Maybe it would be better to stay in the plane, where at least there was a modicum of cover. But the Megafortress would be a target for whomever was attacking; he turned and yelled at Kick, who still hadn't moved off the deck.

"Yo, Kick boy, time to get the hell out of here," he yelled to his companion. Once again he draped the other pilot across his back, wobbling as he snaked around and then up through the hatchway. A green arm appeared over the black skin of the Megafortress as Starship pulled upward. His heart nearly leapt from his chest before he realized it was one of the Special Forces soldiers.

"Let's go, let's go," Starship yelled, more to himself than the soldier or Kick. More arms appeared around him. He resisted as they started to push him toward the ground, then realized they had him; he slipped into the arms of a burly Special Forces sergeant, who immediately pushed him down and in the same motion whirled and began firing at something in the jungle fifty yards away.

Southeastern Brunei
Exact location and time unknown

Every bone in his body felt as if it had been broken, and every muscle felt as if it had been twisted and bent and re-arranged. But for Mack, the worst thing was the horrible taste in his mouth, which for some reason just wouldn't leave him, not even after he gulped water from the nearby stream. He spit, he dunked his head, he stuffed the top of his flightsuit into his mouth—it stubbornly remained.

Mack started walking downstream, along the side of the stream opposite the one he had fallen down on. Within a few minutes he heard the rush of a waterfall. He climbed hand over hand down a scramble of rocks and dirt, descending nearly fifty feet before the ground leveled out in a bog. The only way through was over a jumble of felled trees. As he reached a run of boulders he finally caught sight of the waterfall, a spectacular spray that cascaded over a nearly sheer cliff. Mack, never much of a nature admirer, stared at the spray as it came off the flow, awed by it.

The bugs prompted him to move on. He threaded his way through jungle fronds, the stalks and leaves getting thicker and thicker. Finally he thought he might have to turn back and tried rushing ahead like a bull, crashing and struggling until he hit a clearing. Mack collapsed, resting for a few minutes; when he got up he saw that he had come out on a path.

He took it to the left, and within ten minutes heard voices in the distance. He froze, then moved off the trail, hiding as he tried to make out the sounds. They seemed to be kids, which meant he must be near a village; his best bet would be to go there and ask to be taken to the police station, where he could explain who he was.

As he took a step back on the trail, something crashed behind him; Mack spun just in time to see the back of some sort of animal disappearing into the vegetation.

When he turned around again, he found his way blocked by a short, squat man holding a large machine-gun in his beefy hands.

Brunei International Airport
1242

Prince bin Awg's MiG-19 sat in the center of Hangar Two, an access ladder propped to its cockpit. McKenna decided to take that as an omen of luck, rather than an indication that mechanics had been trying to fix something when the attacks began. She spun the tractor she'd taken from the other hangar into position, jumped off, and pulled away the wheel chucks from the plane. She climbed up into the cockpit to check on the brake and found a helmet and parachute stowed there. Those were clearly signs of good luck.

The tractor filled the hangar with thick diesel exhaust as she stomped on the pedal and got it moving forward. The vehicle— its vintage was uncertain, but it had Chinese lettering on the dash—groaned as it tugged the MiG out of the hangar. The two Whiplash troopers helping her were just pulling up with the fuel truck that had been in the other hangar. McKenna threw on the brakes and jumped off the tug.

"Fuel it! Let's go! Let's go!" she yelled, running to unhook the tractor and get it out of the way.

Prince bin Awg's engineers had updated some of the systems, mostly with Chinese equipment intended for the vastly updated J-6, whose design was based on the MiG-19 family. The radio was state-of-the-art, and a small GPS device had been jury-rigged to the right panel. Otherwise, the cockpit remained exactly as it had been when this model rolled off the line at Gorki in 1957—primitive even by Russian standards. McKenna switched on the backup battery and got a tentative read on her instruments, cinching her restraints at the same time.

"All right, that's good," she yelled at the men outside with the jet fuel. Her tanks were more than half full—more than enough to get her where she had to go. "All right, go. We're going. See you at the end of the war."

The twin Tumansky turbojets groaned as she brought them

on line. Even with the brakes set the aircraft moved forward, and in fact when she removed them there seemed almost no difference. McKenna turned left onto the access ramp, snugging the canopy as she went. The aircraft started slightly to the right and she nearly went off the other side over-correcting; her controls felt sluggish and she thought one of the tires might be flat or close to it. A helicopter buzzed off to her left as she brought the plane onto the main runway. It seemed to be firing at someone but McKenna couldn't spare the attention. The MiG was proving more of a handful than she remembered.

But she appreciated challenges.

The engines responded quickly as she goosed the throttle. The plane drifted right as she shot down the runway; remembering her earlier problem she treated the controls as gingerly as possible. As she hit one hundred and eight knots she began her takeoff rotation, lifting her nose wheel five degrees. But the MiG stayed stuck to the ground. Her forward air speed dogged, the aircraft struggled despite its lightish load; finally she managed to get it up, passing one hundred and sixty knots, just enough to lift off the ground. She crossed to the right, trying to stay clear of the area where the helicopters had been, climbing slowly and heading toward the ocean.

Now that she was airborne, the MiG's speed built nicely, climbing up over two hundred and fifty knots. The controls got a bit lighter as she flew, and McKenna felt the pleasant tug of the old metal around her. The MiG-19 was the first supersonic fighter built by the Soviet Union; while it was quickly superceded in the Russian inventory by the MiG-21, the design had a number of virtues. It was built to go very fast and very high, enabling it to threaten the bombers of the day. The MiG's speed would be a liability when she landed, even with the parachute that was standard equipment at the rear of the aircraft; the fact that the brakes hadn't been particularly good was not a good sign.

But there was plenty of time to worry about that. McKenna decided there was no reason not to see what the plane could do. She gave her instruments a quick sweep, checked her altitude and the air around her, then pulled the throttle to afterburner.

* * *

"MIG IS OFF," THE HELICOPTER PILOT TOLD DANNY.

"Pick up our guys," Danny said, though the command was unnecessary—the pilot had already whipped the Quick Bird toward the hangar area.

"Danny, I have an update from the Malaysian air base," said Jennifer. "They're taking heavy fire. The command trailer has been hit by mortar fire. One Megafortress took off. Another is on the ground. They think it got hit. Colonel Bastian is overdue as well."

"They asking for assistance?"

"They've radioed out to a Malaysian unit in the area. They didn't get a response."

Danny leaned back in his seat. Besides the length of time it would take to get there—upwards of an hour, if not more—they didn't have the fuel.

"We're ready to blow hangar one, Cap," said Liu, breaking in. One had the Sabre and the Hunter, which McKenna has said were the most likely planes to be used. "Charges are set."

"All right, Jen, I've got a few things to attend to here. I'll get back with you."

Danny was about to give Liu the okay to blow the planes when he saw the fuel truck on the tarmac near the hangar.

"Can we use their jet fuel?" Danny asked the pilot.

"We can use standard jet fuel, if that's what it is," said the pilot.

Danny clicked into the Dreamland circuit, asking Liu if he knew what sort of fuel he'd pumped into the plane. Liu had no idea. He then switched and spoke by satellite to Dreamland Command, where Major Catsman promised to get a fuel expert on the double.

"If I can smell it, I can tell if it's okay," said the chopper pilot while they waited.

"You sure?"

"Look, jet fuel's jet fuel, right?"

Danny looked around the airport. The only terrorists who had been nearby were either dead or hunkered over by the civilian side of the facility. If he could refuel here, he could fly the helicopters down to the Malaysian base.

Just one helicopter. He didn't want to leave the platform unprotected.

"Whiplash Commander, this is Dreamland Command."

"Freah."

"Danny, I have the man who tuned the Quick Bird engines on the line here, speaking from his quarters."

"Bottom line it, Major."

"Bottom line is you'll blow the warranty if you use commercial jet fuel—yeah, it'll work."

"Thanks."

Pandasan coastal patrol base, Malaysia (north of Brunei) 1243

Dazhou Ti tightened the grip on the pistol as he strode across the dock to the wooden plank that had been thrown over to the side of the ship by his boarding party. He could feel the beat of his blood pulsing in his head, everything a rush. One of his men stepped across the deck as he came onto the ship, saluting smartly.

"The captain is in the bridge," said the sailor.

Dazhou nodded and continued through the hatch into the ship's superstructure, aware that he was being watched, aware that his course now was set and irrevocable. He went up to the bridge, where his men held the captain and another officer at gunpoint.

"You are with us, or you will die," Dazhou told the captain, pointing his pistol at the man.

The ship's captain had served under Dazhou two years before on the *Perkasa*, a coastal patrol ship. Until this moment he might even have considered himself a friend, though Dazhou had not included him in the inner circle of navy personnel who had worked with him on the *Barracuda*.

"I don't know what you mean," said the captain.

Dazhou pressed the pistol against his cheek. "I would think it would be clear enough."

"I am with you, of course, Captain," said the man. "But your aim—I don't understand."

"We are going to assist the forces that have taken over Brunei," said Dazhou. "There is an American force attempting to help them. We will attack them, and then we will find other targets."

"But the government has decreed that we honor our treaty obligations."

"You are very brave," said Dazhou.

Then he pulled the trigger.

As the captain's body fell to the ground, blood coursing from his skull, Dazhou turned to the other officer. The man stood in shock; he did not appear to be breathing.

"Where is the ship's intercom?" Dazhou asked.

Without saying a word, the man went to a panel at the side and held up a microphone. Dazhou took it.

"This is Captain Dazhou Ti. I have been commanded by God to take over this ship to join in a holy war against the western devils who rule Brunei through the bastard sultan and his family. It is a holy war and the rewards of those who truly believe will be eternal and guaranteed. Any who do not wish to join us may leave the ship in five minutes. After that, we will set out."

Allowing some to leave was a calculated risk. The ship's complement was fifty-one; it could be operated with less, but most of the twenty-three sailors Dazhou had brought with him were not familiar with the ship and it would be difficult to operate it if everyone aboard deserted. On the other hand, the appeal to faith—and a religion that Dazhou himself did not share—put the argument to join him in its starkest, most obvious terms.

He handed the microphone back to the other officer. "You too may leave," he told him.

"I am a believer. I stay."

Dazhou nodded, then turned back around. Blood still poured from the captain's head.

"Throw him overboard," he told his men. "Then report to the second officer. We have much to do."

North of Meruta
1243

Dog crouched on his knee behind the tree, watching as something moved about thirty feet ahead through the brush. There was no doubt in his mind that it was the terrorist, but he could not actually see the man. He had the rifle wedged against a shoulder. He cocked his head down so he could see through the scope; the sweat on his palm made the M4 feel oily and he pressed his fingers tighter.

A white rag appeared in the middle of the scope.

Was the man surrendering?

He raised his head, saw only a blur. He was only twenty feet away at most. He had a rifle in his hand.

The white was the shirt he was wearing.

Dog put his head down again, his eye on the scope.

He'd lost his target!

Dog pushed the barrel to his right but couldn't find his enemy. He brought the weapon down, scanning to his right—something moved dead ahead of him. He saw a white swatch, then a face, pushed his shoulder against the weapon and fired.

The gun popped in his hands, the recoil easier than he thought. He swung right, saw something much further away but hesitated, not sure exactly what it was. Finally he saw a rifle with a banana clip against a white background through the leaves and fired. This time he saw that he had hit what he was aiming at; it furled backward, falling to the ground.

Something cracked behind him. Dog swung around, nearly losing his balance. A white shirt loomed in front of him.

He fired point blank into the man's stomach. The bullets didn't seem to affect the terrorist at first. He continued fumbling with the AK47 in his hands, having trouble making it shoot. Dog fired again, still at point blank range.

A bulletproof vest!

Dog started to aim higher, but just then the terrorist began to dance—it was the only way to describe what Dog saw, a kind of macabre shake and jump, a turn to the left and then to the right, as if the man were trying belatedly to duck away from Dog's gunfire. He shook his shoulders, and then the gun dropped from his hands and he fell off to the side, confusion on his face.

Dog started to stand. As he did a shout made him lose his balance and he toppled forward, just in time to hear three short bursts of automatic rifle fire. To his right. Lang burst through the leaves and stood over him, firing again. Dog pushed himself back to his knees but Lang held him down, crouched over and scouting the nearby jungle.

"All right," said the soldier, tugging him to follow. Dog

stumbled and then started to run, moving sideways as well as frontward as they tracked toward the road. His feet sloshed in a wet spot and he nearly fell, but somehow he managed to keep his balance until he reached the road's shoulder. His elbow and shoulder broke his fall and he rolled onto his stomach.

"It's all right, we're clear," said the soldier from his haunches a few feet away. "Cross the road. We'll move down the ditch there. There's a little cover."

Dog glanced to his left, then scrambled over the macadam and got into the vegetation. He started to relax, then realized he should be covering Lang's crossing. He got up and watched as the soldier made his way across the roadway very deliberately.

It wasn't that he went slowly, just that he was under control. Unlike Dog, he'd have been able to react and fire if anything had appeared.

"Let's duck through this run of trees," suggested Lang. "Then angle back."

They began trotting through the jungle, going several hundred yards west before angling back in the direction of the road and the village they had visited earlier. When they had the highway in sight, they stopped to catch their breaths. They couldn't hear anyone following.

"Good going back there, Colonel," said Lang.

"Good going to you, too."

"You want to give that little radio a go again or what?"

"Yeah." Dog took it from his pocket and put it back on voice, making another broadcast. After several more tries, he gave it up, slipping it back to beacon. The battery was limited, but Dog figured that there was no sense trying to conserve it; they'd either be saved or dead by the time it ran out the way things were going.

"Nobody home, huh?" said Lang.

"Not yet."

"We'll just have to take care of ourselves, that's all. You think we should head back to the village?"

"I think that's a better idea than staying here."

"Maybe, maybe not," said Lang. It was the first time since they'd met that he'd expressed anything close to doubt, and Dog felt instantly uneasy.

"I don't like to sit when I can be moving, if you know what I mean," added the soldier. "I say we move."

"I agree," said Dog.

"All right, let's move out then. But listen, Colonel, no bull-shit now—you get tired, you tell me, okay? I mean, no offense, but you got to talk up if you're tired."

Under other circumstances, Dog might have been insulted—or even touched. But now he just shrugged. "Don't worry about me. And you can call me Dog."

"Yes, sir," said Lang, getting to his feet.

Aboard *"Penn,"* over Malaysian air base
1243

Zen launched the Flighthawk and hastily tipped its nose down in the direction of the mortars. The radar beeped as it picked up a shell, and C^3 began a quick set of calculations to determine not only the precise launch point but the best angle for an attack.

"Bree, I have a target."

"I just need some altitude so I can launch one of the air-to-ground missiles," she said.

"If there's anything left of them when I'm through," Zen told her, accelerating into the attack, "you're welcome to them."

The terrorists had set up a pair of large mortars roughly three and a half miles from the base. Five men were working the two tubes, which were either 81 millimeter British or 82 millimeter Russian weapons, in both cases old but reliable and potentially devastating weapons. The guerillas had a van just to the north of the clearing as Zen approached. He put the Flighthawk's nose onto the firing team on the left and pressed his trigger, working in a diagonal through the mortar area and into the van. His first shots missed both the mortar and the men serving it, but the vehicle exploded almost immediately. By the time he turned off it was engulfed in flames.

He came back and looked for another target beyond the thick cloud of black smoke. A long dirt road ran through the jungle toward a paved road to the west; Zen followed along it but saw nothing. He saw a reflection from a ridge to the north as he turned and headed toward it, guessing that there was a spotter using binoculars there. Sure enough, he saw figures scrambling and caught the outline of a gun in the magnified viewer. Zen pushed down to fire at them but by the time he got in range they had ducked away; he pounded the ground with shells but it was like trying to hit a flea with a spitball.

"Ground is reporting that they're no longer under mortar attack," said Breanna. "They have about a dozen guerillas trying to fight their way in from the southwest, near the end of the strip. They've radioed to another Malaysian unit for support. No response yet."

"Yeah," said Zen. He climbed back in the direction of the air base. "If you can get them to mark the position, I'll make a pass with the cannon."

"The guerillas are in white and they're coming up the ravine," she said.

"Yeah, yeah, I see them," said Zen. He pushed the Flighthawk's wing down, swooping into a wide arc to the far side of the ravine the enemy was using for cover. Zen walked the Flighthawk down the ditch, working the cannon back and forth.

"Zen, can you do that one more time? They want to use you as cover for a counterattack," said Breanna.

"Hawk leader," he confirmed, pulling back around and repeating his run from the opposite direction. He could see movement on both sides of the ravine but concentrated on the ditch itself, which had ten or twelve soldiers in it.

"You talk to Alou?" he asked Breanna.

"Negative."

Zen's path brought him over the airfield. He could see the other Megafortress at the end of the runway. Part of its right wing had been chewed off by an explosion and the nose had been mangled. The plane rested on its belly.

"Zen, I'm picking up a distress signal on the UHF band," said Breanna.

"Yeah," he said as the chirp flooded over the circuit. "Did *Indy* get off the field?"

"I don't think so," she said. "Stand by. Let me see if I can track it down."

Zen spotted someone moving near the aircraft. He hoped they'd gotten out and the signal was just a glitch.

"I have the source three and a half miles south of the base," said Breanna. "I'm marking it. Ground's asking for more support back by that ravine."

"Roger that," said Zen, pulling the Flighthawk around.

Malaysian air base
1254

Starship didn't realize that Kick had stayed back near the plane until the gunfire had nearly stopped. One of the Special Tactics people had found a medical kit and was trying to clean and bandage Starship's arm, which he'd bashed up pretty badly somewhere along the way.

"I'm okay. I have to go back and get my friend out," Starship told him. "I'm really all right."

"Just hang on until the area's secure," said the air force special operations soldier.

"Yeah, okay," said Starship. But he stood up and started moving toward the aircraft anyway. He saw a Flighthawk whip overhead and unleash its cannon. The sight locked him in place; he watched the small aircraft whip upward, disappearing in a blink of an eye.

"Kick," he said, moving again toward the plane. "Kick!"

The joints in his knees were so unsteady he wobbled from side to side as he reached the wing of the giant plane. He hauled himself up, using the Flighthawk to get a boost, and then ran up along the top of the big plane. He navigated around the hatchways to the rear compartments and threw himself down to peer inside the opening over the pilot's seat.

Major Alou stared up at him, his face a macabre death mask.

"I'm sorry," he told Alou.

He looked to the right but didn't see Kick. "Kick! Kick! You asshole!" he shouted to his friend. "Get the hell out of there! Kick! What are you doing?"

He thought he heard Kick's voice behind him somewhere. He looked around but didn't see him. There was another shout, and he crawled to the side of the plane.

"Lieutenant, you better get off that plane," shouted the Air Force Special Tactics soldier from the edge of the runway. "You're an easy target up there."

"My friend—Kick, the other Flighthawk pilot. He went back inside."

"No, sir, he's down here."

"He is?" Starship climbed down the front of the smashed up windscreen and bashed nose, jumping to the ground. His knees gave way and he crumpled in what seemed like slow motion. As soon as he hit the ground he rolled back up and started to run to the side of the field.

"Kick, Kick, you idiot, where the hell are you?"

The Air Force Special Tactics soldier caught him from the side with his tree trunk arm.

"Lieutenant. Your friend—"

Starship turned and looked at him. The soldier shook his head. Starship shook his head as well.

"He can't be dead. I pulled him out," said Starship.

"I think he was dead when you pulled him out," said the man. "Listen, we have to fall back to the bunker area until reinforcements come in. We don't know how many more of these bozos are out there in the jungle. We're down to six guys who can handle a weapon, not counting you and me."

"I can't leave Kick," said Starship. "Where is he?"

"Sir, you're going to have to leave him," said the soldier. "Or you're going to be dead, too."

"He can't be dead."

"This way," said the sergeant, starting to trot up toward the bunker.

Starship stared after him for a moment. Then, against his conscious will, his legs propelled him to follow.

Southeastern Brunei
Exact location and time unknown

The man with the gun prodded Mack down the pathway past a cluster of small houses to a turnoff that led to a long wooden platform above the slope. At the far end of the platform sat a small building constructed from chipboard. Inside, Mack found several women holding or sitting with children on the floor of the single room. The far wall was a screen overlooking a rock-strewn slope down to the stream Mack had walked along earlier. A man with a pistol stood in front of the screen; he glanced nervously at Mack as his escort left him, then went back to watching out the side.

Unsure of the situation, Mack decided that his best course for now was to say nothing until he could puzzle out whether the men with the guns were terrorists who had invaded the settlement, or if they were the husbands of the women trying to protect them. But no one said anything, either to Mack or each other, outside of an occasional soft whisper to children who were fidgety.

"Are you for the government?" asked Mack finally.

No one answered.

"Sultan?" he asked. But that didn't draw a response, either.

"U.S.A?"

Nothing.

"Could I have some food?"

Still nothing. Mack propped his hands on his knees and leaned forward, baffled by the situation.

North of Meruta
1348

Dog heard the whispery jet engine approaching from the north and realized it had to be a Flighthawk. He pulled the PRC radio from his pocket and switched it to voice.

"Colonel Tecumseh Bastian to Dreamland Flighthawk. You're approaching my position," he said.

The only response was static. Dog cupped his hand over the earphone as he broadcast and listened again.

"Dog, this is Zen. I should be just crossing overhead," said the pilot finally.

"Yeah, I see you," said the colonel as the black dart came overhead. "We were ambushed further up on the road. The terrorists got one of our guys."

"I saw the Hummer. Danny is en route with a helicopter."

"Danny?"

"He's about fifteen minutes away. Pilot wants to claim a new speed record for an A-6," said Zen. The transmission crackled and faded but then came back. "Can you find a good place for him to land?"

"Plenty of roadway," said Dog.

Zen said something, but it was wiped by static. Dog asked him to repeat it but didn't get an acknowledgment.

"You're talking to the plane?" asked Lang, coming back.

"Yeah. They have a helicopter en route. It's about fifteen minutes away."

"We have to keep moving," said the soldier. "They're only a few hundred yards behind us, on the other side of the road."

"You sure?"

"Yeah. They've been following all along and now they're starting to catch up. Come on."

Dog started to tell Zen that they were being pursued. He got only two words out of his mouth when the by now familiar rattle of an AK47 sounded through the nearby jungle.

Aboard *"Penn,"* over Malaysia
1352

"I didn't get a good location," Breanna told Zen. "I think his battery's dying."

"They may be under fire," he told her. "I see something popping down there. Something's going on."

She flipped on the feed from the nose of the Flighthawk and watched as the small robot made a tree-top pass over the road. There was a flash off the right wing, but the robot plane went by so quickly it was impossible to tell exactly what had fired at it.

"I'd try raking the trees with the gun," said Zen. "But I just can't tell where they are."

"I have a better idea," said Breanna. "Let's show them we're here and maybe they'll back off."

"Bree, they may decide we're a good target—" said Zen, but she'd already started the aircraft downward. The Megafortress cleared the treetops by maybe five feet.

"Trying to break their eardrums?" Zen asked as she climbed.

"If it'll help," she said.

Southwestern Brunei, near the Malaysian border
1352

McKenna put the MiG-19 into a steep descent and got ready for her landing. She had to bleed off speed but keep the engine

up in case she blew the approach in the unfamiliar plane; even
a veteran MiG pilot could find the combination challenging on
a rough field. The tiny runway came up quickly in her windscreen as she descended; she glanced at the dial tracking her
engines' rpms, making sure she had enough power to abort if
necessary.

The MiG's air speed plummeted from 325 knots to just over
200 as she dropped toward the hard-packed surface at the edge
of the runway. Her flaps were open all the way and she was
committed now. The craft sank abruptly, threatening to pancake.
She got past it, the tail twitching slightly but her nose right, flar-
ing up so the plane could help itself slow. But she reached prematurely for the throttle to throw it into neutral—a minor mistake in
another plane, a potential catastrophe in the MiG-19 on a short
runway. Cutting the speed so sharply caused the back end of the
plane to slip downward abruptly once more, this time perilously
close to the ground. She felt her heart thump, and then in the
next instant felt something kick her from behind—her father,
she thought, telling her not to be a jerk.

That was all it took. She managed to get the rear wheels
down solid without scraping her butt on the runway. With her
nose still up to increase drag, her speed quickly fell; when she
slipped under 130 knots she dropped the front of the plane and
went for the brakes and chute and brakes.

And brakes and brakes and brakes. She stopped with her
nose over the end of the field.

"Never a doubt," she said as she climbed out of the plane.

"My MiG!" exclaimed Prince bin Awg, materializing from
the back of the crowd that ran out to greet her.

"She's a beauty," said McKenna.

"How did you rescue her?"

"She kind of called to me," said McKenna.

The prince looked at her, then smiled. "For your bravery,
you deserve a present."

"I'm not much for medals, Prince," she told him. "Besides, it
was mostly the Dreamland people. The terrorists made a move
to the Megafortress and they decided they had to keep her on
the ground. They took her rear stabilizer off and wiped out the
fuel truck they'd brought in from outside the city somewhere."

"The Megafortress was destroyed?" asked the prince.

"Temporarily disabled. They blew the back section of it off. It'll fly again someday."

"And my planes?"

"I saved this one," said McKenna. "Best I could do."

The prince nodded grimly, as if lamenting the passing of a dozen old comrades—which in a way he was. "You deserve a reward," he said. "It is yours."

"What is?"

"The MiG."

"Really?" McKenna looked back at it. "No kidding?"

The prince looked at her solemnly. "My uncle owes you his life. I would give you twenty such planes."

"I'll settle for this one and a new set of brakes," said McKenna. "Mind if we get some grub? Those Dreamland people were nice, but the only thing they had to eat were MREs. One more peanut butter and jelly sandwich in a tube and my stomach would have hit the eject button."

Brunei International Airport
1352

Sahurah watched as the men pulled the last of the metal from the wrecked hangar entrance. Two of the hangars at the prince's side of the airport had been completely destroyed, but only the doorway to this one had been blown up. A large aircraft sat untouched a few yards away.

"It may be of use," said Yayasan, the pilot who had deserted from the sultan's air force. "It hasn't been used often, but it was flown recently. The Russians called it a Tu-16. The Western nations referred to it as a Badger. This model was used for maritime patrols, and some bombing."

"Could we use it against the sultan's forces?" asked Sahurah.

"Certainly. There are machine-guns, those racks are there for bombs or missiles. Missiles, but we could use bombs."

"Can you fly it?"

"I have never done so."

"That is not my question."

Sahurah looked into the pilot's face, filled with fear. Sahurah knew from his own experience how difficult a foe fear was. He wished he had the ability to inspire others to face it, but realized he did not. Sahurah turned and started to walk away.

"I will try, Commander," said the pilot behind him. "I will try."

North of Meruta
1402

Dog tried the radio again, but once more all he got was static. The terrorists had stopped firing their weapons but they were still in the jungle somewhere across the road.

"I think they'll follow us all the way to the coast," Dog told Lang as they crouched in the weeds, catching their breath. "They're persistent bastards."

"No, they won't go that far," said the sergeant. He pointed to the south. "There's another group coming up on our side. Look."

Dog saw the last man in the small column as he ducked over a hilltop in the brush about a quarter of a mile away.

"Shit," said Dog. He picked up his radio to broadcast again.

"Wait," said the sergeant. "Listen."

Dog raised his head and heard the chopper approaching from the distance.

SITTING IN THE FRONT SEAT OF THE QUICK BIRD AS IT whipped toward the area where Colonel Bastian had been located, Danny caught a glimpse of the Flighthawk darting back and forth in the sky. It looked like a crow protecting its young from a prowling cat.

"I see you, Zen," Danny said over the Dreamland satellite circuit. "Are you in contact with them?"

"On and off. I haven't had anything from him in the last ten minutes, but I have a rough idea of the location. The terrorists are very close by."

He gave him GPS coordinates, and then described the spot as just west of the highway, about a hundred yards from a sharp bend.

Danny discussed it with the pilot, who thought their best bet would be to take the Quick Bird directly in while the Flighthawk laid down some covering fire near the terrorists. The pilot told Danny they could hover above the highway; if Dog came out they could pick him up, and if the bad guys came out they could fire at them themselves.

It was a risky plan, but the pilot claimed he'd done things twenty times as dangerous when he was flying with the 160th SOAR, the Army's special operations helicopter regiment. Danny didn't doubt that he was telling the truth.

They flew south a mile and a half, then made a wide turn on the side of the jungle where Zen thought Dog was. They dropped low and hovered over the road as the Flighthawk dipped down toward the trees, looking for something to shoot up.

"There," said Boston. "On the left, your left, just in the ditch near the road."

"And there," said Danny, pointing ahead. "Terrorists at two o'clock."

DOG WATCHED AS THE HELICOPTER WHIPPED OVER THE ROAD behind them and then started to turn. Before he could get up and run for it, it began firing at the row of trees to the north. The terrorists there answered, one of them firing a rocket-propelled grenade. Dog watched in horror as the grenade flew toward the cockpit of the plane and then seemed to disappear inside it. Fortunately, it had actually sailed to the side, curving like a baseball hit down the line. By the time it exploded in the jungle, the Quick Bird had unleashed a pair of TOW missiles into the tree line.

Lang began firing his M4, and Dog whirled around just in time to see six or seven terrorists throwing themselves down about three hundred yards away to the south. He too began to fire; as he did, something darted down overhead and he heard a roar and a grating sound, the kind of thing a garbage truck might make it if digested a load of steel.

"To the road, to the road," Lang shouted, pulling him away as another grenade flew through the air. Dog fell backward; bullets flew nearby and he seemed to be breathing dirt.

"Stay down, stay down!" Lang yelled. The Flighthawk roared right overhead, its cannon roaring.

"The helicopter," said Dog.

Lang didn't reply. Dog raised his head, then felt something push it down as a fresh gunfire erupted nearby. Something hot creased the back of his neck.

"Let's go, let's go!" yelled Lang, and Dog found himself running up onto the road. The helicopter appeared on his left, moving along slowly with its skid a foot from the ground. One of the Whiplash people, dressed in his black body armor and helmet, leaned out and started firing his gun toward the rear, while someone else leaned from the front of the cockpit. Dog threw himself toward the helicopter, grabbing for it; as he did he felt it lifting away from him. His M4 slipped away but he knew better than to fish for it; he felt himself falling to the rear and his stomach revolted for a moment. Green and black swirls passed before his eyes and his head rattled with the roar of the engine. He saw something green below his feet and realized he was not quite inside the helicopter, even though they were lifting up above the trees.

ZEN SAW THE HELICOPTER DART UPWARD. THREE FIGURES were clinging to the side.

"Clear," Zen told Breanna.

"Launching."

The bomb fell from the belly of the Megafortress, sailing on a direct, short dive to the roadway where the terrorists were emptying their assault weapons at the helicopter and Flighthawk. The helicopter managed to clear away before the weapon exploded, but Zen had doubled back to keep the terrorists interested, and the blast of the thousand-pound warhead was so immense that the small plane stuttered momentarily, tossed so severely that Zen thought he'd lose it.

"Good shot," said Zen finally, back in full control of the plane.

"How's your fuel?" Breanna asked.

"Have to tank inside twenty minutes. How's yours?"

"We're fine for four or five hours. Let's escort the helicopter back, then set up a refuel. We may have to head back to the Philippines or to one of the Malaysian airports," she added. "I don't know that they're going to be able to move *Indy* off the end of the runway any time soon."

"Roger that," said Zen, sliding over the Quick Bird.

* * *

DANNY PULLED COLONEL BASTIAN INTO THE HELICOPTER
and held him as they rushed to get away. He pressed his weight
down against Dog's back as the chopper whipped over the
nearby tree tops.

"We're all right," said the pilot as the airstrip appeared
ahead, but Danny didn't stop leaning against Dog until the helicopter's engine had been cut, a few minutes later.

"You look like hell, Colonel," he told him as he helped the
colonel out onto the concrete.

"I feel better than I look, I think," he said. "You okay,
Tommy?"

The SF soldier started to grin—then leaned over and threw up.

"My stomach feels like his," said Dog, taking a step away.
"What happened here?"

"Base was hit by a mortar attack," said Danny. "That's all I
know. What happened to you?"

Dog recounted how they had been ambushed, and what had
happened to the driver. By the time he finished, the Special
Forces soldier who had stayed behind had found them. He
filled them in on the casualties, which included Major Alou
and Kick.

"Why the hell did they try to take off when they were under
fire?" said Dog. The cuts on his face had turned deep red.
"Danny? What the hell did they do that for?"

"I don't know, Colonel," said Danny. "Maybe they were trying to save the planes."

"God damn it. God damn it."

"It's lucky for you they did," said Danny finally.

"Losing two of my people is not lucky for me," said the
colonel angrily, stalking toward the hangar bunkers.

Southwestern Brunei, near the Malaysian border
1420

Prince bin Awg waved his hand over the map as he finished
his summary of the situation. All over the country, people had
shaken off their initial shock and were fighting back against the

madmen; there were uprisings throughout the areas held by the terrorists.

That was the good news. Here was the bad: the terrorists were slaughtering many innocents, indiscriminately killing women and children as well as legitimate combatants.

"It is a grave, grave sin and evil," the prince told McKenna and the local commanders, whom he had gathered for a briefing. "To spare our people, the army must launch its attack against the capital as soon as possible. The sultan has ordered it."

The army was already on the move. Two separate columns of armored cars, augmented by pickup trucks and a few private vehicles, were now within ten and fifteen miles of the capital, approaching from different roads. They were being helped by intelligence flowing in from Dreamland's LADS system, which was fed directly through a video hookup at the sultan's head-quarters.

"Troops should reach Bandar Seri Begawan by nightfall," said Prince bin Awg.

"By nightfall?" asked McKenna.

"The people are rising everywhere. We cannot move quickly enough."

"Well, fuel my plane and let's get going," said McKenna. "We'll fly out in support of the column, bomb whatever we see, come back, refuel, and bomb some more."

She punched her wingman's arm. "You too, Seyed," she told him.

"Yes, ma'am," said Captain Seyed.

McKenna turned to the techie who'd come in with the prince to maintain the planes. "Can we put the bullets from the Drag-onfly into the MiG?"

He shook his head. The bullets were the wrong caliber and there was no way to adapt them or the gun so they could be used.

"Can we put bombs on, at least?" she asked.

"Bombs, sure. You have four hardpoints."

"Do it."

"The MiG is not much of a bomber," said the prince. The sight on his MiG was an afterthought, added by the Poles after the aircraft had become too antiquated even for them to use as an interceptor. Bin Awg had purchased the plane through an intermediary when the Poles surplused it after years of storage; it was likely the plane had never dropped more than a dozen bombs, and those had all undoubtedly been dummies.

"Not much of a bomber's better than no bomber at all," said McKenna. "Let's load her up."

Southeastern Brunei
Exact location and time unknown

Mack felt his leg starting to go to sleep. He rose, shook it, and then walked back and forth. The man with the pistol paid no attention to him.

What would happen if he just walked away?

He had started toward the door when the man who had brought him here came in, followed by two others whom Mack had not seen before. The men started talking to the man with the pistol excitedly; they seemed to be arguing.

"Say, uh, you mind if I ask some questions?" said Mack finally.

One of the men gave him a disdainful look, then signaled for the others to go outside.

"Don't leave on my account," said Mack, watching them go. He sat back down.

"They're arguing about what to do," said one of the women near them.

"You speak English?"

One of the other women reached to stop her but she pushed away, defiant. "They said they would kill us and our children if we spoke. They've taken the men who were here. They arrived two days ago. They wore white uniforms until today. Now they seem scared."

"Where did they take the men?" asked Mack.

The woman said nothing, instead looking toward the door.

The two men Mack had seen before came in. They walked to the nearest woman, yanking her up so ferociously her baby slipped from her hands. They pushed her, not letting her bring the child.

"What the hell?" said Mack as they left. "What the hell?"

The answer came a few seconds later, with the muffled crack of a pistol fired into a skull at very close range.

Off the coast of Brunei
1720

Jennifer watched the display as LADS Vehicle One tracked the two ships approaching from the north. Both were Malaysian navy vessels, according to their markings and flags. The first appeared to be a Spica-M class attack craft; the computer ID was tentative but Malaysia had several, and it was of roughly the right size.

The second ship, larger and better armed than the first, was clearly the *Kalsamana,* an Italian-built corvette obtained only a month ago with her sister ship, the *Laksamana.* The *Kalsamana* packed Aspide anti-aircraft missiles and Otomat anti-ship missiles, along with a sixty-two-millimeter cannon and a twin forty-millimeter gun.

"Sergeant Garcia, what do you make of this?" Jennifer asked, calling Garcia over to the control station. "These are Malaysian navy ships."

"Maybe they're looking for those bastards we took care of the other night," said Garcia. "They claimed they were rebels who had stolen the ship."

"Maybe we should send the helicopter up, just to get it off the platform so we don't call attention to ourselves," said Jennifer.

"Let me get Sergeant Liu," said Bison.

Liu and the helicopter pilot came down and took a look at the screen, staring at it as Jennifer explained how she had tracked the two ships.

"The Malaysians are our allies," said Liu.

"I know," said Jennifer. "But I don't trust them at all. I think we should launch the helicopter and lay low."

"Agreed," said Liu.

The pilot nodded. "I'll loop away, then come in from the north, ask them what's going on."

"Have you received an update from the base in Malaysia?" asked Liu.

"Colonel Bastian was recovered," said Jennifer.

Liu nodded. They already knew that Merce Alou and Kick had been killed. The helo kicked up above, and the building shook as it took off.

"Ships are probably nothing," said Liu.

"Probably," said Jennifer.

"I'm going back to my lookout post. We'll take turns eating at 1800."

"Sounds good to me," said Garcia.

Just as Liu walked out, the LADS system emitted a loud beep. Jennifer looked down at the screen, where a warning flashed:

LAUNCH DETECTED.

"They've fired a missile at us!" she yelled, jumping up from her chair.

VII
"Hang On"

Brunei International Airport
1720

THE LARGE RUSSIAN AIRCRAFT LOOKED LIKE AN ANGEL astride the ramp, its wings giant arms that extended over the turf and dirt. Its silver skin gleamed in the low sun, and as he stared at it Sahurah felt himself drawn to the craft, as if beckoned by Allah himself. The throb in his head vanished; the cacophony of the others around him, his assistants and lieutenants with their reports and demands and updates—all faded as he looked at the plane. Truly, God had sent it. Two brothers who were mechanics had come forward from the city to volunteer their knowledge of the aircraft. They had found the fuel tanks nearly filled—the hand of the Lord, obviously. It was the only explanation.

Yayasan and the other pilot would fly the plane. The second man had experience with large jets, including the 737 sitting on the civilian side of the airport. That experience, Yayasan said, would serve him well with the large Russian plane, whose multiple engines and big body made it complicated to fly.

It seemed to Sahurah as he stared at the plane that he could fly it himself. God had sent it for him—to carry him to heaven.

"Commander, the Badger is ready," said the pilot. "Do we have your permission to take off?"

"I am going with you," Sahurah told him.

"To survey the city?"

"I am going with you."

"Yes, of course, Commander. Come and let us fly while we have plenty of light."

Off the coast of Brunei
1722

Jennifer grabbed her laptop as she ran from the small room, following Garcia and trailed by Liu. As they reached the door, the system beeped with another warning—a second missile had been launched at the platform.

The Otomat ship-to-ship missiles fired at the platform carried a 210 kilogram warhead, just under five hundred pounds. Developed by the French and Italians, the missile traveled close to the speed of sound; that gave them roughly two minutes to get off the platform and as far away as possible.

Jennifer turned to climb up to the roof.

"No," yelled Liu. "He's going to take on the ships. Come on. We'll use the boats. This way."

The sergeant pulled her down to the lower deck, and then prodded her toward the ladder. Garcia had reached it already, and with Bison had revved the motor on one of their two Zodiacs. Jennifer jumped into the other, scrambling toward the engine; Liu unlashed it and pushed it away from the dock so fiercely that he fell into the water as the boat bobbed off. By the time he got back aboard Jennifer had the motor working; she revved it and went forward so fast she nearly struck the small dock, veering off at the last second.

"Down, down!" yelled Liu at her as they flew across the waves. Jennifer started to duck but couldn't see to steer; afraid of running into something she put her head up, steadying herself with one hand against the boat's neoprene gunwale.

The missiles skimmed over the water on their final approach on the platform. The first soared almost directly over her head. Jennifer spun around in time to see the missile pass between the platform's piers without hitting anything. The sky burst gray and white behind the steel gridwork; a moment later the sound cracked and the small boat seemed to lift forward with it. Just then Jennifer saw the second missile strike the upper deck, spewing black shards and circles into the air as it exploded. The sound this time pushed her down sideways, all the way to the bottom of the boat.

When Jennifer finally looked back, she saw the deck area on the northern side was blackened and battered. The superstructure leaned sharply to that side. She steered around in a circle, taking the boat toward the other Zodiac, where Bison and Garcia were scanning the horizon with a set of binoculars.

"There's one of the ships on the horizon," said Bison, pointing toward it. "The smaller one."

"Our best bet is to get as far down the south coast as possible," said Liu.

"I should have taken the LADS control unit with me," said Jennifer. "I didn't switch control over to Dreamland either."

"There wasn't time," said Liu.

She looked back at the building. "It has to be destroyed."

"Not worth the risk," said Liu.

"If we don't switch it over, Dreamland can't take control," said Jennifer. "The sultan's army will stop getting information once the units are destroyed."

"You can't rig something up with your laptop there?" asked Bison.

"No, not without the hookup unit and the satellite antennas. I should have turned it over to Dreamland."

"It's not your fault," said Liu.

"I can climb up there. It's easy."

"It's not a question of difficulty," said Liu. "It's a question of safety."

"We have to destroy that unit," she told him.

"We could get some of our weapons, too," said Bison. "All we have right now are pistols."

"Ships are a good distance off," said Garcia. "I think they know they hit it. Helicopter'll keep them busy for a while."

Liu nodded, then looked back to Jennifer.

"If the ships come close, or if the platform is too dangerous, we can leave," she told him. "But we have to try."

"All right. Let's take a quick look," said Liu, frowning as he turned the boat toward the shattered platform.

Southwestern Brunei, near the Malaysian border
1729

McKenna checked her instruments as the MiG-19 climbed. Not quite used to the old-style panel, she found herself staring at each of the round dial faces, making sure the information on rpms and pressures and the like registered in her brain. Four 250-pound bombs were strapped to the plane's hardpoints, but the MiG seemed barely to know they were there, speeding through the air without a complaint.

"Brunei MiG to Brunei Army One," McKenna said, trying to contact the ground controller in the column heading toward the capital. "How are you reading me?"

There was no answer. She tried again a few minutes later with the same result, and then twice more before getting a response.

"Brunei Army One reads you, MiG. What a glorious day to liberate our country."

"Kick ass," she replied.

The controller, an army major who had taken a course in working with aircraft from the U.S. air force, gave her a good brief on their present situation, then asked for intelligence on the capital.

"Give you a verbal snapshot in zero-five," she said, double-checking her position on the paper map. "Hang on."

Southeastern Brunei
Exact location and time unknown

As soon as Mack heard the pistol shot, he went to the side of the doorway, flattening himself against the wall. The woman who had spoken to him earlier handed off her child to another mother, then got up and went to the other side, reaching it just as the two men came in.

Mack hesitated for half a second—the smaller one was closer to him, but there was no way to change positions with the woman. He threw himself forward into the man and they crashed down to the floor, the terrorist's pistol flying across the room. Mack's fury erupted and he pummeled the man's head with an insane, obscene rage, pounding the flesh with a ferocious force that rose not from him but from the earth itself. Mack's bare fists crushed the bones of the man's jaw and nose and even the side of his skull. Blood gushed as he leapt out toward the pistol, grabbing it and rolling backward in the same motion, crashing against the wall and firing into the two forms that appeared in the doorway with their rifles. He kept firing until he emptied the gun; it took that long for both men to totter backward.

Mack scrambled to get up. He reached his feet in time to see the last terrorist standing above the woman who had helped him, pistol drawn. Mack launched himself as the man began to shoot. His momentum took the man down and they tumbled against the wall. This time, rage wasn't enough. Mack's hands suddenly went limp, his fingers raw and his wrists sprained from his earlier assault. He struggled to hurt the other man, hitting him with his elbow and leg, rolling his body against him and trying to batter him with the side of his head. The man had lost his pistol but pounded him with the flat of his hands, the blows like the shock of an ice pick hitting Mack's kidney. With a scream Mack tried to get his feet under him, levering himself away. He pulled the terrorist up with him, and they pushed each other against the side of the doorway. Mack felt something swipe him on the side—his enemy had taken out a knife.

Mack threw his head forward and bit at the side of the man's face, wholly animal now, wholly a creature of violence determined to survive. He threw every part of his body against his enemy and the knife clattered away. But Mack tumbled down, out on the wooden walkway, thrown by the other's fury. Mack's face landed against something soft and wet; he smelled salt and sweat. Realizing he'd landed in the chest of one of the men he'd killed, he looked for a weapon; he found the hilt of a knife and pulled it from the man's belt.

The other terrorist had recovered his knife and charged him. Mack thought he would impale him as he came but he missed, his enemy ducking away in a bizarre dance and toppling to the ground. Mack tried to jump on him but tripped, as well. The knife flew toward the other man, who managed to duck it.

As Mack sprawled he saw one of the rifles. He grabbed at it desperately, trying to swing it up and fire. But he couldn't reach the trigger quickly enough and the terrorist kicked it away.

Mack grabbed at the leg, pushing forward just enough to make the man lose his balance. As the terrorist's knife waved in front of his face, Mack grabbed at it but missed. He was able to hit the terrorist's leg and groin, but his blows were weakened by his injuries and pain and the terrorist fell back, regrouping.

The gun, thought Mack. The gun. He threw himself on it. His enemy came once more, diving toward him with the knife.

This time, Mack's finger found the trigger. The rifle roared beneath his chest, and his whole body reverberated with its ferocious roar.

Aboard *"Penn,"* over Malaysia
1730

"Dreamland Command says the oil platform has been attacked," Breanna told Zen. "I can't get them on the radio."

"Do they have a feed from the LADS?"

"Dreamland Command does, but they don't have control of the blimps or the system."

Zen checked their position. They were about two hundred miles from the platform; it would take roughly twenty minutes to get out there.

"I say we have a look," he told her. "Let's launch Hawk Two."

"I agree. I'll inform Colonel Bastian."

"Roger that."

Off the coast of Brunei
1735

The dock floated serenely at the base of the platform, as if there had been no attack at all. Jennifer got out of the boat and lashed the line around the large steel hook.

"Wait!" yelled Liu as she reached for the ladder.

"I'm fine," she shouted, starting up. "We don't have much time."

If he said anything else she didn't hear it. The first ten feet or so up the ladder remained exactly as it had been, rising perpendicular to the waves. But at that point the ladder twisted with the structure and she found herself climbing on a slant and then twisting with it as it turned on its side. Jennifer was an experienced rock climber, but going up the off-kilter ladder was nonetheless an odd experience. She reached the first deck and put her foot up, holding herself against the railing and then working to the second ladder, which rose up through a hatchway a few feet away.

The platform seemed to move as she got onto the deck, reverberating maybe with the footsteps of her companions who were just now coming up the ladder. Jennifer tried to ignore the gentle shaking, climbing up the second ladder to the charred and mangled upper deck. A large hole had been blown in the front of the deck to her right where the missile had hit. Metal twisted every which way, and she could see that the double-girdered pier no longer connected to the structure. The building looked as if it had been punched; part of the roof cantilevered up, almost like a baseball cap whose peak was pushed upright. A sooty black star with two dozen arms covered about half the front of the building, but the shock of the explosion had not mangled the interior, and as she crawled out on the sloping deck she could tell that the building itself had not caught fire. Two of the windows, in fact, had managed to somehow stay intact.

The floor of the building angled roughly thirty degrees to the side, sharper than the deck outside. One of the large suitcases that held the LADS control gear had been thrown against the rear wall so hard that it had embedded itself there. But the control panel itself—a pair of large LCD screens that folded out of a long trunk—sat on the desk where they had been mounted at the start of the mission. One of the feed windows on the left-hand screen was blank, but the other showed the ships approaching, with the Quick Bird dancing in front of them.

Jennifer hunched awkwardly in front of the station, one hand against the desk to keep her balance as she punched the keyboard with her right hand. She selected the handoff sequence from the command tree, but after she authorized it the screen seemed to freeze. Cursing, she was about to try again when the superstructure groaned, and the list increased five degrees. She lost her balance and slid all the way to the wall, smacking her head against the deck.

* * *

DAZHOU TI WATCHED THE HELICOPTER WITH HIS BINOCULARS, his anger growing with every second. The crew of the *Kalsamana* continued struggling with their sea-to-air missile battery, unable to lock on the target. The Aspide missile had an effective range of up to 18.5 kilometers; they were now within ten. Because of their incompetence, the gunship that had joined him was now coming under fire.

The *Gendikar* had been his last command before the *Barracuda;* his old executive officer was now its captain, and Dazhou knew he could count on his loyalty to the death. The ship had been instructed to stop him—and as soon as the radio instructions were received, its captain had radioed Dazhou to tell him that he wanted to join his crusade.

The Bofors cannon at the front of the other ship began to fire at the helicopter. Something flared from the chopper; it fired a salvo of rockets or missiles at the bridge area of the *Gendikar,* then bolted away.

"Have you locked the missiles on the helicopter yet?" demanded Dazhou.

"No, Captain."

"Do it quickly," he said.

When he looked back, he saw that the other ship had stopped firing. The helicopter had managed to put it out of action, at least temporarily.

The American bastards! He would take revenge with his bare hands if necessary.

"Captain, we have a lock," said one of the men behind him.

"Fire, damn it!"

The Albatross Quad launcher shrieked and hissed as a pair of Aspide missiles flew upward. The missiles rose for a short distance, then began angling downward. The helicopter jerked to the right, firing flares and speeding away as the missiles flew toward it. Dazhou gripped his binoculars tightly as he watched first one and then the other missile veer off, exploding harmlessly. As he cursed, a second salvo was launched. This time, four missiles left the ship.

The helicopter seemed not to realize that it had been targeted again. It started back toward the *Gendikar,* firing another pair of its missiles. Suddenly it veered away, zagging left and right. It ducked the first Aspide but the second found its side, igniting with a red and white spark. The helicopter reared upward, then seemed to slide into another missile. It crashed into the sea, a white and black smear on the waves.

As Dazhou watched the steam and debris settle, he finally felt some of the satisfaction he had longed for. He scanned the ocean; they were now within sight of the platform area.

"It still stands," he told his crew. "Ready another missile," Dazhou said. "Strike it again. And let us see to *Gendikar*."

As the order was passed, the radar operator called over the other officer. The man looked down at the console and then over at Dazhou with a puzzled expression. "The radar detects something overhead," he said.

"Where?"

The man pointed in the sky. Dazhou searched the area with his glasses but saw nothing.

"Where?"

He handed the glasses to the other man, who searched in vain. Dazhou stared with his naked eyes, but still saw nothing.

"It appeared immediately after the missile struck the platform. There may have been some sort of radar jammer there."

"You're sure it's not a malfunction?" Dazhou asked.

"I don't believe so. It's hovering, like some sort of spy plane, but the signature is small."

"Shoot at it. Target it and shoot it down."

DOG WAS WAITING FOR HER IN BED, BECKONING TO HER.

"We should get married," he told her.

"Married? How?"

"We find a minister—"

"I mean, how would that work?"

"It would work, like now."

Like now? Not better?

Like now with her head slammed up against the wall, her legs tangled up, and the platform swaying?

I'm on the platform, she realized, not in San Francisco.

I have to get out of here!

Jennifer crawled back to the desk. The words CONTROL TERMINATED flashed in the center of the screen. Dreamland now had control of the blimps.

She collapsed the control box, pushing out the large cable that connected it to the power and antenna feeds. One of the detents at the bottom failed to clear; she leaned against the cable and the metal sheered off from the box. But though it looked light the control unit weighed nearly two hundred pounds; she tried to pull it off the desktop but it fell to the deck, the crash reverberating and the list increasing.

"We must go now," said Liu, looming above her.

"Help me get this out."

"We must go," he said, taking one end of the control box and pushing it up toward the door.

Jennifer scrambled to follow. Outside, Liu struggled to get the control case up the inclined deck. Jennifer watched as he pushed it past the open hatchway.

"Where are you going?" she asked, and then she realized.

"Don't!" she shouted, but it was too late—Liu pushed it over the side and the one-of-a-kind-control unit, built at a cost of at least a million dollars, fell into the sea.

"There's no time," said Liu. "The ships are coming. Come." He grabbed her wrist and pushed her down the hatchway.

Malaysian air base
1735

With their forces stretched thin, Dog oversaw the grim task of removing Major Alou's body from the Megafortress himself, working with two of the Malaysian soldiers as the dead pilot was carried from the wreck to the bunker area. Lieutenant James "Kick" Colby had already been brought to the small, fetid underground room, along with a Malaysian who had been killed from fragments from one of the shells. Dog pressed his teeth together, ignoring the stench that had already gathered around the bodies; the odor was a final cruelty, depriving the dead men of their last scrap of dignity, reminding all who lived that they, too, would decay.

Starship appeared in the outer bunker area as Dog left.

"Lieutenant," said Dog, nodding at him.

The young man seemed to want to say something. Dog recognized the look in his eyes, the question—the demand, really, for something that would make sense of the deaths of his friends.

No words could do that. Dog simply shook his head.

"We have to carry on as best we can," he told Starship.

Tears began to slip from the young man's eyes, though he tried to fight them back. Dog felt a surge of sympathy for the young man, and yet he shared his impotence. He said nothing else, pressing his teeth together and walking toward the wrecked Dreamland Command trailer. Danny Freah had retrieved some of the backup radio gear and set it up in the shade behind it.

"I've just been talking to the Brunei army command. They're about to attack the capital," said Danny when the call ended. "They have the terrorists on the run."

"What's *Penn*'s status?"

"They're trying to reach the drilling platform and find out what's going on with the Malaysian ships. The Malaysian navy claims they've been hijacked by the terrorists. Colonel, the platform was hit by at least one missile. The helicopter managed to disable one of the ships but was shot down. Dreamland's been watching the whole thing, but they haven't been able to communicate with the Whiplash people since the attack. It may just be that they're too busy."

Jennifer was with the Whiplash people aboard the platform. Dog resisted the impulse to ask if she was okay—he didn't want to hear that she wasn't.

"*Penn* should be there in a few minutes. There's a possibility the sultan's forces will be in control of the capital by nightfall," added Danny. "The people in the city are rebelling against the terrorists. They want their lives back."

"I can't blame them," said Dog, sitting at the portable communications console so he could get an update from Dreamland Command. The console was actually an oversized laptop attached by wire to a satellite antenna.

"Colonel, the platform has been attacked," said Major Catsman from the control center.

"I've heard."

"We have control of the system, but we have to make some changes so that we can broadcast the signal over to you.

Dr. Rubeo has an idea of how to do it by changing the programming in your com units. He needs some technical people to implement it."

"We have very limited personnel here," said Dog.

"I'll take what I can get, Colonel," said Ray Rubeo, appearing on the screen. The scientist's frown seemed surprisingly reassuring on the small screen.

"All right, then," said Dog. "Tell me what it is you want me to do."

Over Brunei, near the capital
1745

Sahurah had only been aboard two airplanes in his life, and never one like this. There was a gunner's post in the center of the cabin behind the pilot and copilot stations; he sat in the seat, looking up at the blue vastness of heaven.

"There, Commander—armored cars on the ground," said the pilot, Yayasan. "Look!"

Sahurah stared at the sky for a few more moments, soaking in the moment. He wanted to believe that God had sent for him—he felt it strongly. And yet it couldn't be true.

"Commander?"

The pain at the side of his head returned. Sahurah lifted the microphone on his headset and responded to the pilot.

"The sultan and his troops are marching, Commander. We can radio the command to be prepared."

"Do so," said Sahurah. He undid the wire that tethered him to the interphone system, and worked his way past the two pilots to the nose, which had an old-style window section for an observer.

He could see a long row of vehicles snaking toward the capital a few miles away.

Was this why God had called him, to stop the demon in his tracks?

"We will strike them," he said after he plugged his headset in.

"Yes, Commander," said Yayasan, his voice trembling. They had no bombs, but the guns were filled with ammunition. Besides the defensive weapons at the rear and atop and below the fuselage, the pilot could fire a twenty-three-millimeter cannon in the nose.

"Are you afraid, pilot?" he asked.

"Yes, sir."

"So am I. God will give us courage."

"Yes, Commander."

"I will be there in a moment," he told him, starting back.

Aboard *"Penn,"* off the coast of Brunei
1745

Even without the computer's automatic identification library, Breanna would have recognized the aircraft synthesized in her radar screen. Only one plane like that flew over Brunei—Prince bin Awg's famous Cold War era Badger, the same plane that Mack Smith had ridden to accidental fame in an encounter with the Chinese. She tried contacting the plane on the radio but it didn't respond. The plane was fifty miles away.

"I see it," said Zen. "But we better concentrate on the platform and those Malaysian ships."

"I agree," she said. "Should be in range in five minutes."

"Keep up with me, *Penn*."

"Keep up with yourself, Hawk leader," she told him, touching the throttle to make sure it was at the last stop.

Over Brunei, near the capital
1746

McKenna saw the radar contact maybe sixty seconds before she saw the plane with her own eyes, the large Badger swooping down at tree-top level above the western outskirts of the city. She started to call back to the ground forces to make sure the Americans hadn't liberated the big-tailed bomber but then realized it wasn't necessary—bullets shot from the nose of the aircraft as it attempted to strafe the line of government troops surging toward the capital. McKenna watched the plane pull up awkwardly; its strafing had been ineffectual but that was beside the point. She leaned on her stick and put the MiG into a crisp turn that put her on the back of the big aircraft, perfectly positioned to shoot the Badger down.

Except that she had no bullets in her cannon.

"Son of a bitch," she cursed.

The Badger added insult to injury by lighting the twin NR-23 in its tail, filling the sky with shells. McKenna buzzed over the plane, ducking another stream of bullets from a gun at the top as she dove across its path. The Badger reacted in slow motion, turning back toward the city.

"Come on, you chickenshit," she raged at it. She goosed her throttle and streaked over the top of the plane just behind the wings, so close that she thought the tailfin would strike her. Bullets flew out from all of the plane's guns, black streams of lead littering the sky.

"I'm going to take you down," she said, swinging around. "Just wait."

ONE BY ONE, THE RED LIGHTS ON THE WEAPONS PANEL CAME on, indicating that the cannons were no longer capable of shooting. Sahurah did not understand how this could be; he had only fired the weapons for a few moments. Surely the guns must carry more than a few hundred rounds of ammunition.

"Why are my guns not working?" he finally asked the pilot.

"We had only a hundred rounds for each one," said Yayasan. "You've probably fired them all."

The plane shuddered and then pitched sharply to the right. Sahurah saw a silver dart thunder past the forward window.

"He's toying with us," said Yayasan. "He'll shoot us down soon."

Sahurah looked up through the observation dome above the gunner's seat. The sky remained as blue as ever.

"I'll try to return to the airport," said the pilot. "I can't guarantee we'll make it."

"All right," said Sahurah.

Suddenly he knew why God had called him to board the plane.

Malaysian air base
1750

Dog finished entering the string of digits and hit the return key. The screen remained blank.

"Is that dish antenna facing the right direction?" he yelled.

"Yes, sir," said Boston. "Uh, Colonel, no need to shout, sir. I have the headset."

"Sorry," said Dog. He flipped the com channel back to Dreamland. "I have nothing, Ray."

"Give us a minute," said the scientist.

"I don't even have the feed I had earlier."

"Give us a minute," repeated the scientist.

An image of the ocean popped onto the screen. It looked peaceful, but slightly out of whack—there was an oil platform at the left-hand side, and Dog thought the image's perspective was pushed over. Then he realized the image wasn't askew; the platform was.

There were two ships on the opposite side of the screen. Something flashed from one.

"Colonel, do you have an image?" asked Rubeo.

"Yes. What's going on?"

"It would appear the blimp that is providing the video image right now is being targeted," added the scientist in his vaguely condescending voice. "We believe they knocked out the jammer when they struck the platform and now realize it is there. Press the 'D' and 'E' keys on your keyboard simultaneously."

"Now?"

"Now, Colonel. After the screen flashes you should be able to select any image you desire. It may take a moment longer if they strike the blimp."

Off the coast of Brunei
1754

Dazhou watched as the second missile shot upward. From working with the *Barracuda,* Dazhou knew there were many different varieties of electronic countermeasures, but the ability of the American device—surely it had to be American—to so thoroughly confound the radar aboard the corvette seemed incredible. Not only was the shipboard radar convinced that there was an object hovering eight thousand feet overhead, but the guidance system on the missiles had declared it was there, as well. Yet both veered off to the west, obviously confused.

"Try firing the gun," he ordered.

The twin forty-millimeter weapon began to revolve, firing its shells in a wide pattern. Black dots filled the sky.

Dazhou started to put his binoculars down in disgust. As he did, a gray rectangle appeared in the sky to the right of the stream of bullets. It was as if a panel had been knocked from a ceiling; it folded outward then blew into twisted spirals of black and red.

"A blimp!" said one of the officers nearby. "How did they make it invisible?"

"Clever Americans," said Dazhou. "Prepare the missile to fire at the platform."

"It is ready, Captain."

"Fire."

THE SHIFTING OF THE PLATFORM HAD TORN A LARGE GASH IN the deck on the second level, making it impossible to reach the ladder.

"We can go over the side," suggested Bison, pointing to the rail. "Then climb around on that girder there."

"Good!" yelled Jennifer. "Last one in the boat's a rotten egg," she said, sliding through the railing.

Jennifer had two advantages over the burly Whiplashers: She was considerably thinner and shorter than all of them, even Liu. She also wasn't trying to hump packs of gear and guns. She made it down to the ladder before them, and tested it with the weight of one foot; it remained solid. But after two steps it started to slide away toward the ocean; Jennifer scrambled down two rungs and then leaned over to the girder, grabbing on as the ladder collapsed downward in slow motion.

"Whoa, shit!" yelled Bison above her.

"I'm all right!" Jennifer leaned around the girder, trying to find a way for the others to get down. The path to her pier was now blocked, but each of the others had a narrow work ladder that ended a few feet above the water. If Bison and Liu could climb up and then across the girder near them, they could make it to the easternmost pier and have the boat pick them up.

"Worth a shot," said Bison as Jennifer explained it to them. "Either that or climb out to the pole at the center there and slide down."

"You'd have to go all the way back up to reach that."

"That or fly," he said.

Sergeant Liu began working his way over, picking through a mangled gate of metal and thick wires to reach a solid, open girder that ran about ten feet across open water. "It's doable," he said, starting across.

Jennifer watched as Bison followed. Taller than Liu and much bulkier, especially with his bulletproof vest, he had a hard time getting through the narrow passage a third of the way across.

"Get rid of the packs," she told him, but either the sergeant didn't hear or, like all Dreamland personnel, was pig-headed when it came to accomplishing a mission. He made it to the girder and began climbing across. About six feet out, the metal, which looked to be a good foot thick, snapped.

Jennifer watched in shock as Bison fell six feet, then stopped abruptly in midair. Her mind couldn't comprehend what had happened—it looked as if God had reached down and grabbed him, holding him over the sea. Incredulous, she climbed back up to the point where the deck had snapped, then reached over to the nearby girder—it was only twelve inches, but the fall looked like forever. She reached it, pulled herself up, and began making her way toward Bison, going hand over hand on a three-inch pipe for twenty feet until she reached the metalwork directly over him.

A piece of jagged metal had snagged his vest and one of the backpacks; he was literally hanging by threads, his body twisting.

"You with me, Bison?" she shouted down.

"I think." He sounded dazed.

"You are one lucky motherfucker," she said.

All of a sudden, Bison seemed to become fully aware of where he was. He started to reach for the metal that held him. He couldn't quite get it.

"No," said Jennifer. "I think you can climb up and grab the girder overhead, then come over to this pier and come down. It's a better bet than jumping."

"I don't think it'll hold."

"The girder?"

"This metal. I think I'll just unhook and jump."

"It's too far. And if you miss, you'll smack into the metal below."

"I ain't going to fall."

Bison pulled on the pipe, trying to swing.

"It's not going to work, Bison," said Jennifer. She could see from where she was that the gap between the Whiplash trooper and the metal was nearly ten feet—much too much to jump. "Go up."

"Maybe that is the best way," he said. He started to pull himself up, then lost his balance. As he swung down, the pipe shifted an inch downward, taking him further away.

"I don't like this," he said.

"It'll be easier if you let go of the packs and the two machineguns," she said.

"No," said Bison. "I can make it with them."

"Let go of the fucking packs!" she yelled at him, furious.

Bison looked around and, finally, dropped the guns and pack that hadn't snagged. They crashed against the metal, then rebounded into the water. He pulled himself up, groping over and across the girder to a large flange at the side of the pier where she was. The metal, about the size of a manhole cover, formed a kind of seat and he rested there for a few moments. Jennifer scrambled up to see how he was.

"You got a dirty mouth for a girl," he said when she reached him.

"And you're as stubborn as a mule."

"As a buffalo. That's how I got the nickname," he said proudly.

They climbed down about thirty feet to a platform that completely surrounded the pier. The only way to get down would be to hang off and try and get a foothold on the girder before stretching down. It was impossible to see the work ladder from above. Jennifer thought she was nimble enough to do it, but might not be tall enough to reach back easily; Bison, on the other hand, looked tall enough but exhausted. One of them was bound to slip.

Another girder extended out over the water a few feet above the platform; a pulley set at the bottom of the metal beam was all that remained from a small lift that had been used to move equipment.

"I think we should jump from there," she told Bison, pointing.

"Jump?"

"Look, it's only twenty feet from the water. As long as we keep our balance to the very end and go out there, we won't hit anything. It's like a diving platform. The others can pick us up."

"Shit on that. Twenty fuckin' feet."

"Easier than snaking under this platform, I bet."

"Twenty fuckin' feet. Maybe thirty."

"I bet you did worse than that at Lackland when you went through special operations training."

"Yeah, but that was Lackland. Everybody was out of their mind there."

"Come on. You go first," she told him.

"Ladies first."

"We'll both go first. Come on."

"You ain't walking out there, are you?" he said as she climbed up.

"Should I run?" she said, standing on the girder.

"Jesus," said Bison. He pulled himself up and started to crawl out behind her.

Jennifer waited until Bison was on behind her, then started resolutely toward the edge. She felt her right foot slip, and pushed forward—she did run now, pushing her momentum so that she was sure she would fall far from the metalwork. As gravity took her, she pushed her legs together and brought her arms in together, covering her upper body.

The water punched at her so hard that she was convinced she had struck the metal. Her lungs rebelled; she pushed upward, flailing desperately. Finally she saw light just ahead, but two strokes failed to bring her to the surface. She felt despair, tasted the salt water in her mouth.

But she'd hit rock bottom a month and a half before, when the air force seemed to turn against her, launching an investigation that targeted her. She'd survived that; she could survive anything.

A shock of cold jerked her body as if she'd touched a power line. Jennifer's head bobbed upward, breaking the water's surface. She gasped once, twice, then felt herself lurching backward.

Liu pulled her into one of the Zodiacs. She sat upright just in time to see Bison pulling himself onto the other a few yards away.

The motor at the rear revved. The lightweight boat bucked forward, picking up speed quickly.

"Down!" yelled Liu.

Jennifer wasn't sure why he was yelling, until she saw the platform explode over his right shoulder.

Aboard *"Penn,"* off the coast of Brunei
1755

Zen brought Hawk One into a shallow dive to strafe the nearest ship, the smaller of the two. He saw as he came on that the bridge area at the front of the superstructure had already been struck by something; he slid his cannon fire into the center of the gun in front of it, riding the stream of bullets through the housing as the barrel swung in his direction. He flashed overhead, spinning back for another shot. Since the gun no longer moved he slid toward the missile launchers atop the rear deck; they looked like a pair of long garbage cans angled toward the sky.

It wasn't clear which of the ships had launched the missile at the platform earlier, but by the time he laid off the trigger it was clear that this launcher wasn't going to be used again—a secondary explosion erupted from the front of the tube as Zen cleared upward.

There were two more missile launchers on the port side of the ship. As he started toward them, the radar warning receiver erupted with a message—the second ship, about a half-mile to the north—was attempting to lock its anti-aircraft weapons on him.

"You're up next," Zen said to himself.

PENN WAS JUST CLEARING FIFTEEN MILES SOUTHWEST OF the corvette, nearly in range for the JDAM GBU-32, the last weapon in her bomb rack. The GBU-32 was essentially a thousand-pound bomb with a set of steerable fins on the back that could be programmed to strike a specific GPS point. The bomb, still being tweaked for regular military use, was extremely accurate, but it had been designed to hit land targets that didn't move, not ships at sea.

On the other hand, airplanes had been taking on ships since Billy Mitchell's salad days, and Breanna had worked out a solid attack plan with the help of the Megafortress's computer. She intended on launching inside five miles, which would decrease the possibility of the ship outmaneuvering the weapon.

"Zen, I'm about a minute and a half from launch," she told him. "I'm going to open the bomb bay. Can you take out their missiles?"

"Roger that."

Over Brunei, near Brunei International Airport
1756

McKenna swung around, getting ready for another run at the Badger.

If she only had bullets in her cannon, she could take the slimer down. Hell, she had half a mind to fly next to the big SOB, whack open the canopy, and wing the pilot with her pistol like they did in World War I.

Hell, she'd even throw a brick at him if she had one.

She did, actually. Four of them, each loaded with 250 pounds of explosives.

Bomb another airplane?

Why the hell not?

The bombs might not explode, but if she could match the other plane's speed, she could get them right through the wings.

Matching his speed was just a BS aerobatic stunt, the sort of gimmick Ivana used to have her do all the time to close a sale.

McKenna pulled off to the right, taking a wide circle south of the Badger as she tried to decide if she was crazy to even think about taking a shot. What the hell, she decided as she came through the wide arcing turn. She leveled off, trying to slow the MiG-19 down to match the Badger's speed. The two planes were very different, and she couldn't quite get it; she pulled close again but the MiG tugged at her, trying to slide off to the right. By the time she got the plane steady she was beyond the Badger's right wing. She tried swinging out to the right and then tucking back in a kind of weave, but she was still going too fast. The Brunei airport loomed ahead; obviously the Badger was going to try and land.

Maybe I'll wait until it lands, she thought to herself as she accelerated and turned ahead.

Then she noticed that the gun turret at the top was revolving, following her.

That did it. She didn't wait for it to fire again. She took the turn, letting her speed bleed off precipitously; the plane seemed to whine at her but she resisted the impulse to nudge the throttle. Wings barely clutching the air, she walked the MiG slowly toward the tailfin of her prey, which was now on a glide toward the concrete runway. As McKenna slipped overhead, losing her view of the Badger, she hit the bomb release. The MiG, now a thousand pounds lighter, shot forward. McKenna went for the throttle, jacking her speed and rocketing upward.

It took more than thirty seconds for her to climb up and come back around to a position where she could get a look at the runway. When she did, she saw that the Badger had landed—without its right wing.

Off the coast of Brunei
1800

Miraculously, the debris from the missile and platform didn't strike the Zodiac, but the nearby ocean boiled with the rumbling wake. The small boat, designed to withstand anything less than a typhoon, bucked and tumbled with the waves but remained afloat.

The missile had sheared the platform off into the water, leaving only three stalks above the waves.

"Where's the other boat?" she said to Liu. "Where's Bison?"

"Ahead of us," said the sergeant, nodding with his head.

DAZHOU WATCHED FROM THE BRIDGE AS THE SMALL AIRCRAFT started a fresh attack on his other ship, which had stopped defending herself. His crew had been unable to lock on the knife-like aircraft, which danced around the sky like a dervish.

"Use the cannon," he shouted. "Sight it by eye if you have to."

As Dazhou turned to the helmsman to tell him to steer closer to their stricken sister, his second in command shouted a fresh warning. "The plane is coming for us!"

"Shoot it down," he said angrily.

* * *

ZEN COULD SEE THE ANTI-AIRCRAFT MISSILE LAUNCHER turning in the direction of the Flighthawk as he closed on the second ship. He fired point-blank into the side of the launcher's structure; his second or third shell ignited one of the missiles and started a secondary explosion.

"He's toothless," Zen told Breanna. "I'm going back on that first ship."

UPSTAIRS, BREANNA GAVE A LAST-SECOND UPDATE OF THE target parameters and then nudged the Megafortress into a shallow dive and then a swooping turn, tossing the bomb in the bay at the target. The JDAM left the Megafortress's belly just inside four miles from its target, a point-blank shot for the weapon. The bomb sailed downward, made a slight correction, then nosed down toward the GPS point the Megafortress and Breanna had calculated for it—the bridge of the *Kalsamana*.

THE SHIP REVERBERATED WITH EXPLOSIONS AS THE FIRE IN the missile battery behind the superstructure spread. Dazhou could taste the acrid smoke in his mouth. But he would not give up; he would not abandon the ship, nor flee his destiny.

"Use every weapon you have!" he demanded. "Everything! Everything!"

As the crew moved to comply, the bomb struck the port side of the antenna mast and crashed through the roof of the bridge area directly below, carrying through the deck without exploding. Dazhou turned in time to see something rushing through the cabin directly behind him—a ghost fleeing the demons of the past. The rush of wind seemed to him the swell of voices, the many voices of those who had tormented him in his life, returning one last time to torture him. Every mistake he had made, every man he had lost, every moment of foolishness pressed in around him.

And then the thousand pounds of explosives in the warhead ignited, and neither earthly vengeance nor human failings were of any more concern to Dazhou, or most of the men on the ship.

Southeastern Brunei
Exact location and time unknown

Hours seemed to pass before Mack Smith could make himself get up from the floor. Three of the four terrorists lay in the room dead; the last huddled around a pool of blood at the side.

The woman who had helped him was sprawled on the floor, eyes open, hands unclenched.

"Are you all right?" he said, kneeling over her. "Are you all right?"

Her mouth remained agape and her stare fixed on the ceiling.

Slowly, the others in the room started to move. And then, as if by some secret signal, all the women and children began to wail.

"Stop," whispered Mack. "Stop."

The fearful cry continued.

"Stop!" he shouted finally, and one by one the wails turned not to silence but to softer sobs.

"Are there others? Other terrorists?" He had to ask the question three times before he got a response from an older woman at the side.

"These were the all who we've seen," she said in broken English.

"Take me to the men," he said.

She got up, jaw trembling, and walked toward him. Another woman, much younger, grabbed his arm. "Our savior," she said. "Our hero."

"She was the hero," said Mack, pointing at the dead woman. "I'm just lucky. Now take me to the others."

On the runway at Brunei International Airport
Exact time unknown

Sahurah felt his body lifted by a thousand angels. His pain had finally ceased. After his long, torturous journey, he had reached Paradise. The angels carried him through the golden gates, up the winding marble stairs to the vast throne room. The Messenger himself waited on the landing to greet him, surrounded by a veritable sea of angels. Light glowed behind him.

Paradise, he thought. Paradise.

And then the pain returned and Sahurah felt his body fall the hundred miles from heaven, felt it roll and slam and slap against the earth. He felt fire and cursed his existence, cursed his sins and dark desires. Something grabbed him from behind and pulled, dragging him through the black jaws of dragon-snakes that snapped at his body.

"Commander Sahurah! Commander Sahurah!"

It was part of the dream, he thought—the imam stood above him, peering down from above. The Saudi was nearby, his eyes watchful.

"Commander Sahurah!"

No dream this—Sahurah was on the runway, a hundred feet from where the Badger had crashed. Someone had pulled him out in a misguided attempt to rescue him.

Why was the Lord so cruel to such a devoted servant? Why did he deny him the final glory of paradise?

"Sahurah—the devils are overrunning our defenses," said the imam. "We have a pilot, and the passenger plane that was parked at the airport. Come. We will leave and return to fight another battle."

Was this the devil tempting him? Or an angel sent to rescue him from damnation?

The imam bent down and looked at him quizzically. "Sahurah? Come, little brother. There is a time for everything. Now is our time to retreat."

The Saudi seemed to frown.

"No," said Sahurah. "I will stay and fight. It is jihad."

"The Malaysians have turned against us," warned the imam. "It is time to retreat. American warships are only a few hours away. We will regroup and wait. Our time will come again."

"I must stay."

The imam frowned. The Saudi said something in Arabic Sahurah could not decipher.

"We must leave now," said the imam.

"I stay to do the Holy One's work."

The imam nodded and then turned. Sahurah knelt, deciding to pray to the Lord that he had made the right decision. But words would not come; he could not even remember the simple prayers he had learned as a child. The throb at the side of his head chased all thoughts from his mind, and it was all he could do to stand and walk in the direction of the city.

Malaysian air base
1810

Thanks to Rubeo's software hacks, Dog now had limited control of the LADS observation system and could switch through the video feeds. One of the airships near the oil platform had been destroyed, but a second one just to the southwest showed Dreamland's two Zodiac boats. There were four people inside them—all of the Whiplash people, and Jennifer, lovely, beautiful Jennifer.

What if she had been in *Indy?*

Two patrol boats were heading toward them from the west. The boats had left occupied territory, but it wasn't clear if they contained terrorists or the vanguard of the sultan's troops, who were pressing into the northern part of the country, vanquishing their foes.

"Dreamland Malaysia Base to *Penn*," said Dog, keying into the communications line. "Breanna, our two Whiplash boats are running toward a pair of patrol craft of undetermined allegiance."

"We're on it, Daddy," she said.

For once, Dog didn't yell at her for calling him that.

Off the coast of Brunei
1815

Zen flew over the ship a few seconds after the bomb exploded. It looked from the air as if it were a child's toy with a thick hole drilled through the top. The superstructure and hull had been badly mangled, and when he took another pass he saw the corvette-sized craft had already started to slide down into the water.

"They're out of it," Zen told Breanna. "Going for the Zodiacs."

"I'm right behind you."

The Whiplash team was about five miles from the coastline and just over eight miles from the platform that had been destroyed. Two patrol craft were five miles from them on what looked like a direct intercept. Both were Russian-made Matka-class gunboats; they had been purchased a few months before by Brunei, but it wasn't clear whose side they were on.

Zen tucked Hawk One down toward the water, streaking ahead of *Penn*. The Whiplash people in the raft had not answered any hails, and neither had the ships. Neither patrol vessel flew any flags.

"Think we can get them to turn around?" Breanna asked.

"If I had skywriting gear, maybe," said Zen. He rode the Flighthawk down and then held her on her wing, taking a show-boat turn in front of the Zodiacs.

"Still on course," said Breanna.

He took another pass.

"I think somebody waved," said Breanna, who was watching on her feed on the flightdeck.

"Yeah. Listen, let me take a run over the patrolboats. Maybe we can at least find out if they're hostile or not."

"Go for it."

JENNIFER WATCHED THE FLIGHTHAWK SPIN OFF TO THE WEST. She leaned against the side of the boat, exhausted from the earlier climb and plunge into the water, not to mention everything that had come before. As she stared, the waves formed themselves into anthills in the distances.

Ships.

Ships!

"There's something up ahead, ships in the water," she yelled to Liu. "I think the Flighthawk was trying to warn us."

Liu cut the engine and waved at Garcia and Bison to do the same.

BREANNA SAW THE FRESH CONTACT ON HER RADAR—A 737 had just taken off from Brunei IAP.

Terrorists leaving a sinking ship?

Or a jerry-rigged bomber planning an attack?

"Zen, we have a 737 climbing up from the airport," she said.

"Roger that. You sure it's a 737?"

"Affirmative. Should we try and stop it?"

"Why?"

"The terrorists were in control of the airport. It has to be them," said Breanna. "They may have it set up as a bomber."

"I can't just shoot it down."

"We can't just let them fly away."

"I can put Hawk Two on it, and see if they'll at least identify themselves," he told her. "But then you won't have an escort."

"Do it."

ZEN GAVE CONTROL OF HAWK ONE TO THE COMPUTER, telling it to overfly the gunships nearing the Zodiac, then switched his control set and pulled Hawk Two out from its post ahead of *Penn*. As he began to accelerate he saw that the 737 had turned northeast, heading out over the water. Its course took it away from the Zodiacs; they had to choose to go after one or the other.

To Zen, the choice was a no-brainer—his people were more important than a plane that might or might not contain terrorists.

But Breanna seemed to disagree.

"Zen, he's not answering my radio calls and he's picking up speed," she told him.

"Yeah, listen, by the time we catch him we're going to be out of range of Hawk One. I won't be able to cover our people down there."

"Maybe we can bluff him," she said. "I can transmit a warning."

Zen didn't think that was worth her breath, but she tried twice anyway, trying to get the pilot to acknowledge. At the same time, she shifted her course to stay close to the Flighthawk pursuing the plane. Within a few seconds C³ warned that he was about to lose contact with the Flighthawk over the Zodiacs.

"Turn back, Bree," said Zen.

"We have to stay with the terrorists' plane."

"They clearly have no hostile intent. Let them run away if that's what they're doing," he told her. "We have to protect our own people. Tell the Filipinos to take care of it. We need to get west."

After what seemed an eternity, the plane lurched back toward the Zodiacs.

THE TWO SHIPS WERE MOVING AT A DECENT SPEED; THEY were now about two miles away. Both had weapons on the bow.

"Think they're friendly?" Jennifer asked Liu.

"I don't know. They came out of the terrorists' territory."

"What are we going to do?" Jennifer asked.

"Wait for another signal from the Flighthawk," he told her. "We can always run into shore if we have to."

Jennifer looked at the ships. If they kept on their present course, they would come within a mile of them. Retreating seemed like a poor option, given that there might be more Malaysian ships beyond those that had attacked the platform. Nor did it seem like a good bet to try running out to sea.

Beaching wasn't a no-brainer, though. As far as they knew, the shoreline was controlled by the terrorists and Liu was the only one who had a weapon.

Malaysian air base
1823

DOG HAD THE LADS CAMERA AT ITS MAXIMUM RESOLUTION. There were people moving around on the narrow deck near the gun at the bow.

Jennifer was in one of the boats. More than anything else he wanted to be there with her—with all of his people, but her especially.

The ships started to turn toward the Dreamland boats.

"Bree! The ships are turning," he blurted over the Dreamland com channel. "They're going for the Zodiacs."

Off the coast of Brunei
1825

Zen angled Hawk One toward the prow of the first ship, charging downward. He had only a few dozen bullets left in the guns. Hawk Two, still catching up, was another minute and a half behind.

The targeting pipper in Hawk One blinked yellow. He didn't have a shot yet.

"THEY'RE COMING TOWARD US," JENNIFER TOLD LIU.

"What's the Flighthawk doing?"

"I don't see it—wait, here it comes. He's diving on them."

"Attacking?"

Jennifer stared at the small black dart diving toward the water. If he was attacking, she'd know in a few seconds.

THE MATKAS LOOKED LIKE SOUPED-UP AMERICAN PT BOATS, with a large single-barrel gun at the bow and a pair of large boxes on either side from amidships to the stern. The boxes housed anti-ship missiles in this case, though the vessels could also carry surface-to-air weapons. Zen put his nose on the rounded superstructure just aft of the cannon; it was no larger than the cabin you'd find on a good-sized pleasure boat back home, though rather than fiberglass it was padded with armor.

A man stepped from the cabin as Zen's weapons indicator turned red. Zen saw him clearly in the center of the screen. He hesitated, then realized why.

The man was waving his hands.

No, he had both hands up.

Zen couldn't see what was going on at first. He had to circle around and drop his speed, taking a pass from the rear. There were three men on the stern of the ship, all with their hands raised in the air.

"Hey, Bree, I think they're surrendering."

"To us or the Zodiacs?"

"Does it matter?"

"Well, I hope it's the Zodiacs," she told him. "Because water landings are hell on the landing gear."

VIII
Paradise Regained

THE CEREMONY TO HONOR THE DREAMLAND FORCE FOR ITS bravery and indispensable aid liberating the country was moving enough that every one of the honorees had tears running down his or her cheeks by the end.

All but one—Zen Stockard.

Maybe losing the use of his legs had made him cynical. But as he listened to the sultan's speech and the promises to bring "gradual democracy" to the nation, the air force major found his skepticism growing. The sultan might want to do the right thing— most people had good intentions, Zen thought—but when push came to shove, giving away power and money took a heck of a lot more than words.

But he didn't share the cynicism with anyone else. In fact, he found himself in a rather good mood as the ceremony continued, smiling as his friends were honored. Deci Gordon had grown a scraggly beard during his stay in hiding; except for that, he was in fine shape, accepting a medal for having helped a small contingent of local citizens retake a police station around the time the attack on the platform had been thwarted. Deci was given the keys to the police station; he joked that he hoped he'd never need them.

There were medals for everyone, from Dog to the maintainers who had pitched in and cleared the Badger wreckage from the field at Brunei IAP. Mack Smith seemed to become almost humble as the sultan honored him in what seemed to be a knighting ceremony, making him officially "A Constant Protector of the Kingdom," a title that seemed to have been invented especially for the occasion, and one which apparently gave Mack a million dollar a year pension for life.

It figured that Mack would land with his boots in lucky shit.

Starship had taken the loss of Kick pretty hard. Zen didn't blame him. Dog had already arranged some time off for the kid, and suggested that he spend it in Hawaii—where, it just so happened, the MC-17 was bound this afternoon.

And, another coincidence surely, the sultan of Brunei happened to own a nice hotel suite that wasn't going to be used by the royal family for the foreseeable future.

Prince bin Awg, who before the revolt had had a reputation as a lightweight partier, had proved himself anything but. Zen's cousin Jed Barclay had told Zen last night that the prince was working behind the scenes to make sure his uncle kept his promise about bringing democracy to the country sooner rather than later.

Maybe he would. He had proven remarkably resilient, even taking the destruction of his aircraft collection in stride. Zen decided he would try to keep an open mind—at least for the next eighteen hours they were to spend on Brunei.

"So you ready to resume our picnic?" Breanna asked him as the ceremony finally ended.

"I don't really feel like picnicking," he told her.

"You want to stay for the reception?" She glanced toward the side of the large palace room, where the crowd of dignitaries was heading toward the first of several large parties planned in their honor.

"Of course not," said Zen. "Dog said we could slip out, and I'm taking him at his word."

"What then?"

"Why don't we go to the restaurant at the hotel, sit in the quiet corner way in the back, have lunch—then go upstairs for some personal time in the room."

Breanna raised her eyebrows.

"You look good in that scarf," Zen told her. She'd had to cover her head for the ceremony—even heroes were expected to be modest, at least when they were women.

"Maybe I'll wear it at after lunch," Breanna retorted.

"I don't think so," said Zen. And then, remembering their last telephone conversation before things got tight on Brunei, he added, "Maybe we can discuss the kid thing later."

"The 'kid thing'?"

"Yeah. We can talk about it." He shrugged, trying to be nonchalant and honest at the same time. He wasn't so sure about the former, but the latter was a must. "I haven't made up my mind. We need to seriously talk."

"We are," she said. She bent over and kissed him.

"Fight fair," he told her.

"Who's fighting?"

JENNIFER HAD DONNED A LONG DRESS WITH AN ELABORATE scarf as a sign of propriety for the ceremony. It was everything Dog could do to keep himself from staring at her the whole time. He managed to get next to her as they walked to the reception room in the palace and gently touched her elbow.

"You're the most beautiful woman here," he whispered.

"I'm the only woman here," she said.

There were others, actually, but Dog had a ready answer. "As far as I'm concerned, you are."

"That's good," she said, sliding her arm through his. "I'm sorry I didn't get to talk with your wife."

"What?" said Dog.

"I thought it might be fun."

"You're out of your mind."

"Should I be threatened?"

"Hardly."

She reached up and touched the side of his face. "I want to know everything there is to know about you."

Dog looked into her eyes. He felt an almost irresistible urge to sweep her into his arms and kiss her. The only reason he didn't was the certainty that he'd never settle for a kiss.

"Colonel, excuse me. Can I have a word?"

Dog turned. Major Mack Smith—now Sir Lord Protector of the Kingdom Mack Smith—stood next to him.

"You have poor timing, Major."

"I'm sorry." He turned to Jennifer. "I'm sorry. Excuse me just a second. I really am sorry."

"You feeling okay, Major?" asked Dog. Ordinarily, Mack didn't apologize to anyone, not even him.

"I'm fine. Can we talk? Over here, out of the way."

Dog followed Mack toward the side of the room, away from the swirl of dignitaries and officials filling the hall.

"I want to come back to Dreamland," said Mack.

"But you're rich. You're a hero here."

"This isn't for me. I don't want the money."

Dog looked at Smith. He'd been through a lot, not just during his brief captivity but in the weeks leading up to it.

"You can't just walk away from the sultan and the prince. The air force needs you."

"They have McKenna," said Mack. He pointed across the room, where the Brunei air force commodore—in a dress, no less—was holding court with other members of the central defense ministry. "She's ten times as competent an administrator as I was, she has those bozos eating out of her hand. And between you and me, Colonel, she may even be a better pilot than I am."

"Mack, I don't think I've heard you say that about anyone," said Dog.

Smith shrugged. "Can I come back?"

"Well, uh, sure. Of course. I mean, I don't know if I have a specific slot but, of course. We can work it out."

"Thanks, Colonel. I appreciate it."

"Where are you going?" Dog asked as Mack turned around.

"Take a walk, get some food. Get my gear. Say good-bye for me, would you?"

"Mack—"

Smith didn't stop.

Bandar Seri Begawan (capital of Brunei)
24 October 1997, 1320

Sahurah made his way slowly down the street. With each step, the pain pummeled the side of his head. But soon—very, very soon—he would be free of pain.

He would be in Paradise.

When he was fifty feet from the entrance of the hotel, he saw a man walking toward him. At first glance, something about the man caught his attention. It was not simply the fact that the man was a Westerner. There was something about the stride that was hauntingly familiar. Though the sides of his head pounded, Sahurah stopped in the street.

It was the man who had saved him at the airport, Smith.

How was it that he was still alive? And here?

Only if he was a devil, surely.

Sahurah started to run toward the hotel.

MACK SAW THE MAN IN THE LONG COAT GLARE AT HIM, THEN bolt for the nearby building.

Weird stinking place, he thought to himself.

Then he realized who it was.

"Hey!" he yelled, chasing after the man. "Hey!"

The man reached the threshold of the hotel. Mack yelled at the doorman to stop him. As he did, he tripped over the step and lost his footing, flying headfirst into the ornate pillar that separated the portico from the building. He managed to get to his knees and somehow slid forward, pushing himself toward the man.

"Stop him!" he yelled, pushing past the guards.

Sahurah glanced over his shoulder as he entered the doorway of the restaurant. Mack half leapt, half fell, stretching out his arm in a desperate attempt to grab the terrorist.

"I'LL BE RIGHT BACK," SAID BREANNA, GETTING UP FROM THE table. "I have to use the powder room."

"I'll be here," said Zen. He maneuvered his chair slightly to get a glimpse of the pianist, who was set up in the corner near the front of the large room. Breanna had had to insist that they be given a table back here off to the side; the waiters felt it wasn't dignified enough for national heroes and wanted the couple up front where everyone could see them. Zen would have ordered room service instead; he didn't want to be gawked at. In his mind, the hero stuff was just cover to "sneak a peek at the geek in the chair."

He turned and watched his wife walk down the hall. The ladies room was at the far end, providing a fine opportunity for an extended view of his wife's very attractive figure as she walked.

He was just turning back around when he heard a commotion at the front of the room. Someone screamed, and then Zen felt himself being slammed backward to the floor.

BREANNA FELT THE EXPLOSION JUST AS SHE CLOSED THE door to the restroom. The floor rumbled and someone shrieked; she slipped as she pulled the door open, falling to her knees. Six or seven people ran past as she finally opened it. Dust was thick in the air. The lights blinked out. She started back toward the dining room where she'd left her husband.

"No! No!" yelled a man, stopping her.

"I must get my husband."

"Suicide bomber! No," said the man. He started pushing her back. Breanna resisted, but another man, this one in uniform, grabbed her and together they carried her down the hallway and out a back door.

"DO YOU WANT TO WALK?"

"What the hell kind of question is that?"

"Do you want to walk?"

"How?" demanded Zen.

"Do you want to walk?"

"What do I have to do?"

"Do you want to walk?"

Zen decided it was a trick.

And then a face appeared, a small pinkish-white face, the face of a baby.

"Do you want to walk?" asked the voice again. It didn't come from the baby, but the baby was all he could see.

"Well, who the hell wouldn't want to walk?" said Zen finally.

"Then come with me."

"No," said Zen. "No."

"Do you want to walk?"

Zen shook his head. "No, I don't want to walk!" he yelled. "I don't want to walk!"

The baby's face morphed into a dragon's snout, leering at him. Zen closed his eyes.

"Are you there? Are you there? Are you there?"

"I'm not here," he said finally.

"Are you there?"

Something moved to his side.

"Are you all right?" said the voice again.

"Yeah, I guess I'm okay," he said. He saw that he was on the ground, in a little space formed by part of the ceiling, which was angled against the pillar that had been near his table.

"We're going to get you out," said the voice.

"Fine with me," he said.

"Your legs are pinned."

"It's all right."

"Can you move them?"

"I'm a paraplegic. I haven't been able to move them for a long time," he said. The words were loud and strong, almost as if he were bragging.

Maybe he *was* bragging. Imagine that.

"I couldn't use my legs before the explosion. I'm okay. Just get me out."

Of course I want to walk, he told himself as the rescuers pulled off the debris piece by piece. Who the hell doesn't? The question is, where?

"ZEN! ZEN!" SHOUTED BREE A FEW MINUTES LATER AS THE Brunei rescue people carried him on a stretcher to the back of the building, where a triage center had been set up.

Zen raised his head. "Hey. Hope you had a good leak."

"I'm glad you can joke," she said.

"So am I."

He could tell she had been crying, but Breanna had daubed her face so he wouldn't think so.

Ever since the accident, Breanna had tried to never let him see her cry. He knew she was doing it for him—the doctors had probably told her she had to keep his morale up—but it irked him sometimes. Not now, though. Now he was just glad as hell that she was okay.

* * *

IT SEEMED TO MACK THAT IT HAPPENED IN REVERSE. IT seemed that he found himself covered with ice, then felt incredible pain, then saw the bomb exploding. Only after it exploded did he reach out.

By then he was already dead.

Except that he wasn't dead. If he were dead he would not feel pain, and he felt incredible pain.

And ice under his back.

Maybe you did feel pain when you died. Maybe saying that you felt no pain was just what people said. After all, who would know?

He knew. Because he had died and then the bomb exploded and then he was alive, in ridiculous pain.

"You will be okay, Minister."

Mack blinked his eyes, struggling to get them to focus.

He was in a hospital bed. At least he assumed it was a hospital bed—he heard machines, saw white, smelled something antiseptic.

His back was tremendously cold.

"You will walk again."

Who was talking to him?

Mack forced his eyes to find Prince bin Awg, who stood on his right.

"Is this a dream?"

"No, Minister. You're awake. And alive." The prince had a faint, slightly patronizing smile. "The doctor says it is a temporary injury, very severe but temporary. You will walk."

"Don't let them operate on me," he told the prince.

Bin Awg looked embarrassed. "The operation was two days ago."

"Two days?"

"You had many injuries."

"I had many injuries?"

The prince nodded grimly.

"I—I'm not going to stay. I have to go back to Dreamland," Mack said. "I'm sorry—this administrative stuff, the job isn't for me."

"Rest," said the prince, putting his hand on Mack's chest. "Rest."

"I have to go back."

"You will."

Mack tried to push his elbows up beneath him. He got the left one in place but the right one didn't move. The right one felt as if it didn't exist.

In a panic, he looked over to the side of the bed, then turned away, then looked back.

But his arm was there; even though he couldn't feel it, at least it was there.

He couldn't feel his legs either.

His toes?

Nothing on his legs. They were like—a buzz? No, it was more like a thought of something that he just missed seeing. His back felt ridiculously cold and the side of his neck—that buzzed.

"God, my legs," he said.

"You'll be okay," said the prince. "You'll be okay."

"I tried to stop him. The suicide bomber. I tried to stop him."

"You kept him from getting very far. He detonated himself so close to the doorway that there were not many injuries. Your friends were all okay. They've been waiting to see you for four days now. Do you wish to see them?"

God, my legs, thought Mack. *Oh God, my legs.*